# Heartland

# Other books by Davis Bunn

## Novellas

*Tidings of Comfort and Joy*

*The Quilt*

*The Book of Hours*

## International Thrillers

*Elixir*

*The Lazarus Trap*

*Imposter*

For a complete list of books by Davis Bunn,
please visit davisbunn.com

## Praise fo[...]

"*Heartland* tells the story of [...]
an act of Providence finds hi[...]
ful TV series based on his li[...]
corruption, greed and other [...]
each one of the characters, cast and crew to discover what's good about themselves. *Heartland* is a fantastic read. It is hard to put down. Like the best in literature, it makes you laugh and cry, sometimes at the same time. While it uncovers the corruption in Hollywood, it also helps the reader understand his own failings and perhaps even to discover the solution."

— *Movieguide Magazine*,
in granting *Heartland* its highest
rating ever for a book

"*Heartland* is T. Davis Bunn at his best! From the first page until the last I was captivated by the creatively-developed, fast-moving plot. Warmly enriched by believable characters and laced with timeless principles, reading this book was just pure pleasure! I heartily recommend it to all of us who love a good story, well told."

— Anne Graham Lotz,
Bible teacher and award-winning,
best-selling author

"Readers beware: this is one you won't put down until you've reached the final page. Davis Bunn has woven a plot so intriguing . . . so fascinating . . . so FUN . . . I can hardly say enough good things about it! *Heartland* is on my 'you *have* to read this' list I give to all my friends. It will find its way to yours, too."

— Eva Marie Everson,
author of The Potluck Club Series

"He's at his best in this absorbing . . . suspense thriller."

— *Publishers Weekly*,
regarding *Imposter*

"I am amazed a guy who isn't a long-time Baltimore cop wrote [*Imposter*] . . . Suspenseful, thrilling, action-packed, and incredibly real."

— Mike Hammel,
Senior Homicide Detective,
Baltimore Police Department

"[*Imposter* is] a sweeping crime drama of political ambition, personal corruption, and military intrigue, all rolled into a can't-put-it-down read . . . a masterpiece."

> — Mark Mynheir,
> former homicide detective and
> author of *Rolling Thunder*

"[*Imposter* is] an absolute cracker of a suspense thriller. The story explodes off the page."

> — Hy Smith,
> Senior Vice President, United
> International Pictures

"*The Lazarus Trap* is a masterpiece. It will keep you on the edge of your seat from page one right through to when you reluctantly finish."

> — Eddie Bell,
> former chairman and CEO,
> HarperCollins UK

"Bunn has comfortably made the transition from evangelical to mainstream readers, and his popularity shows no sign of abating."

> — John Mort,
> *Booklist*

# Heartland

**Davis Bunn**

THOMAS NELSON
*Since 1798*

NASHVILLE   DALLAS   MEXICO CITY   RIO DE JANEIRO   BEIJING

Published in Nashville, TN, by Thomas Nelson. Thomas Nelson is a trademark of Thomas Nelson, Inc.

Thomas Nelson, Inc books may be purchased in bulk for educational, business, fundraising, or sales promotional use. For information, please email SpecialMarkets@ThomasNelson.com.

Scripture quotations are from the GOOD NEWS TRANSLATION, SECOND EDITION, Copyright © 1992 by American Bible Society. Used by permission. All rights reserved; and THE NEW KING JAMES VERSION®, copyright © 1979, 1980, 1982 by Thomas Nelson, Inc., Publishers.

Publisher's Note: This novel is a work of fiction. Names, characters, places, and incidents are either products of the author's imagination or used fictitiously. All characters are fictional, and any similarity to people living or dead is purely coincidental.

**Library of Congress Cataloging-in-Publication Data**

Bunn, T. Davis, 1952–
   Heartland / Davis Bunn.
     p. cm.
   ISBN-13: 978-1-59554-203-8 (hardcover)
   ISBN-10: 1-59554-203-5 (hardcover)
   ISBN-13: 978-1-59554-295-3 (trade paper)
   ISBN-10: 1-59554-295-7 (trade paper)
   1. Accident victims—Fiction. 2. Television programs—Fiction. I. Title.
PS3552.U4718H43 2006
813'.54—dc22
                                               2006022260

*Printed in the United States of America*

07 08 09 10 11 RRD 6 5 4 3 2

This Book Is Dedicated To

Tony Collins
&
Ember Wilcock

*Glad Tidings,*
*New Beginnings*

# Chapter 1

JayJay aimed on setting the ranch in his rearview mirror two hours earlier, only his sister followed him from room to room while he packed his meager belongings. Clara, who had raised him after the floods swept their parents off in his tenth winter, had never been one for quarreling. But she did her best. "Think of everything we've been through to keep this ranch! Evil bankers, greedy oil barons, locusts, tornadoes, typhoid, hail, snakes, and now you're going to just walk away?"

JayJay's only response was to slip into his boots and stomp down on the heels to make them set right.

Clara pointed through the living room window, past the shed holding the pickup, back to where the cottonwoods tracked the creek leading off the stream. To the tombstones by the meadow's border.

Clara's voice rose an octave and a half. "You mean to tell me you can just walk away and leave all that behind?"

JayJay shouldered his canvas duffel and said, "I reckon so."

He couldn't take their lone truck and leave Clara without a way to get to market, and his horse, Skye, was still lame. So JayJay hoofed it down to the highway and thumbed a ride to Simmons Gulch. There he waved down the bus for Los Angeles, the only city serviced by the only bus that still called on the only town he had ever known.

JayJay hesitated there on the first step of the bus and took a last look around. He was about to enter a world he'd never had any interest in

1

before. Which of course was why his fiancée had dumped him for that feller who traveled the rodeo circuit riding wild bulls.

That recollection was painful enough to drive him into the bus.

Soon as he took a seat, the bus rumbled to life and pulled away. He tilted his hat down over his eyes and dozed off, dreaming of better days.

The grinding sound of the accident almost woke him. The bus jolted hard, and there was a flashing pain, and it was almost natural to stay asleep and let everything go . . .

"Peter?"

"Upstairs."

Cynthia clambered up the steps to his attic office. It was a tough climb, as she was eight months pregnant with twins. "Why aren't you getting dressed?"

"The script is due tomorrow and I'm still stuck on the same scene."

"Poor Peter." His wife had changed out of her current favorite T-shirt, which read "frontloader." Instead she wore a frock that billowed like a navy-blue sail. "How long have you been working on it?"

Peter stared at the computer screen. "Three weeks and one day."

"Do you want to tell me about it?"

Normally Peter responded to such questions with a look. The one that said, *I'll talk about it when I'm done.* This time, however, Peter replied, "I've got JayJay leaving the valley. The bus has an accident. Then nothing. JayJay Parsons has been napping on the LA bus for twenty-two days. He's as good as petrified."

Cynthia walked over and hugged him from behind, pulling his hands from the keyboard. "I thought you told me you had the sense in your prayer time of everything being okay."

"That was then. This is now." He had come upstairs on a whim, hoping he could finally make some headway. What he felt right now was *power*. Despite his dissatisfaction over the lack of progress, the room felt electrified. "We both know what's going to happen tomorrow."

"It's just more rumors."

"No, Cynthia. Not this time." He touched the edge of the laptop. The force hummed so powerfully he could feel his entire body vibrate. Yet he still could not write a single word. Which was ridiculous. "I feel so alone."

"That's the one thing you're *not*. The church has been spreading word all over. People are writing from places we've never heard of promising to pray—how many e-mails did you get just today?"

"It doesn't matter. The show is doomed."

"This is not the way you're going to start our anniversary evening." Cynthia reached over him and turned off his laptop. "For six years, people all over the world have found a hint of goodness and light in *Heartland*. I'm as sorry as you the show's in trouble. But this is—"

"No you're not." Peter swallowed hard. "Nobody's that sorry. Not even you."

Cynthia did not argue. "Don't do this, Peter. Keep the fire alight where it matters most. In your creative heart."

Peter kept his fingers on the keyboard. Even turned off, the computer seemed to hum with a barely repressed force. He wondered idly if there was a short in the connection. "Tomorrow I'm meeting with the studio chief. And he's going to tell me what everybody on the set has been saying for weeks. That *Heartland* is finished."

Cynthia ran the fingers of one hand through the hair at the base of his neck. Rubbing him like she would a cat. Saying nothing.

Peter caught her expression reflected in the plate-glass window beyond his desk. The emotion etched into her features brought a lump to his own throat. He swallowed hard and asked, "What am I going to do?"

"You're going to come downstairs and get dressed. Tonight we're going to do our best to put all this aside and give thanks for the blessings we still have."

"And tomorrow?"

"Tomorrow we'll pray that you have the strength and wisdom to face whatever happens." She pulled him from the chair. "Now you come with me."

As he started down the stairs behind his wife, Peter cast one final look back at his desk.

He could almost hear the computer humming.

# Chapter 2

There was no doubt in JayJay's mind. He had died and gone somewhere. The sound of the bus wreck still echoed faintly in his brain. To be honest, he didn't have any real problem with dying. The problem was, he couldn't decide where he'd been sent.

Although his body still resonated with his injuries, he no longer felt pain. Actually, he was feeling great. Which suggested he had gone to the higher place. The preacher had made it pretty clear what to expect downstairs, the heat and the smoke and the gnashing of teeth.

He was seeing some gnashing, all right. But they didn't seem to be experiencing any pain.

He was situated in some kind of warehouse. It was dark. Between him and the only door he could see, two people gnashed away. The lady was good-looking enough to be called an angel, all right. And the guy, well, perfect was the word that came to mind. But JayJay didn't recall the pastor ever mentioning angels wearing what these people had on. Which for the lady appeared to be a suede bikini and Indian headdress, and the guy was in armor and oil. Nor could he ever recall the pastor mentioning that angels would gnash like they were. Because they were definitely going at it. Oh yeah. He could hear the two of them from across the room. Like hogs at the trough.

The outer door opened. A woman's voice said, "All right, this isn't a playpen. Get a room, why don't you. We're serious people doing serious work."

The pair broke off. The lady refit her leather and the guy did something with his armor.

"Hang on. I recognize you two." The light streaming through the door was certainly bright enough to be heavenly. But the woman sounded like she had chewed off the business end of a cement mixer. "You. Tall guy. You're late for your screen test. And honey, they're busy looking for another Pocahontas. If I were you . . ."

But the pair were already gone.

The woman sniffed and might have said, "Extras." JayJay wasn't sure. He should have been paying more attention. But he'd just realized he was nude.

Stark naked. Not a stitch of clothing on his frame.

JayJay crouched lower still. He wasn't sure what was proper in heaven. And he probably shouldn't care about what to wear in the lower place. But his momma had brought her baby up proper. And he wasn't about to pop up unclothed in front of a strange lady who might or might not be standing in for Saint Peter.

The woman walked away. JayJay could hear her moving about in another room. Cautiously he scouted around. When he didn't see anybody else, he rose in stages, ready to do his jackrabbit imitation.

The warehouse looked like it was nothing more than a huge closet. Row after metal row of clothes stretched out behind him. The racks were on wheels. Each rack had a little handwritten sign attached to one corner.

JayJay gasped. The sign on the rack in front of him read, *Heartland*. Which was the name of his spread.

"Who's that in there?"

JayJay tore off the first clothes he touched. The metal hangers clattered at his feet.

Footsteps started his way. "I better not find you two back for another round."

JayJay double-hopped into a pair of jeans. He slipped on a shirt that looked too much like his own. Which spooked him so bad he made a mess of the buttons.

"I don't like coming down on extras, but in your case I'll definitely make an . . ." The woman stepped into the chamber, spotted JayJay, and clutched her chest.

JayJay gripped the waist of his trousers to keep them from falling off. "Howdy, ma'am."

"Who . . ."

"Sorry to startle you."

She released her hold on the dress over her heart. "I remember now. You're the new fellow."

"I reckon so, ma'am."

She took a step closer. She tilted her short body with each step, like her spine had permanently stiffened. "You didn't give me half a shock, mister."

"That makes two of us, ma'am."

"You're so late, they'd just about given up on you. That must be why Casting sent you straight to Wardrobe." She turned around and motioned for him to follow her. "Come on in here. I need more light to fit you. Gladys, you got to get a load of this one."

A voice from the other room said, "I'm busy."

JayJay used his other hand to grip his unbuttoned shirt and shuffled forward. Though the clothes looked just like his own, they were five sizes too big.

The dumpy woman said, "Well, just un-busy yourself and come meet a ghost."

The second room held no more answers than the first. JayJay stepped into a large chamber, forty feet to a side and surrounded by windows. And upon the windows splashed a brilliant golden light. But the room was for *working*. A roller system traced along the high ceiling. Three long tables held sewing machines and irons and magnifying glasses on long stems and lights on spindles. And a hundred different-colored threads. And scissors and measuring sticks and pencils and diagrams and working charts and drawings and easels and . . .

"Oh my word."

A second woman rose from the central table. She was almost as tall as JayJay and wore cat's-eye glasses that sparkled in the light. She was as old as the first woman and peered at JayJay with the same spooked expression.

The squat woman said, "Can you believe it?"

"I'm looking straight at him, and I don't trust my own eyes." The tall woman moved in close. "Where on earth did they *find* you?"

"T-the bus to Los Angeles, ma'am."

The angular woman chuckled. "Well, come on over here, and let's get you fitted up proper."

The tall woman tugged and drew lines on his clothes. The shorter woman picked up a phone, punched in a number, and said, "It's Hilda over in Wardrobe. Your replacement JayJay is here." She listened a moment, then her voice turned flinty. "You know what? I was so busy trying to clean up your messes I forgot to ask."

Hilda turned to him and said, "The peon who calls himself an assistant director wants to know why you've kept everybody waiting."

"Ma'am, all I can tell you is, the bus took a hit while I was fast asleep."

The tall woman spoke through a mouthful of pins. "Sounds to me like you're going to fit in around here just fine."

Hilda said into the phone, "His bus was in an accident. No, I have no idea why he traveled by bus. You want details, you can get them yourself . . ." She cradled the phone a second time. "King Peon wants to know how long."

Gladys replied, "I've got to take the pads out of the shoulders, else he's going to look like a hairless ape. And take in six years of flab. He's got a dancer's waist."

Hilda said into the phone, "Five minutes. Okay. Right. I'll tell them." She hung up and said, "His Royal Pain in the Neck says to hurry."

"Like we ever took it easy around here." She patted JayJay's arm. "Okay, hon. Let me have those clothes."

"Ma'am, you got to excuse me, I don't have nothing else on."

"You hear that, Hilda? The cowboy here is shy. Just step behind that screen there, hon."

JayJay did as he was told. As he handed his clothes around the corner, he said, "I was just wondering. I mean, is this heaven?"

Both women laughed at that. "Only if they offer you a contract, hon. Otherwise you're just a sheet to tear off their clipboard. What size shoe do you wear?"

"Thirteen and a half, ma'am. But I was always partial to boots."

"Thirteen and a half, you hear that, Gladys?"

"The one part of him that didn't get shrunken or swollen."

"Ma'am?"

"Never you mind, son. What's your name?"

"JayJay Parsons, ma'am."

The ladies laughed again, full-throated and long. "Oh, that's rich."

"Takes you back, doesn't it?"

"Right out of my past, that boy." A hand snaked around the screen, holding a pair of jeans. "Try these on."

"Why, they fit like they was made for me."

"Let's hope you're around long enough to claim them, sport." A shirt came next, then boots. "You won't need a hat. They'll want to shoot you with your face exposed."

"Shoot?"

"Hurry it up, sport. Let's have a look at . . ." The voice trailed off as JayJay stepped into view. The two women moved in close together. Their eyes mirrored the same astonished expression.

"Is something wrong?"

The shorter woman nudged her neighbor. "Gladys."

"What?"

"The kerchief."

"Oh. Of course. Hang on, I just had it . . ."

"Right there by your machine."

"Oh. Sure." Gladys fumbled for it because she seemed unable to take her eyes off JayJay.

"Thank you, ma'am." He rolled the kerchief cowboy-style, flipping the ends and then slipped it around his neck. He spied his Arapaho collar ring, the one Clara had given him for Christmas a while back. Which was as strange as anything this day, on account of having lost it down the well, oh, it must have been two years back. But JayJay didn't say anything, the ladies were looking at him strange enough already. He slipped the ring up tight and set the kerchief's edges front and back of his right shoulder. Lying there on the table was the blade he'd taken off the biker who'd been threatening the ladies in Simmons Gulch. He slipped it in the back of his belt, tilted so it wouldn't ride up when he sat down. Like he'd been doing it all his life. His every motion made the ladies go more round-eyed.

He cleared his throat. "Y'all are making me right spooked."

Hilda started like she was coming awake. She gripped his arm and spoke in a shaky purr. "Come on, sport. I got to see this."

"You aren't going anywhere without me," Gladys declared, moving around to his other side.

# Chapter 3

O kay. Here's your choice for the day." Martin Allerby addressed Peter in what the writer considered full studio-chief mode. "I'll give you the version for public consumption, or reality. It's your call."

They were situated in the penthouse of Centurion Studios' main office building. If an office building with only five floors could claim to have a penthouse. But Hollywood was all about status. Mythical or real mattered less than whether people believed it or not. Martin Allerby was the head of Centurion Studios. Naturally, his office would be located in the penthouse. Even if it was in the basement bomb shelter under the back-lot cafeteria, it would still be the penthouse. That was Hollywood.

The leather chair squeaked as Peter shifted uncomfortably. An offer of this much truth at nine in the morning could only mean bad news. "Whichever will let me keep my job."

"A survivor. Good. I like that in my employees." Martin Allerby reached for one of the five cigarettes he permitted himself each day. Allerby was a spare man. He lived the high life, but in moderation. Martin Allerby was a survivor in a world that generally ate its own young. He did so by keeping his vices in check. He did not care what others did unless it affected the studio's bottom line. He had produced a stream of television shows that made money for the networks that bought them. He was not cold so much as utterly disconnected.

Allerby smoked Cuban cigarettes that came in a hard box with gold foil. The cigarettes were an odd ivory color. The smoke smelled like cigars. Rich and pungent. It was of course against California law to smoke in a public office. Six months back, an actress being interviewed for a role had complained. As a result, she had been barred from ever entering the studio. Not publicly. But it happened. That was Martin Allerby. He was not a man to cross.

"Okay, here's the straight deal." Allerby smiled across his desk. "And if you ever breathe a word of this to the press, you'll never have lunch in this town again."

Peter gulped audibly. "Maybe I don't want to hear it that bad."

"Too late, Peter." He released a thin stream of smoke toward the ceiling. "Townsend is a basket case."

Neil Townsend was the actor who played JayJay Parsons. "I've heard the rumors."

"Sure you have. You saw how he was at the end of last season. We closed the set and made everybody understand their jobs depended on keeping the secret. Which is why we managed to keep the lid on. But nothing and nobody could control Townsend when he was off duty. I'm surprised the secret has been kept this long."

Allerby made a process of dumping his ash. "I'm telling you this so we can both save some time. My guess is, you arrived today with your spiel all worked out. You were going to remind me there's nothing like this on television today. Our rankings come and go, but there is a core audience that sticks with us through thick and thin. We generate more fan mail, our advertisers are happy, yada yada. How am I doing?"

The balloon Peter had been carrying since waking abruptly deflated. "I can write around him."

"No you can't. JayJay Parsons *is* the show. And Townsend knows it."

"So the news I've been reading about the show having run its course—"

"Rubbish. Total hogwash. But the public we're aiming at wouldn't swallow the truth."

"Which is?"

"Townsend is finished." Allerby pronounced the sentence with no emotion whatsoever. "He's a boozer, a druggy, a sex fiend. We've put him into rehab four times at studio expense. He switches addictions for the time he's inside, going for sugar when he can't get any other drug. His weight explodes."

Peter felt the sweat trickle down the length of his spine, cold as an iced dagger. Ready to plunge in and cripple his career. He had held the job of *Heartland*'s scriptwriter for the last season. The original writer was an old dog named Ben Picksley, who'd worked the Hollywood trenches for thirty-seven years. Picksley knew the players and the wars and the locations of too many corpses. He'd gotten his start on a Texas series where an old man and his three sons fought off the bad guys every Thursday night at nine. Ben had given Peter his first chance because Peter came cheap. Ben had also liked the fact that Peter didn't carry any film school habits, like smoking French unfiltered black-tobacco stink bombs or using terms like *erudite* or *predilection* in every sentence. Ben's formula for *Heartland* had been simple: one moral drama and one tornado per episode. The moral drama could have no more weight than a wet puppy, and the tornado had to come cheap. When Picksley had retired, Peter had gotten the tap. His fate and Townsend's were inextricably united.

Peter said, "He can lose the weight."

"He could do a lot of things," Allerby agreed. "He could shape up. He could rein back the bad habits. He could stop hitting on every female extra that comes within radar range. He could learn his lines. He—"

A roar from the outer office silenced them. Allerby's only sign of displeasure was the way he thumped out his cigarillo. "Speak of the devil."

The noise did not sound human at all. "That's him?"

Allerby's smile was rapier thin. A slit of humorless, bloodless flesh. "Don't you recognize our leading man?"

The door slammed back. Peter was so astounded by the sight he could not even rise from his seat.

The voice of Allerby's secretary emerged from behind the mountainous flesh. "I'm sorry, sir. He just would not listen."

"That's all right, Gloria."

"Off the show? *Off the show?*" The words were so slurred Peter could hardly make them out. "You cretin! I *am* the show."

"Sit down, Neil, or I'll call Security and have you tossed from the lot. How would that look to the tabloids, I wonder. Leading man sprawled on the pavement outside the Centurion studios. Again."

It was doubtful Neil Townsend understood what Allerby said. His eyes did a glazed trackless wander around the room. But the chief's frigid calm subdued the actor. Townsend grunted something unintelligible and started toward the chair next to Peter.

"No, not there. We'll need a crowbar to lever you out. Take the sofa. Gloria, give our star a hand, will you. That's it. Now then. What will you have, Neil? Coffee? A week at a fat farm?"

The man could have played a caricature of himself. His features were bloated, his skin splotchy, his eyes almost blind from whatever coursed through his veins. He spoke, but the words dribbled from his lips like crumbs.

"Yes, well, whatever it is you're telling us would be fascinating, I'm sure. If only I had time to find a translator well versed in Drug-eese. Which I don't." Allerby turned to Peter. "I assume I don't need to say anything further."

"I-I had no idea."

"No, no one did." Allerby fished out another cigarillo and poked it toward Townsend. "After last season's final episode I gave our star there an ultimatum. Sober up or else. So off he went to rehab. Five weeks later I got a call. Townsend had vanished. That was the last anybody heard from him until this weekend, when his agent phoned to say our Neil was home. The agent was less than pleased when I insisted on going by."

Allerby lit his cigarette with a slim Dunhill lighter. He snapped the lid shut, blew out his smoke, and said, "I was right to fear the worst."

"So it's over." Peter stared, not at the mound of flesh but rather the end of his own career. One season of writing for a show that got the ax was nothing to light up his résumé. His body felt numb from the blow.

"Brace up, Peter. Your work is solid enough. Which is why I wanted to see you this morning."

Peter knew what was coming. Hollywood was a very small town. People talked. Centurion had a prime-time drama that was in trouble. Peter had read several of the scripts. It was typical evening soap. A medical drama including incest, greed, murder, and too much wealth gone bad. But it was work. And regular work was hard to find. He had nothing else on offer. He'd be a fool to turn it down.

"We are looking for a writer with your savvy to help turn around—" Allerby was halted by a knock on his door. "What is this, LAX?"

But the head that poked in belonged to Britt Turner, director of *Heartland*. "Martin, hey, Gloria said you were busy but this can't wait. Hey, Peter." Then he saw the man on the sofa. "Oh, wow."

"Shut the door, Britt."

"Sure. Right. But it won't do any good. This will be all over the lot in ninety seconds flat." Britt moved toward the sofa. "Poor Neil."

"He's not dead and buried yet, Britt."

"Might as well be." But the news did not seem to bother him. The director turned back to his boss. "You guys have got to come with me."

"As you can see, we're busy with—"

"Martin, you've got to come *now*." Britt was normally one of the most quietly contained men Peter had ever known. He directed his shows with a voice like a silken lash. Today, however, he was bouncing from one foot to the other. "We've found our new JayJay."

Allerby's second cigarette of the day was pounded into the ashtray. "We've been through all that. The public won't go—"

"The public is going to eat this guy up, Martin. Forget a side order of fries. They're going to take him *raw*."

Martin was already shaking his head. The studio chief knew hype when he smelled it. "I'm not buying. How many screen tests did we sit through?"

"Too many. So many I didn't even bother to come in for this one."

Martin frowned. "I didn't authorize another test."

"I know. But I was in my office when my AD phoned and said they had this guy. Look, just take a walk with me, okay?"

"You did a test this morning and you've got the film ready to show?"

"We didn't shoot anything yet. I stopped by the set and came straight here. This guy, Martin, don't look at me like that. I've never steered you wrong. I'm telling you, *this guy is JayJay Parsons.*"

The glutinous mound on the sofa shocked them with a sudden roar. Peter could smell the foul breath from across the room. The star thrashed about so hard he broke one of the sofa legs. He poured onto the carpet. It was a struggle, but he finally managed to make it to his feet. Only then did he emit his first intelligible words since his entrance.

"That role is *mine!*"

Neil Townsend staggered across the office and slammed the door open so hard it broke the top hinge. Somebody in the outer office screamed.

Martin called through the open doorway, "Gloria, have Security send a couple of men over to the *Heartland* set."

His unflappable secretary asked, "Shall I say they have permission to shoot to kill?"

Britt gaped at the empty space as their star thundered down the Centurion hall. "Was it something I said?"

"Look at it this way." The Centurion CEO reached for his phone, already on to the next deal. "All we need is a decent slasher-horror script and we're ready to roll."

# Chapter 4

JayJay Parsons leaned against the warehouse's interior wall. He turned his back to the impossible and focused on what was right there in front of his face. This was real. This metal. This bolt. This paint. This faint smell of dust and disinfectant. He was not dreaming, and this was not a mirage.

"Okay, where's the hick? No, Claire honey. Not you. The other one. Can somebody kick-start the guy?" The fellow talking was a human gnat. Just buzzing around, stinging whoever was closest. JayJay sighed and swung about. He knew gnats. They'd just keep pestering. They were also attracted to the smell of sweat. Well, JayJay was giving the gnat a ton to work off of.

"You. Male hick. You realize you're the reason we're all here, right? Good. Okay, so why don't we finally shoot this thing so we can let you go back to holding up that wall."

The gnat had introduced himself as Kip Denderhoff, the assistant director, and then waited like the words were supposed to mean something. And they might have, if JayJay hadn't just spotted what was there at the other end of the building.

The two ladies had walked him across a huge concrete square, something they called a lot. Gladys and Hilda had led him into this building big as an indoor rodeo, big as outdoors with that afternoon sky painted across the back wall. Then at a snap of a switch the sun had risen inside the building, the lights were that bright. When JayJay's eyes had adjusted, his legs almost gave way.

Which was how he came to be standing by the side wall, picking at a fleck of loose paint.

"No, no, this won't do. The hick has sweated through his shirt. Where do they find these clowns?" Kip Denderhoff hefted his clipboard and did an angry pirouette. "Gladys, go get the hick another shirt."

"I'll have to sew one up."

"You're kidding me, right?" Kip wore a loose red shirt that had to be silk. When he waved his arms like he was doing now, the sleeves looked like sails caught in a nervous wind. "We've already wasted half a day on this idiot, and you're telling me we can't shoot a single lousy take?"

"Maybe if you stopped shouting at the guy he'd loosen up," a voice muttered from JayJay's other side.

"I heard that. You want to reacquaint your shoes with the pavement, keep it up." The assistant director looked at his watch and reeked exasperation. "All right. Twenty minutes, everybody. Gladys, do up two shirts so we don't have to go through this another time. And Makeup, where's Peggy?"

"Right beside you."

"Look, Peggy, darling. His face is running. He might as well be wearing tan lava. Do something."

"I can use the outdoor cake. It's guaranteed not to melt under desert sunlight."

"Any reason why we didn't do this the first time?"

"It's a bear to get off and a lot of people are allergic—"

"If I want a diagram, Peggy, I'll bring in a real artist." Kip raised his voice another notch. "Off the lights! And turn the a/c up a notch, I'm roasting!"

There was a sound like a hammer hitting an anvil, and the lights bright as outdoors dimmed to nothing. JayJay's chest lost its crimping iron band. He managed a decent breath. He pressed his fist to his heart, willing it to stop racing so.

"Here, hon." Peggy was a muscular lady with a flinty voice and eyes to match. She pressed a hot damp towel into JayJay's hands. "Wipe off the gunk and we'll start over."

"I still don't get why I'm supposed to be wearing this stuff anyway."

"Don't tell me this is your first time on a set."

"First time anywhere." JayJay scrubbed his face clean, then saw what he'd done. "Lookit this. Now I've ruined your clean towel."

"That's okay, hon. We've got plenty." Peggy tilted her head to one side. Dark eyes glittered with humor and something more. "You shouldn't let the AD get to you so."

"It isn't him. It's the whole shooting match."

"I hear you." She spun JayJay about. "See that door over there? Go find the welcome wagon and tell him you want a double espresso with a shot of butterscotch and a dollop of whipped cream. I'd suggest something stronger, but they'd come down on us both with a ton of trouble, after the misery we've had with Townsend."

"Who's that?"

"Never you mind." She prodded JayJay forward. "Just tell them you want one of Peggy's special pick-me-ups for a very hard day."

JayJay managed to cross the warehouse floor without looking once at the thing cast in shadows now that the lights were off. But it didn't do him any good. He couldn't just pretend it had gone away. He had seen it. He had *touched* it. And the result had been a branding hot as any iron straight from the fire.

The shadows could not completely hide the fact that there, taking up the left-hand side of this huge building, was his home.

But not his home.

This cabin was segmented, like a giant had attacked it with scissors. Each room was split off from the other. One wall was missing from each room. His whole life, his whole *world*, chopped up and split apart.

And everybody kept watching him.

JayJay couldn't get a hold on how many people were in the building because they kept coming and going. JayJay had offered the strangers a couple of polite howdy's, but they'd just stared back. Mute as nervous cattle. All clustered together and staring at him like they were watching a ghost cross their path.

But soon as he pushed open the rear door and stepped into the sunlight, things only got worse.

Because leaning against the little chuck wagon was his sister. Clara. Wearing a blouse he had picked out for her special. Her sunbonnet was off and sat on the counter. And she was *smoking*.

"Clara!"

"Oh, please." She dropped her cigarette to the concrete and ground it out with her boot. "Not you too."

"You don't smoke!"

"Wait, let me guess. You're straight out of method school. Where was it, Chicago?" She looked at him, Clara but not Clara. His sister, but hard-eyed and giving him an attitude like he'd been caught doing something awful. "Never mind. This is the real world, bub. I don't care how much you look like my long-lost little brother. You want to do television, you arrive on time and you hit your mark and you deliver your lines. You read me?"

JayJay felt like his mind had been force-fed a pile of rocks, not words. Nothing she'd said made the tiniest bit of sense. He was trying to figure out what to ask her, when somebody or something bellowed from inside the building.

"Oh no." Clara paled. "Don't tell me."

The metal door slammed open. A beast staggered out.

JayJay gripped the counter. The nightmares just kept piling on top of one another.

He felt like he was staring into a funhouse mirror. This distorted beast of a twin lurched toward them, his arms waving and a foul stream spewing from his mouth.

JayJay flushed at what he was hearing. Or at least what he thought the stranger was yelling. The words were so slurred and distorted it was hard to be certain. But he knew a drunk. And his sister was scared. There was just one thing to do.

JayJay stepped forward. "Now you just hush up, mister. There's women in range."

The man blinked and swayed. JayJay had seen bulls do the very same thing. Trying to decide whether to charge. "Don't you go pawing the earth, now. You just turn yourself around and head on back where you came from."

The stranger lifted his arms and roared his first clear words. "The role is mine! *All mine!*"

He took a wild swing at JayJay. If it had connected it probably would have taken his head off. But JayJay just backed off a notch. The stranger might as well have mailed JayJay a letter with the day and time.

JayJay let the fist swing past, then stepped in. And hammered the stranger straight over the heart.

The stranger coughed a fetid breath. His eyes went wide. His arms dropped.

JayJay could have stopped then. He probably should have. But his sister was not somebody to be talked to in such a way, not even if she was a stranger walking around in Clara's skin.

So he popped the guy on the chin. A measured blow. His fist didn't move more than twelve inches. Just enough force to cause the guy's eyes to drift back.

JayJay was there to catch him. The stranger's weight caused him to stagger a little. But JayJay had been raised lifting cattle from the byre. He shifted the guy around to the rear of the chuck wagon and settled him down on the pavement with his back against the wall. "You rest easy, friend. And lay off the hard stuff, that's my advice. A man's gotta know his limits, or he don't have any business setting down that road."

Clara said, "I know that line."

JayJay took a step back and stared down at the stranger. "Like looking at my evil twin, ain't it?"

"Wait, wait, it'll come to me. The episode with the three tornadoes, right?"

"Clara, you ain't making any more sense than that stranger I just decked." He stared more closely. She *looked* like his sister. But the edges of her eyes were pinched up tight. And her voice might as well have been beaten out on the blacksmith's anvil. "You mind if I ask who you really are?"

"Really?" She smiled. Once again it was her and not her. Clara with a citified edge. "You just saved me from a man I've spent six seasons loathing. Right now I could be just about anybody you'd like me to be. How does that sound?"

JayJay backed off so fast he stumbled over the stranger's sprawled legs and almost went down. "Now you just keep your distance, whoever you are."

"What, you never liked the idea of a little incest?" Clara fished another cigarette from the pack by her sunbonnet and pointed at the stranger, who was now snoring. "He sure did."

"That's it. I am plumb done with you and everything else around here, wherever *here* is."

But the only way out of the alley was back through the building. And once inside the building the first voice he heard was the gnat's. "Okay, everybody. The male hick has decided to grace us with his presence. Gladys, give him his shirt, and Peggy, would you *please* do something about his face! Somebody find us little miss country tramp, maybe we can wrap this thing up and go—"

JayJay didn't mind being called a hick. Why should he. He *was* one. Matter of fact, he always thought it was a sideways compliment. And he shouldn't get too riled over what the gnat was saying about Clara. Especially since he'd just been thinking the very same thing. It was more the way Kip Denderhoff stood over there, all five-foot-nothing of him, waving his arms and doing that little twirling two-step, bossing and throwing scorn at everybody in reach. Not even that was much of an excuse. But just then, the lights came back on. And JayJay was trapped once more in the headlights of this mysterious place, staring at his disemboweled home.

"You there, hickster! Stop gawking! We're on the clock here! Tick, tick, time is money in Gotham. Peggy, do his face, darling, and this time get it right or you'll be out fast as hickster there. Lighting, lighting! I *told* you to damp that kitchen, it looks like you're trying to parboil the table! And *why isn't the a/c cranked up?*"

JayJay spun about, plucked out his knife, and sent it flying.

The blade caught a billion lights as it spun across the room. Somebody gasped, maybe a couple of people. JayJay knew he was being watched again by everybody in the room except the gnat. Maybe that was why the little guy had such an attitude problem, he hated being ignored. JayJay had time for all those thoughts before the blade slammed into the door beside the gnat. Bam! The gnat saw the blade and shrieked. It was the most satisfying sound JayJay had heard all day.

The door opened. Two people stepped through. The first man said, "Why aren't we filming?"

Kip's voice had lifted a full two octaves. "That man just threw a machete at my head!"

"On account of you making the whole world nervous." JayJay walked over. "I swear, you make more noise than a herd in a twister."

Whatever the assistant director saw in JayJay's face caused him to shriek once more and flee. Or try to. But he got his feet tangled in a folding chair and went down hard. "Somebody *save* me!"

The newcomer watched JayJay pry the knife from the door and said, "Out here, fellow, we have other ways of warning somebody to be quiet."

"I wasn't warning nobody." JayJay eyed the gnat as he slipped the knife back into the sheath. "I missed."

The newcomer's laugh echoed through the silent hall. He clapped his hands. "All right, everybody. Let's get this action on film!"

# Chapter 5

C enturion Studios was one of the few midsize production units that had managed to survive the merger craze of the nineties. Old Carter Dawes controlled the majority of Centurion stock. And he wasn't selling. Carter Dawes' grip was subtle. So long as Martin Allerby kept delivering hits and did not stray from Carter Dawes' directives, Martin Allerby was allowed to rule Centurion as his own fiefdom.

Even so, Dawes' control chafed on Martin Allerby. His general loathing of Carter Dawes and everything he stood for had steadily increased over the seven years Allerby had held the position. And nothing abraded Martin Allerby more than the directive that Centurion's business was strictly television.

Centurion held the enviable position of having prime-time hits running on two of the three networks, known as majors, and two cable stations. They averaged nine movie-of-the-weeks a year. A new pilot from Centurion normally resulted in a bidding frenzy.

But Centurion was still television. Centurion's lot encompassed forty-three acres in the wasteland between Riverside and Barstow. Most of their staff lived in the San Bernardino Valley, light-years removed from the mythical realms of Beverly Hills and Bel Air. Malibu Beach might be forty miles away, but the average Riverside family saw the Pacific Ocean less than once a year. This isolation from Hollywood's wealth promoted both loyalty and frugality. Whenever Martin Allerby had trouble getting an actor for the price Centurion was willing to pay, he invited the star and their agent out for lunch on the lot. One look around the neighborhood was worth a billion words between dueling attorneys.

Martin Allerby hated their studio's second-rate location with a silent, seething passion.

A typical valley haze obliterated the afternoon as Martin Allerby left his office and took the stairs down three floors to the viewing room. He slipped into the central sofa. The table to his right held a phone and a notepad and a carafe of coffee. Once a young director had decided to sit in Allerby's place when Allerby had been in New York. The director had been sacked even before Allerby had returned to LA, his contract paid off, and he had never worked for Centurion again. As far as Allerby was concerned, a simple act like this served far better than a thousand interoffice memos.

He nodded to the assembled crew and punched the speakerphone button. "I skipped lunch. Anybody want something?"

Britt Turner was so nervous he almost danced in his seat. "I'll have a tuna on wheat, lettuce and cucumber, hold the mayo."

"You get that, Gloria?"

His ever-calm secretary asked through the speakerphone, "What about you?"

"Chicken salad, rye crackers, Perrier with ice and lemon."

"You want the Sinatra or the Chasen's?"

"What's the difference?"

"Sinatra is oil and a trace of vinegar, Chasen's is mayo."

"Whichever you can get here faster. And bring us some more coffee mugs." He cut the connection and said to Britt, "What's this I hear about a knife fight?"

"It wasn't a fight. He tossed the blade to shut up my AD. Knowing my AD, the guy probably deserved worse."

"Okay. Tell me why I'm here."

Britt bounded from his chair. "You got to understand, the guy has never seen a script before."

"What, *any* script?"

"Not a script, not a studio, not a camera."

Allerby realized the director was not nervous. He was thrilled. "You're wasting my time over some wannabe who's totally new to television? In case you've forgotten, rule one in television is you don't introduce—"

"A new face to a hit series. I know the rules, Martin. I *wrote* some of them. This is different."

Martin Allerby prided himself on never losing his cool. Never showing the blade in public. The old adage had always worked well for him. Never complain, never explain. If somebody stepped out of line, do them fast and silently. The fear factor was amped as a result. Nobody ever knew for certain where they stood.

Martin nodded his thanks as Gloria entered and set the tray down beside his elbow. She distributed the mugs, placed Britt's lunch beside his chair, poured coffee, and left. Martin disliked thinking Britt might be slipping. They had enjoyed some good years together. But that was the trouble in this business. Things changed. If not the people, then the public's tastes. Times like this, Martin was glad he never let anybody too close. There was no need for him to share the dagger's pain.

When the door clicked shut, Martin said, "What's he done, stock theater?"

"I don't know. And it doesn't matter."

Martin hid his displeasure by digging into his lunch. The time wasn't a total waste. He needed to eat.

"The only reason I mentioned it, his copy of the script never arrived. So we had him read off the teleprompter. But this kid, he didn't have the sense to turn away. So it looks wooden."

Martin shrugged. "Townsend's acting the last two seasons has resembled a carved totem."

"Right. Exactly. So we shot the one scene in the living room, you know, from the final script Peter's still working on. And then we did something a little different. What you're about to see hasn't been cut at all. I mean, we haven't edited a single second."

Martin wished he had brought his cigarettes. "Enough talk, Britt. Let's see what you've got."

"Right. Sure." The director bounded back to his seat, keyed the phone and said, "Roll the tape."

The lights dimmed. There was none of the flickering of old film. The last season, they had shifted *Heartland* to digital tape. Like most studios, Centurion had fiercely resisted the shift. They had finally taken the plunge because digital filming meant they could inspect takes as soon as they were shot. When dealing with someone in as poor a state as their former star, moving from scene to scene as swiftly as possible had been essential. There simply had not been that many hours when Townsend could function.

But there had been a lot of problems in the beginning. The lead cameraman, a devotee of the old school, loathed digital. He had lit it as he had been doing it for years, leaving the scenes looking flat, the colors too harsh, the sense of three-dimensional reality totally lost. But Martin had backed Britt on the decision. Then Panavision had reworked the lenses, a critical issue with digital film. The focal viewpoint with a digital camera was less than one-twentieth the size of a standard film camera. Which meant the lens had to be ground to NASA specifications. A digital camera lens cost more than a Lexus. But digital film saved so much time on editing it could earn back the extra cost in one decent series. Still, Martin missed the old days of flicker and focus and anticipation.

The screen counted down. The electronic clipboard snapped. The scene was there in total digital clarity.

Martin leaned forward. His half-finished plate dropped unnoticed to the carpet at his feet.

"We used two cameras," Britt said. "I know it's not normal with a screen test, but—"

"Be quiet," Martin snapped.

The close-up circled the pair. Off-camera Britt's voice said, "Just hold it there, that's it. Now say your name for the camera."

"You know it already. JayJay Parsons."

Someone off-camera laughed. Britt snapped, "Either shut up or take a walk. No, not you. I wasn't asking for your stage name. What's your other name, JayJay?"

On camera the actor looked confused. But his speaking voice was excellent. More than that. It was *incredible*. "John Junior."

"Okay, Mr. Junior. Look at Clara now. Good."

Martin realized he had risen to his feet only when his head protruded onto the screen. He stepped to the left.

JayJay Parsons was clearly uncomfortable under the lights. Twice his eyes flickered toward the camera, a serious no-no in filmdom. But it did not matter. Nothing did.

The close-up camera swung in a gradual arc. Filming JayJay from every angle. Even the rear. The resulting three-dimensionality left Martin shivering.

"Okay," Britt said off-camera. "Read your lines on the teleprompter."

Clara took her brother's hand. Her voice carried a flirting edge. "You sure you can't make it back in time for dinner?"

"I done told you already."

"But I've got your favorite dessert already half-finished, JayJay." She swung his hand back and forth, holding it with both of hers. "Blackberry cobbler with molasses and a hint of fresh ginger."

"That don't change a thing, Clara." Slowly but forcefully JayJay drew his hand away. "I got six hours of riding in each direction. There ain't no way I can get back tonight."

Clara pouted and looked at the man from beneath her long lashes. "I don't like being here on my own, JayJay. The nights just go on forever."

"I'll leave you the rifle."

"No, I couldn't sleep thinking about you out there in wolf country with nothing but your six-shooter and your knife."

Martin's shivers only strengthened. The man was wooden, sure. And his gaze tracked the words. JayJay read the lines without inflection. But this was television. Hits had been launched with worse. A certain household name had become a star playing a cowhand on a cattle drive. Nobody thought the public would have any interest in week after week of marauding Indians and panicked steers. But the thing worked. And the fact that thirty years later the actor was still known around town as the Wooden Nickel did not matter at all.

JayJay said, "Them wolves are taking our calves, Clara. You know how I feel about them little ones. I got to round them up and bring them back."

Clara did not look like any sister Martin had ever known, not as she drew one fingernail slowly down the front of JayJay's shirt. The nail's passage left a dark imprint where the man's sweat stained through. She asked, "How long will you be gone?"

"That depends on how you act when I get back, woman. Now keep your paws to yourself."

"Cut! Okay, JayJay, just read the lines."

"You tell this conniving woman she ain't to touch me like she was working the back room of Baker's Taproom."

"What's the matter, JayJay?" Clara pouted. "Don't you want to give your sister a good-bye kiss?"

"That's enough, both of you." Britt stepped into camera range. He slipped the headphones from around his neck and tossed them off-camera. "Look, JayJay. What say we just take a little walk out back. I'd like to shoot you in the natural light."

"Long as *she* don't come along. Else I'll be shooting her with something besides that camera."

"Bye-bye, brother," Clara sang. "I'll be waiting."

"You just chill, okay? Come on, JayJay. She's pulling your leg."

The portable followed them through the mammoth soundstage. JayJay gave everything they passed a nervous glance, then turned away. Like he'd be burned if he looked at anything too long.

Britt took him through the double doors marked "Corral." The camera adjusted with digital swiftness to the change in light. Britt said, "Give us another close-up here."

While JayJay was still getting his bearings, the camera swooped in so tight Martin could see where the makeup lay uneven on JayJay's neck.

Britt obviously noticed it as well, for he turned in his seat and said, "JayJay basically melted his first makeup. Peggy must have missed that bit there."

Martin waved it aside. On the screen, JayJay was staring ahead like a drowning man spying dry land. The camera shifted around so that Martin could see what JayJay was looking at.

"Hey, girl," JayJay said. "If you aren't a sight for sore eyes."

The mare flicked its ears and whinnied.

JayJay vaulted the corral fence and whistled once. The horse came trotting over.

Martin said, "I don't believe what I'm seeing."

"Tell me about it."

JayJay let the horse nestle against his chest as he stroked its forehead. He bent down and touched the right foreleg. "Let me see that hoof, girl."

The horse obligingly lifted its leg. The same leg that had threatened to separate Townsend's head from his shoulders. The horse sniffed JayJay's back as he bent over and inspected the foreleg. Martin heard the horse whinny again.

JayJay straightened. "Why, you're as good as new, aren't you? I guess them docs were right after all. Rest was the only thing that'd cure you."

Britt turned in his chair so he could watch the studio chief's response. "At least he's seen the show."

Martin nodded agreement. They had written out the horse after it bit Townsend's shoulder so bad he needed forty stitches and a skin graft. Martin had resisted months of attorneys and agents yelling for the horse to be destroyed. For one thing, Skye had cost upward of a quarter million dollars. For another, the horse had only done what almost everybody on the set had wanted to do for months.

The mare was a dappled gray with the most astonishing silver mane and tail. Skye shook her mane and whinnied louder still.

JayJay responded by leaping onto the horse bareback. "Giddap there!"

The horse bolted. Or so it seemed to Martin. The view jerked as the cameraman tried hard to follow the unexpected action. Horse and rider did a loping run around the corral's perimeter.

JayJay then guided the horse toward the derelict exercise ramp in the middle of the sawdust-covered circle. The horse accelerated and leaped over both hurdles together. JayJay laughed as he rocked down hard on the horse's neck. He recovered swiftly and guided the horse twice more around the perimeter, before leading the mare back to where a crowd had gathered. The horse pulled up sharply, then rose up tall as a dappled mountain on its rear legs. JayJay Parsons kept his legs tight to the mare's ribs and gripped the mane with one fist while his other hand came up in a traditional salute over his head. A salute they had dropped after the second season, when Townsend's rising-star status meant he could begin indulging his bad habits.

But Townsend had never ridden bareback. Not in a zillion seasons.

JayJay dropped to the sawdust-covered earth. He stroked the horse's neck. And he smiled.

The camera did not need to zoom in to catch that smile's power. Martin felt it in his gut. It was not just a good smile. It captured the sunlight and drew it down with pinpoint accuracy.

The screen went blank. The lights came up too fast, catching Martin before he was ready.

Britt grinned. "We're back in business, aren't we."

Martin punched the speakerphone. "Run the tape again. Put it on the small screen."

The camera operator asked, "You want spots or the whole deal?"

"Show me everything."

The lights dimmed once more. Early in his reign, Martin Allerby had positioned a television to the right of the main screen. Too often the big screen did not reveal what the folks at home saw. But this was not the real reason why Martin wanted to watch JayJay a second time.

He needed a chance to recover.

As the scene ran on the smaller screen, Martin had to struggle not to shout out his rage.

Martin Allerby was not just looking at a star.

There on the tiny box was a man who had just become his enemy. Martin Allerby needed a moment to mask his frustrated fury. And decide which knife to use. And how.

# Chapter 6

---

JayJay Parsons had never reeled anywhere in his entire life. He had seen enough of the wrong sort of folks staggering out of Baker's Taproom. He had even fought a couple that threatened the peace of Simmons Gulch. But JayJay did not reel. Especially not in broad daylight, leaving someplace called Centurion Studios. But that is exactly what he did.

He staggered down the cracked sidewalk, around the corner, and almost wound up planted on a sixteen-wheeler's front bumper. That woke him up a trifle. He leaned against a lamppost and took stock. Or tried to.

He was surrounded by ugly. The traffic was constant, the street an asphalt river six lanes wide. When the light went red again, he stared at the oddest vehicle he had ever laid eyes on. The sparkling rims kept spinning even when the car was still. Music loud as a jackhammer thumped through the open window, shouting an angry tirade. The passenger wore bulbous insect-eye sunglasses and a shirt with every button open. Three gold chains thumped against his tattooed chest as he rocked back and forth to the beat. He noticed JayJay and grinned. "What's the haps, Pops? Where's your horse?"

"Back at the corral," JayJay replied.

The stranger laughed and spoke to the driver in Spanish. Everybody leaned over to stare at JayJay. The stranger made a gun from his forefinger and thumb and took aim at JayJay. The driver shouted over, "*Vaya con Dios, vajero,*" then gunned the motor. The car roared away.

35

The buildings were all stained yellow with the dry desert dust. Scrubby weeds and scraggly trees dotted the otherwise lifeless street. The only people he saw were in cars. The only crops that thrived were billboards and telephone poles.

He walked because it gave his body something to do while his mind struggled to make sense of everything he had seen. The day just didn't add up.

"Hey, guys! Take a look, will you!"

JayJay winced and shied like a nervous filly as somebody rushed toward him. A voice yelled, "I don't *believe* this."

"Hold fire there, stranger."

"Sorry, sorry, yeah, sure, you must get a lot of this. It's just . . ." The newcomer had too large a grin for his young face. "You're him, right?"

A young woman raced up so fast she bounced off the young man. "It's *you*."

Another man bounded up. And two more women. "It can't be."

"The studio's only a couple of blocks from here," the first guy pointed out. "You're him. You've got to be."

JayJay did what any man who'd been brought up proper should do. He offered his hand. "JayJay Parsons."

"Oh, man, this is just too much." The girl was tiny and Oriental. She jumped up and down, turning a circle in the process. "I was *raised* on you."

He stood in the center of a growing crowd. All of them shone with the enthusiasm of youth and good health. The first guy to have approached was slender and Oriental, with high cheekbones and jet-black eyes. "Can I just say one thing, sir? My family came over here on the boats after Nam. Not me, I was born here. But my grandmother and my parents."

He spoke in such a rush he had to stop and breathe, then, "I know you hear this all the time. But I've got to tell you anyway. My grandma doesn't speak much English and my Vietnamese is lousy. But every week, man, I wish you could see what it's like. Eight o'clock Tuesdays, we are *there*. Planted in front of the tube. It's the only time our house is quiet. Tuesday nights and church, that's our time together, all of us." Excitement squeezed tears into the kid's eyes. "And every night when the show goes off, my grandmother, she says the same thing to me. 'Go and be like him. That's why we came to America. For you to become a man like him.'"

JayJay allowed the kid to take his hand. "I don't rightly understand what you've said, mister. But I'm much obliged just the same."

The young woman who looked like his sister asked, "Can I have your autograph?"

"Don't bother him with that, silly. He gets that all the time."

"I don't have pen nor paper, miss." He looked out over the throng. There had to be a couple of dozen now. All of them in their teens and twenties. "What's going on here? Y'all are the first people I've seen out in the daylight."

They all laughed like he had just told a joke. "Yeah, that's LA for you."

"We're headed for the fires."

"Fires?"

"You haven't heard?" A dozen voices all started talking together.

The Vietnamese kid shouted, "Quiet!" When the chatter subsided, he went on, "Wildfires, JayJay."

A kid with a serious dose of freckles said, "That's not his name."

"It is as far as I'm concerned. What *is* your name?"

"John Junior was what I was called as a kid. Nowadays JayJay fits well enough."

"There, see?" The kid pointed at the bus and explained, "Our church is sending out volunteers to try and put a fire line between the closest blaze and some homes."

Suddenly he did not want to be alone, or separated from these people with their honest gazes and easy talk about things that mattered—church and homes and a very real danger. "Y'all need another set of hands?"

Eyes grew round. "Are you serious? You want to come? With us?"

"Sounds like you're off to do the right thing." He couldn't say why they were so thrilled to hear him volunteer. But it made him feel as good as he had that entire strange day. "Can't see myself doin' anything less."

"There he is. With the kids."

"I see him."

Peter sat in the car of his best pal from the studio, Derek Steen. Derek was African American with skin the color of sourwood honey and hair cropped to a black knit helmet. Derek was the number two cameraman on the *Heartland* series. Like a lot of people working behind the camera, Derek was a quiet guy, and very strong for his slender build. Derek played guard on Peter's church basketball team. Peter had seen Derek lay out a forward twice his size when the opponent thought he could just run Derek over, and instead discovered he had struck a concrete barrier.

Derek asked, "Who are these people?"

"I don't know. But they're dressed for hiking or something."

"No. Wait. See the gear? Sure. I heard of them. They're going—"

"To fight the fires. Right. I heard them make the announcement at church, same as you."

"Look. He's helping them load the bus."

"He can't be." But he was. This new JayJay Parsons was now part of the conga line, humping a huge pile of protective clothing and water and axes and sleeping bags and ropes into the baggage compartment of the church bus.

"Stars don't do that," Peter protested.

"This one apparently does." Derek spun around and leaned over the rear of his seat.

"What are you doing?"

"Probably wasting some perfectly good film." Derek had rescued a broken last-generation camera, jerry-rigged a 35mm lens so that it fit the tighter digital nozzle, and spent his spare time running down stories for several local news stations. Derek had three children, a fourth on the way, and needed the extra income.

When Peter started shifting in his seat, Derek said, "Don't open your door. I don't want them to see us."

"I'm just reaching for my phone."

"You won't get a signal." Derek focused through the front windscreen and clicked the trigger. The camera gave a gentle whirring. "Apparently the cell-phone companies think the valley doesn't have anything worthwhile to say."

Peter shut the phone and stowed it away. "None of this makes any sense."

"What, the new JayJay?"

"Of course the new JayJay. Just look at the guy. He's . . ."

"Incredible, I know." Derek stopped filming and settled the camera into his lap.

"You don't sound worried about it."

"How long have we been praying for a miracle to rescue the show?"

"Since the beginning of last season."

"Exactly. Then what happens but our pastor suggests we get the word out, since there are so many others who love the guy JayJay is supposed to be. Now we've got prayer groups all over the country praying for rain." Derek pointed with his chin through the front windshield. "You know what I see out there sweating in the desert heat? A future. Want to guess how many starving cameramen there are in LA?"

"Not as many as there are starving writers."

"Exactly. So this guy comes out of nowhere and walks into the role like he was made for it. So what?"

"No. Like he actually *is* JayJay Parsons."

"Whatever. The facts stay the same. The studio powers have bought into this guy. Which means you're not just another guy with a laptop and a legend of once having written for a hit series." Derek picked at a bit of loose tape binding the camera's cover. "Personally, when I say my prayers tonight, I'm going to give a lot of thanks that this guy popped in from wherever."

Peter sat up straighter. "What's he doing now?"

Derek squinted through the windscreen. "This isn't happening."

JayJay Parsons accepted a meal bag and a bottled water from a smiling young woman and followed an Asian guy onto the bus. The motor fired up.

"Can we follow him?"

"You kidding me?" Derek started his car. "When you get a signal, call my agent. Tell him I've got some footage he can take national."

When he found a signal Peter called his wife and left a message that he would be late. He then called Derek's agent and gave her secretary the requested message. The PA heard him out, then told him to hold. The agent came on, totally LA, all brusque energy and hustle. "Who is this?"

"Peter Caffrey."

"Who?"

"A friend of Derek's. He asked me to call."

"He won't talk to me himself?"

"We're on a mountain road and Derek drives a stick shift."

"So what you said to my PA, it's true?"

"JayJay Parsons is going off to fight the wildfires with a team from a Riverside church."

"You mean Neil Townsend."

"No. Townsend is off the show. His replacement."

"What's his name?"

Peter stumbled on that, and decided, "JayJay Parsons."

"Sure. I get it. You're stressing continuity. But it still won't wash. A replacement who hasn't been tested on-screen could fly to the moon and it wouldn't be news."

"Hold on a second." Peter cupped the phone. "Your agent says it won't wash."

"Plant the phone to my ear."

"This is silly."

"Just do it, okay?" When the phone was within range, Derek said, "Have I ever steered you wrong?" He listened a moment, then, "And I'm telling you this guy is more JayJay Parsons than Townsend ever was. No. You've just got to take my word, is what. I'm about to hand you a major exclusive. All I'm saying is, you should make the calls."

Derek motioned with his head for Peter to retrieve the phone. "Agents."

"You can have mine anytime you like."

"No thanks. They're like bottled water. The only thing that changes is the packaging. Inside it's all the same and tasteless."

"But essential."

"I hope so. I'd like to think I'm not wasting fifteen percent of everything I make."

"That's debatable." It was an old conversation. Peter dialed the studio operator. "Could I have Casting, please?"

Derek asked, "What are you doing?"

"Just checking on something. Hi, this is Peter Caffrey. Who am I speaking with, please?"

"Phyllis Gleason." The woman had "No" permanently implanted in her tone. "Who did you say this was?"

"Peter Caffrey."

"Oh. Caffrey. Right. The scriptwriter on *Heartland*." The voice lost a bit of its rough edge. "Sorry. I thought you were an actor looking for a bit part. They start calling about this time every afternoon."

"Sure. Listen, the guy you sent over for the JayJay Parsons role. I was just wondering where—"

"Who?"

"The new actor."

"What new actor? I haven't sent anybody for a couple of weeks."

"Somebody else, then."

"Look, Caffrey. We're a small shop over here. If anybody had come across another Parsons, I'd know about it."

"But . . ."

"Besides, Britt Turner stopped by, when was it?" A voice in the background spoke up. "Beginning of last week, that's right. Told us it was a waste of time."

"I don't get it."

"Get what, hon?"

"A new JayJay Parsons showed up and did a test."

"He can't have."

"But he did." For some reason, Peter found himself sweating. "I watched the filming and then sat in when they showed it to Allerby. He loved it. We're supposed to start filming a new series."

"So what's the actor's name?"

"That's why I'm calling. All I've heard is JayJay Parsons." Peter wiped his face. "Britt said Casting sent him over."

"That's impossible."

"I heard the AD say it." AD, as in assistant director. Kip.

"Well, that little pest never got anything right. He entered the world backward and never got turned around since." Phyllis spoke more loudly, "Anybody send over a new wannabe JayJay?" Then back to the phone. "Either you heard wrong or the pest is off by a mile. Again."

"You haven't sent anybody over?"

"What I just said, hon."

"Thanks."

"You tell Britt to make sure this new guy has his guild card. If he doesn't, we need to jump on this."

"Okay."

"He's not talking about some bit actor here. If we get caught using a noncarded actor in a starring role, we'll have the unions down on us like the Mongol hordes."

Derek cast Peter glances as he wound the car up a steep incline, close behind the wheezing bus. "Look at it this way. You asked for a miracle. You got one. I was kneeling right there alongside you. I never heard you pray for logic."

# Chapter 7

---

The first hour or so, the bus ride was noisy as a fair-size rodeo. JayJay relaxed for the first time since coming to inside the warehouse of used clothing. The kids were too natural to hold him in awe for very long. He did not understand why they all seemed to know him so well. But as the bus wound its way into the northwestern hills, he decided it really didn't matter. Their joy was as genuine as their excitement.

But when they hit the high plateau, their mood turned tense and the noise dropped away. The northern reaches were cut off by a billowing dark wall. Overhead the high desert sky remained so blue it appeared almost black. Up ahead, however, there was no sky at all.

JayJay had an aisle seat about midway back. While boarding he'd shaken the hands of two pastors and a number of ladies who had stared at him with that same astonished wonder. He was seated beside Ahn Nguyen, the Vietnamese kid. Ahn's younger sister, Minh, sat across the aisle and one row up. She was small like her brother and painfully shy over her mouthful of metal. But she watched him with her brother's bright-faced eagerness. JayJay found himself drawn to the young woman, and now, as the bus drew quiet, she asked, "You're not from around here, are you?"

"Not hardly, miss."

She blushed scarlet and cradled her arms on the seat back so she could use her elbow to hide her braces. She asked, "How did you come to be here? In Hollywood, I mean."

"All I can tell you for certain is, one minute I was snoozing in the back of a bus. Then lightning must've struck, because the next thing I knew, everybody was staring at me."

The folks within listening range erupted in laughter. Those who had not heard it the first time had it repeated for them, until JayJay's words were echoing up and down the aisle. He would have been ashamed over the attention were it not for seeing Minh laugh so fully she momentarily forgot her braces.

The pastor rose from the front of the bus, smiled JayJay's way, and raised his hands for silence. "Okay, we've gone through everything a dozen times, but once more won't hurt. We work in teams of four."

The kid in the row ahead of them, Robbie Robinson, turned around and whispered, "My girlfriend had to back out. She sprained her foot. Want to hook up with me and Ahn and Ming?"

"I'd consider it an honor."

Once more he was rewarded with a from-the-heart smile from Minh. The pastor continued, "What's our first and only rule?"

The bus shouted in unison, "Stay safe, stay together!"

"Right. You folks who are doing this for the first time, your team leader has been out before."

"That's Ahn," Robbie said.

"No wild heroics. Keep your team in sight at all times. Follow orders. Questions?" When the bus remained silent, he said, "Okay, let's bow our heads and pray."

The bus wheezed to a halt just as the pastor intoned his amen.

People lifted their gazes to an utterly different world. The clearing was full of trucks and equipment and smoke-stained people in fire-retardant gear. A fist banged on the bus door. A burly man with red eyes, a three-day beard, and a smoke-roughened voice climbed the stairs and said, "Name's Sears, like the stores, and no relation, I'm sorry to say."

He got a few chuckles, but not many. People were too busy getting used to the proximity of danger. His helmet was stenciled with one word, *Boss*. "I'm your section leader. Anybody asks, this is section two. You find somebody wandering alone out there, you bring them back here. Firefighters or civvies, it makes no diff. You bring them here. Everybody clear on that? Nobody but nobody works the fire line alone. Let me hear you're listening."

There was a chorus of assent. He nodded. "Team leaders, raise your hands. All of you have been on a fire line before, right? Good. Everybody know your team? Okay. Pile out, grab your gear, and head for the woman at the assignment board. She's over there by the chuck wagon. Only team leaders speak to her. Otherwise things get chaotic. She'll tell you where to go and what to do. No arguments, you hear me? You do what you're told or you sit it out on the bus. Let me hear you're listening."

This time the response was stronger. "Our job is to finish a fire line between the burn along the western ridge and the houses to our east. We could have a code red today. No chance of rain before tomorrow. Latest meteorology report warns of rising winds. If you hear the claxon, you *run*. Tell me you're listening."

This time he got a shout in reply. He nodded. "Now tell me, what's rule one?"

"Stay safe, stay together!"

"Right. And rule two?"

There was a confused silence. A grin split his blackened and bearded face. "Same as rule one. Okay. Let's go fight some fire."

Derek stopped his car along the curve leading into the clearing. "This is as close as we want to park."

Now that they were there, Peter faced a rising dread. "You've done this before?"

"My first shots on national news came from a wildfire."

Reluctantly Peter rose from his seat and walked around to the back of Derek's aging hatchback. "My throat hurts."

"You get used to it." Derek flipped open a metal box. "Well, actually what happens is, in about ten minutes you'll be too busy to pay your throat much attention."

Peter watched the crowd including the studio's new JayJay Parsons cluster around a woman with a bullhorn. She stood beside a park bulletin board that had been covered with a plastic-encased map. She pointed to the map, then to one of the upraised hands, made a note on a sheet, then turned back to the map. Again and again. Peter asked, "Too busy doing what?"

"Staying alive." Derek handed him a thick padded belt. "Here. Make yourself useful."

"You're actually enjoying this."

"You kidding? Far as I'm concerned, they could charge admission."

Peter watched as a sudden blast of smoke obliterated more than half the clearing. He tasted the acrid stench far below the level of his taste buds. Then it was gone. All but the feeling in his throat. He appeared to be the only one who even saw it. "I'm pretty sure my wife would tell me to stay in the car."

"Yeah, mine too." Derek handed Peter an orange canvas vest with *Press* written in black letters across the front and back. "Good thing they're not here, right?"

Peter let his friend stuff lenses and cloths and extra film into the belt's various pouches. "Remind me what we're doing here."

"You're the one who told me to follow JayJay from the studio."

"Stop calling him that."

"So what name should I use?"

"That's exactly what worries me. I have no idea." He turned to where JayJay Parsons was slipping into an orange fire-retardant jacket and helmet. "Who *is* this guy?"

Derek slapped a press cap onto Peter's head. "I already told you. Our paycheck, is who." He hefted the camera. "Okay, let's move out."

A blood red sun glared down from an acrid sky. Angry streamers poured up from the west, black and gritty and laced with heat. Loudspeakers hanging from the chuck wagon's corners blared "I Am a Man of Constant Sorrow." Three soot-blackened firefighters sprawled on the earth beside the paramedic station, coughing into oxygen masks. They watched JayJay and his team stride by, wearing their pristine fire-retardant jackets and their axes and shovels sparkling in the wretched light. The bedraggled firefighters didn't say anything. They didn't need to.

JayJay said, "Don't worry about it, friends. Come sunset, we'll be just as dirty."

Minh was the only one who managed a smile. "Have you ever fought fires?"

"Been through a lot, sister. But this here is a first."

As they entered the forest, a woman so hoarse she had lost all but the last shred of her voice stood in a fork of the trail. "The line is three hundred meters straight ahead. Listen for the claxon. If the wind rises we've got to clear out of here fast."

The trail was rimmed by fire hoses that writhed and slid like canvas snakes. They passed through a clearing that held a half dozen houses. Families frantically packed SUVs. People hosed down roofs. Two women standing in the nearest home's front drive hugged in tear-streaked terror.

"I'm frightened," Minh confessed.

"I'm sure glad to hear it," JayJay replied. "Hate to think I was the only fellow scared out of his tiny mind."

Robbie asked, "What's that sound?"

Ahn replied, "Take a guess."

But it didn't sound like a fire. It sounded *alive*. A growling roar rose ahead and to their left, an angry rumbling JayJay felt in his chest.

They followed the sound of chain saws and bulldozers. The fire line was such an astounding sight they froze at the point where the trail opened. Another woman was clearly used to the response, for she started grabbing sleeves and pointing them ahead. Another man waved to them. He pointed to the shrub. Then to the people scurrying to either side.

"Come on," JayJay yelled. "We got work to do."

"Hold it right there, you two."

Derek pointed to the yellow letters on his vest. "Press."

"Hey, I'm so impressed I can't hardly stand it." The bearish guy's soot-stained helmet read *Boss*. He turned his head and coughed. His throat sounded semiruined. "Out here you either follow my orders or you leave, got me?"

"Sure, Boss."

"You ever been on a burn?"

"I have, Boss. More times than I can count."

"Then you should know better than to head out on your own."

"We're trying to catch up with JayJay Parsons."

"What, the actor from *Heartland*?"

"He was on the church bus with those kids."

The guy grinned. His teeth looked impossibly white. "This is a joke, right?"

"No, Boss. No joke."

"Okay, but you still got to team up." He scouted around. A trio of weary firefighters were gathering their gear from a pile by the oxygen tanks. "You guys headed back out?"

"Got to get that line done," one replied, then had to cough from the effort of speaking.

"Take this pair with you." To Derek and Peter he said, "Grab coats and helmets from the pile by the ambulance."

The firefighters glared at where *Press* was written on their vests. "Why us?"

"They need a team, you're it. And keep an eye out for JayJay Parsons."

"The actor? For real?"

"All I know is what these two are saying. But if you find him, do us a favor and keep the six o'clock news from telling the world we toasted my favorite TV star."

# Chapter 8

There was no room for anything but *speed*.

The din was earsplitting. Bulldozers driven by insane men with lightning reflexes shoved down tree after tree. Chain saws chopped off the branches. JayJay and his team joined sweaty, soot-blackened workers pulling the debris into mountains on the opposite side of the line from the approaching burn. The line was a hundred and fifty feet wide and ran off in both directions to where ridgelines became swallowed by smoke. Their task was to widen the line. The four of them wrestled mammoth branches and fragments across the stumpy earth. No one needed to tell them to hurry. Every hint of wind carried the threat of the enemy.

JayJay welcomed the work. He relished everything about it. The people, the hoarse commands he couldn't understand, the sweat, the aching muscles, the heaving chest. This was *real*. The sparks that floated in the air and burned the exposed skin of his neck were not just painful. They *anchored* him. The tormenting thoughts were banished. He was among new friends. He was doing something useful. Something important.

He had never felt so alive.

Derek's mouth almost touched his ear. Even so, Peter scarcely made out the question, "Do you see him?"

"Are you kidding?" Peter had never experienced such sensory overload. His mind threatened to shut down. He wanted to curl up in a safe corner, close his eyes, and just make the whole thing go away. He could scarcely hear himself, much less Derek. The noise held such intensity it assaulted his brain.

A trio of planes lumbered by overhead, so close Peter thought he might be able to reach up and touch them. They were followed by two helicopters, the big ones with two rotors each. The choppers carried huge buckets on long metal lines. The buckets almost scraped the treetops. Then they were gone, but the noise level remained the same. As though the din had reached a point where it could not grow any louder. Just change in nature. The dozers and the chain saws and the fire formed fists of noise. He had never heard a burn before. But he knew the sound. It could not be anything else.

He jerked as one of the firefighters grabbed his sleeve. The man's words were lost to the din. But Peter read the man's lips. *Stay close.*

They jogged across the clearing. The fire line was frightening in its unnatural straightness. And the people. Hundreds and hundreds of people. All of them moving at breakneck speed. Gestures took the place of words. Everybody worked in frantic coordination.

One of Peter's team grabbed an idle chain saw. Peter flinched as the man gave the handle an easy toss and the machine whined to life. He had always hated the sound of those things. Now he was surrounded by a hundred of them. All screaming and biting and cutting.

Derek punched his shoulder. He pointed to a group of four people who came and went in the drifting smoke. He said something Peter missed entirely. Then he started walking.

"Wait!" Peter glanced nervously at the guys they had arrived with. But the firefighters were intent on a felled tree. Peter stumbled after Derek. The earth was rutted and jumbled, the going made treacherous by deep bulldozer furrows and exposed roots. The mud was glutinous. Yet even carrying the camera, Derek sprinted toward the foursome.

Peter followed only because he was terrified of getting lost and never finding his way out again.

Derek stopped without warning and dropped to the earth. He was still thirty paces from the four. He braced his elbows on the highest stump in the clearing. He focused. Took a slow breath. Then hit the trigger.

Derek did a slow sweep of the entire scene. Taking in the dozers and the saws and the workers and the angry sky. He lingered on the smoke overhead. Then he drew in close and tight. Taking aim at one group in particular. Four people hauling a branch. Four out of hundreds. Struggling with just another huge branch.

Then Peter saw him.

JayJay's face was streaked like an Indian's. His teeth were drawn back in a snarl of sweaty effort. The reddish-gold hair emerging from his helmet was matted to his forehead. The four of them were dwarfed by the pine branch they carried. Even so, they *ran*. JayJay Parsons and three others. Two of whom were Oriental. The fourth guy had freckles and looked about seventeen. They were all clearly very scared. They dumped the branch. Kicked it well back out of the clearing. Stood breathing hard for a minute. Then they turned and headed back across the line for the next branch.

Peter found his breath returning to normal. He took a more comfortable position on the ground beside Derek. He took mild notice of the wet seeping through his trousers. He no longer cared. His mind had moved into creative mode.

He did a slow three-sixty, trying to embed everything into his brain. He did not need to watch JayJay. Derek would do that for them both. What he needed was to get all of this down so tightly he could go back and make it live on the page.

He came back around. And found Derek grinning at him. The camera was propped on the stump. Peter moved in so close their helmets clicked. "This is the first episode for next season!"

"Now you're thinking!" Derek pointed ahead. "Let's change position so I can shoot them against the sun!"

"What sun?"

"Exactly!" Derek clambered to his feet. His legs were caked with the viscous mud. Ash speckled his coat. His face and hands were gray-black. His eyes were on fire. "Let's go!"

The wind caught them totally by surprise.

One moment the four of them were wrestling just another branch across the line, with the mud clinging to their boots like red claws. The next, the world vanished.

JayJay started coughing before his mind fully registered the change. The world was *gone*. At first he thought it must have been another of those giant choppers passing too close overhead, clamping the smoke to the earth. Only he could not hear the rotors' deep thrumming. Yet the air was pushing *down* on them. Not from the north where the fire burned. Straight down. Compressing the air and the smoke to the earth. Blinding them. Making his lungs burn like he had taken a double helping of ash.

The claxon added a ghostly panic to the invisible scene. The alarm whooped up and down the scale. But from which direction? The wind was as great an enemy as the fire. It made the noise come from all directions at once. It rammed the smoke and the flames down JayJay's throat.

JayJay dropped his hold on the branch. He tried to shout, but the words barely croaked from his throat. "Where's my team?"

If anything, the smoke grew even thicker. The sky overhead ate the sun completely. He heard coughing. He groped in the direction he thought the cough came from. His glove gripped another shoulder. JayJay flung his arms around the unseen figure. The man was almost his height, which meant it had to be Robbie. The way Robbie clung to him, JayJay knew he was not the only one who had panicked. Feeling the young man's muscled strength beneath the jacket drew JayJay back from the brink.

He stripped off his belt, reached around, and found Robbie's arm. He planted one end of the belt into Robbie's hand. He drew his helmet in tight to Robbie's. "Don't let go!"

"Where are the others?"

"Stoop down and hunt! One hand only!"

JayJay found the body by stumbling over it. He had no idea whether it was Ahn or Minh. Only that the body was small and still except for tremors that did not quite form into full coughs.

The chain saws and the bulldozers grew silent. The fire still roared at them from all sides. Other hoarse voices called out names and confusing directions. The claxon whooped and shrilled and offered no clearer a course than the fire.

JayJay clearly heard Robbie croak, "I've found Ahn!"

Which meant it was Minh that JayJay was slinging onto his shoulder. "One of you strip off your jacket!" He did not recognize his own voice. "Grab hold of the arms. Everybody stay together!"

"Where is Minh?"

"I've got her."

"Where do we go?"

"I'm working on it." JayJay shifted Minh so that she rode easier on his shoulder. At least it was the lightest of the team that had gone down. He squinted and looked straight up. Ash and burning cinders pelted his face. He blinked away the blinding tears and forced himself to keep staring at the unseen sky.

A panic-stricken voice shrilled, "The flames! They're coming! *I can see them!*"

"Hold hard there, brother. You ain't burning yet." Then it came. The one solid opening he had been waiting for. There and gone in a single frantic heartbeat. But enough for JayJay to get a sighting on the sun. But he also lost hold of his belt. "Where are you at!"

A panicked voice tremored, "Here."

"Here don't mean nothing in this soup. Follow my voice. Okay, I got you, no, don't grab, I'm carrying somebody."

Ahn cried, *"Minh!"*

"You stay calm too. I got your sister." JayJay heard other voices calling with the authority of having made the same sighting as him. Which added to his confidence. "Everybody listen up! Grab hold of anybody you get within reach of, but only use your free hand! I spotted the sun. Okay, let's move!"

They had only gone about thirty paces when JayJay tripped over a coughing form and almost went down. Half turning, he called back, "Robbie!"

"Yo."

"Grab my jacket. I need my other hand." He scooped up the unseen figure. "You got to help me, mister. I'm too burdened down to bear your weight."

The guy tried his best. But he was coughing and hacking so hard he kept wanting to fold again. "Mister, you got to stay up, we don't have that far to go." Each word raked another furrow in his throat. JayJay hacked and came up dry. "Come on, keep walking, that's it. We're almost there."

But he wasn't sure where "there" was until he recognized the hoarse female voice that had directed them off the trail and into the fire line. "Okay, y'all get ready. On my count, we're all gonna shout together, 'The trail is over here.' Ready? One, two, *three.*"

They didn't make much of a dent, even calling together. But the news was caught by those closest and passed back. At JayJay's command they did it again. Then other shadow figures were closing in. And JayJay was still holding a supine form. "Let's go!"

He took the trail at as close to a trot as his exhausted legs could

manage, what with a body on one shoulder and his other arm supporting a coughing, stumbling man. The farther they moved down the trail,
the more condensed became the crowd and the clearer the claxon.
Finally they stumbled into the clearing. The smoke was marginally less
dense back here, but only as a matter of degree.

JayJay heard the paramedics shout, "Only those needing serious
care. Everybody else stay back!" But he couldn't for the life of him tell
where the sound was coming from. The noise from the claxon masked
all directions.

Then a chopper flew over. For the very first time, the bellowing
machine was a friend. The downdraft blasted away the smoke. The
chopper hovered not over the clearing, but rather farther along the
trail. It was soon joined by a second, and then a third. People poured in
a constant filthy stream into the clearing. JayJay dropped the coughing
man. To his amazement, JayJay recognized him as the guy from the studio. But JayJay didn't have time to worry about that just then. The
young woman on his shoulder was not moving.

He humped his load over to the ambulance. The machine was surrounded by coughing, singed, supine forms. JayJay grabbed a passing
medic, who wordlessly spun JayJay around. Ten seconds was all she gave
him. Then she slapped a minibottle of oxygen into his hand and shouted
in his ear, "Three mouth-to-mouths, then feed the oxygen and count to
ten. Then repeat. Got that?"

"You bet."

"I'll be back."

JayJay lowered Minh to the ground, then had to push Ahn back
before he could pinch Minh's nose closed and do the three breaths. He
fitted the nozzle over Minh's face and twisted the handle. Counted to
ten. The chopper noise was awful, but at least the smoke was reduced.
Ahn was crouched on his sister's other side. JayJay removed the mouthpiece and gave her another three breaths. Then back on the oxygen.

Minh coughed. Her body convulsed. She opened her eyes.

Ahn dropped back into the mud, covered his face, and sobbed.

Robbie pounded JayJay's shoulder and shouted something JayJay could not understand. JayJay looked over and mouthed one word. *Water.*

Robbie vanished.

Minh's eyes teared up and streaked her face. She watched JayJay with gradually returning focus. Ahn recovered enough to take his sister's hand. Beyond them, the guy JayJay had helped down the trail was turning in a slow circle, coughing and shouting a name that might have been Derek.

Robbie returned with an armload of water bottles. JayJay took a swallow, removed the oxygen breather, lifted Minh's head, and helped her drink. He turned back to Robbie and gave him another one-word order. *Towel.* The kid left and returned in an instant. The cloth he held looked impossibly clean. JayJay accepted the cloth, then nodded toward the guy from the studio, who was searching the returning faces. Robbie understood. He walked over and handed the guy a water bottle. The guy looked dumbly at it, too shocked to understand at first. Then he was trembling and struggling to get the thing open. Robbie took the bottle back and unscrewed the top. The guy drank too fast and choked. Robbie patted his arm. Slow.

JayJay used his teeth to strip off the glove not holding Minh's head. He poured a little water onto the towel and used it to clean her face. Minh captured his hand. She didn't try to speak. She just stared at him.

The medic returned. She was a cute brunette with the lithe compactness of a serious athlete. She fitted the stethoscope to her ears, listened to Minh's breathing, checked her eyes, kneaded her neck. She nodded and gave JayJay a thumbs-up. JayJay grinned his thanks.

The medic's head cocked to one side. She pointed at JayJay. The words were lost to the downdraft. But JayJay understood just the same. You're really him.

This moment was good enough for him to keep hold of his smile just the same.

Peter finally spotted Derek when the exodus began. His legs went so weak he stumbled to his knees again. Then he was up and pushing through the crowd headed toward the buses and safety. "Are you all right?"

Derek gave him a smoke-streaked grin. "All right? Man, this is *fabulous*."

"Are you nuts?"

"I got it all, Peter. Every second of JayJay Parsons and the rescue." They let the crowd push them across the clearing and out toward the vehicles. Derek stripped the water bottle from Peter's hand, drank hard, then poured the rest over his head. "I've been dreaming of doing that."

"Where were you?"

"On top of a fire truck. I waved at you. But you were too busy being scared to see me."

Peter slugged his friend's shoulder. "I thought you'd gone down!"

"Yeah, I saw that too." Derek grinned at his friend. "Nice to know you cared, man."

Suddenly Peter was laughing. It was crazy. But he couldn't help it. Laughing and coughing and stumbling in his exhaustion. Giddy with relief and excitement. He had been there. And he had survived. The feeling was incredible. "Hey, don't kid yourself. I was just worried about having to deliver the news to your wife."

"Whatever." Noise from the claxon and the choppers gradually eased. Derek grabbed two more water bottles from a torn box. He passed one over. "My arms are two feet longer from hauling this camera around."

"Want me to take it?"

"I won't say no."

Peter was scarcely able to hold himself upright, but he took the extra weight anyway. He pointed to a bus up ahead. "There he goes."

"Yeah, I see."

JayJay turned in the process of climbing on board. The Oriental girl still clung limpetlike to his neck as he carried her into the bus. He spotted the pair and nodded at them. An easy gesture from one firefighter to another.

Peter said, "He saved my life out there."

Derek could not stop grinning. "Yeah, I got that too."

# Chapter 9

We're not talking about art. You want art, I know a good dealer down on Rodeo, he'll show you a sketch by some dead French guy, you can shell out twenty thou and hang the thing on your bathroom wall. Forget art. We're talking money here, Harry. The only kind of numbers that matter. Big ones."

Martin resisted the urge to reach for his cigarettes. He had already smoked four today, and he was due at some interminable dinner that night. He rarely went out to such LA functions. But tonight was special, an intimate dinner at the home of a film producer Martin actually admired. Not the man, of course, the man's work. The man was merely a vehicle Martin intended to steer toward Martin's dream. The same dream that had brought him here.

"You know what my kind of art is, Harry? Art is a line at the box office. And that's what Martin and I can produce for you. Art that sells in Kansas City. You've been in this business long enough to know that if you can't sell it in KC, you're dead. The land that Hollywood has forgotten for far too long. That's what we intend to take back, Harry. With your help, we are going to reconquer America."

Milo Keplar was Centurion's director of sales. Martin Allerby ran the studio with just two number twos, a director of production and Milo. Milo Keplar hated Centurion's location with a passion that surpassed Martin's. Milo referred to the San Bernardino Valley as Tombstone West. A place of buried dreams. A place to flee from at the first possible opportunity. Which is why they were here. To escape.

Harry Solish was the unseen face of Hollywood. Only the top execs in the business even knew Harry Solish existed. At any one time, there were never more than five or six people like Harry Solish. They, as much as any other force operating within the film world, determined what got shown on the silver screens.

Harry Solish was money. Big money. Enormous. So big the numbers did not matter. Only the power the money represented. If Harry Solish's consortium green-lighted a picture, it got made. It was that simple.

In any season, about ninety major features were green-lighted. A major these days was a film that cost sixty-five million and up. Add another third on top of that for marketing and distribution. Harry Solish and his group held pieces of as many as forty of these ninety feature films. Without Harry Solish's approval, more than half of these would never have been made.

Harry Solish was a product of modern science. His age was as big a secret as the names of the investors he represented. Martin Allerby guessed Solish's age at somewhere between sixty and a hundred and forty. Harry Solish looked as perfectly groomed and lifeless as a guy wearing a coffin and his final suit. Even his voice held no sign of life.

"Box office sales are down," Harry Solish replied. "What do I want with a stake in a new studio?"

"Not just any studio, Harry. A studio that is dedicated to producing a steady stream of hits."

"And the others aren't?"

"Sure, okay, yes. Of course they all want every film they make to strike gold. But look at the *other* things they count as important." Milo gave no sign he was stressed. He was a small man with a flair for expensive suits and subtle gestures. Martin knew his family had fled Communist Romania, and Milo had sent himself through Dartmouth on government loans. Milo was rabidly American, and fervent about one thing above all else—Milo Keplar's rise to the top of the Hollywood pile.

Martin had no problem with Milo's ambition. Milo was also loyal. Loyalty trumped almost anything in this business.

Milo began counting points off his almost ladylike fingers. "Most studio execs want to be big with the critics on both coasts. They want attention on Oscar night. They want the top names. They want to do what is *fashionable*. They want to be *leading-edge*. But the Centurion Studios we intend to build will care about only one thing, Harry. Generating profit for our investors. A *lot* of profit."

Solish had been nipped and tucked so many times he did not have the spare skin on his neck to let him turn to where Martin sat beside him without swiveling his body. "You've been awfully quiet today, Martin."

Martin held to the party line he and Milo had worked out over the nineteen weeks it had taken to set up this meeting. Their spiel was centered upon the one point his spies had confirmed. "America's middle-class core has been left behind in this postmodern craze for the dark and the dreary and the hopeless. The films of the forties and fifties represented classic storytelling. That's what we want to bring back."

"And not just the films," Milo said, retaking the lead. "We want to develop new faces to match the new stories."

"And thus cut down the costs," Martin added.

"But also the box-office potential," Solish countered.

"Only at first, Harry. Only at first." Milo's only sign of nerves was the way he repeatedly ran one hand down the front of his woven silk tie. "And any face we bring in, we *own*. Just like in the old days. As the star's name rises, they are associated only with our sorts of films. Sure, we can loan them out to other studios. But only on films where we have preapproved the script."

Solish looked from one man to the other, then supplied the line. "And taken a share of the profits."

Martin leaned back and breathed deep for the first time since entering Harry Solish's home office. Not just drew in enough air to keep from passing out. Really breathed. "Not profits, Harry. A percentage of the gross."

Harry settled farther into the sofa and opened the prospectus. Harry Solish was famous for his year-round tan. People who knew Harry, or wished they knew him, spoke with awe about his Caribbean Island getaway. Not a home. A whole *island*. Harry had paid the fifty-seven million dollars with a check from his personal account. Six years on, the Beverly Hills realtor who had handled the deal was still recovering from the shock.

Harry Solish worked from his home on the ninth green of the Bel Air Country Club. He had purchased the homes to each side, torn them both down, and put in a pool lined with limestone tiles embedded with prehistoric animals. Probably reminded Harry of all the careers he had made extinct by simply saying no. The pool house was six thousand square feet and neo-Gothic in design. It contained Harry's office suite. Through wrought-iron glass doors facing the golf course, Martin watched a trio of self-satisfied men putt beneath a sunset-streaked sky. Martin would happily make a fourth, once Harry Solish signed on the dotted line.

There was a knock on the door. The same assistant who had shown them in said, "Sorry to bother you, Harry."

"What is it?"

"There's something I think you'll want to see."

The aide was a typical film-school snot. Martin despised them and their foppish traits. Five years ago the style had been a faux Persian accent and wispy goatee for the men, aggressive man-hating scorn and square black glasses for the women. Now all the guys wore French-cuffed shirts without cuff links and the tail outside the pants. A Rodeo Drive version of floppy prison garb. They emerged from university certain they held the keys to future filmdom. They could waste fifty million dollars on a true stink bomb of a film, then take pride in the fact that nobody went to see it. Martin exchanged a glance with Milo. His sales director was so furious at the interruption the edges of Milo's mouth and eyes had gone chalk white. Martin gave his head a fractional shake. Don't blow it now.

The aide picked up the controls to the massive flat-screen television and hit the switch. "CNN started covering the story in the last half hour. It's so big I thought they might play it a second time. Yes, here it goes now."

Martin's ire vanished in a flash of televised smoke and flames. The professionally cheerful announcer said something he probably should have listened to. But his attention was captured by the image of JayJay Parsons rushing out of a smoking forest with wind-driven flames rising up behind him. His helmet was gone. His face was pulled into a rictus snarl with the strain of carrying one unconscious firefighter over his shoulder and supporting another by the guy's collar. Martin was fairly certain he recognized the grimy face of the firefighter rescued by their actor. Then the image switched to JayJay giving mouth-to-mouth to an unconscious young Oriental woman.

The actor's features were streaked with soot. His left eyebrow was singed. He released the woman's nose and fitted an oxygen mask onto her mouth and nose. When she coughed, JayJay's features turned waxlike with relief. The young man seated beside JayJay began weeping. The camera was relentless in its coverage. Gently JayJay cradled the woman's head and helped her drink, then wet a cloth and began tenderly cleaning her face. His own face was so black it looked charred. But here he was, caring for this young woman, not giving himself a thought.

Only when the scene was replaced by a commercial did Martin realize the three of them had joined the film-school clone standing in front of the television. He and Milo and Harry Solish, all captivated by what this image meant.

It was Milo who said it. "They're going to play that for days. *People* magazine, *Newsweek*, I'm thinking the cover of both."

Harry Solish pointed at the now-vanished star. "I assume this is one of the rising names you have signed to your new venture."

"Absolutely," Martin lied. He held his true feelings down where no one else could see them. Masking his internal broiling cauldron of bitterness was one of his most valued abilities. He had no choice now. He had to work this phenomenon, twist it to his advantage.

Harry handed their prospectus to his aide and said, "Have our people run the numbers." He offered Martin his hand. "Why don't we get together again next week."

He and Milo dared not show any of their glee until they were back on Sunset Boulevard. Milo used the pause at a stoplight to turn and say, "Did that really happen?"

"I wish the boost had come from some other angle, but the timing was phenomenal," Martin agreed.

Milo did not need to ask what was behind Martin's response, as he loathed the *Heartland* series as much as his partner. "You think Solish bought our spiel?"

"We'll know soon enough." Ahead of them both lay a week of tense waiting and sleepless worrying.

Milo drummed his fingers on the steering wheel. "Maybe we should have gone with the other option."

"We've been through all that." Everything they had just laid out at poolside was a calculated scam. Martin Allerby could not have cared less about Middle America and its outdated values. Like his first boss in the film world liked to say, principles were for peons. "And it's too late now."

Milo fretted, "But the numbers on the soft porn, especially taking in the Internet, they were sky-high."

"And I'm telling you my sources claim Solish won't have anything to do with the skin trade, no matter how soft." To hype a guy like Solish, they had needed something nobody else was doing. Something *unique*. Centurion was known for satisfying Middle America's penchant for television's thirty-minute answers to every problem. Of course, neither of them planned for a minute to hold to such a course once the deal was signed. They would make what they wanted. But in the beginning, they needed to at least *sound* unique. It always came back to the same old quandary, how to pry the cash from tightfisted guys like Solish.

Milo was back on the news footage. "If we had bribed CNN a million bucks, they couldn't have worked the timing better." Milo gunned through Sunset Boulevard's winding curves. "One minute I wanted to shoot that film-school phony. The next I could have kissed his three-day growth."

"We need to ride this," Martin said, thinking aloud. "Do an out-of-season special. JayJay Parsons and the wildfire."

"Blend in this actual footage," Milo agreed. "I wonder who owns it?"

"We will," Martin promised. "Before midnight."

# Chapter 10

JayJay saw the news report six times. Not because he wanted to. Because Minh's grandmother plucked at his arm and drew him back in front of the television. Every time they ran it, she grabbed him and bent him over far enough to plant a wet kiss on his cheek.

Ahn, her grandson, loved it. "The mah-jongg circuit is gonna hear about her kissing JayJay Parsons for years."

The grandmother had been the only one home when they returned. JayJay had no idea how much she actually understood as he carried Minh into the little home and laid her down on the living room sofa. But there had been no question of his leaving. Which was fine by him, as he had no place else to go. He had sat at the dining room table and sipped cups of steaming tea, while Ahn phoned his parents and gave them the news. JayJay knew from what Ahn had said on the bus ride home that his folks ran a mini-mart in the San Fernando Valley and could not return until closing time.

JayJay watched the old woman totter back into the kitchen. She swayed like a ship in heavy seas as she walked. She was never still. And she talked all the time. Everything in Vietnamese, jabber jabber jabber, the singsong punctuated by resounding consonants connected to what sounded to JayJay like *oing*. And cooking. The house was one huge smell, all of it good. "I feel like my belly is connected to my backbone."

"You hear that, MahMah?" Ahn called from his place beside JayJay. He switched to Vietnamese. Instantly the old woman teetered back into the front room and planted a bowl and ceramic spoon and another cup of steaming tea in front of JayJay. She patted his shoulder. When JayJay grimaced in anticipation of yet another kiss, she cackled and walked away. Ahn complained, "What about me?"

She replied in Vietnamese and retreated into the steamy kitchen. Ahn planted his chin in his hands. "MahMah says I've got to wait 'til my folks get home."

"Thought you told me you don't speak the lingo."

"He doesn't," Minh said, her voice still very hoarse. "He gets every other word totally wrong."

"Oh, and you're so perfect."

"Better than you."

"Here, we'll share." JayJay slid the bowl over and they dug in. The soup was spicy and sour at the same time, filled with slivers of beef and bamboo, and delicious. "Man, can that lady ever cook."

"Tell me."

Ahn's sister lay on the sofa where JayJay had settled her. Minh was covered with a fuzzy blanket. Her gaze never left JayJay's face. For once, the fact did not bother JayJay at all. He glanced over, warmed by what he saw in those dark eyes. "You doing okay, missie?"

"My throat hurts," she murmured, then coughed.

"Guess that's to be expected."

Their grandmother returned and said something to Minh. Minh whined a response. JayJay asked, "What is it?"

"She wants me to eat, but I know it'll hurt my throat."

"Probably do you good, though." He rose from the table and walked over. He had showered twice in the children's bathroom and was dressed now in the only clothes they had that fit—a cutoff T-shirt and gym shorts. The T-shirt ended just above his navel. There was nothing he could do about it just then. He had no money, and his clothes from the studio were ruined. He could still smell the smoke from someplace, or perhaps it was just the memories. "Mind if I join you?"

Minh winced as she pushed herself to a sitting position. Their grandmother did the same thing every time JayJay moved about, which was to clap her arthritic hands and jabber. Minh said, "MahMah thinks you're a hunk."

"Right. Like you don't." This from Ahn.

"That's enough." JayJay took the bowl the grandmother was holding. He swished the white glop around with the ceramic spoon. "What is this, grits?"

"Rice gruel."

"Reckon it'll be the easiest thing for you to get down. Why not give it a try." He turned to Ahn. "Wipe that smirk off your face and go get your sister a glass of milk."

Minh accepted the bowl. She took a small bite. JayJay saw her wince and heard her swallow. "Just take it easy. But you need to eat if you're gonna keep your strength up."

But she dropped the spoon in the bowl. Her chin trembled as she whispered, "Thank you, JayJay."

He knew her tears embarrassed her. So he drew her over and let her hide on his chest. "I tell you what's the truth. I was stumbling around in that fog like a blind man. Couldn't find enough breath to call your name. When I found you lying there, I would've been the happiest man alive if I hadn't been so scared."

Which was how the parents found them. They came tumbling through the door, weary from a day of work and extra worry, calling out the children's names and a torrent of words JayJay did not need to understand. He stood by the sofa as the Nguyens embraced first one and then the other child. Minh wept openly, and even Ahn could not be quite as brave as he would have liked. Both of them repeatedly pointed at JayJay. When the grandmother squawked and started for him again, JayJay backed away. "Somebody tell her it ain't necessary to keep smacking me every time she gets in range."

Mrs. Nguyen was a porcelain doll with perfect skin and eyes that wept even when they were clear. She halted her mother with a single word, approached JayJay, and bowed. She spoke very formally. "My husband and I are forever grateful for the lives of our children."

JayJay felt himself blushing anew. "Ma'am, it was what anyone would've done."

"You are a good and brave man." She enunciated each word as though writing them in her mind. "We are eternally in your debt."

"No ma'am, you're not. I'm the one who's grateful. These kids of yours are swell."

The father approached but remained a step behind his wife. He met JayJay's eyes with an expression of relief and bone-deep fatigue. He handed over a plastic bag and spoke in English so accented it was hard to follow the words. "My son, he say you have no clothes."

"I'm much obliged, Mr. Nguyen." JayJay opened the bag to find an LA Lakers T-shirt and sweatpants.

"These were the largest clothes we had in the shop," Mrs. Nguyen said.

"They're fine. Thank you. If you'll excuse me, I'll go change into these."

He returned to find Ahn and Mrs. Nguyen and the grandmother busy loading the table. The father held a chair. "Please, Mr. JayJay. You must take place of honor."

"Not a chance in this world, sir."

"Better do as he says." Ahn set another steaming bowl on the table. "Take it from me. Pop is small, but he's stubborn. We could be here all night."

The food just came and came and came. Duck and lamb and an incredible stew that elevated a simple chicken to divine heights. Three different kinds of rice. Fish in a piquant sauce. More vegetables than JayJay could count. JayJay ate until his sweatpants' expandable waistline threatened to cut off his circulation.

But when he set down his fork, Mrs. Nguyen protested, "Please, Mr. JayJay. You have not touched a thing."

"Ma'am, I'm begging you, don't put anything more on my plate. If you do I'll eat it, and then we'll both be sorry."

The grandmother had not seated herself until last, and then ate hardly a morsel. She had become far more subdued since her daughter's arrival. Mrs. Nguyen said, "I must apologize for my mother's behavior. Here in this country, her life is for our children. But still it was inappropriate." She struggled valiantly over that last word.

"It's fine, ma'am." JayJay glanced across the table. The grandmother gave him a tentative smile. "Please tell your mother I can see where her daughter's and granddaughter's beauty comes from."

All three ladies smiled at him. "You are my mother's American hero."

"Ma'am, don't let Miss MahMah get the wrong idea. I'm just an ordinary Joe."

Ahn laughed. "MahMah means 'Granny'!"

"You have been happy using that name all your life. It is a fine name," his mother said. "Please, Mr. JayJay, may I ask what your real name is?"

"John Junior."

Their eyes grew round. "So your name truly is JayJay!"

"It is late." Mr. Nguyen rose from his seat. "Please. It is my honor to drive you home."

JayJay struggled with that one for a time, before finally saying, "Far as I can tell, sir, I've lost the only place I've ever called home. Or maybe it's just lost to me."

The news was met with a rising clamor. But the table was silenced by a single soft word from the father. "Then you must please stay here."

"And church," Ahn said, his eyes alight with the prospect. "He can come with us tomorrow, right, Pop?"

"I will telephone to Robbie Robinson," Mrs. Nguyen decided. "His father is the same size as you, Mr. Junior. That is, if you would do us the honor of accompanying us."

"I couldn't think of a single thing better," JayJay said to the family. "But I don't want to be a bother."

"Mr. Junior, you have given me back my children. What is bother?"

Ahn added, "We made an apartment out of the garage. We usually rent it out, but it's empty now."

Minh's voice was reduced to a soft croak. "He doesn't want to stay in Riverside."

"Can't see why not," JayJay replied. "If it's good enough for folks like yourselves, it should do me just fine."

# Chapter 11

---

"Peter? Honey? Wake up, darling."

He felt as though he fought himself up from a very great depth. He rubbed his eyes and sat up. For a minute he could not remember where he was, or why.

"Here. I made you coffee."

He took the mug as his wife eased down beside him. "What time is it?"

"Almost ten. Why didn't you come to bed last night?"

"Didn't want to wake you."

"What time was it when you stopped writing?"

"No idea. Late."

She stroked his back as he finished the cup. "More?"

"Please."

She used his shoulder for support and pushed herself from the sofa. When she returned, she rolled over the chair from his desk. His writing chair had stronger lumbar support than the old sofa he kept in his office for naps. Cynthia studied her husband's face and decided, "You had a good night."

He reached for her hand. "The best."

"That's good, dear. Here. Give me your mug. Now go wash your face. No, don't ask me questions. Just go."

When he returned, she settled him into the office chair and stood over him. Cynthia had become pregnant the month Peter received his first bonus as the new screenwriter on *Heartland*. Cynthia had insisted they remake the attic into an office. Their home had three bedrooms, and the money could have gone to a dozen different needs, especially when rumors were already surfacing that the show was in trouble. But Cynthia had been adamant. The babies would bring disruption. Peter needed a space that was isolated from the coming clamor. Cynthia liked him working at home, and he deserved a reward.

So the old metal hideaway ladder had been replaced with a circular staircase. Carpenters had fitted a new ceiling, a/c, a window, and two long walls of bookshelves. His battered old desk now overlooked the last three olive trees from the grove that had once populated their hillside. On good days, the ochre slopes descended to the valley floor and then rose to distant snowcapped peaks. Those nights the valley became a universe of twinkling lights. Today, however, the smog had already obliterated everything beyond fifty feet.

Cynthia handed him the phone. "Martin called."

He might have two coffees in him and his face might be clean, but his brain was still muddled from a very long day followed by a night of hard writing. "Martin."

"Your boss."

"Martin Allerby?"

"Good. You're awake. I was beginning to wonder."

"Allerby called *here*? When?"

"About three minutes before I woke you. I told him to call back. Don't look at me like that. I told him you had been up until almost sunrise working on something new. Something big. He liked that."

Peter's heart rate slowed a fraction. "He did?"

"Yes, Peter. Martin Allerby liked it very much."

"What did he say? Exactly."

"Exactly? Hmm. Let's see." She crossed her arms above her tummy and played at pensive. But before she could speak, the phone rang. "I guess you'll have to ask him to repeat it *exactly*."

He waved her away. "This is Peter."

"Allerby here." Being Allerby, he did not apologize for calling on a Sunday morning. "Cynthia tells me you've been hard at it."

"Most of the night. I wanted to get it down while it was all still fresh."

"Then apparently great minds think alike, Peter. Because I want us to move straight into a two-hour special."

Peter watched his wife blow him a kiss and start down the stairs. "JayJay Parsons and the wildfire."

"Introducing our new star, and incorporating the footage. Who was that young woman he saved?"

"I have no idea. But I'll find out. Derek shot those pictures."

"I've already spoken with Derek and secured the rights. It would be good if we could have a look at those pages of yours tomorrow."

"I'll deliver them myself, Mr. Allerby." Peter lowered his voice then added, "He saved my life as well. JayJay did."

"What impresses me as much as that news is the fact you and Derek were there at all. Which brings us to the next point. Where is the actor residing?"

"I don't know, Mr. Allerby."

"This is absurd." The cold edge Allerby normally kept hidden sliced over the lines. "Casting has no idea where to find him. The *director* labeled the footage he shot as Parsons Two. I won't permit such shoddy work at my studio."

"No sir." Peter could not quite keep the tremor from his voice.

"We'll know by nightfall or heads will roll. I'll see you in my office tomorrow at nine."

Peter hung up the phone only to discover his wife's head emerging above floor level. "Repeat that sentence for me. The one that mentioned JayJay Parsons saving your life."

"Honey—"

"Saved your life from *what?*"

"It was pretty hairy out there. The wind came out of nowhere. One minute we were . . ."

She gave him the flat palm and the tone that absolutely halted all argument. "Do I need to remind you that you are a soon-to-be-father?"

"No, Cynthia."

"With responsibilities that mean you can't go out and be a teenager when the whim strikes?"

"It wasn't . . ." The palm lifted higher, as clear a warning as a wife ever made. "No, Cynthia."

"Good. That's settled, then." The hand dropped, but the tension was still in her face. "Your breakfast is ready and we're late for church."

# Chapter 12

Ash and smoke drifted into the valley that Sunday morning. But the wind had died with the setting sun, and the line had held, and the homes were safe. What was more, rain was forecast for that afternoon. Thunderclouds had been building since before sunrise, or so JayJay heard as he followed the Nguyens into church. All he could see from the church's front steps was a blanket of haze, not white, not orange. So thick most of the cars entering the church parking lot had their lights on. A lot of the talk he heard was over fear of lightning strikes.

Robbie Robinson's dad had brought over clothes for JayJay to wear. Word had somehow spread he had lost his home in the fire. JayJay didn't dissuade the rumors. It was better than trying to explain what he himself did not understand.

He recognized the preacher from the bus trip. The pastor started the service by welcoming their special visitor and thanking John Junior for saving the lives of two of their flock. The audience applauded, then those within reach smiled and shook his hand while the Nguyens beamed.

Whatever JayJay had hoped to find in church was not there. Answers, peace, wisdom, direction. None of it. He stood and sat and sang and tried to listen. Folks stared at him here as much as they had at the studio, but he felt no less comfortable for all the attention. The Nguyens were known and liked. He was made welcome. An oddity for sure. But welcome just the same.

Afterward the crowd coagulated around JayJay and filled the central aisle. He endured the smiles and the handshakes. And the hugs. He signed a couple of Sunday bulletins and stretched his weary face for flashing cameras and cell phones.

Then the pastor came over, still in his robes, and asked in a loud voice, "Are we making the gentleman welcome or are we taking advantage of his kind nature?"

There were sheepish chuckles and people began drifting away, at least most of them. A final pair of older ladies reluctantly allowed the preacher to steer them about and direct them toward the exit. The pastor then said, "I guess I'm not much different from the rest of them, sir. But I can't let you go without thanking you for what you did yesterday. We didn't get properly introduced on the bus. I'm Floyd Cummins. I've been pastoring this church for nineteen years. The Nguyens are the kind of folk I'd give my right arm to have more of. Devout, steadfast, leading by example. Their children are bright, honest, honorable. I love them like my own."

"I'm only into my second day with the family. But I feel pretty much the same."

The professional exterior slipped, the worry was exposed. "Did I do wrong, taking those kids to fight that fire?"

"Sometimes doing the right thing means taking risks, Reverend."

Floyd Cummins liked that enough to say, "You strike me as a troubled man, Mr. Junior. I hope you don't mind my speaking frankly."

"Can't hardly do that, not while we're standing in God's house." JayJay took a hard breath. "And not while you're speaking the truth."

"Come on over here and sit down." He steered JayJay into a pew, then scouted about and spied a departing chorister. "Janet, would you tell the Nguyens to head on home, I'll drive Mr. Junior back myself."

"Sure thing, Floyd."

The pastor was a rugged man, with the big hands and heavy features of farming stock. "Hollywood has a habit of laying the strongest person out flat on his back."

"I reckon I've seen my share of hard times. But there ain't nothing I've ever known to compare with this. All I want is to head on home and make things go back to how they were before."

"A lot of people would take that as a line. But I believe you're telling me the truth." The pastor's gaze did not unsettle so much as peel away. "Did you ever stop to think that maybe God was behind your coming, or that He placed you here for a divine purpose?"

That rocked JayJay back into the pew. "Can't say as I have."

"We've known for some time *Heartland* is in trouble. It probably sounds silly for a pastor to be talking about television in church. But we've got a lot of our folks working in the industry. And that show is the only one going where our faith and our values aren't scorned. Some of us figure that's why it's been slated for cancellation. There are people praying all over the place for some kind of miracle so the show might survive."

The air between them seemed to ring with the portent of that word, *miracle*. The pastor asked, "Can you tell me the name of one fellow out here in Hollywood who stands for what is important to folks like me? I don't mean me, the pastor of a Riverside church. I mean me, Middle America. Name one person in the Hollywood spotlight I can hold up in my church. Because make no mistake, the focal point of our culture is entertainment."

JayJay shifted in his seat. "You're making me feel like I was sitting on top of a branding fire."

"Point me out one Hollywood star who loves his God and his country. A man who wants to do right by his family and his community and his nation. A man who *prays*. A man who prays for us to find a way to *heal*. A man who feels overwhelmed by all the troubles that loom beyond the doors of this little haven." The pastor's voice rose to where it turned the heads of people collecting the hymnals. "A man who remembers the virtues our Good Book calls us to. Love, joy, peace, patience, kindness, generosity, faithfulness, gentleness, self-control. Remember what Paul says about these?"

JayJay knew a test when he heard one. He responded with the next line from Galatians, "'Against such there is no law.'"

Floyd Cummins slapped the pew. "There. You see? That is *exactly* what I'm talking about."

"Reverend, you're mistaking me for a man who understands what's happening to him."

"I'm sorry, but you're wrong. I know all there is to know about human failings. I know you're not perfect, and I don't *care*. What matters is your heart. And brother, I can see the same thing those Nguyen kids and Robbie Robinson saw yesterday standing out there on the street."

JayJay inspected the toes of his boots. "Reverend, I've got to tell somebody." The words burned his craw as they emerged. "I . . . I got the strongest feeling I'm not real."

Floyd Cummins laid a hand on his shoulder. "Brother, I want you to listen carefully to what I'm about to say."

JayJay wrestled his gaze up from the floor. Floyd Cummins watched him with a depth and a concern that filled every hollow corner of JayJay's being. "We're all just dust and water, just clay on the potter's wheel, until God sparks us with His holy fire."

The pastor's hand rose and fell in soft cadence. "I'll tell you what I think has happened here. The Lord God couldn't find what He needed for His work. So He scooped you up from wherever you came from. And asked the question He does of all His servants, 'Who will go and speak for Me?'"

JayJay replied, "The prospect of God being in on this has got me sweating."

Floyd Cummins surprised him by grinning. "I take that as a good sign. Would you like me to pray for you?"

JayJay felt the words wash over him, though he could not recollect them even as they were being spoken. Afterward he let the pastor lead him up the aisle and out into the sunlight. If anything, the haze had thickened. As Floyd Cummins drove him back to the Nguyens', images swam suddenly from the gloom and disappeared just as fast. Billboards and telephone wires and mini-marts and faceless sprawl. JayJay murmured, "Where *am* I?"

"Riverside is a place most folks are desperate to leave behind. All those potholes are drilled by folks desperate to escape the San Bernardino Valley."

When Cummins pulled up in front of the Nguyens' home, JayJay confessed, "We're talking the same language, but you're not understanding what I've been trying to tell you about how I got here."

"Are you sure about that?"

JayJay glanced over at the simple fifties-style ranch house, the tiny front lawn bordered by painted concrete blocks. A dusty Toyota sat at the curb. JayJay watched Mr. Nguyen emerge from the front door. "I reckon the only way to say it is, I'm not from this world."

"You think they are?" Cummins rushed his words to finish before Mr. Nguyen arrived. "He ran an electronics company before America pulled out of Saigon. He bribed his family's way onto a boat. He, his wife, and his wife's mother are the only survivors from fifteen who set off. They live for their faith and the future of their children. Now you try and tell me you fit in less than they do."

Mr. Nguyen opened the pastor's door and said in his formal broken English, "Reverend, you would honor our home to eat with us."

"Thank you, brother. But my wife already has my lunch on the table." Floyd Cummins patted JayJay on the shoulder. "Remember what I said, brother. Hollywood *needs* you."

# Chapter 13

JayJay spent his entire Monday walking around a valley filled with the same ash and acrid smoke. But the people he saw were mostly too busy to miss the absent sky. Their faces were tight and grim and tired in the manner of city folk. The surroundings matched their mood. Riverside was not a pretty town. The streets ran weary and riven and deadly straight until they were swallowed by the smog that burned his throat. Billboards shouted messages JayJay couldn't be bothered to read. People stared at him from inside their air-conditioned cars, wondering at the cowboy who had the sidewalks mostly to himself. He passed gangs of youths who played their fist-on-fist games and observed him with bitter, pain-filled eyes. Street vendors served people who did not even emerge from their cars to shop. A few other pedestrians almost ran in their haste. Many held handkerchiefs to their mouths. No one returned his howdy's or met his gaze. After a time he just went silent.

His wilderness training kept him from getting lost. The country where he had lived did not offer the luxury of street signs. The pastor's words remained strong in his mind.

As the sun began its sullen descent, JayJay stopped on a weed-infested corner. Two four-lane roads merged with the highway's on-ramp. A rainbow of dusty cars thundered past him. JayJay stared at the ochre buildings, then raised his head to the smoke-stained sky. He said the words aloud. "Okay, God."

His only response was the rumbling traffic. But he kept his gaze uplifted. The words came natural. As though it was only here, in a world that made no sense, in a place where he didn't belong, that he could hear what his heart was yearning for him to say. "I don't understand any of this, Lord. But I reckon I'm not the first of Your servants who didn't have a clue. So if this is really You at work, all I got to say is, I'm here and I'm listening. I don't know if I can do what You want. But I'll try. Well, I guess that's about everything, so I'll just say amen."

He dropped his gaze and had to grin at how absurd it must have seemed to the rushing tide of metal and noise. A cowboy with his Stetson planted to his chest, head aimed at an invisible sun, talking words that were drowned out by the traffic.

That is, if anybody bothered to glance his way at all.

The Nguyens' garage apartment was a snug fit for a man of JayJay's size. The double wooden doors had been sealed shut and pine slats fitted over the concrete floor. The kitchen ran along the back wall, separated from the minuscule sitting area by a counter, the back of which contained shelves for his plates and utensils. There were two stools, a love seat, one high-backed chair, a chest for a center table, and a television. Stairs ran up the side wall to the bedroom loft, which contained only a mattress and a throw rug and a loudly clicking clock. But the place was clean as a whistle. And just out of range lived a family who cared for him. That evening JayJay ate the supper Mrs. Nguyen had left on the counter and slept well.

Tuesday morning he was dressed in the clothes dropped off by Robbie Robinson's father and breakfasting on instant coffee and toast when Ahn knocked on the side door. "You're awake, good."

"Never could sleep easy past the dawn." JayJay lifted his cup. "You be sure and tell your mom I'm much obliged for the supplies."

"She and Pop are long gone. You can tell her yourself tonight."

"If I'm here," JayJay reflected out loud.

Ahn tried hard to hide his disappointment, but failed. "You're leaving?"

"May not have any choice in the matter. How's your sister?"

"Better. I can tell. But she's giving MahMah the whine, getting breakfast in bed and making me do all the work."

"Why aren't you in school?"

"It's June, remember?"

No, he did not. But there was no need to go there. "So what do you do with your days?"

"I help out at the shop. It's pretty boring. But my folks like having us around. Otherwise I'm working on my honors thesis. I'm midway through my MBA."

"You don't hardly look old enough to be out of high school."

"I know, I know. I look sixteen. I get carded at Starbucks." Ahn shrugged that aside. "Whenever you're ready, there's somebody waiting for you."

JayJay set down his cup and followed Ahn from the apartment. A light wind was drawing clouds and misting rain off the mountains. The air was no clearer, but the pungent odor of diesel and chemicals was gone. Pulled up in front of the house was the longest limousine JayJay had ever seen. A uniformed driver popped out from behind the wheel soon as JayJay emerged. "Morning, sir."

JayJay stepped over to where the window awning protected him and Ahn from the rain. "That thing for me?"

The chauffeur unfurled an umbrella the size of Dallas and walked around to open the rear door. "Yes sir, the studio's sent me to collect you. Mr. Allerby says it's urgent."

"Who?"

The chauffeur cocked his head in confusion. "Martin Allerby, sir."

"That name supposed to mean something to me?"

It was Ahn who responded, "Martin Allerby. The greenlight guy at Centurion."

"Pretend I only speak English and give that to me again."

Ahn was clearly loving this. "Hollywood studios have more titles than a major bank. A hundred different varieties of vice presidents, associate producers, assistant directors, it's all just salad. Only one title matters."

"The greenlight guy," JayJay said.

"Or GG for short. There's only one in each studio. The guy who says the project is a go. The king. At Centurion, that's Martin Allerby."

"How come you know all this?"

"My thesis is on Centurion's business model." Ahn wiped away a raindrop that caught his forehead. "My dream is to break into the business side of Hollywood."

JayJay motioned to where the chauffeur stood waiting. "Want to take a ride?"

"Are you serious?"

"Hop on in."

Ahn almost danced around the limo. "I sure hope Minh is watching."

When they were on their way, JayJay asked the driver, "How'd you know where to find me?"

"No idea, sir. They gave me the address, I came."

Clearly this guy was not going to give him anything he wanted. JayJay turned back to Ahn. "Do me a favor."

"Sure."

"Assume I don't know a thing. Talk me through what's up around that next bend."

Ahn liked that. "Which do you mean—Martin Allerby, Centurion, or *Heartland*?"

"The whole shooting match."

Something very curious happened. The kid just plain vanished. In his place appeared a young man. A *small* man, but a man just the same.

Extremely focused. Incredibly intelligent. And excited. "*Heartland's* been in serious trouble for a while now. The lead actor, Neil Townsend, is a lush. And thoroughly hated. You look incredibly like him, but I guess you know that. I mean, how he *used* to be. Back when he was still a regular guy. Before he turned into Frankenstein's monster. Like some stars are prone to do."

"I think I met him on the back lot."

"Then you know. Initially, *Heartland* had firm standing as a money-spinner. You know that term?"

"I told you. Saturday morning I got dropped into this pit. Before then I didn't even know this place existed." JayJay leaned forward and said to the driver, "Do me a favor and pull over here."

"Sir, Mr. Allerby said you were to go straight to the studio."

"Listen up, friend. We got two choices. Either you stop here for a while or we're climbing out at the next red light. Which means we'll be arriving wet *and* late. But it's your call."

The limo swerved over and halted by the curb. "Much obliged." JayJay turned back to Ahn. "You're saying this *Heartland* thing is making money."

"The first couple of seasons, the show was *printing* money. But then it started sliding. Not because of the show itself, well, maybe a little. I mean, how many tornadoes can you have in one season?"

JayJay rubbed the side of his face. Hard. Trying to make sense of both the words and his own rising internal tumult. "A passel."

"Tell me. But the viewers who made *Heartland* a hit didn't like watching their hero bloat up and talk like he was drunk. Like he was coasting through the show. Like he didn't care."

JayJay observed, "You take this personal."

Ahn's eyes glinted angrily. "Three weeks before the last season ended, MahMah got up in the middle of the show. She walked over and cut off the TV. She stood staring at the screen for a while. Then she just sighed and walked out of the room. I wish you could have been there."

"No thanks. I believe I'd rather face another twister."

"That's why she was so excited over having you come home with us. I mean, because you saved Minh and all too. But there in front of her was this guy, the way he was supposed to be. Her *hero*."

"I'm not comfortable with you talking about me like that."

"Get used to it." Ahn the young man used a tone that brooked no argument. "Word is, Martin Allerby didn't want to do *Heartland*. But orders came down from on high. 'Do it or find another job.' The rest is history."

"I thought you said he was the—whatever you called him."

"Greenlight guy. He is. But there's always somebody higher." Ahn stared at the rain trickling down the side window. "Allerby is from Van Nuys. Except his morals. They're from the basement. I read that somewhere. Centurion is the last of the small independent studios. It's owned by Carter Dawes, a real mystery man. His family controls a lot of the oil and gas rights around LA. Word is, he still farms out in the Central Valley."

"Sounds like a man I could spend some time around."

"No way. He doesn't do meetings. Even sends his lawyer when the Centurion board gets together. But what I heard is, he's the reason *Heartland* got made at all. He basically ordered Martin Allerby to come up with a show where the lead role was a down-home hero. A man who knew his Bible. A man who loved his family. A man people could look up to."

JayJay stared at the unfocused gray day beyond the window. Things were no clearer now than when Ahn had started. The pastor's words pressed at him like a goad to his ribs. Whatever lay ahead could not be put off any longer. "Okay, driver. Thanks for being patient with us."

"No problem, sir."

When they pulled up in front of the studio gates, JayJay rolled down his window and read the guard's name off the lapel tag. "Morning, Mr. Twyford."

"Mr. Allerby says you're to go straight to Soundstage Four, sir. He'll meet with you after you're done filming."

"That's fine." JayJay motioned to Ahn. "I've brought a pal along for the ride. Any chance you could fix him up with something?"

"No problem, sir. What's the name?"

"Ahn Nguyen."

"Spell that for me, please."

When Ahn had done so, JayJay went on, "I reckon this fellow knows more about the place here than most folks on the payroll. Any chance he could talk with somebody in the business?"

The guard was already reaching for the phone. "I'll have a word with Mr. Allerby's secretary. Ask your driver to drop him by the admin building."

"I'm much obliged, Mr. Twyford."

"Just call me Hardy, sir."

"Well, I'm very grateful. You have a good day now." JayJay rolled up his window.

Ahn handled the guest badge like he'd been granted a day-pass to paradise. "This can't be happening."

"I'd go along with that, sure enough." JayJay felt the rumbling of nerves. "Any last-minute advice for the greenhorn?"

Ahn slipped the pass around his neck. "Ask the guidance of the little people. I hear that from everybody I talk to in the trade. Stars never do it. But the folks behind the camera, they know a whole lot. And they'll love you for staying on their level."

# Chapter 14

JayJay Parsons entered the soundstage feeling a lot better than he might have expected. Better, probably, than he deserved. The reason was simple. His first stop had been Wardrobe, where he'd stood on a little stool while Hilda or Gladys—he couldn't get the ladies straightened out—pinned him into a new set of clothes. Then he moved behind the screen to disrobe, an action the two ladies still chuckled over, and did what Ahn had suggested, which was to repeat the words "You got any advice for the greenhorn?"

Hilda or Gladys made her voice as much Western-range as her Brooklyn accent permitted. "Well, stranger, I'd say treat this day like it was your very last chance at the big time."

"I like that." JayJay accepted the jeans and slipped them on. "Only way to break a bronco is to go at it like you got one ride left in you. Else that horse is gonna know you're holding back. And he's gonna do his best to knock you into next week."

"You actually did that? Rode a bronco?"

"Got the spurs and the scars to prove it." JayJay stepped into his boots, walked back around, accepted his hat, fitted the crown just so, and touched the brim. "Much obliged, ma'am."

Hilda or Gladys turned coquettish. "The way you say that makes a gal go all weak at the knees."

The other half of the pair was smiling too. "Go get 'em, tiger. Or should I say, stallion."

So JayJay entered the soundstage with the grin still in place. And as luck would have it, the first face he saw belonged to the foppish little assistant director. Kip Denderhoff waved his arms like he was winding himself up for the day ahead. The AD hissed a stream of nasty at a man handling a huge light and trying his best to appear untouched by the little guy. Then the AD saw JayJay approaching and did his imitation of a squid, going pale and boneless and searching for a rock to hide under.

"Just you hold up there. I don't aim on restarting where I left off." JayJay stepped between the AD and the back exit. "Matter of fact, I came over to apologize."

"Stop making fun." The little guy looked miserable. "And don't you dare hit me. I've got a hundred witnesses. I'll sue."

"And you'd be right doing it. Stand still for a minute, will you? I said I wasn't taking aim. Shouldn't never have started in on you the other day. You were right and I was wrong."

The AD froze. "Excuse me?"

"I was late. I kept y'all waiting. I didn't know what to do or where to go. You had all the reasons in the world to take a piece outta my hide. So I wanted to tell you I'm sorry." JayJay crossed his arms. "Now you just go ahead and yell."

The AD cocked his head. "Don't tempt me."

"Well, I reckon you'll have plenty of reasons to come down on me, green as I am. Comes time, you just fire away."

"Don't worry. I will."

"Well, Mr. Denderhoff, I'd say it's a pleasure but we both know I'd be lying. Just do me a favor and hold off yelling at the ladies. I've always had a hair trigger on their account. You find a need to shout at somebody, come looking for me." JayJay nodded affably and walked away. He offered a couple of howdy's to the people he saw staring at him, feeling good enough over what he'd just done not to let the stares bother him too much.

"Mr. Junior? Did I get that name right? Hi, I'm Amber, the script girl? Would you like your pages?"

JayJay accepted the bound pages from a young lady who resembled a very tense elf. His name was scripted in red across the cover. "Do you make a question of everything you say?"

"Am I doing that? Oh. Yeah. I am. I don't . . ." She bustled away.

The pages were clamped into a simple plastic binder. The title was in bold. *Heartland on Fire.* He turned the page. The script was not in any order he'd ever seen before, blocked out in places and written down the middle in others. Names were in big, tall letters. Strange-sounding orders were also capitalized, like CUT TO, FADE OUT, PARA DIA.

But he had grown up on oddities of the English language like manuals for farm equipment and Sears catalogs. That was not what had him searching with his free hand for someplace to sit down before he keeled over. His hand found a canvas chair and he lowered himself down, all without taking his eyes from the script.

A voice said, "If you think saying a couple of nice words is going to let you get away with *this*, mister, you've got another think coming."

Reluctantly JayJay lifted his gaze. He looked uncomprehendingly at the little AD.

Denderhoff carried his script rolled up tight. He had a trio of lenses strung around his neck. He was sweating. And angry. "Nobody sits in my chair."

"Yours?"

"See the name on the back? Moi. Mine. Now up."

"Sure thing."

The gnat flitted off.

"Here, Mr. Junior." Someone slid a stool within range. "Take a load off."

"Thank you, sir." He did not even see the man clearly. He had already turned his attention back to the pages in his hand.

The words marked for him to say felt as though they had been drawn from his own brain.

He flipped the pages. Same thing every time. JayJay shut the script. He stared into the soundstage's far shadows. The words did not just sound right. They were *his*.

A perspiring young man with bulky headphones around his neck and a stopwatch on a string raced over. "Fifteen minutes, Mr. Junior." Then he was gone.

JayJay asked the empty air, "Does anybody move at a normal pace around here?"

"Hon, this is calm. You're only shooting trials today. Try going live. Nothing beats a live broadcast for pure frantic." Hilda or Gladys grabbed his sleeve and snipped at a loose thread. She lowered her voice. "See the young lady standing all by her lonesome? She's your new love interest."

"Say what?"

"She's almost as green as you, hon, and twice as nervous. Go give her a smile and a howdy." The older woman batted her eyelashes. "First time I've ever been sorry they didn't ask me to dress up for the cameras."

JayJay found it marginally easier to examine his chopped-up home. The structure was built on steel pilings and elevated about three feet off the soundstage floor. The lady leaned against the edge of his living room. As JayJay approached, he decided she did not look afraid. She looked irate.

But she sure looked good doing it.

All the eyes in the soundstage that weren't on him were on her. And for good reason. She drew every light in the room. Her jeans were spray-painted onto legs about six miles long. Her hair was too dark to be truly blonde and framed her face in a tawny mane. She had a cowgirl's rangy muscles. Her feet were the reason they invented boots. Emerald eyes watched his approach with wary intent.

JayJay touched the rim of his hat. "Morning, ma'am. I'm—"

"I know who you are." Her gaze returned to the script. "Let's get one thing straight. All that success of yours? It doesn't leave me weak in the knees."

"You're thinking of that other guy."

But she was on a roll. "And another thing. I've heard you figure grabby-paws is a clause written somewhere in your contract."

He watched her hands, and saw how she could not completely hide the tremble as she flipped through pages she probably didn't see. "That's the other guy again."

"You think I'm kidding?"

"No ma'am, I surely don't." JayJay set his hat on the cut-off floor beside her. "Matter of fact, I'd say you were being pretty temperate in your warning."

She cast him a sideways glance. "Nobody says 'temperate' anymore. It's a law they passed somewhere."

"Guess I missed that. My first day here was Saturday. The feller over there with the lenses around his neck?"

"The mosquito. Yeah, he already drew blood, but he flitted away before I could smack him."

"He set on me like a spark on dry tinder." JayJay drew the knife from his belt. "I whanged this into the doorpost by his head. Which is why I'd call your warning there a polite form of hello."

"I got the long version of that set-to from your fan club in Wardrobe." She studied the sheafed blade. "Is that a genuine Bowie?"

"I can't say for certain about this thing. But a Bowie is what I use back home. You know knives?"

"My daddy has a Bowie. The handle was carved from the first buck's antlers he took." Her gaze softened with her tone. "He was sixteen."

"Don't hardly get any finer than hunting the high country and waiting for that first snow. You from Montana?"

"South Dakota. You?"

JayJay shook his head. "Hard to say."

"Yeah, I know what you mean. This place is so intense I can't remember much of anything from before I walked in the door over there."

"How about your name?"

"Sorry." She wiped one hand down the leg of her jeans before offering it. "Kelly Channing."

"John Junior, Miss Channing. It's a real pleasure to make your acquaintance."

"Well, you talk nice, I'll give you that much." Her features held to their narrow caution, but her tone eased a trifle. "How did you wind up here?"

JayJay hesitated. "Miss Channing . . ."

"I'd say first names are called for. In case you hadn't noticed, they've got us kissing on page thirty-three."

But he didn't want to start thinking on that. "Kelly, I have a mind not to answer you. I don't want you running off telling folks you've been hooked up with a man straight out of the piney woods."

She was not the least bit impressed. "Tell you what, when we're done here we can compare tales. Make a wager over which one of us has the wilder story for how we got to where we are."

"I wouldn't want to take your money."

"You won't. Believe me."

"So how about dinner?" Soon as he spoke the words, he wished he could take them back. The day was already too confusing to go chasing after a lady, even if she was about the best thing he'd ever seen in denim.

Though her gaze remained wary, she responded with a tight nod. "Winner chooses, loser buys."

JayJay gave up on his desire to retract the offer when the steel outer doors clanged open and two men entered the room. First to enter was Peter, the writer JayJay had last seen at the fire. JayJay had met the other man when they'd had him read those lines with his fake sister Clara and then followed him around with the camera. Britt somebody. But JayJay could be excused for having been a little unfocused on

Saturday. This morning the whole scene was crystal clear. Whatever title the guy might be wearing, this Britt fellow was the Business.

"Over here, Mr. Junior." He vaulted up onto the raised half cabin and waved JayJay into his chopped-up sitting room. "I'm Britt Turner, director of *Heartland*. What should I call you?"

He pulled a chair over from the kitchen table. "JayJay's worked my whole life long."

"And we thought a Claire playing Clara was too weird for words. Going to take some getting used to, an actor with the exact same name as his role." The director shared a look with his AD. Denderhoff was stationed behind the sofa holding Claire and the writer. "PR ought to be able to make something of it."

"I'll have a word."

"When we're done here, JayJay, you need to head over to Allerby's office. Admin is working on your guild card, and Publicity will want to get some shots for the promo they're setting up."

"You're the boss."

Britt passed him a quick smile. "Nice to hear an actor say those words." The director wore comfortable no-nonsense clothes, a loose cotton shirt and khaki pants. "Quick intros. You've already met Claire Pietan, right?"

JayJay realized he was speaking of his false sister. He nodded in slow awareness. Shifting the name that little bit helped him fit her into a new mental box. "Not by name."

"And this is Kelly Channing."

Claire's voice was acidic. "Oh, they're already *good* pals. Aren't you, little brother."

"I met Miss Channing this morning," JayJay confirmed, as Kelly gave the other woman a careful study.

"Great. Peter Caffrey here is *Heartland*'s chief writer. And Derek Steen is acting first cameraman today."

JayJay gave them a wave. "Nice to see you gents still up and breathing."

"And clean," Derek confirmed. "Thought I'd never get the smoke out of my hair."

Peter Caffrey remained silent and gave him the sideways look of somebody who wasn't sure he liked what he was seeing. The director went on, "We didn't know where to locate you, so we weren't able to get the pages to you before now. Just the same, our thought was to try a few scenes on for size. Your lines will be on the teleprompter. We'll be filming, but just for study. It's all rehearsal."

"The full script won't be done for another couple of weeks," Peter warned the director. "I'm pulling what I can from the episode we never shot. But it'll be a while."

"We're rehearsing," the director repeated. "But we're going to light it and shoot it so JayJay here can get used to performing for the camera. You're new to this game, isn't that right?"

"First time up at bat."

"We're not after breaking records here. We'll walk you slow through the process, work things at a comfortable pace. You got any questions, now is the time. Or comments. And once again, don't worry about not knowing your lines."

JayJay figured now was as good a time as any to say, "I reckon it won't take me all that long to learn what you want me to say."

That stopped traffic all through the soundstage. The director leaned forward. "Run that one by me again."

JayJay hefted his script. "The words here sound like they were plucked from my head. I don't know how to say it any clearer than that."

"Hear that, Peter? An actor who doesn't feel any need to play with your work." The director stood up and made a process of dusting off his khakis. "Let's light this and see what we've got."

# Chapter 15

P eter waited until they were into the fourth take of the second scene. He sidled up to where Derek was fiddling with an extra light for the kitchen. "This is crazy."

Derek stepped back to the camera. "Good crazy or bad crazy?"

"Too much of both."

Peter's best friend was lighting this practice scene like he was working for his first Oscar. "You ask me, I'd say we're cooking with gas."

JayJay had slipped out the back door. Kelly was enduring some unwanted comments from the AD. Claire was fishing cigarettes from her shoulder bag. Britt was huddled over the remote at the back of the warehouse. A principal advantage of digital filming was how a director could flip the film from the camera, step to the remote, and get a first-hand glimpse of what they'd just shot. The remote was hidden behind a little white tent with "Director Only" written above the entry in Day-Glo orange. No actor was permitted inside the remote's tent. There was too much risk of them turning into mini-directors, looking to control their roles. Britt flipped the cover back and called over, "Derek!"

"Yo."

"We need to mute the lighting on that side of the kitchen."

"Working on it."

Peter waited until the director had submerged to go on. "John Junior."

"So?"

"Episode two? Your brain go back that far?"

Derek used a wrench with a taped handle to tap the light over a fraction. "Before my time."

"John Junior is the character's childhood name. We used it once, then let it slide. The whole world had already accepted him as JayJay." When Derek's only response was to step back behind the camera again, Peter added, "And the speed he's learning his lines. One time through, then he knows every word down cold."

"So we're working with a sober star for a change." Derek turned around and called, "Britt, I think we're ready!"

"In a minute."

Peter stepped closer. "A guy who's never been under the lights before, he's smoothly working his way through a five-scene script? That doesn't strike you as even marginally strange?"

"Yeah. It does." Derek leaned against his camera. Gave him a flat-eyed stare as only Derek could. "So where are you going with this?"

"I don't know. I just wanted to hear somebody else say it besides me."

"Yes, Peter. I am as astonished as our director over there. I came in to do some rehearsal work. And I discover we're shooting finished takes. Everybody in here is so surprised they can't talk about anything else. About how we've got ourselves a JayJay Parsons who is going to reignite this series. About how we've got a future." Derek crossed his arms. "So I'm asking you again. Where are you going with this?"

Britt chose that moment to flip back the remote's cover and say to the assembly, "Okay, everybody. We're cooking. Where's my AD?"

"Here."

"Get everybody in place. You, Channing. Has he been giving you a hard time?"

Kelly Channing looked ready to chew nails. "I'd give that an affirmative."

"Well, don't worry about it. That last take looked solid. I want you to do it again exactly the same as before. Think you can do that?"

"Absolutely." She stuck out her tongue at the AD, who sniffed in response.

Britt walked over and said to Derek, "Show me."

Derek waited while the director studied the kitchen through the camera lens. Britt straightened, nodded, said, "Very professional work."

"Thank you, Mr. Turner."

"As acting principal cameraman, I'd say you can use my first name," Britt told Derek, then turned to Peter. "What's the matter, Caffrey. You look worried."

"Oh, he's just concerned about bringing the next batch of scenes together." Derek's look was distilled caution. "Isn't that right, Peter."

JayJay stood under the chuck wagon's awning and listened to the water drip. The cook was a taciturn fellow with a book open on the counter. Everything about his stance and his expression said he had no interest in small talk. Which suited JayJay just fine.

There was a peculiar sweetness to how rain smelled in the desert. As though the parched terrain sighed an earthy perfume in relief. Even here, where everything was paved over and citified, the fragrance was strong enough to draw him back home. Wherever that was.

Without asking, the cook lifted the pot off the stove and refilled JayJay's cup. JayJay nodded his thanks and took another sip. The coffee was real. The rain, the scent, the quiet moment out here on his own. Every now and then somebody peeked through the rear door and frowned at the rain, like water falling from the sky was some alien menace, then retreated inside. JayJay took another sip. He liked the solitude just fine.

Taking stock of the day was a confusion in itself. He had been greeted by an Oriental young man with a brain faster than a revolver in the process of expelling a bullet. He had taken his first ride in a limo. He had been given pages of words he already knew. He had been positioned under lights strong as August sunlight and told to playact with a pair of women, one of whom *looked* like his sister and *sounded* like his sister but sure to goodness *wasn't*. And the other lady, well, she had a magic all her very own.

A stronger curtain of wet descended, cutting them off from the rest of the world. JayJay stared at the torrent and reflected upon the pastor's words. It all came back to that. There weren't a whole lot of options. Either he was just plain nuts, or something had happened to him. Something so wild, nothing else came to mind except divine intervention.

But why him?

And what did it mean about the life he had left behind?

And why did even thinking about that leave him feeling like he'd been gored by the day?

The rear door clanged open and expelled his fake sister. JayJay tried but could not recall the woman's real name. She raced over, shielding her head with her script. "Give me a cup of that, will you? Straight up."

She fished in her shoulder bag and came up with a cigarette. She offered her lighter to JayJay. "Make yourself useful, why don't you."

He did so because it would have been impolite to refuse. "You shouldn't smoke."

"In case you hadn't noticed, I'm a big girl, John or Junior or whatever name you go by."

"JayJay will do."

She shook her head, spraying smoke in a semicircle. "I can't call you by the name of your character. No matter how many PR types gyrate with excitement at the thought."

JayJay retreated inside his cup.

Her eyes glinted hard in the gray light. "I saw you over there playing pals with the hired help."

But JayJay definitely did not want to spend time running down that trail. "What's with that writer fellow? He's been looking at me like I'm part of a nightmare he couldn't leave behind at dawn."

She made a shrug out of blowing smoke. "Can't see why. He was due to write for one of those medical shows where all the doctors look like they need drugs worse than the patients. They specialize in a different mystery bug every week. They're sponsored by a toothpaste company. The critics call it Plague and Plaque. Around here it's known as purgatory."

JayJay could not help leaning in for a closer look. The more she spoke, the less this woman resembled his sister. "Who *are* you?"

She gave him what JayJay thought of as a honky-tonk smile. The kind that had about as much warmth as the teeth on a wolf trap. "Treat me right, honey, I'll be just about anybody you want."

JayJay tamped down the first half dozen or so responses that came to mind. He took his time over a final swallow from the cup. Set it down on the saucer in slow time. Making a process of turning back to her. Trying to give her in actions what he was not going to do in volume. "Remember the first thing you said to me? How you'd been treated wrong by the fellow whose place I'm taking?"

She dropped her cigarette to the pavement and ground it hard with her heel. She said with the final lungful of smoke, "Now why would you want to go and ruin a perfectly good moment by bringing up that trash?"

"On account of how I'm asking you not to treat me the same way he did you."

The deep-down ire that seeped through even when she smiled boiled up closer to the surface. "What, I've already lost out to the new girl on the block?"

JayJay fitted on his hat and stepped into the rain. "This here is only about me and you, Clara. I don't know how to say it any plainer."

She shrilled at his departing back, "I told you not to call me that!"

When he walked back through the rear door he almost collided with the AD. "Look at you! How are we supposed to start filming when you're all wet?"

JayJay stepped by the little man. "Hot as I am right now, I'll bake it off in no time flat."

There was enough flammable energy under the lights to incinerate the entire studio.

Obviously Peter was not the only one mesmerized by what was going on in front of the camera. He had been joined at the back of the chamber by more than a dozen idlers from other spots around the studio. A couple of the front-office execs stood next to a truly stunning brunette dressed in what appeared to be a suede Gucci bikini. And the two execs did not look her way *once*. The actor to their right had come straight from the hospital show and was still dressed in trauma-unit blue. He murmured, "I sure hope they haven't got any open flames in that room."

And nobody laughed. The tempers under the light were that hot.

But that did not matter nearly as much as the fact that up there, in a split-open kitchen that was looking somewhat frayed after nine seasons under the lights, those three actors *cooked*.

What was more, Britt the director knew it. And he was rushing to get as much of it on film as he possibly could.

Derek was lighting the new scenes with Britt there beside him. The two of them scurried through takes like there was no tomorrow. Forget what Britt had said about taking things easy.

They had five scenes set in the house. The other nine Peter had completed were exteriors. Peter could see what the director was after, which was to get an initial take on all five scenes. In one day. Which would have been tough with seasoned actors. With two who had virtually no experience under the lights, it was impossible. Ask anybody. They would have said the same thing. It couldn't be done.

Except for the fact that this new kid on the block, the one with a face made for billboards and fan clubs, the guy who had never even *seen* the business end of a camera before Saturday, never flubbed a line. Not once.

The fake surgeon standing next to Peter asked the nurse on his other side, "Can you get over this guy?"

No, as a matter of fact. Peter couldn't. Britt told JayJay where to stand. How to time his movements. Where to look. What beat to give his words, inflection, everything. And JayJay did it. First time, every time.

The nurse whispered, "I used to love this guy. Back, you know, before he started looking like a blimp on bourbon."

"I wanted to *be* him. Ride the range, rescue the girl, get the bad guys." The surgeon watched them run through another take, the three of them sparking every word with a tension that radiated through the room. "Who *is* he?"

Peter shook his head. He had no idea.

But he was going to find out.

They had a ten-minute break while lights and cameras were switched to the living room. Claire was out back again, this time sheltered from the rain by an umbrella bigger than the cab on JayJay's pickup, held by the script girl with the question mark permanently planted at the end of her every breath.

When the makeup giant named Peggy finished messing with Kelly's mouth, she asked JayJay, "Where's the snake woman?"

"Back by the chuck wagon having another smoke."

"Must've run out of venom."

"None of that, now."

Kelly made a quiet humph and shut her eyes while Peggy applied a fashionable streak of what was supposed to be soot to one cheek. "I don't know how much more I can take."

JayJay waited until the makeup lady departed to say, "Unless they've managed to build the big outdoors somewhere around here, I'd say this is going to be our last scene."

"I still can't get over how well you're handling your lines."

"That makes two of us."

"I never thought I'd be happy with just washing my face and getting into clothes that don't pinch." Kelly placed her hands on her hips and tilted one way, then the other. "I hate these jeans. Wardrobe made me stand on a stool and sewed me into these things. I'm supposed to be a firefighter. I'm dressed like a bar girl. I have to swing my legs like a robot just to move. The blood to my toes has been constricted down to a trickle. One deep breath and my top button is gonna take out somebody's eye."

This was the scene where JayJay was supposed to kiss the lady. Britt had walked him through it like he was selling cucumbers at the truck stop. Just one more little job before they closed down for the day. "I'll stand well clear."

"Not much chance of that." Kelly tried for casual, but missed. "What with the face time we got coming up."

JayJay worked at ignoring the crowd of folks at the warehouse's far end and swallowed on a serious case of nerves.

The rear door opened. Kelly snipped, a little louder than necessary, "Oh, look. Bat lady is back."

Britt the director stepped from behind the camera. "All right, places, everybody. This is a take."

JayJay kept his gaze on either the director or the floor by his feet as Britt walked him through the scene. There was a little strip of tape with his name set in the floor. Hit the tape and wait while the ladies set off some sparks, was near about what it all boiled down to. Then say his one line, get smooched, and hold hard while his sister and Kelly continued with their whanging match. Britt went on a fair while over how JayJay was to look worried about his cattle on the back forty, separated from the main pastures now by the spreading wildfire. Then he moved to the ladies and explained how their basic goal was to set up an antagonism between the female firefighter and Clara.

JayJay doubted that was going to require a whole lot of acting on either lady's part.

Britt jumped down from the stage. "Sound?"

"We're good to go."

"Clapper."

The AD stepped in front of the principal camera, the one Derek manned, and said aloud what was lit in red electric letters on his little board. "Scene nine, take one."

"And . . . action."

Clara walked toward where Kelly was hanging her helmet and fire-coat on the wooden hooks by the front door. "How much saccharin do you take in your coffee, hon, one shovel or two?"

Which, of course, was not the line from the script.

Kelly hesitated a fraction, long enough for Britt to call a cut. Instead, the director stood just offstage and frantically rolled his hands. *Go on.* So Kelly accepted the cup from Clara and said, "Thank you, darling. A little bit of bile goes a long way."

Again, not exactly what the script had on offer.

Clara gave Kelly an expression that brought to mind a hungry vermin. "Oh, dear. Where are my manners. JayJay, honey, ask your little guest if she'd like to stay for lunch. I'm sure I could roast her up a rat or two."

"I'm tempted to show you some of the tricks I learned from my daddy." Kelly again. "The ones that require a sharp knife and a fish you aim on cooking."

"Thank you, dear. Try talking to my little brother. I'm sure he'd be delighted with any tricks you learned in the gutter you crawled from."

Kelly set the cup down with the exaggerated care of somebody working hard not to use it as a mobile launch vehicle. She strolled to where her name was taped on the floor, using it like a line in the sand. "What do you say, JayJay. Want to go fight some fires, or would you rather stick around with this *delightful* reptile here?"

"Cut!" Britt stepped onto the stage and directly in between the two women. He was the only one on the stage who was smiling. "I'd say we've reached the end of this day."

"Fine by me." The woman playing JayJay's sister jumped down from the stage. "The odor of rank beginners is overwhelming."

"All right, enough. We're going on location tomorrow. Hear that everybody? The bus rolls out of here at nine sharp." Britt pointed at JayJay. "Time for you and me to meet the big guy. You too, Peter. Let's go."

# Chapter 16

My formula for a successful television series is very simple, Mr. Junior. Make a film version of a Big Mac. Tasty, cheap, and full of everything the public wants. Forget what's good for them. Prescriptions for the public good change as fast as tastes. Give them a big dose of whatever will keep them in their seats. And do it as inexpensively as possible."

Peter had never heard Allerby talk so openly before. But then again, he had not ever sat in on a negotiation with a new star. And that was what this John Junior certainly was. No longer an actor. Across from the studio chief sat the leading man of a show that could once again become a serious hit. Three days after the wildfire, the cable channels were still playing the tape of JayJay emerging from the fire with the girl draped over one shoulder and him stumbling along beside. Derek had started leafing through Lexus catalogs in his downtime.

Martin Allerby went on, "I've seen the dailies. And I'll tell you what you've probably already heard around the soundstage. You have the makings of a good actor. You are as clearly made for this role as anybody I have ever met."

The office was large enough to seat them all comfortably. JayJay and Britt Turner sat in the two leather chairs in front of Martin Allerby's desk. Peter was joined on the sofa by Milo Keplar, Centurion's sales director. The three adjoining chairs were taken by Phyllis Gleason from Casting, Centurion's chief counsel, and a woman from Publicity that Peter did not know. Gloria, Allerby's personal assistant, had rolled in a chair from the adjoining boardroom and sat to one side, laptop at the ready. Back in the far corner by the boardroom's entrance, just inside the door, sat a young Oriental man whom JayJay had requested be allowed to join them. Peter recognized the kid from the fire. Ahn somebody. He looked seriously spooked to be where he was.

Martin Allerby continued, "But Centurion has been down this road once before. The *Heartland* series is unique. Our leading man needs to set a certain example. We can't have you taking on roles that conflict with what we're trying to achieve here."

From his position, Peter could openly study JayJay at close range. The man defined rawbone. Even seated, JayJay exuded a remarkable power. He encompassed the still force of a whirlwind yet to strike. His face was both strong and attractive, yet also vulnerable. He sat slightly hunched over, watching the chief while twirling his hat between his knees. He still wore his trademark denim outfit. Yet he did so with the ease of a man born to nothing else. He was not so much tanned as leathery. His shoulders were huge when compared to his waist. And the knife jutting from his belt fitted as comfortably as his boots.

"We want to establish you not merely as the star of a popular series, Mr. Junior. We want to make you a brand." Allerby could not read JayJay's expression any better than Peter. And he didn't like it. "Tell me you understand what I'm saying."

"Looks to me like you want to tie me up proper," JayJay replied slowly. "And you want to do it cheap."

Britt laughed. He tried to cover it with a cough and failed.

Allerby gave a tight smile. "Who represents you? May I call you John?"

"I've always been partial to JayJay, Mr. Allerby."

The chief shook his head. As jarred by this as everybody else. The woman from Publicity was busy making notes and smiling. She filled the silence with, "Where are you from, Mr. Junior?"

"I was born in the Central Valley, miss."

"And now?"

He studied his hands for a long moment. "I reckon here is as good a place as any to hang my hat."

Allerby repeated his question. "Who's your agent?"

"Don't have one, sir."

"You're telling me this is your first role?"

His hat twirled faster. "I left the ranch. I got on the bus. I landed here. I don't know how to say it any better than that."

"Well, Casting has outdone themselves, locating you like they did."

Phyllis Gleason shifted uncomfortably in her seat, but had the sense to remain silent.

"We're in a touchy situation here, Mr. . . . JayJay. We've actually started filming a two-hour special and we don't have you under contract. What I'd like to suggest is we allow our counsel to draw up a temporary contract—"

"A handshake would work fine by me, sir."

Allerby's smile had nothing whatsoever behind it. "This is Hollywood, JayJay. We live by what's down on paper."

The actor leaned back with a sigh. Settled his hat on his knee. Tapped it a couple of times. "I never did like the feel of that word, *temporary*. Has the same feel as dangerous."

"What do you suggest?"

JayJay used his hat to point toward the Oriental man. "Ahn here can do my dickering."

The kid might as well have become plugged into the wall socket. "*Me?*"

Allerby said, "You're suggesting we appoint this young man as your agent?"

"Nobody said nothing about agents, sir. You want to work out a contract. I'm saying Ahn can lay the groundwork and point me in the right direction." JayJay glanced over. "You can do that for me, can't you?"

"Well, sure, I mean, one of my professors is a former agent. And the guy who taught me business law—"

Allerby broke in, "I'm afraid it doesn't work like that here, JayJay. Hollywood agents and attorneys are licensed. You will need one or the other to give you formal representation. We'll be happy to refer you to someone good."

"Somebody who you know and I don't, you mean."

Britt laughed out loud. Allerby studied his director before replying, "For our sake as well as your own, the contract must be drawn up by recognized professionals."

"Eventually," JayJay finished for him. "If I'm staying."

"If you're—" Allerby's cold edge emerged. "You're thinking of leaving?"

"Not directly, no sir."

"Most actors would donate all four limbs for the offer I'm making."

"That's what we need to decide on, though, isn't it. Whether I'm an actor or not."

Peter had never seen the chief's face so taut. Or his voice. "I can't bankroll a series based on a man who isn't sure he's got the staying power."

JayJay appeared unfazed by the chief's ire. "That makes sense. How long will it take to do the series you're talking about?"

Britt Turner responded, "Six months. But we wouldn't want to do just one, JayJay. The public is going to want this to run forever."

"Well, only God can talk about that sort of timing. What say I give you my word I'll do everything in my power to be here through the end of your series?"

Allerby didn't like it. But all he said was, "You'll give us an exclusive for the duration?"

Ahn spoke up then. "For Townsend's salary and benefits, he will."

Allerby looked aghast. "You can't expect me to offer a green actor what our star received."

"Your star was dumping this show right in the ratings basement." Ahn went through a remarkable transformation. He was tight and cold as Allerby in his response. "You want an exclusive, fine. This is what it's going to cost you."

"I can't agree to that."

JayJay rose to his feet, making the same action Peter had seen ten thousand times before. Until now, however, it had always been on the little screen. Using the brim of his hat, Jayjay brushed off the front of his trousers. The reflex of clearing away the trail's dust was so ingrained he did not notice. But everyone else did. Neil Townsend had mocked the action and all it stood for, a down-home hick who didn't know enough to put on clean pants. This particular JayJay did it without thinking. Everyone in the room watched.

JayJay said, "Looks like you and Ahn can work this out without me."

Allerby was still locked on the actor's hands. "I'll have a limo run you home."

Britt added, "And pick you up tomorrow."

"No limo," JayJay replied. "I can't say I like being driven around like I was somebody special."

"You prefer to drive yourself?"

"I might. Only my truck is broke down, I don't have a red cent to my name, and I misplaced my driver's license."

"The license is no problem. The local authorities are very helpful. Gloria?"

"I'll see to it as soon as Publicity can give me a head shot."

"Done," the lady replied, still making notes. "Mr. Junior, I need a few minutes of your time for background—"

"Not today," JayJay said. "I never thought standing around and jawing could get me as tuckered out as I am right now."

Britt said to Allerby, "We covered all five scenes. In one day."

Allerby repressed his excitement well. "Gloria, let the gentleman have something from petty cash. Would five thousand dollars do you, JayJay?"

He had the easy smile of a man carrying little unseen baggage. "I was hoping for a twenty."

When the room stopped laughing, JayJay asked, "How much did this Townsend fellow earn, anyway?"

Allerby was reluctant to divulge this. "One fifty per."

"One fifty what?"

"A hundred and fifty thousand."

*"Dollars?"*

Allerby was not enjoying this exchange. "What did you think, yen?"

JayJay shook his head. Started for the door. Said to Ahn, "Go easy on this fellow. Sounds to me like he was kidnapped and held for ransom."

"I hope you're listening good," Allerby snapped at Ahn. "All right. Britt and Legal stay, please. Everybody else, thank you for your time."

JayJay was still chuckling when he got to the front gates and found the lovely Miss Channing deep in conversation with the studio guard, Hardy Twyford. They were apparently using a break in the rain to discuss baseball. From the deep-set angle of the guard's right arm, JayJay assumed he was describing a curveball. The fact that Kelly actually seemed interested only made the woman more attractive. As did hearing her say, "That so-called stupendous throw you're describing. Is that the same one Lopez knocked over to a week from next Thursday?"

The guard dropped his throwing arm. "Yeah, well, you know what they say about a steady diet of steroids."

"I tell you what I think," Kelly replied. "The Dodgers couldn't win against the Yankees if they packed Uzis and Mace."

"Riverside's own," Hardy said. "A town and a team made for heart-stopping moments and nights of pure dread."

"Capital of drive-bys and assault by car stereo," Kelly agreed. She re-aimed at JayJay. "I detect a fresh limp, but I don't see any gaping wounds."

"They didn't even wing me," JayJay said.

Hardy felt comfortable enough with the moment to say, "Never known Martin Allerby to fire blanks before."

"Actually," JayJay said, "I was protected by that fellow who came in with me."

"What, the kid?"

"He's small, but he's got a dead-solid lock on smarts."

Kelly said, "Old slugger here's been filling me in on the game I missed yesterday. On account of my being paid to pretend there's nothing that'll ever make me happier than dressing up like a stick of cinnamon gum."

"You only missed a finish that put half the stands in the ER with cardiac arrest," Hardy said.

"I have the perfect excuse," Kelly said. "I was sick with that dread virus called overdue rent."

"I know that one," JayJay said. "Brings me out in the worst case of rash."

"From the sounds of things," Hardy said, "neither of you folks are gonna have to worry about that particular infection for a long time."

Kelly snorted. "I'll believe that when my landlady stops meeting me at the front door."

JayJay motioned for her to join him. "I got something I need to tell somebody before I explode."

Hardy waved them off and hummed something that sounded like "Love Is in the Air."

Kelly called back to the guard, "You do a great play-by-play, Hardy. Next time, I'll bring the grill, you get the dogs."

"I'd say you got yourself a date," Hardy replied. "Except for the lock that other guy's got on your arm."

The studio was fronted by a postage stamp of green and a border of fussed-over flowering plants. JayJay stopped by the concrete wall blocking them from the street. "I just heard how much they want to pay me for this particular game of dress-up."

"And?"

"A hundred and fifty thousand dollars a year."

Kelly actually hit a falsetto. "What?"

"I know. It's a sin."

"It's worse than that, it's robbery!"

"What, you think I should give it back?"

"Give . . ." Awareness flashed clear as humor in her gaze. "Sweetie, are you really that green? Or is this just a line I haven't heard before?"

"You pick, long as you call me that again."

"What, sweetie?" The smile actually broke through then. "Tell me exactly what they said."

JayJay had difficulty recalling what they were talking about, the impact of her smile was that strong. "I asked what they were paying that other fellow."

"Townsend. And?"

"One fifty per. Those were his exact words."

"You're sure?"

"You think I could ever forget a thing like that?"

"JayJay, here. Sit yourself down on this bench." She nestled in close enough beside him for JayJay to catch her scent, wildflowers and clean hair and country.

For the first time in far too long, he stopped worrying about the confusion these days had carried. He looked into emerald eyes sparked with down-home humor. Eyes that carried no threat. Eyes that did not need to look beyond this moment. Which, from where he was sitting, was pretty good indeed.

"Now. Take a deep breath, because you're in for a serious shock." Kelly was clearly having the time of her life. "Okay. You ready?"

Martin Allerby smoldered his way across the hall to Milo Keplar's office. The place had the plasticized look of a condo display unit. Testimony to how much time Centurion's sales director spent at the studio.

Keplar demanded, "So?"

"We're in."

"And?"

Allerby shut the door. "It cost us."

"You're telling me you couldn't handle the runt?"

"The kid is not human." Allerby slumped into the chair across from Keplar's desk. "I got in real tight. Under his tongue there's an imprint that reads 'Authentic Dell Parts.'"

Milo did not laugh. "How much damage are we talking?"

"One fifteen per."

Milo might have squeaked out a *what*.

"Plus escalation."

Milo's mouth did the goldfish thing, all action and no sound.

"Another fifty for every two points we rise in the ratings."

Milo grabbed his heart.

"And not from when we were at the top. Where we are now."

Milo gasped. "You didn't sign."

"Our mini-Dell borrowed Gloria's laptop and wrote out a deal memo. Invited me to do it then or wait until he's back in school and can get his professor's input. Wait to *film*, Milo. As in, I sign or we don't do the special." Allerby fished out a cigarette and lit up. Milo did not even protest. He was that upset. "Two ten for the special. Half up front. Claimed his man needed the funds to set himself up. His *man*. The mini-Dell left with the check."

Allerby lifted his cigarillo. As in, what to do with the ash. Milo did not even bother to respond. Allerby walked to the window. The rain had ceased, but the sky remained gray and brooding. He opened the window and flicked. "But I got him. Oh yeah. John Junior is ours for as long as we want him."

"That's something," Milo muttered.

"Not enough." Allerby's cigarillo only added to the moment's acidity. He flicked it out the window. Slammed it shut. Said to the glass, "I'm going to find a way to stake that kid out somewhere his screams won't be heard."

They drove to what passed for downtown Riverside in Kelly's battered Yukon. The bank was where Ahn's parents did their trading. He knew they kept late hours because he handled the family's deposits. The drive was punctuated by Ahn making Kelly tell the story nine times, and laughing so hard he couldn't give directions.

When they pulled up in front of the bank, JayJay said, "Y'all have got to come in with me. I can't carry all that money by myself."

"It's a check, JayJay."

"Ho, ho, ho, Ahn."

"Them zeros are heavy suckers." He tried to give her the envelope. "Here. See for yourself."

"It's your money, JayJay."

"What if they discover it ain't mine. And they call the cops and SWAT takes me down. I don't want to go through that alone."

"Hee, hee, hee."

They were barely through the bank entrance when a voice shouted, "Hold it right there!" An elderly security guard approached with his hand on his revolver. "You can't bring that in here!"

"I told you," JayJay said. "Even he knows this is bogus."

"He means your knife, JayJay."

"Ho, ho, ho."

"Hang on a second." The guard loosened in segments. First his hand dropped from his holster. Then his neck rose, drawing the rest of his scrawny form with it. "You're him. Ain't you. That guy."

"Here." JayJay handed the guard his knife. "Better take it before I do something to old funny bones here."

"What's wrong with the kid?"

Kelly answered, "He's studying to become an agent. Agents are all crazy. It's in their contract. Come on, JayJay."

The teller was a narrow lady with skin of polished ebony. Her face was a repository for circles. Round eyes. Big "O" of a mouth. Before she could speak, her supervisor emerged from the side office and said, "Can I help you?"

JayJay lifted his hat. "Afternoon, ma'am. I'd like . . . What do I want again?"

"Open an account and make a deposit."

"What she said."

The teller breathed, "You *are* him. Aren't you. The hero."

"Helen," the supervisor admonished. She was a large woman in rust-colored tweed who held herself impossibly erect. She asked JayJay, "Do you have some form of ID?"

"But it's *him*!" The teller did a two-step in place behind the counter. "My daughter wants to grow up and have your babies. Oh, I can hardly stand it." She scrambled for pen and paper. "You got to sign this. Say to Larissa. With love. Sign it JayJay Parsons. She will *die*."

"Helen, please." The supervisor gave a proper banker's smile. "Perhaps I should help you, sir. If you'll just—"

"No, no, Ms. Bell, please. Let me." The teller did her best to straighten up and fly right. "You just get yourself right over here please, Mr. JayJay."

"That's not his name," the supervisor said.

"Actually, it is," Kelly replied.

"Oooh, I've gone all cold. Look. My skin looks like a plucked chicken." A glare from the supervisor sobered her. "What name should I make it out for?"

"John Junior, ma'am."

"My goodness, you sound just like him."

"Of course he does," the supervisor said.

"Address?"

JayJay glanced at Ahn, who replied, "One fifteen Andeles."

The circles grew bigger. "You don't mean . . . You are living here in *Riverside*?" Another glare. The teller bent over the form. "River-side.

There. I can't hardly write the words. What amount did you want to deposit?"

JayJay slipped the envelope from his pocket, and the check from the envelope. But he couldn't bring himself to pass it over.

"Sign the back," Kelly said.

"It's like putting my name on a lie."

She patted his arm. "I know, honey. But it will pass. That's the problem with money. What looks like too much today won't be nearly enough tomorrow."

"I doubt that." JayJay signed it John Junior because it just seemed better than getting into explaining what he hadn't worked out. "Here you go."

The teller slid the check over to where the supervisor could have a look. The supervisor said, "Well. I see. Naturally we would normally want to have this clear before we could credit your account. But in this case, since Centurion is a client, I can call their accounting department while you wait."

"Thank you, ma'am, but that won't be necessary."

"Yes it will," Kelly interjected. "He's new to the area."

"His house got burned in the fire," Ahn added.

"Oh, you poor, poor man." The teller patted his hand. Then realized what she was doing. And shivered. "Where are you living, honey?"

"With my family," Ahn replied.

The supervisor said, "You're the Nguyens' son. Of course, I would have recognized you except . . . If you'll excuse me, I'll just go make the call."

When they were alone, JayJay took the slip of paper and said, "What is your daughter's name again?"

"Larissa. Oh, Mr. JayJay, can I call you that?"

"It's my name, ma'am."

"My daughter is going to just fall over and never get up." She folded the paper and slipped it into her purse. "She thinks the whole world would be right if they'd just make you president for a day."

Kelly said, "He's going to need some temporary checks."

"No problem." She studied Kelly. "Are you somebody famous too?"

"Not yet," JayJay said. "But soon."

"Oh, will you give me your autograph too?"

"Sure thing." Kelly signed another sheet. "First time for everything."

"Tell me about it." JayJay waited until the teller had stowed it away to ask, "Can I make a transfer?"

"The transfer's gotta wait until the money clears. But you can write it up now." She leaned in closer. "You look sooo much better now you've lost all that weight."

"Do you know," Kelly said, "I've been thinking the very same thing."

"Even my daughter, and she's your number one fan, well, she started calling you the Goodyear Man. You know. Like the blimp?" She gave JayJay's form an appreciative hum. "But not anymore. I told her when we saw you fighting them fires, that man has done some serious work on his bootie."

"Okay." He turned to Kelly. "How much does one of them agent things make?"

"Agent things. I like that. Ten percent is the norm."

Ahn slid up out of nowhere. "No way."

JayJay pointed at the transfer sheet the teller held. "Make it out to Ahn Nguyen."

Ahn protested, "JayJay, you can't—"

"You just hush up." To the teller, "Write me out a transfer for, what's ten percent of this?"

"Ten thousand, five hundred dollars."

"Sounds about right." He turned to where Ahn was suddenly struggling for breath and said, "Ho, ho, ho."

# Chapter 17

The Thirty Seconds that Shook Derek's World.

Even as a working title, it wasn't much. But Peter was tired. At least he was there for the moment. He was waiting to give his best buddy a ride home. Derek's car was in the shop. Again. Probably an overdose of smoke.

Eleven hours as stand-in chief cameraman had left Derek gray with fatigue. He did not even make a pretense of pulling back when Peter took the box of lenses from him. Derek just stumbled along beside him, muttering words that didn't connect. Still running through shots in his head, and not even aware he was speaking the fragments out loud.

"Derek, good. I was afraid I'd missed you."

Britt Turner was two men. On the surface he was affable and calm and quick. Underneath, however, there was what Peter thought of as the Hollywood edge. As in, scalpel-sharp. There to slice and dice at a moment's notice. No wonder his buddy turned scared.

Britt wore the day's efforts as well. His khaki shirt was stained and his hair was matted from the headphones and sweat. "I just had a word with Larry's agent." As in, *Heartland*'s chief cameraman and Derek's boss on the set. "Larry is filming some safari in Costa Rica. When he gets back he's booked for two weeks on a shoot in Calgary. Plus, between you and me, Larry never was totally in sync with our move to high-def."

Like a majority of senior cameramen, Larry looked down his nose at video. Film was richer, film was standard op for cinema, film gave greater depth of focus. Yada, yada. The truth was, high-definition digital required relearning an entire trade. But Derek had always felt that hi-def was tomorrow. He had learned film and he loved it. But he also devoured everything available on hi-def.

Britt said, "I liked the work you did today and so does Martin. So we've decided not to bring in a new face. Think you can handle being DP on location?"

DP, as in Director of Photography. The official title for chief cinematographer.

Derek was either numb enough or tired enough to respond calmly. "Sure thing."

"I think so too." Britt nodded, the deal settled. "Have your agent contact Accounting."

Derek watched Britt walk off. The new chief cameraman's shoulders remained bowed by an overdose of fatigue and sudden shock. He swiveled his whole body toward Peter and asked, "Did that really happen?"

"Congratulations, man. This is fantastic."

"I didn't even thank him."

"There's always tomorrow, right?" Peter thumped his shoulder. But not too hard. Derek might have keeled over. "Your bus has finally arrived."

Derek fumbled for his pocket. He needed three tries to snag his phone, then had even more trouble getting it open.

"Allow me." Peter pretended not to see his friend's eyes welling up. He took the phone and punched in Derek's home number. "Here you go."

Peter hefted the lens case and headed for the camera warehouse. Giving his friend the gift of privacy. Smiling when he heard Derek's voice go all shaky over those first words. "Honey? Hi. No, I'm fine. Listen, I've got something to tell you."

# Chapter 18

---

Martin Allerby's house was in one of the culs-de-sac off Mulholland Drive's peak. On good days, the view was stupendous. On bad, he was often above the worst of the LA air. From the road, Allerby's house was nothing much, a single-story ranch. Five windows with wrought-iron barriers fronted the road. Garage. Tiled roof. The postage-stamp lawn and blooming hedges were as pristine as a weekly Japanese gardener could keep them. The only feature of note was a peaked Gothic-style door, banded by iron and plugged with fist-size nails.

Inside, however, the house exploded. That was the image that came to mind. An explosion of light and space. The house perched on a very steep ridge. From behind, Allerby's residence was four stories, all glass and steel and redwood. The floors were patterns of hand-cast Mexican tile and Carrera marble. The carpets were Isfahan and all larger than his front lawn. The lighting indirect. The paintings real. Allerby had bought the place the year he had taken over Centurion. He could sell it now and retire to Santa Fe. But Allerby wasn't after retirement. He was after the most elusive of Hollywood titles.

A name.

Allerby wanted to be known. Pointed out wherever he went. A man sought by the top people. A man the stars fought to work for and the critics fawned over. A man able to green-light a feature. A man the investors like Harry Solish waited nineteen weeks to see.

And one thing was for certain. Martin Allerby was not going to get where he wanted to go with projects like *Heartland*.

"I hate that show," Martin muttered. "Every sanctimonious episode."

Milo Keplar did not need to ask which one. He leaned against the balcony railing watching a pair of hawks ride the updrafts. "At least you're able to set other people in motion, then hole up in your office and pretend it isn't happening. I've got to go out and sell the thing."

"It's not that easy."

Milo wasn't done. "Makes me want to gag, talking up that show."

Martin walked to the portable bar and freshened his drink. "You know, I think that's what ruined Townsend. Not the stardom. Having people expect him to *be* that guy. Honest and straight and strong and true. The red-blooded American hero."

"Don't forget religious." Milo took a deep belt from his own drink. "That show's made us the laughingstock of Hollywood. Even when it was at the top of the ratings, we were still the backwater studio nobody wanted to touch."

Allerby gripped the railing and said nothing. He knew all about what the Hollywood greats thought of him and his studio and his show.

One of the longest-lasting oddities about Hollywood was the status of television versus film. The money was in TV. A hit series or game show printed money for years. Success in film was greater when it came. But each feature required starting over from scratch. Television income was far steadier and lasted longer.

But there wasn't a single television director, actor, or studio executive who wouldn't have traded his next of kin for a slot in features.

A story making the rounds was about a writer who pitched a modern version of *Faust*. He set it in Hollywood, where a director was offered the chance to move into film if he gave up his soul. The studio exec heard the writer out, then said in all seriousness, "There's no way I'm turning my autobiography into something you watch at the local cineplex." Allerby had no doubt the story was true.

The doorbell rang. The pair listened as Allerby's Nicaraguan maid opened the door. Allerby asked, "Ready?"

"I got to hand it to you, Martin. You know how to impress."

"Thanks, Murphy. Coming from you, that means a lot."

Allerby disliked bringing business home. His privacy was critical. He needed a haven removed from the Hollywood struggle where he could drop his mask and relax. But this was an exceptional situation. The meeting had to happen. And it had to be where privacy was guaranteed. But it also had to impress. And charm. Allerby had cast about for weeks and come up with no better alternative. From the looks of things, he had chosen right.

The dining table was situated under the balcony roof overhang. A gas fireplace set into the house's outer wall fought back the evening chill. The sun was giving them an LA send-off, the haze forming a purple-and-gold veil. Down below glimmered the billion false stars of Los Angeles.

Murphy Watts, also known as the King of Sleaze, was the only man at the table in a tie. His dress was part of his trademark. His suits all came from a bespoke tailor on Savile Row. His shirts were Turnbull and Asser. His shoes handmade by Church of Jermyn Street. Murphy Watts owned a Regency manor in Dorset. He preferred living, it was said, where no one connected his money to his morals.

Allerby had come across Murphy Watts early in his career. Among other things, Watts ran a string of high-end call girls, the kind of ladies smart enough to avoid the Mob. Watts promised quality and discretion, things prized by studios entertaining on the sly. Though Watts rarely associated directly with such a relatively trivial portion of his empire, Allerby had made it a point to seek Watts out. Allerby always liked a man who delivered.

Allerby's maid arrived with their starters of salmon terrine and Beluga caviar. Watts watched her use the silver tongs to settle crustless brown toast onto his butter plate and said, "I doubt I could do better at the Connaught."

"We aim to please, Murphy." He toasted Watts with his glass. "And make us all rich."

"I'm already rich, Martin."

"Wealth comes in more forms than bank balances, as you well know."

Murphy might be wearing clothes worth more than a new S-Class, but underneath he still looked like a glossy plumber. He stood six-three in his stocking feet, weighed in at over two fifty, and possessed the coarse features of generations of heavy lifters. His eyes were ghostly pale, his age somewhere over sixty. Murphy Watts had started his first skin magazine while still a teenager in the Bronx. He had soon graduated to Los Angeles for two reasons. California's liberal courts had fought down all attempts to control the growth of porn. And there was a constant supply of new talent, drawn west by the lure of stardom. When the doors of Hollywood proved stubbornly shut, Murphy Watts was there to offer another way to play beneath the lights.

Allerby asked, "You have any objections if we talk business while we eat?"

Watts nodded at the maid filling their glasses. "Is it safe?"

"One of Lucia's most endearing qualities," Martin replied, "is her complete lack of interest in the English language."

Watts' meaty hands made a mockery of his table manners.

"So, Martin. Other than a great view and better food, what do you have to offer?"

"I'd say a chance of a lifetime, but you'd probably laugh."

"Not to your face," Murphy Watts replied. "I admire you too much for that."

Watts was accompanied by a man he had introduced simply as his associate. Martin's research had identified him as Irving Wexlar. Wexlar's nickname around the Watts empire was the Cadaver. Wexlar had a reputation for polishing every one of Watts' dimes before letting it go. He was a bloodless man with skin like wet wax. He did not look at anyone directly. He never spoke. But Martin knew what few others did. Irving Wexlar had a weakness. One Martin intended to exploit mercilessly.

"So let me lay it out, and you tell me whether it's as good as I think it is." Martin set down his fork. Dabbed his lips with his napkin. Set that aside as well. Claiming center stage. "I want to offer you what you've been denied for far too long. A chance at legitimacy. Part ownership of a Hollywood studio."

The mildly mocking smile dissolved. "Centurion is not for sale."

"It will be. Sooner rather than later."

"You're sure about this, are you?"

"The lawyer who is handling the deal has risked his bar license by breaking confidence with his client."

"Now why would a good upstanding Hollywood attorney do that for the likes of you?"

"Because," Martin replied, "I offered him five percent of the company."

Milo then performed his one role of the night. He made sure Murphy's attention was elsewhere, then nudged Wexlar. Once. A move subtle enough to either be ignored or misinterpreted. Except for the look Milo gave when the Cadaver glanced over.

Murphy Watts was a typical New York mick. He had brawled his way to the top of a very ugly pile. He paid Wexlar very well for his services. But Wexlar wanted what Murphy Watts would never give him. Wexlar wanted ownership. He wanted a piece of the pie and a seat on the board.

Wexlar lifted his narrow face a fraction and looked straight at Allerby for the first time since entering. Allerby made no sign. Just met the man's gaze.

"So Centurion's going on the block." Watts made a pretense of unconcern. "So what?"

"Not the block, never the block. Carter Dawes is sick. He will soon be approached by a buyer. He—"

"You?"

"Indirectly."

"You have financing in place?"

"Half of it."

"That's what you want from me? Money?" Watts pushed the plate aside. "I don't do minority deals, Martin. I'm surprised your research didn't come up with that."

"You'll never be accepted as principal of a studio. The moral parasites back east would parade you in front of Congress. The majors would shut you out of distribution to protect themselves. You know that as well as I do. Even the softest of your products isn't taken by any of the networks. For the same reason."

Murphy Watts touched the knot of his tie, as though taking reassurance from the silk. "I've done all right."

"That's not what we're talking about, though, is it? Doing all right."

"So what do I get from this other than my name on the role of a third-rate company that's lost in the wilds of television-land?"

Milo flushed and started to respond. Allerby silenced Milo with a look. Watts caught the exchange and smirked.

"We intend to launch a new reality show," Allerby said. "Two hundred contestants. The top twelve will be given costarring roles in a movie we will film and market. A movie that will carry the same title as the program."

"Which is?"

"*Vegas Stripper.*"

Milo spoke for the first time. "The tagline will read, 'Innocence on Display.'"

Watts studied him intently. "You have a buyer?"

"Two cables are bidding," Milo replied.

"Which ones?"

"Filmbox and Movietime."

Allerby knew what that meant. Both had refused to even take a meeting with Watts or his team. Watts said, "They'll slap you with the eighteen rating and slot you in after midnight."

"That's why they invented TIVO," Allerby replied. "Think for a second, Murphy. We're not talking about just another soft porn. We're talking about selling innocence. Think of what a young actress would do for the chance to go from nothing to actually starring in a feature."

"A feature about skin," Watts corrected.

"Reality shows are already as close to peddling flesh as the watchdogs permit," Allerby replied. "We're taking it to the next level, and we're doing it on a major cable network."

"Where's your other money coming from?"

Allerby knew Watts expected him not to say. Which made it even sweeter. "Harry Solish."

"He know you're talking with me?"

"Of course not."

Watts actually smiled. "Let me guess. You've promised Solish you'll keep doing the same old schtick. Then you'll bring me in. And even though you'll have just a minority stake, you'll actually control the studio, because your two principal investors hate each other with a dedicated passion."

"And we're going to make a killing," Milo said.

Watts rose from the table and walked to the railing. He said to the night and the shadows of eucalyptus trees, "Yeah, you probably will."

Wexlar looked up a second time. Straight into Allerby's face. Allerby nodded. Once.

The deal was as good as done.

# Chapter 19

The Nguyens' farewells were a bittersweet moment, and followed an argument that had lasted through dinner and into the evening, then restarted over breakfast.

Though *argument* was hardly a word that fit their soft voices and exquisite politeness. They merely gave voice to their concerns. Over and over and over. How JayJay could not possibly think their young son deserved such a gift. No, no, please do not call this work. Ahn has no experience, and he dreams of entering the movie business, and you give him this wonderful opportunity, he should pay *you*. How could we accept your money and remain honorable people? We would be insulting you, and be dishonorable to our God. And of course such a fine gentleman as yourself would not seek to cause us such distress.

Like that.

Ahn said almost nothing. He simply watched. Minh also. They both translated occasionally when the English words escaped their parents. But that was all. The hard-nosed jester who had held up the president of Centurion Studios was gone. Which JayJay found intensely moving, how this kid would show his parents such deep respect. Which left JayJay arguing more fiercely, since he was standing up not for himself, but this kid.

The one bad moment came two hours after dinner, when they had halted and asked if JayJay would join them for an episode of *Heartland*. Ahn reminded them that it had starred the other guy, which was the one point where MahMah became voluble, showing her disgust with a queenly drop of her hand.

JayJay viewed the episode with nightmarish dread. There upon the screen was a rerun of his own life, starring a man who slurred his words and kept his gut in place with lycra. This fake used JayJay's truck to wrangle up a herd of young calves in a lightning storm. He *remembered* the time. During the commercials JayJay wiped his face and studied the sheen on his hands. The family saw his distress, but said nothing when JayJay excused himself and went to bed.

His night was one long tumbling dream of whirlwinds and plagues and evil bankers, and he couldn't say for certain whether the nighttime images were more real than what he called his own past.

The next morning, when the parents started back in on Ahn's payment, JayJay found himself unwilling to hear more of the same. "Look here. We're not either one of us budging. It's time we moved on."

"But Mr. JayJay, if you will just listen—"

"I done heard you five times already, Mrs. Nguyen. I don't mean any disrespect, ma'am. But I tell you what's the truth. I'm headed out this door to catch a bus. The last time I got on one of them things I fell asleep and landed up in a world that don't make no sense. But I'm here, at least for now. And your pastor's words really hit home. He told me to do the best with what God's put here before me. And I'm starting with you folks."

From the way their foreheads scrunched up, JayJay knew they hadn't understood a lot of what he'd just said. And it didn't matter. "So this is what's happening. Ahn is keeping the money."

"But Mr. JayJay—"

"No, now excuse me. But it's your turn to listen up. Okay. The money is your son's. If accepting it disrespects you, give it to the church. Or take it out back and heap it in a pile and burn it all. That's your choice. But I'm not taking it back. What I'd suggest, though, is you treat it as a gift. Ahn is headed off for more schooling, right? So you've been nice to a stranger. You've taken him in and fed him and clothed him and given him a roof over his head—"

"You are not a stranger. And you saved our children's lives."

"I was a stranger then, ma'am. And please let me finish. So this money is Ahn's. I'd call it a college fund and let it go as that. But here's the thing. I *need* your son. I want him to keep working for me whenever something comes up with them folks over at the studio. So what I want to know is, what am I going to pay him next time?"

"No pay," Mr. Nguyen protested. "No more."

"Sorry, sir, but that ain't happening. I've paid my way since Pappy died and I got stuck with the ranch, and that's the way it's going to stay. Ahn is working for me unless you tell me otherwise, and I'm gonna pay him." JayJay folded his arms. "Y'all want to see stubborn, you try and tell me different."

They had settled on half what Ahn said a Hollywood lawyer received. Four hundred dollars an hour. The sum clogged up Mrs. Nguyen's tongue and bulged her husband's eyes a bit. But Ahn got down a book and showed them a page, and they looked at each other and shook their heads but said nothing more. Except for one thing. JayJay had to promise that he would treat their home as his own, whenever he was in the area.

He left for the studio feeling like he had escaped the battlefield singed but not badly wounded.

Ahn drove JayJay to the studio in the family car. Hardy waved them through the gate with a two-handed slugger's swing. Ahn stopped in front of where a crowd boarded a bus. Clara stood by a limo smoking and squinting at JayJay sitting there in the tight little sedan. Ahn's voice carried the same glazed state as his eyes. "I can't thank you enough. I ought to say it better, but I can't."

"You don't need to say a thing. I've been poor before. I know what it means to find myself looking at a pile of cabbage with my name on it."

Ahn looked at him. "Not just the money. The trust. The *chance*."

JayJay wanted to reach over and hug him, but he wasn't sure how the kid would take it. So he made do by punching Ahn's shoulder and saying, "You just be good and ready for the next time they lay down the bear traps."

They wanted JayJay to travel in the limo with Clara and Britt. He was having none of it, which caused Clara to go all snippy about him needing to make time with the hired help. JayJay purposefully chose a seat far away from Kelly, which she seemed to understand, at least enough to cast him an easy smile. Derek, the camera guy, took the seat next to him. Derek fretted and chewed his lip pretty much the entire five-hour journey. JayJay welcomed the silence. Now that he had left the Nguyens' shelter, the previous night's television program scrolled across the yellow-desert landscape. JayJay closed his eyes and tried to pray for guidance. But the images just kept rolling inside his brain. That fat old fraud in a girdle hugging JayJay's sister and then waddling off in JayJay's boots to drive JayJay's truck and save JayJay's cattle.

He opened his eyes and pretended to study the terrain. Anything was better than trying to make sense of the desert storm raging inside his head. All dust and turmoil and empty noise.

The hours rumbled by. The interstate was a dry river of heat. The surrounding vista was yellow rock and scrub and hills of hopeless ardor. Finally they started climbing, passing through one mesa after another. Somebody passed out a box lunch. Derek opened his and studied the contents like he was reading hieroglyphics. JayJay asked, "You want to talk about what's eating at your craw?"

"You ever been given what you've always wanted and wished you never asked in the first place?" Derek fumbled over shutting his box. "I never knew confusion could feel this bad."

JayJay slid his own box under his seat. Sighed back around to stare out the window. "I can't say I've ever started off like you're saying. But it sure feels like I wound up in the same hole."

Derek gave him a shadow of a smile. "You mean being a big star isn't all bluebirds and buttercups?"

"When I meet me a star," JayJay replied, "I'll be sure and ask him."

The hardest moment of all came around the final bend. Worse than losing Minh in the smoke. Worse than coming to buck naked in that little shop of horrors. Worse than the night he'd just finished. Bundle them all together and let them stew, they still wouldn't compare with how it felt to come around that bend and stare at his old home.

The hills were there. All his old friends, the ones he'd sat and watched grow from ghostlike to stately in dawn's gold.

The stand of cottonwoods growing by the spring.

The corral where a field hand was releasing his horse with a pat on its rump.

The fields.

The front vegetable garden.

His daddy's old well.

The house.

"Unless you want to head on into town with me, mister, you better get a move on."

JayJay wrenched himself away from the sight. "Excuse me?"

The bus driver pointed his thumb at the open door. "I'm supposed to go drop the personal effects by your hotel."

JayJay needed both hands to manage the steps. He stumbled away as the driver wheezed the door shut and rumbled off.

"Hey, you!"

JayJay had trouble placing the lady taking long strides toward him. Kelly said, "The crew's got hours of work and we don't start rehearsals until tomorrow. What say we go find us a place that knows how to cook real grub?"

JayJay turned back to the cabin. "I don't think so."

Kelly planted both fists on her hips. "You make a habit of turning down the best thing going?"

JayJay pointed at the cabin. "That ain't real."

"Doesn't need to be, since we do all the interior work back on the soundstage. Remember?" When JayJay did not respond, she closed the distance between them. "Hey, look at me a minute. You remember how you came over that first day on the set? Did you have any idea how scared I was?"

"Gladys told me. Or Hilda. I can't recall which is which."

"Remind me to thank them both. Truth is, I was about ready to bolt. Then this handsome fellow came over, first one I'd met in Hollywood who didn't treat me like I was ice cream on a stick. I don't remember exactly what it was you said to me. But I know how good it felt, just making a new friend in all that strangeness."

"Is any of this real?" JayJay's voice cracked under the strain of voicing very real fears. "Am I?"

"I can't speak for this place or this work." Her voice changed then. It was a womanly thing, how she dropped the hard shell and showed him who she was underneath. "But you're just about the strongest dose of real I've had since leaving Dakota."

She gripped his arm and tugged. "Come on, cowboy. Let's go see if that limo guy knows how to spell honky-tonk."

# Chapter 20

Martin Allerby was crossing the lot and talking into his cell phone when he spotted an unlikely figure up ahead. "Hold on a second, Eddie." He raised his voice. "Peter, over here if you please."

The writer scuttled. Allerby had seen the response a hundred thousand times and still found pleasure in fear on display. Like a film scene so well plotted and choreographed he could run it every day and never tire of its precision and beauty.

Allerby pointed to a spot in the concrete at his feet, signifying that Peter should stand and wait. He said to the phone, "No, Eddie. No. I'm sorry, Eddie, talking faster will not change my mind. Now here's what you do. Go back to your client and remind her that we had seven hundred actors respond to that particular casting call. Wait, I'm not finished. We winnowed this number down to six finalists. Any of which would do fine. We chose your client not because she was the best, but because she fit our criteria. She was peppy, and she was cheap. Do you understand what I mean by the word cheap? Fine. I'll expect the signed agreement messengered to my office by the day's close, or I'll select someone else to fill the role."

He snapped the phone shut. The writer's eyes had glazed over slightly. Hearing the stats always had a chilling effect upon talent. Allerby asked, "What are you doing here?"

Peter jerked. "Working on the next set of scenes, Mr. Allerby."

"I understand that." He felt the late-afternoon sunlight drill them with the precise force of a close-up lamp. "I meant, what are you doing *here*. On the lot. And not out with the others on location."

"Mr. Allerby . . . my wife?"

"A charming lady, I'm sure."

"Sir, she's eight months pregnant. With twins."

"How very good for you both."

"I thought . . . that is, I just assumed . . .'"

Martin watched the writer's carefully worded arguments fade to dust and blow away. "You are not paid to think. You are paid to complete the script we are already shooting. Am I making myself clear?"

"There've been some complications—"

"As there always are when you move a half-finished script from dis-cussions to filming." Martin chose to misunderstand. "Which is why it is essential for you to be out there. Close at hand. Ready to help them with rewrites on a moment's notice."

The protest, though feeble, still emerged. "I could do that from here."

"Theoretically. That's what we're talking about, isn't it. Theories. Theoretically your wife might have problems, which may or may not arrive in a day or a week or in six weeks' time. Theoretically she might need you. At which point you are only four hours away."

"More like six."

"Fine. Call it twelve if you want. Call it three days. Call it a trek across the Gobi." Martin slipped the blade a fraction from its sheath. "If that would help you explain to your wife why you have been dropped as principal writer of this series. Do I make myself clear, Caffrey? Excellent. I'm so glad we cleared that up."

Allerby kept his smile contained until he entered the soundstage and could aim it at a director with whom he had argued the previous day, confusing the poor woman enormously in the process. Which made the moment even sweeter. Confused talent was talent operating on its toes. Allerby leaned against the side wall and pretended to watch them set up the next scene.

This really was turning into a splendid day.

# Chapter 21

----

JayJay and Kelly stopped by the hotel long enough to check into their rooms and change. The hotel was on the outskirts of Salton City, a nice enough town according to the limo driver, whose name was Gerald and who proved to be not only a font of information but a guy seriously intent on hustling tips. The hotel was family owned, a fifties-style two-story affair that had been done up by the son and his wife. This according to Gerald. The hotel's exterior walls were flagstone. There was a little central courtyard with a flower garden and pool area. The road-ies got a view of the highway so they'd feel at home, was how Gerald put it as he pulled into the forecourt. JayJay started to make a fuss when he learned he was assigned a suite, but Kelly gave him one of those looks, the kind women patented about a thousand years ago that were meant to stop a man dead in his tracks.

JayJay didn't have any clothes except his studio gear and what Robbie Robinson's dad had loaned him. He stopped by for a shower and a couple of circuits around his suite, which wasn't much bigger than the corral where they were keeping Skye penned. Then he walked back to the conference room behind the lobby, where he'd spotted the two wardrobe ladies sorting through piles of this and that. He knocked on an open door and asked if they had anything besides jeans that might fit him.

"Oooh, another man who hates to shop."

"I'd have an easier time of it," JayJay replied, "if they could somehow separate the shopping from the bit about spending money."

During the fittings, JayJay finally got the ladies straightened out. Gladys was the taller one, Hilda the stockier and more sharply focused. Both women had Coney Island rock-candy exteriors with marshmallow hearts. They dressed him in a Mexican-weave shirt, dun-colored slacks, Tony Lama ostrich-skin boots, and a jacket of suede so soft it brought to mind half-melted butter.

He stared at the stranger in the mirror and said, "Now we get to the hard part. How much do I owe you?"

They acted like he'd said something hilarious. Gladys patted him on the arm and said, "You two young people go have yourselves a lovely time."

"How'd you know I was going out with Kelly?"

They both played like he was a comic again. "Honey, when it comes to the stars, there are no secrets on a set."

"I'll keep that in mind."

Kelly chose that moment to show up and say, "I saw you folks through the back window. It looked like such a good time I thought I'd come join in."

She wore fawn-colored slacks and high-backed sandals and a sleeveless knit top the color of clouds at sunset. She'd done something with her hair, so it was partly loose and partly slung over one shoulder. And she looked like spun diamonds. That was the thought that sprang to JayJay's mind. It didn't make any sense, but he was too hammered by the sight of her to care.

Which was why the only reply JayJay could manage was, "Whoa."

They came out of the hotel parking lot and started away from town. Sooner or later JayJay was going to have to take that route in the opposite direction, see how his supposed memories meshed with the place he had always thought of as Simmons Gulch. But right then he had just about all he could handle, walking alongside the prettiest gal in six states. Nice enough looking to slow traffic on the road. Nice enough to have him wishing his arm was about nine feet long, so she still could hang on to it like she was doing, and he could sneak back a couple of paces and get a load of this woman's walk. Maybe give off a holler or two for good measure. Yes *sir*.

The place they were headed for was called Goody's. Their choice was the result of a lengthy negotiation between Kelly and the limo driver, then continued with the lady behind the hotel counter. Done all serious, like Kelly'd been planning to invade a medium-size country instead of find a place that served up something hot. But there were three restaurants in town that had dance floors and the sort of clientele who knew what to do with a night off. What clinched it for Goody's was when the check-in lady related how the name had previously been Good Time Bar and Grill. Then a twister had taken off everything but the first word, and the owner had changed it to what folks already called it, which was Goody's. Then two weeks back he had lost one *o*, the stem off the *d*, and the last *s* to shotgun blasts from a couple of clients. The check-in lady had related all this with the tired humor of having been there herself, and finished with, "I guess them good-time boys didn't like the band."

Kelly had slapped her hand down on the counter and declared, "This is what I was after all along. A place that serves up a story with their rice and beans."

The sun was nothing more than a golden afterthought, but the sidewalk gave off enough heat to bake a casserole. They took it slow, enjoying the stroll. She saw him grinning at nothing and asked, "What's on your mind there, Slim?"

"You're looking at a man happy just to push the world to one side."

She gripped his hand tighter. "That's why God invented the two-step. Didn't you read that in Sunday school?"

They knew they had arrived because the lot was packed solid with pickups and dusty high-wheelers. A heavily damaged sign flickered and buzzed on top of the roof. The sign's only working lights spelled out "Gooy." The crowd snaked out the front door and down the six steps to the lot and spread over hoods of close-parked cars. Every now and then a loudspeaker called out a name. Folks leaving the restaurant all had to stop and shake hands and chat with friends. They were a mixed bunch, city folks and country, Anglo and Hispanic, a lot of three- and four-generation families.

A young man leaning against the stair-post spotted them crossing the lot and nudged his neighbor. By the time they arrived at the stairs, every eye was upon them.

Kelly took it in polite stride. "Evening, all. Can somebody tell us what's the right way to get our names down for a table?"

A woman by the door said, "Y'all just head on inside."

"We don't aim to go breaking in line," JayJay said.

"I don't imagine they're gonna give you much chance to argue," the woman said.

Word had already passed inside to the three ladies behind the check-in stand, an older woman and two younger versions. All shared the same wide-eyed expression. The older woman started off all formal, "Welcome to Goody's. Can I help you?"

"It's really you, isn't it," the youngest said. "Him."

Her sister said, "His name is JayJay, silly."

"I know that. You're him, aren't you?"

The older sister was far enough into her teenage years to offer a bit of lip. "I thought you'd gotten fat."

That turned their mother around. "Now you just hush up, unless you want to spell Ernesto at the dishwasher for about sixteen years." She turned back to her clients. "Welcome to Goody's."

"You already told them that, Momma." The teenager wasn't quite done yet. "Daddy says you been wearing a girdle."

"That was the other guy." Kelly patted JayJay's arm. "This is the new-and-improved version."

The older woman snipped, "Well, I guess the only way I'm going to make my daughter *behave* is if I show you to a table."

JayJay protested, "Ma'am, you got people who been waiting here a spell."

"There is no way on earth I'm going to make JayJay Parsons stand in my foyer putting up with comments from Little Miss Big Mouth here." She picked up a pair of menus and marched away. "Do you have children?"

"No ma'am. That's one pleasure I've missed so far."

"Well, I've got one you can have cheap." She was miffed enough to stop being impressed by who she was serving. "I've got a table clear by the dance floor. But once the band starts up you won't be able to hear yourself think."

Kelly gave him one of those women-only looks. "Oh, we didn't come here to think, did we."

The smiles that followed them across the restaurant made the staring easy to bear. As the woman seated them, Kelly said, "That's an interesting sign you've got on top of the restaurant."

The woman gave Kelly a seen-it-all look and replied, "That was last week's story. Hang around here long enough, we'll probably serve you up a tale all your very own."

They hadn't settled in before a slender man came hustling out of the kitchen, drying his hands on an apron. "Well, I'll be. I guess my wife ain't gone loco after all." He offered JayJay his hand. "Norman Goode. A couple of your roadies showed up this afternoon. I been hoping they might find somebody able to resurrect the only reason I don't shoot my TV."

"The name's John Junior, sir. This here's Kelly Channing."

"'Preciate you brightening up our place, Miss Channing." He wore a grin that was too big for his narrow face as he said to JayJay, "My daughter didn't really ask if you were wearing a girdle."

"To tell the truth, they made us feel so welcome I didn't hardly notice."

He ran a hand over his remaining dark hair and said to Kelly, "It's probably a good thing they don't offer trade-ins on teenagers."

Kelly asked, "What should we eat?"

"The artichokes are in season."

"That's all I need to know."

"I could start you off with some of my wife's cream of artichoke soup, do you up a big plate, grill you some hearts, serve them with strips of corn-fed beef, bowl of some hot sauce on the side, little Parmesan, how does that sound?"

"Better add a few batter-fried," Kelly said. "I been eating that no-fat LA nonsense for too long."

He re-aimed his smile. "Where you from, darling?"

"Sioux Falls."

"Sounds like my kind of country, if you been raised not to run screaming from a little hot grease." He backed away. "We'll ask some friends to make sure any tourists who slip by my daughters don't bother you none. You folks have yourselves a time."

"Thank you, Mr. Goode, we aim to." JayJay waited until the table was theirs again to say, "I declare, you could charm gold from Fort Knox."

She looked at him like she was measuring out some words, but they remained unspoken. Instead, she said, "You recall our little wager?"

"It's not my nature to forget what a lovely lady's said to me."

"So tell. How did you wind up here?"

He leaned back and crossed his arms. Gave her determined. He was having too good a time to disturb this night. "You go right ahead."

"Loser buys, right?"

"That was the deal."

"I'm only asking because there's no way you're going to top this." She did something with her hair, playing it like a talisman. "My best friend back home was a local beauty queen."

"Oh, and you're not?"

"Hush up, Slim. This is my tale. My friend did some modeling, got as far as Chicago. Decided to give Hollywood a run. She came out, did the circuit. Her phone calls were all about how tough it was to break in, find an agent, the casting calls, the dead-end jobs, the struggle to get noticed in a town full of other beauty queens. A while passed, long enough for everybody to accept that our friend had permanently immigrated to la-la land. One day I got a call from her mother."

Kelly was interrupted by their soup being served by the owner himself. "You folks tell me if this isn't the finest you've ever tasted."

When they had tasted and complimented, he backed away with, "Enjoy."

JayJay hesitated then. Kelly asked, "What is it?"

"You mind if we bless this food?"

"No, JayJay. Why should I mind?"

"On account of about six thousand people watching every move we make."

"So what could be better? Here, take my hand. Now say the words for us."

He worked the words around the confusion that was there waiting for him when he shut his eyes. At the "amen" he lifted his gaze to find her waiting with, "That was nice."

"I don't hardly know what I just said."

"Good prayers are sometimes like that."

"You sure are something. Full of spark and full of faith. I don't recollect ever coming across somebody like you before."

"Is that a good thing?"

"You know it is."

"My daddy is a rock-solid country Baptist preacher man. My momma is an Alabama firecracker. Life wasn't what you'd call calm around our house, but it sure was interesting."

The soup bowls were taken away by a younger daughter who moved about in absolute silence. JayJay said, "Thank you, honey."

"You're welcome." She bit her lip. "Momma told me I wasn't to say anything and bother you folks."

"Polite conversation isn't a bother," Kelly assured her. "It's a pleasure."

"'Specially coming from somebody nice as you," JayJay agreed. "What's your name?"

"Heather."

"That's as lovely a name as ever I've heard."

She flushed with pleasure. "I don't care what my sister says. You're the only show Daddy ever stops long enough to watch all the way through."

When they were alone again, Kelly said, "I don't want to scare you, Slim. But I can tell you one thing for certain. You're sitting in the company of friends so good you don't even need to remember their names."

The plates arrived then, a steaming feast of artichoke hearts prepared four different ways and local beef and a hot sauce strong enough to remove one layer of skin from the roof of JayJay's mouth. Kelly held up well under the strain. JayJay ate until another bite would have been genuinely painful.

JayJay waited until they'd declined dessert and been served coffee to say, "You were talking about your friend's momma calling."

Kelly made a process of folding her napkin and setting it aside. "She asked if I'd heard from her daughter. I said, not in a while. But Julie's calls had trailed off so gradually I didn't pay much notice until her mother phoned. Then I realized it was longer than a while. More like five months. The worry in her mother's voice got me to thinking. I called Julie and said I was coming down. She didn't want me to, which only made me more determined.

"My friend was living in this dump off Sunset with four other girls. All of them worked day jobs and ran to casting calls and dreamed of that one big chance. All were beautiful girls from small-town America. Five totally different stories, but all grown into the same hard Hollywood shell. You know what I mean. They'd learned the walk and the hair and they shopped the sales for the hot styles. They studied the moves and they'd all learned how to *shine*."

She was quiet for a while, until JayJay said, "You don't have to tell me any more. I think I know already."

But she went on, "Julie tried to put this smiley face on it. How it was her chance to get into the big time. How everybody did it, guys and girls alike. But she knew and I knew. She was just another pretty face who'd gotten sucked into this big producer's stable of wannabes. She was going to these parties and she wasn't coming home. And there wasn't a thing I could do but hang around and let her know I wasn't buying any part of the package. Just reminding her there was another world out there, no matter what she put down her throat or up her nose to help her forget. And I prayed. Hard as I've ever prayed in my whole life. Just looking for a way to get my friend out of there.

"I'd been there about a week when she went to a casting call. I went along because I didn't know what else to do. I was supposed to be heading home the next day. You know how those things run, right?"

"No," JayJay replied. "I don't."

"There must've been three hundred lovely ladies. So many they all ran together in one huge river of silk and perfume and lipstick and hair spray. It was the most depressing thing I've ever seen in my entire life. A ghetto of desperate beauty. All of them young, all of them so hungry they'd do *anything* for their big chance. They clutched their page of lines. They practiced. They ignored everybody else. They studied themselves in the mirror and worried over every hair, every tiny fault only they could see.

"Then this director comes walking by. He's young, he's a little muffin job, you know what I mean?"

"I can imagine."

"Pudgy, wearing a stained T-shirt and raggedy jeans, just a nobody who happens to be making a movie. And those ladies, I mean, they just went *on*." She tried for a smile and failed. "That director fellow stopped dead in his tracks, looked at me, and said, 'You're the one.'

"My friend just plain freaked. She threw me out of the apartment. Julie gave up on Hollywood and flew home the next day. I called my daddy and told him what had happened. He said he'd call her folks and meet her at the airport and start building bridges. I asked him what he thought I should do. He asked me if I wanted to give this movie thing a try. I said I wasn't sure. I'd been working as an ER nurse in Sioux Falls, I could get my job back in a heartbeat. And by then I'd discovered this film deal, when it's working, it's *fun*. So he gave me three pieces of advice. Never be ashamed of who you are. Leave the place richer for your having been there. And don't ever call the place home."

JayJay found himself rocked back in his seat by what he heard. "Your daddy sounds like a very wise man."

"Yeah, I miss him and Momma almost as much as I do my former best friend."

JayJay let her stare out over the empty dance floor for a time. The band started gearing up for their first set. Finally he leaned forward and said loud enough to be heard over the tuning guitars, "I bet soon as that lady comes to her senses, she's gonna realize just what a great thing you've done for her."

Kelly gave him a look of pure yearning. "You really think so?"

He reached across the table and snagged her hand. "Miss Channing, you're as fine a lady as I've ever met."

She blinked away the sheen of sorrow. "Is it just me, or does life always give you the pie with a hole cut out of the heart?"

"I don't know as I've seen enough of life to answer that."

"Okay. So it's your turn." When he tried to draw away she tightened her grip on his hand. "Don't you even think about backing out on me."

"Kelly, I'll tell you my sorry tale. I promise. But the thing is just so twisted it'd wreck the night for me. And I'm having too fine a time just being here with you to let that happen."

She inspected him. "You'll tell me?"

"If you ask me again. But I'm afraid—"

"I won't run, Slim."

"Don't say that 'til you've heard me out."

She took his arm in a two-handed grip. And repeated the words. "I won't run."

The band played modern country with a solid bond to Southern rock. They sported both a mandolin and a hard-fisted guitar. They followed Roy Acuff with the Allman Brothers. The dance floor filled with people doing everything from the cowboy two-step to the modern wrangle. Closest to their table, a little towheaded boy in pink suspenders swung the hands of a lovely Latina with wildflowers in her dark hair. Kelly slid her chair around and used her grip on JayJay's arm to draw it around her shoulders. Easy and natural, like she'd been doing it for years. They sat and listened and returned the smiles of those who glanced their way. Just another couple out for a night on the town.

When the band took a break, she said, "One question."

"Say what?"

"I get to ask you a question, you answer, and you don't ask the same thing back."

He was too comfortable feeling her closeness to argue. "I suppose."

"How is it that a handsome galoot like you isn't staked out and branded?"

"I loved the wrong woman, is the simple answer."

"What was her name?"

He leaned a little closer, took a deep breath of her perfume and the clean scent of her hair. "Tell the truth, I don't rightly recall."

She turned without drawing away, which brought her face so close he felt her breath on his cheek when she said, "You big fibber, you."

"She ran off with a rodeo rider."

"Sounds like a woman seriously lacking in the smarts department."

"Said she wanted somebody who hankered after a life beyond the next valley."

Kelly's reply was cut off by the owner's teenage daughter approaching their table. She wore a sullen expression and carried a tone to match. "My momma says I've got to come apologize for what I said."

Kelly put some space between them and motioned for JayJay to stand up. "Sit yourself down here, darling. What's your name?"

"Felicity."

"So you did what your momma asked. Now tell me the boy's name."

"What boy?"

"The one your momma would like to stake out over an anthill."

She looked square at Kelly. "Roy."

"And what's this Roy of yours into, tattoos?"

"Dirt bikes."

"Same thing. You want some advice of the been there, done that variety?"

Felicity gave what to JayJay looked like a thoroughly teenage shrug. "I guess."

Kelly looked up to where JayJay still stood by what had formerly been his chair. "Make yourself useful, JayJay. Go ask the band if they know 'Gotta Serve Somebody.'"

Felicity made a face. "He makes you call him that on a *date?*"

"It's his real name."

"Get out."

"For real."

"That is just so totally twisted."

Kelly draped an arm around Felicity's chair. "Honey, twisted is the one word that totally describes Hollywood."

"Are you an actress or something?"

"Or something." Kelly looked up. "What you waiting for, Slim?"

JayJay asked, "'Gotta Serve Somebody' is a song?"

"Tell me you're kidding. As in Bob Dylan?"

"Duh," Felicity said.

"I mean, really," Kelly said.

"Whatever," Felicity said.

The two ladies looked at each other and burst out laughing.

JayJay crossed the empty dance floor and said to the band leader, "My place just got hijacked by a sixteen-year-old girl overdosed on lip."

The guitarist fingered a riff and replied, "My teenage daughter is why I spend so much time on the road."

The drummer called over, "His teenage daughter is why I want to get back." Then he drummed the air over his snare.

The band leader patted his side pocket and said, "I been meaning to shorten the life span of that feller. Somebody send a roadie for the six-shooter I left backstage."

The drummer grinned. "Lucky for me you can't hit the side of a barn at two paces."

He asked JayJay, "What can I do you for?"

"Y'all take requests?"

The bass guitarist said, "We don't do no Hollywood plinkety-plink."

The drummer said, "Does this feller look like a plinkety-plink kinda guy?"

The bass guitarist said, "Hollywood does things. They make you eat squid and pretend you like it. There ain't no telling what he wants. Could be something that killed old Fred Astaire, and then where would we be?"

The lead guitarist said, "Don't mind him. He was born in a bad mood and it's only grown worse. What you want to hear?"

"The lady asks if you'll play 'Gotta Serve Somebody.'"

"That old Dylan number. I believe I heard that somewhere before."

The bass guitarist said, "My momma was always after me to learn that one. I told her I just play the music, I don't live the lyrics."

The drummer pointed with both his sticks and said to JayJay, "I'll even play you some Hollywood plinkety-plink if you'll go ask your lady if she'll come decorate our stage for a while."

"Now there's an idea," the guitarist said.

JayJay said, "I don't know if she can sing."

"Mister, if she's got a voice to match her looks, we're all in trouble."

The band leader pointed a thumb at the mixing board. "We'll just crank the volume down and give all the folks here a reason to stare our way."

JayJay walked back to the table and waited for the two ladies' heads to disconnect. "The man wants to know if you'd like to sing it with them."

To his surprise, Kelly rose and said, "I wouldn't say no." She hugged Felicity and said, "You're a sweetheart."

"This has been so totally cool," Felicity said, and even managed a smile in JayJay's direction. "Bye."

He asked, "What was that all about?"

Kelly patted his arm. "Sorry, Slim. You lack the necessary gene to understand."

Her approaching the stage was enough to draw goofy grins from all the band members. She shook hands with each of them. They stood around and laughed together long enough for JayJay to grow semi-jealous. Then they did some head nodding, talking through the music thing, Kelly giving the impression that she knew just exactly what she was doing.

The lead guitarist stepped to one side. Kelly flipped her hair back over one shoulder, turned around, and plucked the microphone from the stand.

For the first time that night, not a single eye in the place was directed JayJay's way.

Kelly said, "This song comes compliments of all the fine folks at New Road Baptist Church in Sioux Falls."

She turned and nodded to the band.

The drummer clicked them down four beats. The bass and the lead guitarist came in together, the low-driving thunder of electrified Dylan after his conversion experience. Kelly danced them through that first round without moving her feet, just driving them along with a gentle motion. She lifted the mike and dived straight in.

JayJay rose to his feet because the dance floor filled up and he couldn't see. But the folks weren't dancing. The floor was just too full for much motion. He pushed his way through. Folks made way reluctantly. He pressed forward until he was standing close enough to get a full view.

The lady could just plain sing.

Her voice was somewhere below what he'd have expected. A rich, raspy growl, like a proud lioness who just *owned* that mike. The second time through that refrain, she lifted her voice a notch and belted the words with a feeling that punched JayJay right at heart level. It may be the devil or it may be the Lord, but you got to serve somebody. Oh yeah. He couldn't nod strong enough without using his entire body. The lady wasn't just singing now. She was telling *truth*.

When she was done the crowd erupted. JayJay stood there so astonished he forgot to applaud until some fellow started slapping him on the back, like he had to hit somebody and JayJay was closest. Kelly looked down at him and grinned, then waved at the crowd and started off the stage. But the crowd wasn't having any of it. The lead guitarist pulled her back and pleaded with words JayJay didn't need to hear.

She looked at JayJay. He motioned for her to stay where she was. She gave him a different look then, one that warmed him all the way back to his solitary table. One that left him full of something new. Something that was way beyond pride. Something that approached a feeling he didn't even need to name.

# Chapter 22

The Ivy was a Hollywood icon. It had starred in two recent movies. Bookings for lunch in the main room were impossible unless the table included somebody featured in *Hollywood Reporter*. Now there was a second Ivy, known by insiders as the Spillover. Ivy Two was down on Santa Monica Boulevard, three blocks up from the pier. Martin Allerby climbed from his evening ride and said to the parking valet, "How much to leave me a free space on either side?"

"A ten spot should do."

"Fine." He had the bill ready. Ten bucks was still less than parking in downtown New York. Which was a poor excuse for this polite Hollywood robbery. But in truth, Martin really didn't care. After all, Centurion paid.

Allerby's daytime ride was a Volkswagen Touareg. He had packed it with twenty thousand dollars' worth of extras, lifting the sticker within shouting range of a Porsche Cayenne. But Allerby had bought it for the emblem. When agents saw him pull up and park a people's car, their faces fell.

Nighttime, however, he drove a classic sixty-nine Rolls-Royce Corniche. Café-con-leche exterior, dun convertible top, ivory leather interior. Grace Kelly's car. Cary Grant's car. A ride so fine he chose this restaurant because it would take him an hour to drive there.

Milo Keplar crossed the street and said, "Early as usual."

"You were walking through the park? Are you nuts?"

A narrow park lined a fifteen-block stretch of Santa Monica Boulevard, fronting the cliff and the pier and the beach and the sea. Human flotsam flooded there at sunset. A *Los Angeles Times* reporter had recently spent a week undercover, hearing how vagrants from as far away as New Orleans and Toronto used the park as their winter address. Messages were brought in and passed with the evening shadows. Rail mail, the reporter had called it, for the vagrants' time-honored method of crossing the nation. Carried by alcoholics and druggies and psychos. It took months to arrive and cost the drug of choice to receive. Allerby had bought the story's rights and now had a script under development for a television movie. The working title was Allerby's idea: The Park at the End of the World.

Milo replied, "Just taking a stroll down memory lane."

Allerby knew little about Milo's early days, except that after escaping his Eastern European hovel, he had been raised by distant relatives in a gunfire-ridden stretch of Albuquerque. "Have you seen our guest?"

"He's already inside, drinking his third dose of atmosphere on the rocks."

When the hostess showed them to their table, the attorney's first words were, "Robert De Niro just walked by."

"Could be. He's got a place down in Malibu." Allerby offered his hand. "How are you, Leo?"

"Yeah, fine." He shook hands without taking his eyes off a pair of blonde Valley strollers in their matching pick-me-up outfits of microsuede. "Man, this is a universe removed from Ojai."

Leo Gish was forty-eight and still severely bruised by his ex-wife's divorce attorney. He was overweight and balding and wore a suit that shouted lawyer from the sticks. His eyes held the desperate quality of a man who was watching his entire world spin out of his grasp. And every glance in a mirror only heightened his alarm. His days were numbered, and almost all his dreams were gone.

Thump the man, Allerby thought as he opened his menu, and Gish would sound as ripe as a melon.

They spent most of the meal enduring Leo Gish's ongoing tale of woe about his avaricious ex. Gish halted his tirade only to sigh over the Santa Monica flesh market. The Ivy's front terrace was the most expensive show in LA. Allerby barely touched his food, promising himself a decent meal when this tedious business was behind him. "How are things with the man?"

The man, as in Carter Dawes, owner of Centurion and Gish's principal client. "I just finished drawing up his will."

"And?"

"No mention was made of his Centurion holdings."

Milo could not completely mask his eagerness. "So the man is definitely selling."

"Unless he gets better." Gish tracked a trio of high schoolers dressed for the Ungaro runway. "He's recovered before. But this time . . ."

"You think it's different."

Gish dragged his gaze away from the sidewalk. "Our deal is still valid, right?"

"You have our offer down in black and white," Allerby reminded him. "The five percent and the seat on the Centurion board are yours soon as our deal gets green-lighted."

Gish forced himself to focus. "He's ready to cave, is what I think."

Allerby fought for calm. "We'll have our attorney table the offer tomorrow."

"You've got the financing in place?"

"All of it."

"Where is it coming from?"

"Half from Solish and his group. The other half has to remain secret for a little while longer."

Allerby saw Gish flash a momentary concern. "What is it, Leo?"

"Far as I can see, everything is solid. Dawes will receive an offer from a private group offering top dollar. He's always said he wanted to keep Centurion from being swallowed by one of the majors."

"But?"

Gish hesitated, then, "What if he changes his mind?"

Milo's tone was hardened by years of clinching Hollywood deals. "You told us this was exactly the sort of offer Dawes would want, Leo. And the timing is yours. Not ours."

"Leo isn't trying to welsh on us," Allerby soothed. "He's just expressing a valid concern. Isn't that right, Leo."

"Dawes is so secretive," Gish fretted. "I've seen him pull out of deals I'd have called perfect. Done it seated at the table with the signing pen in his hand."

Milo was ready to crawl across the table and cram himself into the lawyer's face. "That can't happen."

"It can," Gish replied. "It has."

A cloud descended over their table, one dark enough to obliterate the street theater.

Then Martin felt lightning strike. He leaned forward. "What you're saying, Leo, is we need a sweetener. Something that would push Dawes over the edge."

Milo knew his partner well enough to say, "You've got an idea."

"How about this." Martin lowered his voice to a point where the two men had to crane forward to hear. "We move the *Heartland* piece from a TV special to a feature film."

Milo gaped. "What?"

"Three times I approached Dawes about moving into features. Three times he told me the exact same thing. Do it with *Heartland* or not at all."

"We ran the numbers," Milo pointed out. "It would have been a total disaster."

"Exactly."

"A full-on failure of that scale would cost us our careers."

"Which is why we haven't moved forward," Allerby agreed. "Until now."

Gish looked from one man to the other. "You lost me."

"Think about it, Leo." Spelling it out for all three of them. "We contact Dawes. No. Wait. Even better, you tell him we've met here tonight. That way, if he ever catches wind of this meeting, you can say it was because we wanted to move forward on the film concept. Maybe he's heard about our new JayJay Parsons, the hero."

"He has. Believe me. He spent half our conference talking about that instead of the will."

"There you go. So Milo and I, we've had a change of heart. We want to ride this wildfire publicity onto the silver screen."

"Perfect." Milo breathed the word. "Starring an actor who's never seen the front end of a camera before."

"Two actors," Allerby corrected. "You're forgetting the new leading lady, Kelly Channing. Her last role was smiling for mouthwash. Or gum. Something memorable."

"It'll be a total mess." Milo's grin displayed rows of overly small teeth. "We might as well put the cash in a wheelbarrow and push it across the street to the park."

Leo asked, "You guys *want* this to fail?"

"In the biggest way possible. You get Dawes to sign off on this feature film he's always wanted to see happen. We set the project in motion. We'll gear up our PR for a major push."

"Then we'll watch the press write up what a total catastrophe Centurion has on its hands," Milo said. "Meanwhile, I'll be out there trying to pitch a film that nobody in their right mind would dream of buying."

"And this mystery group, who are based in a world far removed from *Variety* and *Hollywood Reporter*, will keep their offer on the table."

Gish saw it now. "Dawes would be desperate to sign."

"Exactly," Allerby agreed.

"I got to hand it to you," Milo said. "This is a stroke of genius."

Leo Gish leaned back in his seat. For the first time that night, he looked happy. "You know what this means?"

"Yes, Leo," Allerby replied. Able to give the man at least one dream come true. "You're about to become a Hollywood player."

# Chapter 23

The setting sun glared through Martin Allerby's office window, drenching the chamber and the people in gold. A good DP would have paid with blood for such a shot. Every face was painted in big-screen accuracy. Milo Keplar, his sales director and secret partner in crime, was seated in his preferred corner from which he could observe and calculate. Two senior staffers from Contracts and one from Legal occupied the ring of chairs around Martin's desk. There to warn them of any potential speed bumps. Britt Turner shared the sofa with his diminutive AD. Gloria, Allerby's assistant, was in her standard position with laptop at the ready.

The stage, as they said in the biz, was prepped. It was time for action. There would be no second take.

Martin asked, "How are things going with the shoot?"

"So far, pretty solid." Britt was understandably nervous. He had been summoned back to headquarters on a moment's notice. The phone call from Gloria had arrived about a half hour before the limo to take him to the local airport, where a flying taxi waited to speed him south. No reason given. Just come. "We've rehearsed all the scenes Peter has completed so far. We've gone over some of the connecting action. I like what he's writing."

"And Derek?"

"He's working out well."

"He's young for a DP role on location."

"He's thirty-three. Seven years' experience. He started in ads like most cameramen these days. Took a serious cut in salary to come on board here as assistant cameraman." Britt scanned the faces. "Is that what we're here about? You're naming another DP?"

"Do you think we should?"

Britt shifted nervously in his seat. His AD might as well have been frozen solid. Not even his eyes moved. "It's your show, Martin."

"I'm just asking your opinion."

"Then no, I don't think a change is called for. The dailies we gained from his one day in the saddle on set were solid."

"That was here. Soundstage and location shooting are two different animals."

"We've been on location for nine days. I've been watching him carefully as we work the sets and light the scenes." Britt had difficulty controlling the timber of his voice. "He's blocked out the scene work and laid the lights and cables so we can move from rehearsals to shooting without any lost time. And done it all without a word from me. He's got the makings of a solid professional."

"Then he stays." Allerby watched his director breathe a fraction easier. Britt Turner was in his early fifties, which in Hollywood terms meant he was as good as cremated. He had a dead-straight style of composition that worked well with this kind of story and character. And this kind of medium. Television viewers might not be able to say it in words, but their viewing habits were dominated by straight-ahead stories. Shallow characters, easy plots, nothing that challenged or strayed far from the program's principal task of delivering the audience to the next commercial. Allerby studied the director and watched his tension increase. Fear was such an exquisite tool in the hands of a master. "It's good to see you defend your personnel, Britt."

"Is that it?"

"No." Allerby rose from his chair. His desk was positioned close enough to the center of the room for him to be able to pace easily. The region between his chair and the rear wall was his own little stage. "There's been a change of plan."

"About the special?"

"From this point on, there is no special." He let the moment stretch until he was certain the diminutive AD was going to shriek like the whistle of a steam train. Kip Denderhoff's features were that tight. When it was either speak or watch his employees explode, Martin stopped pacing and declared, "We're going to make a feature film."

The AD actually squeaked. The rest of the room made do with a swift indrawn breath. No one knew anything except, of course, for Milo. Even Gloria gasped.

Britt had gone pasty. "For real?"

"Last night I received confirmation from Carter Dawes' attorney. The financing is in place. *Heartland* is headed to the big screen." He returned to his pacing. "PR and Milo's division will both use the angle that a new star has restored the show's original polish. He's been shown across the nation saving two people from the wildfire. We have received more publicity from those shots your DP took than we could have bought with our entire annual PR budget."

"Fox News is still running the tape as part of their thirty-second intro," Milo added.

"*People* is naming him one of the year's sexiest men," Allerby said. "I just got that from PR."

Martin Allerby could hear the director's mental gears grind from across the room. Like everyone who had ever immigrated to Hollywood, Britt Turner had always yearned to make the leap to film. But if his chance had ever come, he had missed out. Timing, ability, right script, right meeting, whatever. A thousand things must come together in the correct order to build the impossible bridge from television to dreamland. Only one item needed to go wrong. But in Britt's case, Allerby suspected it was simply a matter of talent. Britt Turner was made for the tiny screen. Martin inspected the man, and knew his initial judgment had been sound. Britt Turner was going to take this chance and fail.

Allerby said, "I'm absolutely confident you and your team are going to triumph."

Britt swallowed audibly. "What's our budget?"

"Twelve million."

Allerby glanced at Milo. They had argued for six days before settling on the amount. Twelve million dollars was no-man's land. Television topped out at two and a half million dollars for an hour of absolute top-drawer television miniseries drama. Which *Heartland* definitely was not. Five to eight million dollars was tops for an indie feature or art-house release. These days a feature from a major studio started at forty mil. With another twelve to fourteen on top for marketing. Call it fifty-five mil as a bare minimum. The *average* studio feature cost ninety-seven million dollars to make and market.

Twelve million dollars for a feature was a neither-here-nor-there budget. It fit into none of the standard calculations. It was doomed from the outset.

"That's the absolute maximum we were able to obtain from Dawes and the board," Allerby warned. "Don't come back and ask for more, because there won't be any."

They spent four hours discussing issues that would have been vital if there was any chance whatsoever of success. Gloria's deal memo alone ran to nineteen pages. When they were done, Britt and his AD rose from the chairs like automatons whose batteries had died. Dull-eyed, stiff, barely able to make the door. Allerby personally ushered everyone out, repeating several times to make sure the entire stunned group had it embedded in the memory banks for posterity. "I am absolutely certain you folks are going to bring back a triumph on film."

Milo waited until they were in Allerby's Volkswagen and out the Centurion gates to say, "We might as well pile the old man's money on the pavement and set it on fire."

# Chapter 24

The hotel's inner-facing rooms overlooked a grassy courtyard, garden, and a little pool area. But there was no view of the sunset, so JayJay and Kelly had gone out front and climbed up onto the cab roof of one of the lighting trucks. Like they were up in the high-range country instead of stuck in a hotel parking lot with trucks rumbling down the blacktop. The day had been the first they hadn't worked themselves to exhaustion, what with Britt and Kip called back to the studio. Up until then, these television folks on location had worked farmer's hours, dawn to dusk and long beyond. Come quitting time, JayJay hadn't had much interest in anything more than dinner and bed. Until today.

The sunset turned the world into a fairyland so sweet even the passing truckers were caught up. The highway drifted out of town and ran straight to where the first set of hills took hold and rose up to meet the golden sky. Neighboring orchards blanketed them in sweet fruitiness. Kelly waved at passing freighters and got honks and sunburned arms lifted in response.

It was not until the light began fading that they noticed the strangeness. The windows fronting the highway revealed film crew locked in worry and fret. When they walked back into the courtyard, they found the same thing in one room after another. Derek stood looking at a greaseboard with his arms wrapped around his body. Every once in a while he'd unclench himself long enough to reach up and grab two fistfuls of hair and tug. In the room next to Derek's, the lady who played JayJay's sister smoked and paced and argued into a cell phone. Room after room showed the same air of tense concern.

It seemed natural enough when Kelly said, "We ought to do something."

The computer screen in front of Peter was empty. He had typed nothing for hours. A script ran in the mental space behind his eyes. One he could not use. But it was all he could think of just then.

INT. PETER'S MOTEL ROOM. EVENING.

Peter is working at his desk. The motel room is flooded with the remnants of a desert sunset, his seventh since arriving on location. His room is located in an upmarket small-town hotel: plush carpet, one wall of stone, two beds, sofa, two easy chairs, desk, huge television, one window, view of the interior courtyard and pool. His laptop is angled so the screen is shaded from the sunset. He does not want to pull the curtains because the isolation becomes too great.

The mirror over his desk is lost behind hundreds of sticky-notes. The near bed has become an extension of his desk. As has the coffee table and one of the chairs and the sofa. Scribbled concepts and hundreds of notecards are laid out in a possible shooting sequence. Sheets of white drawing paper are taped to the motel wall, forming a fifteen-foot-long timeline.

Peter turns his chair away from the desk and the laptop. He looks across the room.

CLOSE-UP. PETER'S BEDSIDE TABLE. EVENING.
On the table rest two pictures. One is of CYNTHIA,
Peter's wife. The other is a sonogram of two babies
locked together in a uterine embrace.

INT. PETER'S ROOM. EVENING.
Peter's laptop has idled so long it pings and cuts
off. He turns and stares at it, but clearly can't
bring himself to cut it back on. The fading sunset
illuminates a face locked in anguished regret. He
turns back to the pair of photographs.

PETER
(to the photograph)
I shouldn't be here. I should have argued harder.

Script structure was intentionally very terse. A screen script was a ballad told with an engineer's ear. Poetry in blueprint form. One of the first bits of advice Peter learned was that a screenwriter should count one page of script for every minute of film. Which meant a good script should read far faster than it would show upon the screen.

The second lesson came from the same source, his former boss, Ben Picksley, a grizzled veteran of the Hollywood trenches. The money was ridiculous, Picksley had warned Peter his first day on the set, but so were the demands. Worst of all, studio execs would take his finished script, his treasure, and feed it into the blender of hyperinflated egos.

The way to avoid self-destructing, Picksley advised, was to remember that no matter whether Peter worked on a television script, a short, or a feature, one rule remained the same. The Hollywood writer must never see himself as delivering a finished product.

Basically, a screenplay was a skeleton. Bare bones. When things worked well, the script would then be taken by an incredibly talented team called a production crew. They would pour their creative energies into this crucible he had created, molding something complete. Something timeless.

So far, Peter had been shaping scenes. He and Britt, the director, had worked out a tentative sequencing. Where the major explosions would come, and what they might be. A studio illustrator was housed in the next room, working out the initial storyboard. They had spent the past week rehearsing and scene-setting and lighting. They worked to a typical TV-frantic, on-location schedule, with a tight budget and tighter timeline.

Peter had never worked on a two-hour program before. He had decided, with Britt's permission, to structure it in a three-act format, something more akin to a feature than a TV-special. Even so, all he had been doing thus far was working on images. They still needed the single unifying concept, the *hook*, to bring it all together.

The central action was the same as every *Heartland* episode. The homestead was under threat. JayJay would save the day. He would do so honestly and with bone-deep integrity. Exactly what the most loyal audience in television-land had come to expect.

But the hook. The single emotional concept that made this summer-time special unique. That was the clincher.

Peter went back to what he normally did whenever hitting the barrier. The stone wall. The impossible cliff. Electronic or paper, the unattainable challenge remained the same.

Filling the empty page.

Peter sorted through the pile of notecards beside his computer. In the process of writing a script, he filled as many as three thousand cards with his scribblings. Most were discarded. Cynthia had urged him to sort through the ones not used and garner ideas worth keeping. His garage was walled by floor-to-ceiling boxes of notecards awaiting his attention.

The cards by his computer represented the next scene. He knew it was going to be a dynamite action sequence. The cards almost vibrated in his hand. But this was not the issue. Without a central theme, he was just creating a collage. And one thing was certain. The viewing public might not ever know precisely what was missing. But the show would not keep their attention. And when they reached for the remote and changed the channel, they'd chop Peter's career off at the knees.

Peter heard the footsteps scrape along the sidewalk outside his door. He waited for the knock. When it came, he was tempted to tell whoever it was to go away. More than likely, Derek had come down for a chat. And he needed to get this scene done.

Even so, he called out, "It's open."

JayJay stepped inside and said, "Looks to me like everybody's fighting ghosts tonight."

The sunset silhouetted JayJay in Peter's doorway, rimming him in gold. "What?"

"You been sitting here for an hour, doing as close to nothing as a fellow can with his eyes open. Derek's upstairs wearing a hole in his carpet. The guy next door is laying on his bed arguing with the ceiling."

"You've been watching us?"

"Hard not to." He pointed a thumb behind him. "Kelly and me, we been out there watching the sun go down. All we had to do was turn around to see y'all fret."

"It's this scene," Peter said lamely.

"No it ain't. It's going from full on to idle." JayJay started spinning his hat. "We spend nine days working hard as we can without a pick in our hands. Then the boss is flown back to headquarters. He says he'll be gone a couple of hours. It's been all day and he's still not back. So everybody is sitting and sweating, wondering who's gonna be stood up against the barn and shot."

JayJay didn't give him a chance to respond. "Kelly and me, we been thinking. We figured it might do us all some good to get together. Pull out the Good Book. Spend a few minutes looking where we might actually find some answers."

JayJay stepped back into the golden sunset. "You feel like joining us, we're gonna meet over in the breakfast room. Fifteen minutes."

Sure enough, this was something, all right.

They all had a list of rooms assigned to crew. He'd taken the ground floor, Kelly the second. The motel didn't have a restaurant. But the owner's wife served up a fine country breakfast. Now there were nine of them situated around the breakfast room, a lot more than JayJay had expected to see show up. Double doors shut the breakfast nook off from the hotel lobby. They could hear the television's murmur and somebody answering the phone. But it didn't hardly matter. The sun was gone and the night outside the window was made darker by the streetlights and the passing traffic. The day of rest had not been enough to erase the fatigue from the faces JayJay saw. Or the worry.

Kelly was giving him a woman's look, one that said without words that she was handing things over to him. Which was kind of ridiculous, since this'd been her idea. But now wasn't the time to argue, so he cleared his throat and said, "I didn't have any real idea of what we were gonna do once we got here. Except, well, I had the impression we had some burdens we were having trouble laying down. Which is what we're supposed to be doing."

"Says who?"

JayJay looked over to the far corner. Now that was a real surprise, having Claire Pietan show up. JayJay stared into the face of this woman who playacted his sister. He'd sure been amazed to see Kelly walk through those doors with Claire behind her. Claire was doing the same thing she'd done since entering the room, which is use one arm to hug a sweater to her while the other held another cigarette.

When he didn't respond fast enough for her liking, Claire's voice tightened down. "What kind of jerk would suggest we could just set problems on the ground and walk away from them. Like they were some kind of, I don't know, weight or something."

Derek answered to the floor by his feet, "The Bible says that, Claire."

She blasted out a hot breath of smoke and thumped her cigarette hard into the ashtray she'd brought with her.

JayJay stared at her a long time, seeing not just the woman but all the questions she represented. He spoke the only words that came to mind just then. "I'm sure not any closer to answers for my own worries. But I know one thing for certain. I haven't been doing much of a job of asking for help. I'm strong enough for most things, which is a right hard curse when it comes to knowing when to get down on my knees."

The nine were an odd Hollywood mix, was how it seemed to JayJay. There were two electricians, one male and one female, both lean and close-faced and wearing thick glasses. Across from them sat two grips, which was the word JayJay'd heard them use for the picker-uppers and the haulers. The grips were big men who looked to JayJay like they were on a first-name basis with trouble. But here they sat, the breakfast chairs groaning under the loads of muscle and beards and tattoos. And Kelly and Peter and Derek. And there in the corner, the mystery woman. His fake sister. So hard-faced she appeared ready to bite somebody's head off. Or sob.

JayJay went on, "It was Kelly's idea that we get together. And it struck me as something I should've thought of long before now. So what I reckoned was, maybe we ought to make this a regular thing. Just meet up and have us a little Bible reading and then anybody who wants can talk about what they are worried about. After that we could have ourselves a prayer time. Help each other out in a way that might really do us all some good."

He nodded to Kelly, who opened a well-thumbed Bible and said, "I thought it might be a good thing just to read a few of the passages I've underlined that help me when I'm down. I'll read from Deuteronomy for starters, because that's what I've been studying lately."

She read slowly, in a voice that said clearly this was a natural thing. "'Love the Lord your God with all your heart, with all your soul, and with all your strength.'

"'He is your God, and you have seen with your own eyes the great and astounding things that he has done for you.'

"'I call heaven and earth to witness the choice you make. Choose life.'

"'These teachings are not empty words; they are your very life.'

"'The Lord loves his people and protects those who belong to him.'

"'He guards them all the day long, and he dwells in their midst.'"

Kelly shut her Book and looked at him.

JayJay wished he'd brought his hat. He never knew what to do with his hands when he was talking. Spinning his hat always helped his mind work easier. He looked down at his hands, the fingers laced together in a suntanned bundle. "Since I was the one who suggested it, maybe I'd best be the first to talk about a problem I'm finding difficult to lay down." He took a breath, then spoke the words that burned coming out. "I stared into the mirror this morning, and I didn't even know who I was."

The sound of a woman choking for control lifted his head. Claire had her mouth open wide as she fumbled for another cigarette. Her eyes gaped at the night-blinded window. Her fingers made a mess of the cigarette pack. Finally she gave up, slammed the pack down on the table, and took a two-armed grip on her sweater.

Kelly stood and walked over. She settled an arm on Claire's shoulders. The woman jerked at the unexpected touch. But she did not draw away. JayJay watched Kelly draw a chair closer and sit herself down.

"I've got a problem," Derek said. "Actually, I've got two. One of them is mine. The other is Peter's. But he's a friend, and—"

"Derek." Peter did not look over.

Derek persisted, "Peter is a friend and a brother, and I'm worried for him."

"It's okay."

"It's not okay, Peter. Nothing about the situation is okay."

The exchange even drew Claire out of her tight shell. They all watched Derek tell Peter, "Give me the word and I'll be quiet. But I think maybe prayer is the only answer you've got right now."

Peter sighed and shook his head. But all he said was, "I need this job."

"Okay. Fine." Derek waited. When Peter said nothing more, he continued, "Peter's wife is eight months pregnant. With their first. And their second."

The female electrician asked, "Twins? Really?"

It was Derek who answered. "Yes, really. And there have been troubles."

"Not bad ones," Peter said.

"Bad enough. Cynthia's had to stay in bed for a week and a half. She's up and moving again. But still."

JayJay looked from one man to the other. "So how come you're here?"

Derek lifted his gaze then. "There, you see?"

Peter did not speak.

Derek said, "Martin Allerby basically told Peter if he did not work on location, he'd hire somebody else."

"But why?" This from Kelly. "You're a writer."

"Exactly," Derek said. "This isn't about the show. This is about control. This is about ego."

"Derek," Peter said. Stronger now. "That's enough."

Derek huffed, but said nothing more.

JayJay rose from his chair. He walked over to the window and stood looking out. When he felt like he was back under control he turned around and said, "This ain't right."

"No," Derek agreed. "It isn't."

He returned to his chair. "I shouldn't be getting this mad in a prayer service. Especially one I'm supposed to be leading. But this . . ."

"It's an outrage," Derek said.

Peter sighed, covered his eyes with his hands, and repeated, "I need this job."

"Nobody's saying you did wrong coming here," JayJay replied. "But there ought to be something we can do to help you out."

Derek said, "Amen."

"I'm just thinking out loud here. But what if we all went together to talk with Britt? You think that'd do any good?"

"Martin Allerby is Britt's boss too," Peter pointed out. But there was a different note to his voice now, a slight glimmer of hope.

"Well, all I got to say is, you aren't alone in this, Peter. I know that isn't much, and you're not any closer to your wife."

"No," Peter said. "It means a lot."

"What say we all pray about this now. Then we go sleep on it and see if something comes to mind."

Kelly said, "We can meet again tomorrow morning a half hour before the meeting with Britt."

"Not here," JayJay said. "Folks will be milling about. My suite's got more space than one man will ever need. Six thirty in my living room. Number two ten. I'll order up coffee."

He looked around, got nods in reply. "Anybody else want to talk about prayer needs? Derek, you never said what it was you're worried about."

The guy actually smiled. "It can wait."

When he returned to his room, Peter still felt the prayers resonating inside him. He glanced at his watch. Ten o'clock. Time to call it a night, especially since they were getting together in eight hours' time to pray again. But he was too jazzed to sleep. He seated himself at the desk and smiled at what had just happened. After JayJay had asked for guidance, Derek had prayed for Cynthia. And then there had been a silence, he had no idea how long. Then one of the grips had started in. The guy sounded like a bear growling at the back end of his cave. He had spoken briefly. Just asked for a miracle for Peter and Cynthia. Like the one they were seeing right then. No more than a dozen words. Enough to have Peter swallowing hard on the knowledge he was no longer alone.

Then the attention had turned away, as Kelly had prayed for Claire and whatever it was the lady faced.

The iron woman, the one universally disliked on the set, had started crying. Utterly silent, just some tears and some very hard swallows. But enough for the lady electrician and Derek to get up afterward and go over and hug her.

Now Peter sat at his desk and stared at the blank space at the center of the wall. The place waiting for the central theme.

He did not write. But he knew. He had found what he was looking for.

# Chapter 25

---

**P**eter was downstairs when the breakfast room opened at six because he had grown tired of staring at the ceiling. The sky was desert calm and rosy hued. Country music played over the lobby sound system. To his surprise, fifteen or so of the crew had beat him down and were draining the coffee wagon dry. Derek stood with the two wardrobe ladies and waved him over. "Couldn't sleep either?"

"There are two hundred and seventy-six popcorn panels in my ceiling. That answer your question?" Peter poured himself a cup of coffee. One of the many things he liked about this place was that there was no Styrofoam anywhere. Even the lobby cistern used the kind of heavy white ceramic mugs favored by truckstops. "Cynthia says hello."

Derek was smiling broadly as he said to the taller of the two wardrobe ladies, "Go on. Tell him."

Gladys was one of Peter's favorites. "How's the little lady doing, hon?"

"Okay, only she's not so little anymore. And she misses me. A lot. Is that what you're supposed to say to me?"

"No," Derek said, grinning more widely. "Go on."

Gladys said, "I was walking back last night from a late dinner."

"We both were," Hilda said. "I was there too, you know."

"So you want to tell this for me?"

"No, you go ahead. I can interrupt when you get it wrong."

Gladys sniffed. "I saw the two of them walking toward her room."

Peter did not need to ask who they were. "And?"

"Kelly stops in front of her door. Stands there swinging both his arms back and forth. And smiling."

"I'm thinking love," Hilda said. "Tell him what happened next."

"He kisses her on the cheek. And leaves."

Peter looked from one to the other. "No way."

Hilda is smiling now too. "Yeah, way."

Derek said, "What was it old Ben used to say about stars?"

"Two things you can take to the bank," Peter recalled. "Stars on location are children, and they're rabbits."

Gladys asked, "Is it true they held a prayer meeting last night?"

Derek replied, "Most amazing invitation I've ever gotten. A star shows up at my door at eight and says, how about it?"

Peter said, "What about Kelly walking over and hugging Claire?"

The two wardrobe ladies gasped. Gladys asked, "Claire was there?"

Derek said, "Maybe we shouldn't be talking about that."

"Yeah, you're probably right." He glanced at his watch. "We better eat and run if we want to make the second act."

The instant Peter entered JayJay's parlor alongside Derek, he could see how the crowd was split in two. It wasn't where the folks were seated. The gaffers and grips were sprawled against the far walls, not because they weren't involved but because it was their nature to stay well away from the lights. Claire had one of the dining table chairs pulled to the far corner. But she was there. Watching JayJay and Kelly by the front wall with the hollowed focus of a lady coming off a hard night. No, Peter knew there was a split in the crowd from the expressions. The number was more than doubled to something over twenty, more than half the total crew. But a lot of them were there just to see if this was for real, two actors doing a prayer thing on a shoot. Their expressions said they had seen a lot and heard about more. But this was utterly new.

JayJay started in by thanking everyone for coming. "Me and Kelly, we've talked it over and we'd like to try and do this every morning. But we'd like volunteers to do this when we can't. Anybody feel led to lead?"

Derek raised his hand and said, "I'm volunteering me and Peter." As natural as daylight.

That done, Kelly read two of her underlined passages, these coming from Exodus: "'The Lord will fight for you, and all you have to do is keep still.'" Then, "'The Lord is my strong defender; he is the one who has saved me. He is my God, and I will praise him, my father's God, and I will sing about his greatness.'"

Then JayJay asked if anybody wanted to name a specific prayer request. He pointed at Derek and said they'd not heard what was troubling him.

Derek tried to wave it off. "It's a work thing and it's very technical."

"I don't need to understand every word," JayJay replied. "And I doubt the jargon is gonna bother God."

Derek tugged at his close-cropped hair. A true sign of worry. "The color's not right. Everything looks washed out."

Peter pointed out, "I've heard Britt talking. He says what he's been seeing on the monitor is fine."

"It's not fine." Derek tugged harder. "We're lighting like we're still using film. But digital is a totally new thing. It registers light a lot sharper. Which leaves the scenes too harsh."

Claire spoke from the back wall. "And the faces."

"Exactly." Derek turned around. "Britt is doing this like he's always done for film. And it's not working. Well, it's working, but it's not nearly as good as it could be."

JayJay asked, "So what's the answer?"

"Toss out all but one spot, and mask that with a strong yellow filter." Derek's answer came fast enough to show he'd thought on this for hours. "And use reflectors. A *lot* of reflectors."

JayJay said, "Sounds to me like you know what you want."

Claire answered for Derek, "A brand-new chief cameraman does not second-guess the director on location."

Derek just sighed.

JayJay gave it a few moments, then said, "Anybody else with a prayer request?"

The silence was broken by one of the bearded grips telling his mate, "Go on, man. Say it."

The larger of the two guys said through his beard, "My daughter has taken up with a bad crowd. And it's kinda hard for my wife and me to say much, since it's exactly the same crew we used to run with."

Kelly asked, "What's her name?"

"Rachel."

Kelly made a note on a sheet of paper.

"Anybody else?"

Derek said, "Cynthia, Peter's wife. And the twins."

Kelly said, "I've got them down."

A small voice from the back corner said, "Me."

Kelly looked up. "We're not forgetting you for an instant, Claire."

One of the electricians said, "We oughtta pray when the director gets back, we still got jobs."

"That's a good one."

There were a few more requests, and a lot more looks of astonishment between members of the viewing gallery. JayJay said he'd start and anybody else who wanted could join in, then Kelly would finish. He asked everybody to bow their heads. He prayed for a while, then somebody else, and then Derek, and afterward Peter spoke because it just felt natural.

A lot of words would never fit Peter's concept of television location work. *Natural* and *prayer circles* topped the list. Until that dawn.

There was a knock on the door just as Kelly finished. But the feeling was so strong no one cared to break it. The knock sounded again, louder this time. One of the electricians rose and walked over.

Britt Turner, their absent director, walked into the room. He studied the gathering and said, "I leave for one day and look what happens."

# Chapter 26

Lunchtime at The Grill was as close to a producers' club as Hollywood came. The restaurant was situated down a lane narrow as most alleys, and about as dark. The place had few windows, which was fine for a crowd who wore their sunglasses everywhere but the screening room. The interior was plush in the manner of a fifties diner. There were tables down side walls bedecked with photos, and a double row of dinettes with smoked-glass panels. Most regulars had their favorite spots. The Grill was one of few places in Hollywood where no one table held premier position. Which was vital in a world where fistfights had broken out over who had to sit with their back to the room.

Allerby shared his corner banquette with Alexi Campe, not her real name. But in Hollywood, even the reporters got off on doing surgery on their past. Campe had been born Roxanne Steinbrimmer. She was not from Aspen, as she claimed, but Brownsville, a wart on the chin of New York City. She had spent twenty-seven thousand dollars on plastic surgery and elocution lessons. She never drank in public for fear of releasing her original Bronx cheer. Allerby loved receiving his security firm's reports on these people. They read better than most scripts.

Campe or Steinbrimmer covered the television circuit for *Variety*. Martin Allerby considered her his tame viper. As in, you can never tame a viper, only soothe it momentarily. One wrong move, and the viper will go from somnolent to deadly.

Campe was not so much thin as skeletal. She wore an outfit Allerby could only describe as astounding. Black knit cap, the kind preferred by male Muslim fanatics. Black Hindu-style floppy top and drawstring trousers. Huge rainbow clogs and matching enamel bracelets. And MaxMara sunglasses, the kind that had side stems thick as tree trunks. She picked at her meal of Caesar salad, hold the croutons and Parmesan cheese and dressing and chicken. "I hear your prime-time medical drama has hit yet another snag."

"Not exactly true," Allerby replied. "The actress we wanted as our new female lead decided she could hold out for more money. We have merely shown her just how wrong she was."

"In other words, you chopped her off at the knees."

"I didn't say that. And if you quote me with words you spoke, I'll sue."

"Now, Martin, would I ever do such a thing?"

Allerby smiled. "All the time."

Allerby caught his reflection in her opaque lenses. He actually appeared to be enjoying himself. Amazing how easy the lines came to him these days.

The reporter asked, "How's the new lead for *Heartland* working out?"

"Extremely well."

"From the news footage, I'd say you have a serious hunk on your hands."

"And he can act."

"Is this fodder for the press, or for real?"

Allerby extracted the mini-disk from his jacket pocket. "Raw footage from our dailies. His first day on the set. See for yourself."

She made the disk disappear. "Is this an exclusive?"

"I can give you a couple of days' lead. No more."

Alexi stopped pretending to enjoy her meal. "I can't let your medical drama off the hook for this, Martin."

"You're going to take the word of an agent whose actor got shot down?"

"I like you. You know that. But word on the street is you've got a show that's tanked and your efforts to pull it back into the green have failed."

"I appreciate your being so frank with me, Alexi." He leaned forward. "What if I had something else for you?"

"Such as?"

"Not in here." Allerby dropped his napkin on the table. "Shall we?"

He signed the bill, made the customary gesture to the head waiter, and led Campe out into the shadowed alley. The Grill claimed they swept the restaurant daily for bugs. Allerby suspected it was so the head waiter held a lock on what his own mikes picked up. Martin never said anything in here he wasn't willing to see on the front page of the *Hollywood Reporter*.

When the attendant brought his car, he drove thirty feet up from the restaurant and parked, partially blocking the alley. It was a ploy he had used several times before. The lane was too tight for anybody to pass. Which meant he could limit the conversation to a matter of seconds. He spoke quickly. "We are not doing the two-hour *Heartland* special as planned."

Campe pulled a pen and notepad from her purse. "Trouble?"

"On the contrary. We're going to make a feature film."

She paused. "Come again?"

"*Heartland*. Coming soon to a theater near you."

"You're joking."

"No joke, Alexi."

"Does CBS know?"

"Not yet."

She was scribbling fast. "They are going to freak."

"They'll have first rights to the TV run. You didn't hear any of this from me, all right?"

"Of course not. What's the budget?"

"Confidential. Mid-level."

"Which means you can't recoup on a TV sale if the feature concept falls flat."

"We're not going to fail, Alexi. The public is ripe for a good old-fashioned homespun drama."

Not even her enormous shades could hide her skepticism.

"Think about it. Our numbers were the steadiest on record until Townsend overdosed on drugs and fat and fame. Our viewers are *loyal*. So we have a new star. You'll see for yourself what he can do. And we're going to take him global."

"So even if you fail at the box office, you've made a success," Alexi interpreted. "Put the entire budget down to long-term advertising."

"I didn't say that."

A horn honking behind them signaled an end to the discussion. Alexi opened her door and offered him a seasoned Hollywood smirk. "Thanks for the scoop, Martin. I'll bury news of your medical soap."

"You mark my words, Alexi. This is a sensation in the making."

# Chapter 27

C laire told the director, "It's not what you think."

Britt moved over to stand in front of the windows. Kip Denderhoff, the diminutive AD, stood by the side wall. Britt looked very worried. "How do you know what I think, Claire?"

"I don't. But whatever you're thinking, it's not right."

"It looks to me like a union meeting. What, the restaurant burned your toast?"

JayJay said calmly, "We were having a time of prayer."

Kip Denderhoff laughed out loud.

"Whatever," Britt sighed. "Look, since most of you are here already, how about if we just have the rest come up? I've got something that needs saying."

"You're the boss," JayJay said.

The director pointed at his AD and then the phone.

JayJay asked, "Would you like some coffee?"

"Black."

JayJay moved to the trolley at the back. "How about you?"

"You're asking me?" Denderhoff looked shocked. "White, one Sweet 'n Low."

By the time JayJay made the coffees, other people had started straggling in. Britt asked one of the newcomers, "How come you weren't up here for this meeting?"

The chief lighting guy shrugged. "Didn't feel like it."

"Feel like what?"

"Praying, was what she told me."

"She who, Kelly?"

Claire said quietly, "That's all it was, Britt."

Britt took a contemplative sip. "Okay, enough. I've got some good news." He set his cup to one side. "The special has been canceled."

The room expelled a single unified sigh. Claire, their unappointed spokesperson, asked, "This is good?"

"It is when you hear the alternative," Britt replied. "We're doing a feature."

Peter felt an invisible hand reach across the distance separating him from the director. And grip his throat. And squeeze.

Claire was the only one able to answer. "So tell us the good news."

"Oh, like you get these offers every day?"

"Come on, Britt. A lot of these guys are new enough to swallow this whole. But we've been around, you and me. This just doesn't happen and you know it."

"It has this time."

"What's the budget?"

"That is confidential. Big enough to give you a trailer and a limo. And a raise."

She fished a cigarette from her pack and lit up. She said with the first smoke, "So I'm being bribed not to ask these questions, right?"

"No. You're being hired to do your job."

"I'm a professional, Britt. A professional needs to know what is really happening. We don't even have a finished script yet."

"Which gives us an advantage in making the switch. Come on, Claire. Any number of successful films started shooting without a completed script." Britt shut off her next point by saying, "You want to walk, now's the time."

"These are valid questions."

"Yeah, that's what I thought." Britt turned to JayJay. "You are now officially the star of a feature. Your contract has to be renegotiated. Contracts has contacted the kid you used for your initial agreement, unless of course you'd prefer to go with a more seasoned pro."

"Looked to me like Ahn handled you folks pretty good."

Britt almost smiled. "No argument there. You're also entitled to star treatment. Kelly, your situation has just been upgraded as well. I've spoken to your agent personally." Britt addressed the room at large. "Same goes for everyone else. Notify your agents. As of today, you're moving to feature scale."

JayJay turned and gave Peter a look the writer could not fathom. "Just exactly what does that mean, 'star treatment'?"

"I'm not going to tell you the sky's the limit. You're new to the game and your drawing power is untested. But basically if you have a request within reason, we'll oblige. We're trying to locate better accommodations in the area for the film's principals. Maybe a dude ranch."

"Where we sleep is not the issue," Claire said.

"I'd rather stay where we are now," Kelly agreed. "With the rest of the crew."

Britt asked, "Why is that?"

"The prayer group, for one thing. We can't make it work if we're all spread out from here to tomorrow."

Britt and his AD exchanged another look. "Anything else?"

JayJay leaned forward. "So now I'm a star and I get to make demands. A limo and all that stuff."

"Didn't I just tell you that?"

"Okay. Here's what I want." JayJay pointed at Peter. "I want that feller over there to be moved into my suite. And I want the limo to head back down and pick up Peter's wife."

"This is a joke, right?"

"No joke. And I'm not done. I want somebody to find the best baby doctor they got in these parts. I want, what's your lady's name again, Peter?"

"Cynthia."

"I want Cynthia to know she's gonna come up here and get better treatment for her and them babies than she'd be having back home."

The first thing Britt asked Peter when they were alone was, "Did you put JayJay up to this?"

"Are you kidding? I didn't know a thing until you walked in that door."

It was just the four of them. Derek, Peter, Kip, Britt. The behind-the-camera chief and his deputies. Britt looked like he had not slept at all the previous night. He said to Kip, "Call downstairs for more coffee. Order us some breakfast. Tell them to hurry."

Kip leaped to obey. He had always been silent and attentive in the presence of bosses and front-office types. It was one of the reasons they put up with his attitude to the hired help. But something was different. Not just with the AD. With both of them. Britt had a quiet dictatorial approach around the set. He never raised his voice. He never worried. He rarely showed emotion of any kind. But today the two of them were frayed. Exhausted. Genuinely concerned.

Kip returned to his seat. "Ten minutes."

"Fine." They were seated at a circular table set in the corner opposite the windows. Britt leaned his elbows on the table and rubbed his forehead. "The truth, guys. What was going on down there?"

"What JayJay told you," Peter replied.

Derek added, "We got together last night. Kelly came by my room and asked if we wanted to meet up for a time of prayer. They must've gone by everybody's room—"

"They who?"

Peter replied, "Kelly and JayJay. He was the one that invited me."

"We decided to do it again this morning," Derek continued. "And it looks like we're going to try and keep it up."

Britt looked from one to the other. "We're trying to handle this the best we can. There are bound to be some hitches along the way, switching from TV to feature in the middle of a location shoot."

"This was not union." Peter gave emphasis to each word.

When the silence held, Derek said quietly, "You should include them in this conversation, Britt."

Britt huffed a laugh to the table. "What, you're after a little more mayhem?"

"Derek's right," Peter said. "These guys are not after giving you trouble."

Britt said nothing. Just sat and stared at the wood's grain.

Peter took a long breath, and added, "Three of my favorite films started location work without finished shooting scripts and ended up being successes. *Casablanca*, *Gladiator*, and *The Big Chill*. In all three cases the principal actors were included in story discussions."

Britt did not raise his head. "You're giving up control of your script?"

"No, Britt. No more than you'd stop being our director."

"You heard what JayJay's been saying," Derek added. "You're the boss. I think he means it."

"Me too," Peter agreed. "And if he leads, the others will follow."

Britt said to the table, "Kip. See if they're still in his suite."

When his AD moved to the phone, Britt muttered, "This is a serious mistake."

"I don't think so," Peter said.

When the three principal actors were assembled, Britt continued to address the tabletop. "Everything you were asking I've asked myself. About a hundred thousand times."

Claire sighed but did not speak. She and Kelly occupied the remaining two chairs. JayJay had waved the others back into their seats and positioned himself against the side wall.

"No, I can't explain what's happening," Britt went on. "No, I can't ever recall a television company going to feature with a series that's in decline. Or switching from a two-hour special to feature. Or starting a feature with no shooting script. Or going in with an untested star, a brand-new cinematographer, and a writer who's never worked on the big screen."

Claire said, "He wants us to fail. Allerby."

Britt said nothing.

She looked at the AD. "You're the one with connections to the Hollywood rumor mill. You hear everything almost before it's said."

Kip just looked at his boss.

Britt pushed himself away from the table. "Well?"

"Nothing. I've heard zip. Which is so totally strange I can't begin to tell you."

Britt hesitated, then replied, "Our new budget is twelve million dollars."

"That doesn't make sense."

"No," Britt said quietly. "I agree."

Kelly asked, "What's wrong with the numbers?"

"An hour of television costs out at one to two mil. Three mil tops, for the hottest miniseries." Claire kept her gaze upon the director. "Martin might've wanted to use a feature to announce in a big way that the series is back. But not with this budget. It's an in-betweener, isn't that what it's called these days?"

"Among other things."

"Too big to be costed out in direct-to-DVD sales and a TV gig. And too small to make it out of the art-house theaters."

"A *Heartland* story won't play there anyway," Britt agreed.

Kelly asked, "Why would the head of a studio want a project to fail?"

Britt said nothing.

The silence held until a knock on the door signaled the arrival of breakfast. Britt refused the waiter's offer to serve them. He accepted the plate of food from Kip, looked at it, then shoved it to one side. "I don't have any answers, Claire. Can you live with that?"

"You're the director, Britt. Can you?"

"Yes. I can." For the first time since they had entered Britt's suite, he looked squarely at the actress. "You want to know why? Because I've waited all my life for the chance to work on a screen project. It's why I went into television. It was my dream. I wanted to direct features. At one point I had a chance. But I was under contract at the time to ABC. By the time my series ended, the studio had hired another director. I never got another offer. Until now."

He looked around the room. "So yeah, I think you're probably right. Martin probably has a hidden agenda. But at the same time, he's handed me a chance to work on a feature project. Is it how I'd like to see it play out? No. Would I like to have a more seasoned team and a finished script? Of course I would."

He studied each face in turn. His eyes were rimmed by plum-colored circles. But his gaze was steady. "But will I go with what I've got? Absolutely. So what I want to know is, are you with me?"

When he received the expected chorus of assent, he motioned to Kip, who drew out a notebook and pen. "Okay, let's go through what we've got. Derek, you're first. How much can we keep?"

"The sets have to be tightened. Makeup will have to redo everything. Shoot for the big screen and a lot of what gets lost on TV will show. But from the standpoint of what's already on tape, I think we can keep pretty much everything." When Britt gave him a skeptical look, Derek continued, "I've been working on high-gamma resolution since JayJay's first test. I figured the hi-rez would give me more room to play if I got the colors or the lighting wrong. And I figured Martin was going to watch the dailies on the big screen."

"You figured right. How many more electricians and lighting geeks?"

Derek hesitated long enough for Claire to say, "Go on, tell him."

Britt tightened instantly. "What, you're already working behind my back?"

"It ain't anything like that," JayJay replied. "Derek brought a problem to the prayer group. I don't understand it any more now than before, but that don't mean we can't ask for help."

The director scoped the table. "That was it really, a prayer group?"

"Yes, Britt." Claire said it again, more softly this time. "Derek, you really need to tell him."

Derek took a very hard breath. "I don't want this to sound like I'm criticizing. Especially now."

Britt crossed his arms. Still very tight. "Is that so."

"We're lighting these scenes all wrong."

The director pretended a laugh. "How on earth could I possibly consider that a criticism?"

Derek glanced at JayJay, then Peter. Both of them just gave him the look. The one that said they were with him. He went on, "We're lighting this for film. Film needs the back light, the coloration, the tighter illumination. But digital is *different*. It takes the film lighting and makes it into something that looks sandpapered. The colors are painted, unnatural, rough. The edges become razor-sharp."

He gave Britt a fearful glance, who said, "You're not fired yet. Go on."

His voice trembled, but he persisted. "I say, let's hold to digital. It'd cost us a ton to bring in the new film equipment and switch over. Holding to digital cuts the per-frame cost by a factor of fifteen. Ditch all the lights except for one main and two spots for the close-ups. But keep the electricians. I know them and they trust me. Plus the digital cameras have maybe eight times the cable hookups as film. These guys will handle the wires and the reflectors. I'll need seven reflectors at a minimum, maybe as many as twelve for each outdoor shot."

Britt gave him stone. "You've thought this through."

"A lot." He swallowed audibly. "Can I say one thing more?"

"You're on a roll. Why stop now?"

"With the money we save from the lighting, let me have a second cameraman. And an assistant for each of us. These digital cameras are a monster to shift. And a steadicam for as long as I want."

Even Peter knew the request for unlimited steadicam was a serious breach. Steadicams were rented by the day. They came with their own operator. Steadicams were carried on a gyro-based unit strapped to the operators' bodies. Batteries were held in a canvas belt. The cameras moved on a hydraulic lift that worked with the gyros to smooth out all motion. Even walking over rough terrain was rendered smooth and seamless. The problem with steadicams was weight. A steadicam and gyro frame and battery pack weighed a hundred and twenty pounds. The cameraman was required to move at a slight crouch to keep his eye on the aperture.

A steadicam cameraman was always young and extremely fit. Even so, steadicam operators usually blew out their spines by age thirty-five. Steadicam operators were the only members of film crews who were never covered by studio insurance. Which was why they were always outsiders hired on a daily rate. A steadicam's contract was three hundred pages long, and protected the studio from everything up to and including typhoons. It was not just the cost of steadicam equipment that lifted their per diem into the stratosphere.

But all Britt said was, "I'll think about it."

Derek was still expelling his captured breath as Britt turned to Peter and said, "How do we stand on story?"

Peter knew it was coming. And still felt his gut freeze at the simple question. But he had Derek's courage to stand by. So he spoke more calmly than he felt. "I've never written for a feature. Well, I have. I mean, I've done a couple of spec scripts. They got shopped around and basically shelved. So I can give you what I think might work. But I'm ready to have you tell me that you want something different."

"Honesty. An interesting approach. Go on."

"Okay." He switched his gaze to Kelly and JayJay, basically because he found more encouragement there. "The first writer on the show, Ben Picksley, set the rules that I still follow. One moral and one action per show. We had planned to follow the same for the two-hour special. Commercials would have cut it down to eighty-nine minutes. Basically what we're talking about is adding only seven minutes more to the film time. But time is not the issue. A ninety-minute special would have a series of mini-climaxes timed around the commercial breaks, leading up to the final bang. A film runs to a more classical three-act structure."

He turned back to Britt. "I'd say there are two problems. But neither of them have to do with the action."

"The wildfire."

"Right. That still works. We could just expand it from threatening the ranch to the town."

Britt mulled that over. Then, "Two problems."

It was Peter's turn to swallow. Hollywood Boulevard was littered with failed writers who proposed concepts their directors loathed. "Ben's rule for the moral was that it could never hold more weight than a sick puppy. Cute, sentimental, and reducible to one line of dialogue."

Claire smiled. "I remember him saying that."

"Right. So I want to heighten the moral issue into something that generates a sense of audience identity. Something that *defines* this film. Something so big, so important, it holds equal weight to the action. Something that our core audience will recognize as being a genuine part of their world."

Britt's gaze had hardened. "You're talking about restructuring the core concept behind the series."

"That's right." His voice sounded strangled to his own ears. "I am."

"You've obviously been giving this some thought. Why wait until now to bring it up?"

"Because Neil Townsend could never have carried what I'm suggesting. He would have mouthed the words and made the whole concept a lie."

Britt nodded slowly. "Okay. That's problem one."

"The other is the story's hook."

"You and I have discussed this."

"Right. I think I've found what I've been looking for."

Britt rolled his finger. Action. As in, keep shooting.

Peter continued, "JayJay Parsons could be revealed as a lodestar. A moral compass. Not for the ranch. For the *world*. He stands up for what is right. This isn't about JayJay against the fire or the twister or the runaway cattle. This is JayJay against today's moral drift."

Britt returned his gaze to the tabletop. Deep in thought.

Peter's heart was hammering so hard he was sure the entire table must be able to hear it. Directly across from him, Derek lifted one thumb. And nodded. A small nod. But a nod just the same.

Then Kelly chuckled.

That drew Britt up. He studied the woman's smile, his gaze very tight. He had spent a lot of time watching actors give for the camera. "You find this funny?"

"Don't mind me. It's just . . ."

"What?"

"It's nice to hear somebody say what I've been thinking all week."

JayJay shifted on the side wall. "Y'all just stop."

"No, JayJay." Kelly redirected her smile and gave up something that, even though it was directed at another man, still caught in Peter's heart. "No."

"I ain't nobody's idea of perfect."

"That's not what Peter is saying. Is it, Peter."

"No."

"Sure sounded that way to me." JayJay kicked the rug with one boot. "And from where I'm standing . . ."

He stopped because Kelly reached over and took hold of his arm. "He didn't call you perfect, JayJay. He called you a hero."

Britt said to Peter, "Give me the hook in one line."

But it was Kelly who answered. "JayJay Parsons. The most real man I've ever known."

Britt's mask of stone and worry fractured slightly. At least enough for crinkles to form around his eyes and mouth. "So what we're talking about is a moral drama with strong action underpinnings. Shot completely in digital."

The room held its breath.

Britt said, "I'm giving this a tentative go. I'll let you know about the lighting and the steadicam after we've had a chance to check out the first few dailies."

Derek leaned back, looked at the ceiling, and whispered, "Thank You."

Britt was not done. "I can't tell you how long we've got to make this work. But I think we can all assume that time is a critical factor. Time and quality. We need to make this thing so solid, so *professional*, we give the studio no reason whatsoever to shut us down."

The director looked at each of them in turn. His gaze so intent Peter felt it sear his internal organs. Britt went on, "I'm not just asking for best efforts. I'm asking you all to give me every ounce of greatness you possibly can."

# Chapter 28

The Centurion boardroom was separated from Martin Allerby's office by a pair of double doors. The doors, along with all the room's other fittings, had been stripped from the set of *The Cotton Club*, a poor film but a great set. In Martin's opinion, the twenties-era chamber fit this gathering entirely, as the Centurion board members were totally out of touch with the America of today.

There was one African-American, a pastor. Two accountants, one retired, the other within coughing distance of his third coronary. A retired U.S. congresswoman from Dawes' district. A pair of former studio executives who between them could not have found an original opinion with a map. And Leo Gish, attorney extraordinaire.

Milo Keplar and Glenn Pritchard, Centurion's chief auditor, and Martin's assistant, Gloria, made up the eleven. All but Milo were confirmed Dawes mouthpieces. As usual, the only voice that really mattered was silent, as Carter Dawes was a no-show. Today, however, the empty chair did not concern Martin Allerby one iota. Carter Dawes had already given his approval. This was window dressing. But important nonetheless. They would all report their findings back to the little man on his Ojai Valley ranch. The man who needed to be convinced this was real. And then be forced to accept that his ridiculous excuse for a program was generating one of the most spectacular cinematic failures in the history of Hollywood. So he would finally sell out.

Then Martin Allerby would finally own his dream. A throne in the world of film.

Martin said, "Everybody have a fresh coffee? Fine. Then I'll call this meeting to order."

Leo cleared his throat and said what he did every quarter. "Mr. Dawes regrets that other commitments keep him from joining us. I represent him and hold full powers of attorney."

"So noted." Martin pretended to study the room. As though any of these clones would matter four weeks from today.

Ever cautious, Martin had covered the financial bases before moving. Only when Harry Solish's funds and those from the porn king were deposited in his accounts did he set the machine in motion. Carter Dawes was not the only one who kept a stable of tame former studio execs. Two retired directors with impeccable résumés had fronted a deal to buy Centurion. Lock, stock, and barrel.

The previous day, Leo Gish, Allerby's compliant lawyer, had called with the news. Carter Dawes had tentatively accepted his offer.

Today's meeting was to ensure the old man stayed hooked.

Allerby waited until all accounting formalities were concluded. When Gloria called for new business and no one else spoke, he rose from his chair. "I have something to discuss."

He took a step back so that his face was emblazoned by the same silvery light that bathed the framed poster behind his chair. Allerby had placed *Heartland*'s opening-season placard where he would not need to see it. Now it only added to the moment.

"We are in the business of visual fast food. I don't mean Centurion. I mean the entire studio industry. We supply what people want. Unfortunately for all concerned, fast food is not particularly healthy. If devoured in the sort of doses we see today, it decays the spirit. It weakens resolve. It suggests that all life can be resolved in thirty-minute cycles."

Martin took aim at the pastor. "I don't share your perspective on religion, Reverend. But I do accept that something more is needed.

Something deeper. This is what *Heartland* has been in the business of delivering."

He saw a couple of the heads begin nodding and worked at keeping the triumph from his voice. He knew exactly how to push their buttons. He should. He'd endured their out-of-date posturing long enough.

It wasn't just the actors who could deliver a solid Hollywood line.

Martin pointed to the poster. "For reasons beyond our control, however, the series has entered into decline. All of you are aware of the problems. I don't intend to rehash old business. Some of you may have heard that we've signed on a new JayJay Parsons. If you're interested, Gloria can supply you with copies of his early takes. Or you can simply take my word for it."

Milo touched one finger to the corner of his mouth, determinedly tugging out the first vestige of a smile. Allerby chose to ignore his partner as he continued, "His first day on the set, Mr. Junior went straight from his screen test to volunteering for frontline duty fighting a local wildfire. He saved two lives that afternoon, a local woman and the writer of the *Heartland* show. I assume most of you have seen the resulting publicity."

"Priceless," Milo intoned on cue. "It just keeps coming."

"So what we have is a unique confluence of events," Allerby continued. "We have signed a genuine hero who actually embodies the elements we've sold in *Heartland* for six successful seasons. As a result, we have a chance to revive a program with the most loyal following of anything on television today. An opportunity too good to pass up." He paused for effect, then delivered the killer line. "My intention, ladies and gentlemen, is to translate this into a feature film."

He allowed them a moment to let that sink in, then said, "Milo, have you had a chance to run the numbers?"

His sales director opened the leather portfolio. "Last year's average audience was eight point eight million an episode. Down eleven percent from the year before. Which was down fourteen percent from the previous season."

"How would this translate to screen numbers?"

Milo pretended to consult his figures. "Assuming no increase in numbers and we could bring two-thirds of our audience to theaters, the studio's take should be in excess of twenty-five mil."

"I intend to hold film costs to twelve million," Allerby went on. "Another five for marketing. Release in just under a thousand theaters and let it grow steadily. And remember, we are dealing with rock-bottom numbers here. If we are able to draw in sixty percent of our *highest* ratings, what would we be looking at, Milo?"

Again there was the dramatic pause, then, "Forty-eight million plus."

One of the studio execs protested, "But your ratings decline suggests the program has run its course."

Martin smiled thinly and swallowed his initial retort, which was that this very same executive had forced two knockoff sitcoms down America's throat for years with half those ratings. What he said was, "It's possible you are right. But we have evidence to the contrary. Milo?"

"Audience surveys have shown it's not *Heartland* that has died, but their interest in Neil Townsend. Eighty-five percent of those surveyed who claimed to watch most or all of the previous season's shows said they no longer felt he was a viable character."

"We have one other interesting phenomenon which confirms this. Gloria?"

His unflappable secretary had only one speaking voice, a semi-metallic monotone that implied an absolute authenticity. "Since the wildfire incident, our mailbag has trebled in size."

"Not the *Heartland* bag," Martin emphasized. "We're talking the studio's total daily mail. And what about the website, Gloria?"

"In the past eight days," Gloria droned, "the *Heartland* website has received over a million e-mails directed at either 'the new JayJay' or 'the real hero' or simply 'the Incredible Hunk,' which apparently is a nickname spreading all by itself. According to Yahoo, last week Centurion's website entered the top ten nationwide in terms of total hits."

"Which means, ladies and gentlemen, that *Heartland* has crossed the generational divide." Martin had no genuine evidence this was true. But he was not dealing in fact here. It was, after all, Hollywood. So long as they swallowed, he would feed. "A feature film starring John Junior could become a genuine phenomenon."

Milo toasted his boss and partner with a Perrier. "If they gave Oscars for boardroom antics, Martin, you'd walk away unchallenged."

Martin Allerby did not drive his Touareg so much as wade through the traffic headed west. A million metal lemmings, all desperate to escape the dreary hinterland and pretend they could claim a place in paradise, even if it was only the size of a beach towel. "I wonder if there's any chance of our winding up with what I described. A phenomenon."

"Not on your life." Milo redirected the a/c vent straight at his face. "Remember what we're talking about here. A team who's never worked on a feature. Directed by a has-been. Starring two total unknowns. Working with an unfinished script by a drone who's never written anything longer than sixty minutes minus commercials. Camera work by a guy who until last week made ends meet by chasing firetrucks. Know what that spells?"

"Yes." He used a halt in his lane to slip his sunglasses onto the top of his head and rub tired eyes. He had not been sleeping well.

"Tell me, Martin. I want to hear you say it."

"A disaster."

"No, Martin. A disaster would be something that actually makes it onto the screen. Which this won't. This charade only needs to last until the deal is signed. Then we kill it."

"We might keep the show alive," Martin mused. "See if this John Junior can deliver. At least for another season."

Milo waved his Perrier unconcernedly. "What we have is an insurance policy. And like I said when you came up with it. This is a true work of genius."

"We just need to make sure the set dissolves into total madness," Allerby said. "When the rumors start flying, I want there to be enough juice for the LA Times to carry the tale."

Milo shook his head. "I'm thinking overkill."

But Allerby was already reaching for his phone. He speed-dialed Gloria and said when his assistant came on the phone, "Give me Contracts."

Pritchard came on with, "Legal."

"Glenn, we need to be ready for an onslaught of agents. Hold hard, but be reasonable."

"There's no such thing as reasonable, Martin. This is Hollywood."

"Tough but fair," Allerby insisted. "And fast. I want to make this move without a single missed day. I want to have the feature in theaters before our January season opener."

"That's pushing things."

"That's what I want. Use standard guild levels for mid-budget features right across the board. Remind anyone who balks they can be easily replaced. Oh, and open a new expense line for our star. Whatever John Junior wants, he gets."

There was a stunned silence. "You can't be serious."

"Run anything outrageous by me. But I want this guy to deliver. And if he's the star I think he'll soon be, I also want him to stay good and bought."

Martin slipped the phone back in his pocket. Saw his partner's grin. "What."

Milo said, "You're thinking you can corrupt this guy, ruin him in one season?"

That was exactly what he was thinking. But some things were to be savored in secret. "Don't talk silly, Milo. I'm just protecting our assets."

Milo laughed and turned back to the road. "Whatever."

# Chapter 29

A hn arrived late that afternoon, accompanied by a man who would have looked comic except for the somber way he carried himself. The stranger had white quarter-moons of fluffy hair that grew above his ears, a bald head burned the color of old oak, an eagle's hook of a nose, no shoulders whatsoever, and a beer barrel for a belly. But his gaze was clear and direct and very intelligent. His voice was his finest quality. "Mr. Junior, I'm Barry Henning. I teach the business of film at UCLA. Before I retired I was an agent with CAA. Ahn asked me to join him today. May I call you John?"

JayJay and Kelly had migrated to the ranch because they were growing stir-crazy hanging around the pool. There was no filming that day. But the activity around the ranch was something to behold. All day long, trucks and people kept coming and going. Derek had sprinted by them so often they had stopped counting. The AD kept wandering past, worrying over whether they needed something. All of a sudden Kip's first duty in life was to make sure they were coddled like poached eggs.

He slipped off the rail and shook the man's hand. "JayJay's worked well enough all my life long."

"Yeah, I hear the PR folks are salivating over you and this name thing." Barry Henning eyed JayJay like he was a prize heifer. "Now that we've met, I can see why. And you must be the lovely Ms. Channing."

Kelly sat on the railing beside JayJay's shoulder. She wore his hat far down over her eyes. She accepted Henning's hand without moving from her perch. "Call me Kelly."

Every now and then Skye trotted over to their side of the corral, looking for sugar or an excuse to break free and gallop. Which to JayJay's mind was looking more inviting with each passing moment. "What can I do for you, Mr. Henning?"

"Call me Barry. Ahn here tells me you've appointed him your manager."

"We shook hands on it."

"That is definitely a bad idea, JayJay. You'd be handing your career to a minnow and sending him into shark-infested waters."

"Is that a fact." JayJay disliked the way Ahn held back, picking a splinter from the fence post.

"Yes sir, it is. Now, I'd be happy to make an introduction to my former partners. CAA handles some of the biggest names in the industry."

"What about Ahn?"

"He would certainly have some cachet attached to his record when he graduates, having negotiated an initial agreement on your behalf."

"Ahn, this is the guy you were telling me about?"

"My thesis adviser."

"Well, I guess that means I've got to be polite here. On account of how I think the world of this young man." JayJay pushed himself off the fence. Something in his expression caused the agent to falter. "Now let me tell you how this is going to work out. Him, I trust. You, I don't know. That goes for every single one of those mighty important folks in your alphabet soup of a company. If Ahn here tells me he needs to bring in somebody else to help, that is Ahn's decision. But he stays in control."

"But JayJay—"

"Mister, you keep pressing me, and I'm bound to tell you where you can stick that cachet of yours."

Kelly coughed discreetly. Which the former agent most definitely did not like. "I've watched a lot of new stars wreck their careers, JayJay. It never gets easier."

JayJay retorted, "Who's talking career? I just want somebody I can trust to make sure these fellers don't treat me like a rogue steer, wrestle me to the ground, and brand my backside."

"Your attitude toward this incredible opportunity doesn't make your actions any less of a mistake. Ahn, I'll wait for you in the car."

When the agent had moved off, Ahn said quietly, "He was on the phone the whole way up here. Talking to his former partners. Trying to decide which one of them he was going to pitch to you. Loving how they had to suck up to him. He mentioned me every now and then. Like he was throwing me a bone."

"Like I was already roped and saddled."

"Pretty much." Ahn started kicking the fence post. "He's right, JayJay. This is so far beyond what I can handle it's silly."

"So go out there and hire yourself an expert. That's what they're there for, right?" When Ahn did not respond, JayJay guessed, "Your folks giving you a hard time?"

"They alternate. One minute they're thrilled for me. The next they're worried I'm going to drive your career off a cliff."

"See, that's the same mistake everybody keeps making. I'm not after any career."

"That could change."

"It might. But that is in God's hands. Right now all I want is somebody I trust to count the numbers and keep them fellows honest."

"There are a lot of them. Numbers, I mean. What with the move to feature."

"You're telling me they want to pay me *more?*"

This time Kelly laughed out loud.

"You know what? I don't even want you to tell me."

"You've got to know, JayJay." This from Kelly.

"I'm not dancing that tune just so y'all can laugh at me again."

"Tell him," Kelly said to Ahn.

"Who's giving the orders round here?"

"Go on," Kelly said.

Ahn said, "Your role in the feature is going to bring in somewhere in the neighborhood of two point three million dollars."

Kelly slugged his shoulder. "That's a mighty good neighborhood to be in, Slim."

He staggered away.

JayJay spent the next three days just walking through the routine. Trodding a path from one action to the next. Breakfast. Prayer group. Limo to the site. He waited by the corral between shoots. When the day grew too hot he moved into the shadow of the barn. He avoided the cabin, which was nothing but a hollow shell filled with generators and Britt's on-site office and a growing mass of equipment. He never set foot in his trailer except to change clothes or have the makeup folks work on him. When people spoke to him he responded. Ten seconds after they walked away, he couldn't recall what he'd heard or said. Dinner. Bed. Kelly gave him worried glances, but stopped asking if he was all right when he gave her the same response every time. Fine. He was fine. Nobody died from being faced with impossible facts, or being hollowed by questions that had no answers.

They brought in a couple of extra horses for scenes Peter was writing. The wrangler was a young Latina named Felicita, who spoke little English but dearly loved the horses. She grew used to JayJay leaning against the fence or the barn, saying nothing and seeing less.

On the afternoon of the fourth day JayJay was at his accustomed spot, hidden away from the growing tumult around the ranch. The number of actors had doubled, those behind the camera tripled. He was done with his scenes for the day. He had no reason to remain except that the hotel offered less respite than the barn's shadows. At least here he had hills and a horizon to pretend to watch.

He had no idea how long he had stood there. Long enough for his legs to stiffen. Until a voice carried through the dust storm in his head.

It took JayJay a long moment to recognize the pastor of Ahn's church. "What on earth are you doing up here?"

Floyd Cummins had a grip as weathered and sturdy as his features. "I'm headed to a pastors' conference in Fresno. Thought I'd stop by and see how things are going."

JayJay turned back to the railings. "I wish I knew."

The pastor sidled up to the fence. "Ahn told me how you got spooked by the thought of all that money they're tossing your way."

"I asked him not to even tell me. Still wish I didn't know."

"I don't suppose I need to ask what you thought of that Hollywood agent he drove up with."

JayJay bent down, grabbed a fistful of pebbles, and began tossing them at the dust.

"Ahn seems to think that if you decide to hang around, you'll probably need somebody like that agent in your corner."

"Won't happen."

"What if—and I'm not saying it will happen, mind you—but what if you get done with this work here, get all ready to ride off into your own little sunset, and then you learn God isn't done with you yet?"

"There you go again." JayJay tossed another rock. "Every time I say something you don't like, you hit me with the God thing."

"Some folks wouldn't call being made famous and rich such a hard life."

"Yeah, well, they can have it. I'd give it all just . . ."

"Just what, JayJay? To go back to how it was before?"

He let the remaining pebbles fall to the earth by his feet. Locked and helpless, staring into lengthening shadows, washed by the afternoon sun.

"In the time it took me to park my car and ask where to find you, a half dozen people told me about the prayer group you've started."

"It was Kelly's idea."

"But you're the one who made it happen. Nobody can ever remember such a thing before, JayJay." He moved in closer. "You recall our conversation after church?"

He replied softly, "I can't get it out of my head."

"You told me you didn't have any business being here. And I told you, it's the same miracle each one of us faces when God breathes life into dust, and then allows us to rise and face a new dawn." Floyd Cummins stepped into JayJay's frame of vision. "So God has granted you a miracle. And somewhere down deep, you're expecting everything else to just be clear as day. Every answer laid out in fiery script."

JayJay opened his mouth to object. But the words did not come.

"Some lessons are so powerful the Scriptures repeat them time after time. God performs one vital miracle. And then what happens? He backs off. Now why on earth do you reckon He'd do such a thing?" Floyd Cummins took a half step closer. "So that you the believer remain a vital part of the process. So that you remain in charge of *deciding*. Think on that, JayJay. The most subtle gift the Master of creation has granted us is the power of free will. We can choose to ignore His miracles and His subtle ways. We can pretend that we are masters of all we survey, and that there is no such thing as an all-powerful God. Why? Because He *lets* us. It is His *gift*. We are not slaves. We are *free men*."

The descending sun burnished the pastor's face, making it glow like the fire was there inside his skin, and not merely a reflection of power from above. "So God has performed this one miracle and brought you to Hollywood. Now the question is, what do you do with this miracle? Are you going to let life defeat you? Will the doubts and the problems and all the traumas that come along with free will crush you back into the dust from which you came? Because it may very well do that, unless you accept the *responsibility* of your miracle."

A breath of wind lifted a man-size bundle of earth and spun it aloft.

The red soil danced and weaved in the sun, golden and russet and flaxen in turns. Then the wind vanished and the dust fell, leaving only heat.

"You the believer are a vital part of the process. No miracle will *ever* change this. God acts in our midst all the time. But He is not called to explain. Nor does He intend to supply you with all the answers. Instead, we are called to draw close to Him. Walk through the open door, seek His will, and serve Him to the best of our ability." Floyd Cummins gripped his shoulder. "Remember, wherever you are, whatever situation you face, the critical issue confronting each and every one of us is the same. *Choose life.*"

JayJay walked the pastor to his car and returned to his station by the corral. Skye moved up to the other side of the fence, snorting and pawing the ground with her left foreleg. Tossing her silver-gray mane. Saying in everything but human speech that it was time.

JayJay entered the barn. "Felicita, could I have a blanket and saddle?"

She might not have understood his words, but she saw the direction he was pointing. Her smile flashed wide enough to push aside the shadows. *"Sí, señor."*

"No, not that silver rig. A working saddle. Yeah, that old thing will do me just fine. And I know for a fact Skye don't care." He had to grin. When he finally decided to have a conversation, it was with a lady who didn't speak English. "Thank you."

*"De nada."*

Skye was feeling her oats enough to be ready to vault the fence before JayJay was set in the saddle. He reined the horse in and cantered easy in a tight circle, seeing the other horses clearly for the first time. There was a fine pair of fillies, two years old, three at the most, light enough on their feet to float across the paddock. And two geldings with the stolid calm of gentle rides. Felicita opened the corral door, used her hat to wave the other horses back, and smiled him out. A pair of gaffers he recognized from the prayer group waved as he passed. Britt stood in the cabin doorway and called something. This time JayJay intentionally chose not to hear.

His normal route, the one from his bygone era, would have taken him past the spring and along the trail shaded by cottonwood trees. But JayJay tugged the reins and directed Skye through the western meadow and off the ranch. Skye jittered sideways in her eagerness to push out of the easy trot. Halfway across the meadow JayJay eased his grip and touched Skye's ribs with his knees. Once was enough. The horse snorted and grew wings.

JayJay leaned down low to the horse, one hand resting where the mane met the neck. Skye reached out farther still, the hooves eating up the earth. They flew over the western fence and entered the first slopes. JayJay directed Skye onto a rutted track leading up through the almond trees. The flowers were gone now, the crop just beginning to ripen. Skye hammered up the slope, snorting and digging hard as the rise grew steeper.

When they reached the first plateau JayJay pulled back on the reins. Skye did not give in willingly. But JayJay just tugged the harder, easing his horse into a gentle canter. The trail jinked and headed along the edge. JayJay looked down the slope, back to the ranch. The creek was a golden ribbon carved from the valley floor. On the ranch's other side, low-slung hills bordered the road leading to the highway. The town was a mile or so off, the higher rooftops gleaming in the late sun.

A crowd of roadies and newly arrived bit actors cheered him, the sound rising easy in the still afternoon air. JayJay did the showboat thing, lifting Skye into a two-footed dance and waving his hat. The cheers grew louder. Felicita stood on the corral fence and waved back. Britt stood in the cabin doorway and watched, the only person not making noise. JayJay dropped the horse to all fours and turned away from the ranch and all the mysteries.

He rode until the high peaks took a final bite from the sun, until the growing dark made the going tricky and the starlings overhead carved tight edges from a deepening sky. He took another trail down to the main road, preferring asphalt to an unknown descent laced in shadows. When he returned to the barn he waved Felicita aside, pulled off the saddle and blanket, filled a meal bag with oats, and set to currying his horse.

By the time he led Skye back to the corral the night was in full control. Behind the cabin, workers toiled under floodlights and the instruction of the chief set designer. The lights in Britt's office, where the kitchen should have been, were still on. But not even that could disturb JayJay's evening. He turned away from the cabin and spent a long time studying the sweep of stars and velvet hills. Finally Skye walked over and nudged his arm draped upon the fence. JayJay stroked the horse's forehead and said, "I reckon I've sulked long enough."

The horse snorted quietly. JayJay scratched her between her ears, then stepped back and said to the night at large, "It's time I got on with this craziness called life."

# Chapter 30

JayJay woke up knowing something was supposed to happen. But he had so removed himself during the previous few days he couldn't remember what it was until Peter came over while he was standing in the breakfast line and said, "I can't thank you enough. This means more than I can say."

"Cynthia says to be sure and tell you . . ." Peter stopped as Kelly stalked over.

The lady revealed a full head of steam. "I ask you a dozen times to take me riding, and then you take off after I've left for the day? What is this, Slim, a cowboy's brush-off?"

JayJay noticed Peter had backed off a pace. "I just needed a little time alone, is all."

She crossed her arms. "That's your idea of an excuse?"

"Honest, Kelly. We can go today if you like."

"That depends." She spun on her boot and tossed over her shoulder, "On whether you're over whatever it is that's had you about as interesting as the Mojave in July."

When Peter moved back over, JayJay observed, "That lady walks better angry than most do trying for cute."

"I couldn't say," Peter said. "Being extremely married and all."

Kelly didn't exactly put the Grand Canyon between them at the prayer group. But only because the side wall got in the way of her scooting any farther off. From her position by the window, she gave the day's reading in something approaching a huff. "Deuteronomy, chapter thirty-one, verse eight reads, 'The Lord himself will lead you and be with you. He will not fail you or abandon you, so do not lose courage or be afraid.'"

Instead of asking for prayer requests, JayJay decided there would never be a better time than now to make what amends he could. "That passage pretty much says it all, far as where I'm at today. Kelly, would you mind reading that again?"

She gave him a sideways look full of suspicion, but did so. When she'd finished, JayJay went on, "I've been carrying around a load of questions, so crazy I've been afraid to speak them out loud. I still am. And I've been in a serious funk on account of how God hasn't answered when I've asked what's going on. Deep down, I guess I was thinking that if I sulked long enough, He'd decide I deserved an explanation."

There were nineteen of them gathered. About what they had settled down to most mornings. Only Derek was missing from the regular crew. A few of the curious kept coming, and a couple of the new faces around the set had joined in. JayJay could always recognize the newbies from their expressions of disbelief. He could see them now, painted with the soft glow of a rising sun, listening to this guy they called a star bare his soul.

"I've never been one for talking. Not much on thinking about myself either, for that matter. I always figured I had a cowboy's attitude toward life. Walk a straight and steady line, do what's right, and if evil's got the sense to slither away from you, no need in wasting a bullet. But if you got to shoot, aim straight and hit hard."

He knew he wasn't making a lot of sense. And to tell the truth, he didn't much care. Another night of sitting by the window had cleared up his heart. If his head couldn't find the proper words, tough.

"I've studied the Scriptures some. Not as much as I should, I'll be the first to admit that. But enough to know there ain't no place in the Holy Book that says God is gonna explain what He's got in mind. No sir.

What it says is what Kelly just read. Believe in God. Seek His strength. And He will see you through whatever it is you're facing. What's more, He'll turn the mess into something for good. His good, His will. That's what Jesus told us to pray for, right? That the Father's will be done."

The bearded grips, the two giants who had not missed a day and were now seated on the floor by Kelly's chair, were nodding in unison. One intoned, "Say it, brother."

"The other day, when Derek started talking about them gamma things and I didn't understand a word, was I bothered? Not a bit. Why? Because I trust him. And what I *haven't* been doing is trusting God. So this morning I'm not asking for you to pray so I'll get answers. I'm done asking for that. I'm asking for just enough strength and wisdom to get the job done."

Kelly was the first out the door. JayJay was in the process of following, until his way was blocked by Kip, wearing his trademark chartreuse and smirk. "Britt wants to see you."

"In a minute. I just—"

"JayJay, Britt wants to see you *now*." He pointed at Peter. "You too."

Britt's suite was on the ground floor and across the interior courtyard. His living room was increasingly taken over by equipment and cables. Kip pushed through the open door and said, "They're here."

"Good. You two, have a seat. No, over there on the sofa." Britt and Derek were working at what had formerly been the dining table, fiddling with a computer connected to a massive tape machine. Not even the darkened room could mask the exhaustion evident on both their faces. The computer screen was split in two, showing the same image but from different angles. At the bottom of both ran a counter split into hundredths of seconds. Britt watched for a while longer, then said, "Looks like you were right."

"I can beef the background more if you want."

"No, this is solid." Britt rose to his feet. "We're good to go."

Derek seemed to glow. "Thanks, Britt. A lot."

"Come over and run the tape, will you?" Britt pulled over a high-backed chair. He said to JayJay, "I'm breaking every rule in the director's book here. But I want you to see something. Okay, Derek. Roll it."

The monitor was a massive flat screen connected to a vast array of equipment. JayJay instantly recognized the scene from two days back, the morning they moved from rehearsals to filming. He and Kelly had been standing outside the barn with Skye between them. The shy cowboy using the horse to shield himself from the forward-thinking city lady. About a minute and a half of dialogue. Eleven takes. Half a day's work. The colors were brilliant, the scene as vivid and beautiful as modern technology could render. The only problem was the cowboy. They might as well have dressed up a corpse.

When it was done, Britt asked, "You want to see it a second time?"

"No." JayJay felt a flush crawl from his collar and rise to his scalp. "Don't make me watch it over again."

"Tell me what you just saw."

JayJay could see his reflection in the blank screen. "All I needed was a headdress and a fistful of cigars and you could prop me outside a tobacco shop."

"The morning we talked about switching to feature, I asked you to give me the best you had. What I need to know is, are you delivering?"

JayJay rubbed his forehead. There could be no clearer conviction. "I've been letting problems get in the way of my work."

"That is not what I asked you." Britt pointed at the monitor. "Tell me this is all we've got to work with, and Peter here will write your role down to as few lines as possible. We've all had experience dealing with an actor who can't deliver."

The flat way Britt spoke drove the guilty verdict even deeper. "I can do better."

"I think so too. The question is, *will* you?"

"Yes."

Britt studied him carefully. "Here's the deal. Centurion is screaming for the dailies. You understand that word? They want to blow up everything I've shot, all the takes. There's a mini-studio in the office building. They'll get some of the execs together, Allerby and Milo for sure, maybe the editor assigned to cut this project, a few others. And they'll roll the tape."

"You're killing me," JayJay protested.

"Exactly." Britt pointed at the empty screen. "This is what they'll judge us on. If they pull the plug, it will be because of this. Because of *you*."

"You can't let anybody else see this mess." JayJay was pleading now. "I've let everybody down. Don't make it worse."

Britt's gaze had the acute precision of a judge passing sentence. "From this moment on, you'll give me the best you can?"

"Count on it."

Britt turned to Derek and said, "As of now, this tape does not exist. We're starting fresh. All we've done so far is just rehearse."

JayJay did not notice his sweat bath until then. "Thanks, Britt. A lot."

Britt asked Peter, "You told him yet?"

"I was just going to."

"There's a lot riding on you, JayJay. A lot of jobs, a lot of people's hopes. Don't let us down."

They were out of the hotel and a hundred yards down the sidewalk leading toward town before JayJay managed, "I've just been skinned by a real pro."

"You need to sit down?"

"No, better if I walk it off." He shook his head in painful admiration. "He didn't raise his voice. Didn't say a single bad word or need more than ninety seconds. But he roasted me right down to a crispy fritter."

"The first time I got on his wrong side, I had nightmares for a week." Peter shook his head at the memory. "It was less than a month after the first writer on the series had retired. My chance at a career, dead and gone after twenty-two days. The next time I saw him, it was like nothing happened. But he knew and I knew. Either I performed to his expectations, or I was toast."

The admission drew JayJay up tighter and closed the gap between them. They were just two journeymen, both of whom had shared the lash. "Where are we headed?"

"There's somebody I want you to meet." Peter raised his face to the sun and added, "I've got a problem. Actually, two. Britt said it was my choice whether I talk it over. I still don't know what to do."

"Whatever you think is right by me."

"I'm not happy with the romance angle between you and Kelly."

"Neither is she." JayJay raised his hand before Peter could speak. "Sorry. It just slipped out."

"The later scenes work okay. But I need a better opener."

"Why ask me? I'm just the green kid who's still limping from where the boss winged me."

"I just thought . . . You know, you guys . . ." Peter sighed. "Never mind."

They walked a ways in silence. JayJay found himself smiling.

"What is it?"

"Kelly might just finish the job Britt's started if I tell you."

"How bad can it be?"

"It ain't bad at all, from where I'm standing. But this is a lady we're dealing with."

Peter walked and watched and waited. Not asking, at least in words.

"Okay. Here's the deal. The lady can just plain sing."

Peter frowned. "I don't remember seeing anything about that in her sheet."

"Which means she ain't gonna be happy to hear I'm talking about it." JayJay recounted the night at Goody's. "I mean to tell you, she had that crowd on their feet in a heartbeat. Took her four more songs before they'd let her climb down off the stage."

"I can use this, JayJay." Peter started reading script in the sunwashed sidewalk. "Maybe set it at an outdoor stage, a county fair or something. We'll see."

"I probably just signed my own death warrant."

"No, no. You did right." More definite now. "What kind of music?"

"Christian with an edge. She did one number, a love song between God and man. Even the waiters stopped moving around. The place plain froze up. When she finished, I thought maybe the crowd was gonna eat her alive."

"How was the band?"

"Hot. And they liked working with her. The lead man came over when we were leaving and said he'd sign her in a heartbeat. But she said she only did numbers where the cross shone through."

"Kelly told him that?" Peter liked it. A lot. "Probably why she didn't include it in her sheet. Hollywood thinks the Christian music industry is something for choirs and robes and backcountry churches."

"You said there were two things bothering you?"

"Hold on to that thought a minute longer, I want to work this through in my head."

JayJay subsided and studied his surroundings. To his relief, the town that rose up around them was not the town he remembered. Not entirely different, but not the same either. JayJay took comfort in not being confronted with more mysteries he needed to work around. The road grew into a real gasoline alley, with car dealerships to either side. Peter turned into the Ford lot and walked beneath the strings of plastic flags flapping in the hot wind.

"Well, by golly, I guess the rumors got it right for once." The man wore an electric-blue jacket and a Ford Racing tie and a grin big as a shout. "Pardner, you just got to let me shake your hand."

"John Junior, meet Miller Whitley, mayor of Salton City."

"Howdy, Mr. Whitley."

"Call me Miller. Only people using my last name around here are bankers and folks from Sacramento, and I'd just as soon skewer that lot and have me a Texas barbecue."

His energy disguised the fact that he wasn't a large man. His smile was the grandest part of him, creasing everything from his neck to his forehead. He bounced on his toes while shaking JayJay's hand, as though the delight he felt required every inch of his frame. "I tell you what. When they said that old crook they called a star was gone wherever it is they bury the live ones down in Hollywood, why, I wished I was a Catholic, just so I could go light myself a mess of them candles. But I got hold of that desire 'fore it ever saw daylight, on account of my daddy raised his boy to die deep in the Baptist fold."

Peter explained, "Our man Neil actually got banned from inside the city limits."

"We're close enough to cowboy country to put up with a lot," Miller said. "But when that feller borrowed himself a semi with the driver still asleep in the back and drove it through the front doors of the courthouse 'cause the judge told him he had to pay a speeding ticket, well, we figured it was time to draw a line in the sand."

"Tell him about the ticket," Peter said.

"Weren't all that much. 'Cept it was the ninth time he'd been stopped last season."

"Tenth," Peter corrected.

"Actually, it was the twelfth, since they stopped him three times before they finally got the keys away from him. At gunpoint. But who's counting." He stopped. "Where was I headed with this thing?"

"The ticket Neil had to pay."

"There you go. Our big star had bought hisself one of those fancy Eye-talian cars, the ones that come with a bumper sticker that says,

'You won't be able to read this for long.' So round about midnight on the night in question, our star pulls up to a traffic light and beeps his horn to the patrol car in the next lane. He rolls down his window and says, what was it now?"

Peter supplied, "'I've been all over town looking for somebody to race. I guess you jokers will have to do.'"

The mayor laughed and slapped his thigh. "One thing is for sure and for certain. You'd never be talking about that feller starting no prayer group in the hotel."

"Burn it down, more likely," Peter agreed.

"Yeah, I don't reckon they miss the pleasure of pulling mattresses and televisions and Coke machines out of the swimming pool every morning."

JayJay asked, "Folks are talking about our prayer group?"

The mayor waved it away. "That was last week. Then one of our local good-time boys heard his ex-lady friend was flirting with the feller who runs the Tastee Freeze. Two nights back he lashed the shack with cable and used his wrecker to pull it into the passing lane of I-5. Since then, your prayer meeting is just another curiosity in a hot, dusty summer."

Peter explained, "Miller is deacon in the church Derek and I attend when we're up here."

"Yeah, Hollywood folks who treated my church like it wasn't something that belonged in a zoo deserved a howdy." He pointed them toward the office. "Let's mosey into my office 'fore we melt down to sweaty puddles."

Once inside, however, their progress was halted by what was parked in the far corner of the showroom floor. Standing alongside the door leading back to the repair depot was a carefully restored old pickup. The truck came from the era of rounded fenders and running boards and circular headlights. The hood looked overlong to Peter's eye, and had a hole carved in the middle for a serious set of chromed air vents. Peter had never much cared for trucks. But he watched Miller and all the other sales staff grow grins as JayJay ran his hand along the truck fender.

Miller said to his staff, "Folks, what we have here is about as close to true love as I've seen in quite a while."

The truck was painted a fingernail-polish red so deep Peter could almost dive in. JayJay said, "I've been looking for this little lady all my life. But I didn't know it until now."

Miller called to the guy behind the desk, "Toss me the keys, Piston."

Peter asked, "You've got a salesman named Piston?"

"Yeah, we always figured his momma for a psychic." He accepted the keys. "Your name really JayJay, like Peter here says?"

JayJay was peering through the open window. "That's right."

"Well, you sure fit the part, I'll give you that much." Miller reached through the window and fitted the keys into the ignition. "Fire this lady up and let her sing for you."

JayJay did not need to be asked twice. He opened the door, stroked the white old-fashioned steering wheel, and hit it.

The entire showroom trembled. The vibrations struck Peter both in the chest and through his feet. The engine sounded like something from Daytona, a fluid roar of metal and force.

JayJay's eyes had gone completely round. He looked through the open window at where Miller was grinning at him, and floored the pedal.

They might as well have been standing at the base of a space shuttle with the engines on full.

JayJay gave a cowboy's whoop, so loud it was heard over the engine's bellow. Yee-*hah*.

He revved it once more, then cut the motor. And said in genuine breathless wonder, "Y'all give me a minute here to refit my heart inside my chest."

Miller climbed up on the running board. "Nineteen forty-seven Ford half-ton body. We reworked the frame so it could handle a Shelby Cobra three fifty-seven."

"We?"

"My boy and me. The hood's fiberglass, eleven and a half inches longer than the original. Mag shifter. Getrag transmission. MacPherson gas-pack strut suspension, just like them wild boys use over at Indianapolis. Pirelli racers, fourteen inches wide and ribbed for wet traction. Nineteen layers of hand-polished lacquer."

JayJay stroked the wheel. "How'd your boy let this get out of his hands?"

"Aw, he's moved up to the Bay area. Works in IT. Got hisself a lady friend straight outta Marin County. Which, if'n you don't know, is where they raise Martians in human skin. The lady's into Japanese designer fashion and black fingernail polish. Edna, that's my wife, she and I've been taking lessons so's we can carry a conversation with her through dinner. Learned all about tofu and track lighting."

JayJay could not hide his disbelief. "He gave this up for a lady?"

"What can I say. He's twenty-nine and doing his dead-level best to forget he was ever happy in the San Joaquin Valley." Miller stroked the door. "Guess I finally got tired of missing the boy and the days we had every time I went inside our garage."

JayJay tasted the words a couple of times before asking softly, "How much?"

Miller gave a sad laugh. "I could say a million dollars and you wouldn't blink. Tell me I'm wrong."

JayJay was still playing with the steering wheel. "I never figured I had much use for all the money they were shoving at me until now. That's not the best way to start dickering, though, is it."

Peter objected, "I don't get it. You guys are talking about an old *truck*."

JayJay gave him a stricken look. Miller said, "Don't mind him, son. He's Hollywood. Them folks just plain don't know any better."

It took Peter a minute to realize JayJay was now talking to the truck. "You got to excuse the feller. He didn't mean it."

Miller opened the truck door. "Let's go inside my office and talk about this other thing. See where it takes us."

The office had a glass wall overlooking the showroom. Even when JayJay was looking straight at Peter, his attention remained on the pickup. Miller said, "I got to tell you, when Peter told me his idea, I thought it sounded partly loco and partly like an answer to prayer."

Peter asked, "And now?"

"Depends on the day. Before y'all got here I was leaning more toward crazy. But now that I got old JayJay here sitting in my office and in love with my metal memories, well, I'm thinking this thing might just grow wings and fly."

Peter looked at JayJay. "I need to make sure you're actually listening."

JayJay was still blinking like he'd been poleaxed. "I'm here, ain't I?"

"Remember what Britt told you," Peter said. "This is *vital*."

JayJay focused then. Peter saw it happen. The cowboy stood and turned his chair so his back was to the showroom. Seated himself again. "Okay. You got me."

"You remember when I was telling Britt about heightening the film's drama?"

"Something about playing up the moral side."

"Right. Balancing the action, hooking into a dilemma that is resolved by the same climax." He saw JayJay's forehead crinkle in confusion, but forged on. "What I want to do is use the town and its problems as a true-to-life modern drama. Make the folks here our walk-ons. Use the crisis they're facing. Turn it into the story you're confronting."

JayJay asked the mayor, "You're in favor of this?"

"I got to tell you, this thing just might have some legs." Miller rose and pointed out his rear window at the highway and the town beyond. "Salton City is facing the same predicament as the rest of the San Joaquin. All these towns are split into three camps and fighting hard. There's the farmers and the water crisis. Then we got a huge migrant labor population, poor as the Okies were back in the thirties, and a lot of children living a life we shouldn't be seeing in a country rich as ours."

Peter said, "The migrant camp looks like a picture from Central America. They spread down a valley east of here. No electricity. Plastic sheets for walls. No plumbing."

Miller went on, "For the past ten years we've had an invasion of developers. Building houses and malls fast as they can get the zoning permits. Drawing in folks who can't afford a decent place closer to the ocean, looking for a home where they don't need bars on the windows."

Peter went on, "The new developments have skewed the voting population. The farmers aren't in control of local government anymore. The water rights that keep them alive are being stripped away."

Miller said, "Your pal here and I got to talking after church one day. Then I didn't think any more about it until a few days back, when he comes in and springs his idea on me."

Peter said, "For this new scene, you go before a town meeting. We fill the hall with real people. Miller writes your speech. He uses this to get their attention."

Miller leaned back in his chair, the oversize grin back in place. "Now tell him the good part."

# Chapter 31

Miller did not stick JayJay nearly as hard as he could have over the truck's price. He also agreed to fit a new exhaust system, one that would not awaken the next county when JayJay dug in his spurs, and deliver it to the hotel by close of business.

When they got back to the hotel, JayJay went by Kelly's room. No one answered his knock. He returned to the suite, packed his personal items into a suitcase he borrowed from Peter, and transferred over to the room Peter was vacating. He was hugged repeatedly by an extremely pregnant lady with all the world's warmth shining from her face. One look at the two of them together was enough to assure JayJay they were going to make great parents.

Kelly was also not at the ranch. Nor was the limo. Gladys spotted him pretending not to search every corner and said Kelly had received a phone call, something urgent. Britt had given her permission to take a couple of days off. A family thing, was all Gladys knew.

The next three days were a very intense blur. Cynthia, Peter's wife, took over the Bible reading. She had a warm glow about her that bathed the entire gathering. The first morning, she included a suggestion that they pray for Kelly's grandmother, who had taken a bad fall and was in the hospital. JayJay tried hard to bury the hurt over hearing the news from someone other than the lady herself.

On the set, Claire took up coaching him in basic points of acting. How to extend. How to find an internal source of emotion and fire the

233

flames. How to speak more naturally. How to identify what he was feel-ing inside and turn it to his advantage. How to link himself tightly to some specific trait he'd identified in his character. How to play for his audience, the unseen people watching from the other side of the cam-era. How to work, act, move, speak, *breathe*, from the very core. He wasn't sure how well he was doing with the lessons. But Britt's instruc-tions became increasingly limited to hitting the scene. JayJay worked harder than he ever thought possible, standing around and claiming lines as his own. He did as Claire ordered to make the process real, pick-ing out one person there behind the cameras, and reaching out with everything he had in him, doing his best to *connect*.

Only his target was not on the set at all, but rather off in Sioux Falls, silent and distant.

On his time off he started teaching those who were interested what it meant to ride the high range. Derek had probably the worst seat on a horse of anybody JayJay had ever come across. But the guy was sure game. Peter too. Even Claire started coming out with them. When she was along, though, she made him practice his lines to the forests and the birds and the clouds. Shouting out the words, yelling himself hoarse, learning what it meant to test his limits. He never got over his embarrassment, but he learned to shove it aside, back with all the other questions he was doing his best to leave up to God.

He ate his dinners with Peter and Cynthia. Afternoons she came out to the set by limo and either walked the ranch trails or rested in JayJay's trailer. Soon as they were done, they took off in his truck, the limo driver standing by his empty machine and watching their cloud of dust. They avoided Salton City, where word was out about JayJay Parsons and his upcoming talk. They explored the region, looping through dusty towns and miles of citrus groves and fields of asparagus and arti-chokes. The twisting highland roads left Cynthia queasy, so where possible they held to the valley floors. They ate when they grew tired of driving. Their talk was of life beyond the set, JayJay asking but never giving much. After he deflected their questions a few times, they stopped enquiring. Too close to him now to pry. Satisfied just to forget for a few hours that there was anything out there called Hollywood.

Saturday was the longest workday yet, longer even than the studio shoot. They started while sunrise was a faint eastern promise and worked long after night had taken control. The entire day was spent on the streets of Salton City, doing the setup for Monday's assembly. JayJay worked against a variety of add-ons, actors whose single lines of dialogue were listed in the script under names like "First Developer," "Second Mexican Farmer," "Shopkeeper's Wife." Everywhere they went, they stopped traffic. The crowds were a problem until Britt hired the Ford salesman named Piston to call for silence before each take. Piston had a hog-caller's yell that halted traffic on the interstate. The locals minded him far better than they did Kip.

They had taken over the Main Street Diner as a location center. Deep into a grueling sunset scene, Britt drew JayJay into the diner's back room. "How are you holding up?"

JayJay collapsed into a seat, too tired even to complain when the makeup person started dabbing his forehead. "Wore plumb to a nub."

"I want you to see something."

Derek hit a switch. JayJay groaned. There before him was the same scene Britt had shown him in his suite. Wooden as a plug nickel. JayJay complained, "Why don't you just take me out back and shoot my sorry hide?"

"That was then," Britt said. He waited until Derek gave him the nod, and said, "This is now."

Tired as he was, JayJay came forward in his seat. There on the screen was a man he knew and yet didn't know. A man who wasn't fumbling through words that didn't fit inside his mouth. Instead, he saw a local rancher. A man weary and dusty from just another day with too many chores and too few hours. Talking to his neighbors and his friends. Sharing their woes. A man doing his best. Which wasn't enough to solve the problems they faced. But they faced the problems *together*. JayJay didn't need to say the words. It was there on the screen.

He was one of *them*.

When the screen went dark, Britt said, "You see?"

JayJay had not noticed Peter leaning against the back wall until then. "I wish you could know what it's like, seeing the images in my head come to life like that."

Britt said, "That is *acting*."

The makeup lady whispered, "I've got chills."

Britt said, "I want to shoot one more scene."

JayJay groaned.

"Hear me out. You've come into town, just doing your weekly run. You've wound up hearing the same story told from five different angles. How the town is worried and hurting and doesn't have any answers. How good things are dying before they ever get a chance to live."

JayJay said nothing.

"How the old ways are being lost. How people, *your* people, are adrift and confused. You didn't ask them to talk with you about their problems. But they've sought you out."

JayJay sat and stared at the empty screen.

Britt said, "We can do this another day if you like."

JayJay pushed himself from the chair. "I feel like a gunslinger facing down a wolf pack with one bullet left in his shooter."

Britt actually smiled. "That is *exactly* what I intend to capture."

When they were back outside, Britt continued with his instructions. "You don't want this new concern they're shoving at you. You wish the townspeople would just go away. But you've known these folks and this town all your life. They have come to you because you're one of them. They see in you what you don't want to see yourself."

JayJay stood in the center of Main Street. Traffic was diverted to roads on either side. Derek was to his right, next to the camera on the dolly, a little vehicle with rubber wheels and a collapsible carriage that could move soundlessly from ground level to four stories high. Carpenters had laid out a carpeted lane of wooden planks hooked together that would smooth the dolly's progress and keep the camera from jiggling as it tracked JayJay's walk down the road.

A second camera was next to JayJay, armed with a close-up lens long as a Winchester barrel. Derek checked through the camera viewfinder, then used his walkie-talkie to communicate with the electricians manning the lights. There must have been a couple hundred people packed behind the rope barriers, filling the sidewalks, forming a human half-moon behind them. But they were so quiet JayJay could hear the electricians thumping on the lights with their little rubber mallets, readjusting the aim.

Britt said, "You are going to do the toughest thing an actor ever faces. You are going to communicate the tumult and the confusion and the fear. And you are going to do so without ever opening your mouth."

There were a couple of police officers on crowd-control duty. But they had nothing to do. Children stood at the front of the crowd, but they were as quiet and still as their parents. Somewhere in the distance a bird chirped. Derek's walkie-talkie crackled. A carpenter whacked a final hook of Derek's carpeted lane into place.

"You are going to walk down this road. Up ahead is your enemy." Britt's gesture took in the dark and empty street. "It's not just the night, though, is it."

"No."

"Don't tell me, JayJay. This isn't about telling. *Show* me you understand. *Show* me you see the enemy there inside yourself. Attacking now at your weakest. When you're not just tired. You're terrified. You're afraid of failing. Afraid of letting these people down. Afraid they'll see you for what you know you are."

"Afraid of all the mysteries," JayJay muttered.

This time Britt did not contradict. "These people believe you are the one to help them. The one with answers. But you know all the faults you carry. All the mysteries. All the doubts and questions without answers. They think you are *real*. But you know better."

JayJay nodded slowly. Oh yes. He knew.

Britt let him study the empty road ahead. Giving him enough time to get so totally locked into the moment that all the people vanished. And the lights and the cameras. Until it all focused down to the choice.

"What are you going to do, JayJay? What decision are you going to make?"

JayJay did not look at him. It wasn't about Britt anymore. Or the night. It was just him.

"All right. Now go out there and show me what you've decided to do, and who you are going to be. For these people, and for yourself."

Sunday was just another working day for about half the crew. They were busy turning a derelict dance hall into a civic center, their gift to the community in lieu of actually paying the extras—an idea hammered out between the mayor and Britt. At dawn JayJay held an abbreviated prayer time for those who were on duty—the set designers, carpenters, electricians, and camera crew. Cynthia was there, Peter was absent. Kelly was still away. For once, JayJay welcomed yesterday's residual fatigue. Being so tired made it easier to face having lost a good woman before the connection ever took hold.

He went back to his room and dozed for a couple more hours, then accompanied Cynthia to church. It was a modern facility built with a hometown flavor—stone walls, redwood beams, painted Mexican tiles for decorative artwork. JayJay sort of floated through the service, there but far away. Still coming to terms with the previous day—and what lay ahead. The next afternoon he was scheduled to address the town.

Peter and the mayor found him after the service was over. Miller wore his customary grin. "How's your new ride?"

"Makes getting out of bed worthwhile," JayJay said.

"Had a bunch of folks come by, asking me why that actor feller is out tooling around town in my boy's truck."

"I hope you'll excuse me for saying this. But your son needs a serious reality check, letting that truck go."

"That ain't no newsbreak." He pulled JayJay to one side. "I got a favor to ask."

Peter said, "I thought you wanted me to handle this."

"Yeah, I was gonna play the plucked chicken, but then I saw his face light up when I asked about his new toy. And I figured I was good for one more request."

"Name it," JayJay agreed.

"We're starting a Habitat for Humanity drive. The aim is to build two hundred houses by year's end. Biggest welfare project this town's seen since the Depression days. We just got to get those migrant kids into places with proper floors and running water. Those plastic hovels are nothing but a stain on our Christian walk, and that's the truth."

"You'll be speaking about this tomorrow," Peter reminded him. "It's in your speech."

Miller went on, "Sacramento and the federal government are paying two-thirds of the total. The rest is coming through local volunteer work and donations. Today's the official kickoff."

"I heard the pastor mention something about it."

"Yeah, they're playing it up all over town. We been promised TV coverage, papers from as far away as Oakland."

JayJay finally caught their drift. He asked Peter, "Does Britt know about this?"

"Not yet. Miller called me early this morning out of the blue."

"Just popped up in the middle of the night," Miller agreed. "Like a mushroom in a manure pile."

Cynthia said, "You might want to reconsider your comparison there."

"What I'm trying to say is, we want you to come out and cut the ribbon on this new building project. Say a few words."

Peter said, "I've written something you might want to use."

JayJay said, "Derek's out there right now, isn't he? Getting his stuff in everybody's way. Turning this into a regular three-ring circus."

"Ain't no flies on this cowboy," Miller confirmed. "What do you say, hoss?"

"The only way I'll do this thing is if I really work. I'm not gonna have people saying I showed up to use a pair of silver scissors and then disappeared."

Miller actually laughed. "Pardner, I wouldn't have it any other way."

Monday morning JayJay started off in a fog. He had slept poorly, chased all night by the previous afternoon's images. Cutting the ribbon and saying his few lines had gone well enough for Britt to close after just three takes. But instead of letting him work alongside the others, Britt had come up with the idea of them taking a drive through the shanty camp. Bean Town, the locals called it. Sombrero Flats. Tacoville. The names were like blisters on JayJay's brain. The road was a dusty rutted track that crawled through a stretch of pure misery. They took Miller's SUV. Britt had JayJay squint out the open window, scorched not by the sun or the grit so much as the little faces he passed. Britt preceded them in a flatbed with Derek clinging to the back, filming as they went. All night JayJay's brain replayed the trip like he was watching those kids on his own personal theater screen. A nightmare of dust and desolation.

Four cups of coffee, a plate of scrambled eggs, and a rambling prayer for the kids and their parents left JayJay feeling like he just might make it through what would no doubt be a major day. He drove Peter and Cynthia straight from the prayer meeting to the ranch. The two bearded giants and Derek and a lighting guy and a pair of set carpenters filled the truck bed. When he pulled into the parking area and found Britt there waiting for him, JayJay said, "I feel like finding me a nice spot away from this racket and sleeping until oh-dark-thirty."

Britt just turned around and said, "All of you, inside."

The cabin's interior was undergoing serious renovation. Britt had proclaimed he liked the atmosphere that was building on location enough to shoot the interior scenes here as well. But this morning it was tools down, and an assembly of maybe two dozen people formed a half-circle in front of a podium. JayJay halted midway through the front door and said, "Uh-uh. No way."

"Just listen to me a second."

"Why don't you just paint a target on my belly and give 'em all a load of darts?"

"That's an idea. Derek, make a note. JayJay, front and center."

JayJay looked at the hold Britt had on his forearm. "What exactly did I do to get you this riled?"

Britt led him up to the podium. "Look down at your feet, JayJay. Four yellow marks. Each with a number. One, two, three, four. Same as on your talk. See where I've labeled the script? Big blue numbers. Even a cowboy like you can see numbers that big."

"You're enjoying this."

"Just listen to me. Tonight you're going to stand in front of as many locals as that hall can hold. How many people did we figure on, Derek?"

"Eleven hundred, maybe twelve if they stand in the loft."

"Twelve hundred people. Coughing, hacking, kids crying. It's going to be hot and stinky. They're going to be there for a party. The cameras will play this serious. But you've never worked with extras. I have. And I'm telling you, when you hit the big climax, some joker in the second row is going to be drilling in his nose like he's looking for oil. A small-town rebel will scratch himself and yawn 'til his jaws pop. Three teenage girls on the front row will have a giggle fit and do their best to distract you. We're going to shoot maybe ten takes. They'll be squirming like worms in rayon and hiking boots."

"I'm glad you're telling me all this," JayJay snapped back. "Seeing as how I wasn't the tiniest bit worried about it before now."

Britt said, "What we're going to do here is work you. These people have been ordered to get up and go have a cup of coffee and a doughnut and a stretch in the kitchen over there. And then saunter back in here and sit down. Lean against the walls. Do whatever they want, long as they don't make noise."

"They're gonna hate me."

"Not a chance. I'm *paying* them for this. Work has stopped on the set so you can get used to giving emotion to an audience that doesn't much care what you've got to say. Derek is going to light it. We might even film a couple of takes, in case we have to splice in a word or erase somebody's belch. Which means your little audition is costing the studio somewhere in the neighborhood of six thousand dollars an hour. Do you get my drift, JayJay? Tonight's scene is *pivotal*. Right, Peter?"

From the back wall, the scriptwriter confirmed, "You'll be declaring who you are. To the town and the audience."

JayJay had the sense to understand Britt wasn't talking just to him. He had set this up so that the audience would hear and understand the stakes. JayJay studied the director. The weary stains beneath Britt's eyes grew deeper with every passing day. He wore an old Air Jamaica T-shirt and baggy khakis, boat shoes and no socks. A man far too busy and weighed down to care what came up first in his pile of clean clothes.

Britt said, "In theater parlance it's called the star's soliloquy, JayJay. We'll be moving into act two and hopefully taking the audience with us. All because of what you've got to say."

# Chapter 32

---

The word Martin Allerby liked best to describe the Hollywood spots was *seasonal*. Being Hollywood, he was not referring to a period measured in months. After all, when it came to weather Southern California had only two real seasons—rain and smaze. No, by "seasonal" Allerby meant that either a player was powerful enough to hit the right spot at the right time, or they joined the cattle call of wannabes.

The Polo Lounge at the rear of the Beverly Hills Hotel was a perfect case in point. Since the extensive renovations of several years back, the place had resumed its position as the premier watering hole for behind-the-camera players. Writers, producers, studio execs, directors, senior agents, they *owned* this spot.

But the allure lasted only from twelve thirty to two. Ninety minutes. Which, given the nature of the game they were all playing, held an ironic ring.

During the lunch rush, tables were allotted according to power. The darker booths along the wall leading from the bar to the main restaurant were restricted to serious power. Allerby had spotted three other greenlight guys when he arrived. But Allerby was showing up as they were leaving. Which meant his booth had remained *empty* during the entire lunch crush. The vacuum had drawn gazes from all over the hotel. To have the power to book a *booth*, and know the maître d' would hold it until whenever, that was some serious juice.

His two guests arrived fifteen minutes after he had slid into the booth, long enough for Allerby to greet those he cared to notice, order, and return a couple of calls. Milo Keplar showed up first. The studio's director of sales knew Allerby well enough not to question his timing. Then Leo Gish arrived. Before the man arrived at the booth, Martin knew his plan was playing out exactly as desired.

Gish was so taken with the scenery he got his legs wrapped around his briefcase and almost landed face-first on the marble floor. Except the maître d', who was accustomed to first-timers dropping their glasses or teeth and tripping over their tongues, was there to steer him into the booth.

And it wasn't the potted palms and matching mint-green drapes that captured the lawyer's eye.

During the lunch crush, flocks of would-be starlets chirruped inside the hotel lobby. They pretended to indulge in conversations deep as their respective cleavages. They tossed heat-seeking gazes in the direction of power players coming and going. They bribed whomever they could with whatever they had to take the first empty booth. They made their stroll behind the maître d' a version of the Gucci catwalk. They took it slow, they drew every light in the room, and they *shone*. As the power guys gradually departed for the set or the office or the next viewing, the place became packed a second time. Every emptied table instantly refilled. They toyed with coffees or mineral waters, all most of them could afford. They regaled one another with tales of other wannabes who had found their big break crossing the Polo Lounge. Soon as they were certain the last power guy was gone, they flittered away, migrating to the next watering hole.

Seasonal.

Leo Gish punched his chest like he needed to kick-start his heart. "Are you *believing* this?"

The collection of beauty was overwhelming. America's finest, youngest, fittest, most perfect specimens of feminine allure. Table after booth after bar stool. Models, beauty queens, actresses one chance away from the big time. Anywhere else, each one of them would have stopped traffic. Here, they were just background.

Hollywood.

As though on cue, a svelte brunette with a perfect patina of freckles across her cheeks waltzed over. She had eyes of cobalt blue, a spray-painted dress, and lips ready to cry with delight. Leo Gish made a choking sound when he realized she was taking aim for them. "Mr. Allerby? I'm Hannon Hartley, you won't remember me, but we were introduced when I had a part in—"

"*Doctor's Orders*. Of course. The baby nurse. How are you?"

She beamed with the delight of being remembered. "A lot better *now*, Mr. Allerby."

"Meet my guests. Milo Keplar, our director of sales. And Leo Gish"— he hesitated a fraction for emphasis—"our newest member of the Centurion board."

He could not believe it. The girl actually shivered. Martin would have laughed out loud, were it not for the effect she was having on Leo. "*Congratulations*, Mr. Gish. That is so *awesome*. And Mr. Keplar, I've heard about you for years. This is *such* a pleasure. I can't tell you."

"We're in the process of planning a new series. Why don't you give Casting a call. Tell them I said to have you in for a test."

For an instant he feared he had overplayed it, that she was going to actually crawl into the booth with them. "*Wow*, Mr. Allerby, I don't know *what* to say."

"Thanks for stopping by, Hannon."

Only when she had returned to her table did Leo return from his fantasy trance. "How can you stand this?"

Milo answered for them both. "It's like a buffet, Leo. Mildly interesting, long as you don't overindulge. Then it becomes a distraction and gives you heartburn."

Allerby carefully refolded his napkin and set it aside. "I thought this would be a good place to let you in on our little secret, Leo. First, you have to understand this is strictly confidential. You, Milo, myself, and our secret investor. Those are the only players in the know."

Leo forced his gaze away from the playing field. "What is it?"

"Centurion's first new series, tied from the outset to a major feature." Allerby outlined their plan for the new reality show, *Vegas Strippers.*

Milo took over when Allerby finished. "We could cast the whole thing right here, wouldn't you say, Leo? And as an active member of the Centurion board, you'd have serious sway over any such decisions."

Allerby let him digest that for a moment, then turned up the flame. "What we need to know is, when are we closing?"

"Carter Dawes has had the documents for five days. I've phoned the ranch every morning, as per his instructions. That desiccated man-servant of his keeps telling me to call back."

Carter Dawes lived on a ranch in the Ojai Valley, one Martin had seen only through stills taken by his PI. Dawes had never invited him out. Which rankled only mildly. Martin had no interest in Ojai except for all the viewers hooked to the small screen. Martin knew about Dawes' manservant, however. Since his wife had died five years back, Dawes had used the old rancher as driver, butler, and cook. The two old men lived out there alone. Martin had been rebuffed by the taciturn rancher so often he had stopped calling.

"Leo, look at me." When the attorney reluctantly turned his attention back the table, Martin revealed a bit more of the flame. "Do I need to tell you how easy it is for a deal like this one to go south?"

"What do you want from me?" The guy actually whined. "I can't sign the documents myself."

"It's taken us five years to get this far. We've finally gotten the investors lined up. But this won't keep. We have a project that could turn on us at any minute. A thousand things could go wrong." Allerby got in close. Gave him a taste of the rage he had been banking up for the past seven days and seven sleepless nights. "We are *inches* from losing *everything.*"

Gish was sweating badly. "I'm his attorney, not his boss."

"I don't care what you have to do. I don't care who you have to *murder*. I want you to get out there and *close this deal.*"

Milo slid from the booth and turned into a silent menace who gripped Leo's elbow and tugged. Allerby said, "Get out there and do what you're being paid for."

Leo either rose from the table or lost connection to his arm. He clutched his briefcase to his chest. "Come on, guys."

Allerby planted his elbow on the table and took careful aim. "Hollywood lives by its own laws, Leo. You know laws, right? Here's one you better remember. There are no second chances in this town. Now *bring me closure.*"

When they were alone, Allerby signaled the waiter. The kid was a match for any of the female lovelies on display at the tables. "Yes sir, Mr. Allerby?"

"A double Gibson. I want it so cold it goes down like diesel."

"You got it. Mr. Keplar?"

Neither man questioned how the kid knew who they were. "Same."

"It'll be a pleasure."

Milo asked quietly, "So what's new?"

"I spoke to both our investors this morning. And the bank. The funds are in place."

"So everything is cool."

"For now."

Milo waited while the kid deposited their drinks. "And the film?"

"They're reshooting all of last week's scenes. Britt refused point-blank to send the dailies." Martin sipped his drink. "My source tells me several trysts have disrupted things."

Those who dined on gossip feasted well in Hollywood. "So tell."

"Friday night one of the bit actors, down to play a dopey deputy, a role he was apparently born for, decided to show the chief roadie he wasn't all that tough. The Salton police claim it set a new record for the world's quickest fight. Then on Saturday two teenage daughters of a local restaurateur were caught sharing favors with the assistant set designer, who apparently had promised them starring roles. That fight took longer to unravel, and cost us the only designer with any film experience whatsoever."

Milo inspected his partner's face. "What aren't you telling me?"

"There is nothing I know of to cause us any alarm," Martin said carefully. "What about from your end?"

"We've got a bidding war on our hands. Filmbox and Movietime both want *Strippers* so bad they're salivating."

"They can't leak this."

"It's just me and my one guy in each place. Both want points in the feature. They're ready to write me a check tomorrow." When Allerby's only response was to sip from his glass, Milo demanded, "I thought you'd be doing a hula over that news."

Martin sipped again. The glass was so cold it threatened to stick to his fingers. He felt the oily liquid slide down his throat. "They've started a prayer group."

Milo stopped in the process of lifting his glass. "What, like a church thing?"

"In the hotel. A Bible reading and then a time of prayer. Every morning, apparently. Stars, techies, gaffers, anybody on the set who wants to join in." Martin drained his glass, set it down, and tinged the edge as the waiter passed. "I'm getting daily figures. Seventeen, eighteen, occasionally two dozen."

"About half the crew." Milo finished his drink and motioned for a refill. "That's right, isn't it?"

"Close enough. There's more. Apparently our star has given up both his suite and his trailer. To the writer. Whose wife is heavily pregnant. The only demands our replacement JayJay has made thus far were for his limo to go fetch Cynthia. That's the writer's wife. And for our trusty AD to arrange for a specialist to be on round-the-clock call for this lady. Who does not, I hasten to add, have any connection whatsoever to the star in question."

"It doesn't make him a decent actor, right? I mean, we still have a totally inexperienced crew making a film without a script."

"Yes." Martin nodded his thanks as the waiter returned in light speed with their drinks. "I quite agree."

Milo took his glass like medicine. "So why do I feel the worms gnawing at my gut?"

Martin shook his head. "Perhaps mine are contagious. I have no other explanation."

# Chapter 33

The first indication they had of any problem was when they tried to make the turn onto Main Street and couldn't.

They made quite a convoy. Britt was in the truck with JayJay because, as Britt put it, he wanted to see what it was like to ride in a cherry-red rocket launcher. Claire sat between them, her place awarded because of her role as JayJay's coach. The grips and electricians had claimed the truck bed and padded the back with some old Indian blankets.

At three that afternoon they had returned to the hotel for a rest. Over an early catered Mexican dinner, Britt told the crew that everybody not working the set could do what they wanted with the rest of their day. Apparently what all of the prayer group and a number of the others wanted was to come watch.

Two limos and a trio of taxis followed JayJay's truck from the hotel parking lot. The truck was silent during the ride except for one remark from Britt, which was, "Peter's told me about Kelly singing for you."

"For me and a passel of others."

"Strange she wouldn't put it on her fact sheet." Both windows were open, and the late-afternoon breeze was a wash of heat and orchard flavors. "Most actors use their fact sheets like rubber bands. As in, runner-up in the local Miss Car Wash pageant becomes a finalist at Miss Universe."

"Which means two things from where I'm sitting. One, she won't sing for you unless it's her kind of music. Which is Christian with a bluesy-rock-jazz edge."

Britt humphed a little bounce in his seat, but said nothing.

"And two, when she finds out I'm the one who talked, she's gonna come armed for bear."

Claire offered, "I've got this little thirty-eight, you can sleep with it under your pillow if it'll make you feel better."

JayJay tried to keep his voice calm as he added, "Speaking of the lady, do you know how she's doing?"

"The limo's supposed to have taken her straight from LAX to back-stage," Britt replied to his window. "You can ask her yourself."

But when they arrived at the intersection of the rural highway and Main, the road just froze up. Ahead of them was a solid wall of people.

Britt leaned forward and said, "Is this a joke?"

Kip emerged from the edge of the crowd, so frantic he almost skipped toward the truck.

When he arrived panting beside Britt's window, the director demanded, "Why aren't they inside? You were supposed to get them settled and—"

"They *are* inside!" Kip's wave took in the intersection, the sunset, the buildings, the whole dusty world. "The hall's been full for an *hour*. They just keep *coming*."

Up ahead, Derek pushed through the crowd that had now turned to look their way. He called out behind him then jogged to the truck. He climbed onto JayJay's running board and said breathlessly, "You might as well park here and walk."

Britt was not smiling. "Do we have a problem here?"

Up ahead of them, the mayor of Salton City wriggled through the crowd, patting backs and shouting howdy's. He came over, climbed onto JayJay's running board beside Derek, and poked a sweating face into the cab. "I ain't seen this many people since Salton High played Fresno for the state finals!"

Claire asked, "Are we safe?"

Miller Whitley's laugh boomed inside the cab. "They're pretty calm now, little lady. But I reckon one bolt from the blue and you'd see a stampede to carry home and tell your grandchildren about."

Kip whined, "I can't *handle* them!"

"Don't you worry none," Miller replied. "We've deputized every deacon in three counties. The sheriff's got the whole place locked down. They're turning away everybody trying to slip in under the wire."

Even Britt could not hide his surprise. "You mean there's *more?*"

"There would be if we let 'em in." Miller beamed as he punched JayJay's shoulder. "What can I tell you, hoss. This here is JayJay Parsons country."

Though Kip had no more substance than a brilliant butterfly, he forged a path through the crowd with the force of voice and will alone. JayJay walked in the middle of his own throng like a prizefighter headed for the ring. He heard Miller ask the director, "Wherever did you find that squirt of yours?"

"They sort of spawn around Hollywood," Britt replied. "Kip has his uses."

"I heard them environmental yo-yos say the same thing about cottonmouths," Miller replied. "It don't mean I'd give one a job."

The crowd was remarkably silent and well behaved. A few people, mostly young and female, tried to offer JayJay bits of paper and pens. He let his group's general movement sweep him along. He did not look away from, or directly at, anyone.

Miller stopped when they reached the stairs leading to the hall's rear access. "Might be a good idea if you said something."

"Sure." Britt had an actor's ability to draw attention. He did not shout, but his voice carried well. "My name is Britt Turner, director of *Heartland*. I guess it goes without saying we weren't expecting quite so many people. But we're glad you're here. I think what we'll try and do is shift out the crowd that is inside now after a couple of takes. Does everybody understand that term? We are going to shoot a number of takes of a crucial scene tonight, or at least, we're going to try. My assistant, Kip Denderhoff, where are you, Kip?"

Miller said, "I believe I seen him riding a westbound train for the coast."

When the laughter died, Kip called from the front porch, "Here!"

"Okay. Kip will explain how the take needs to run, and what we'd like you folks to do. I guess that's all, except to thank you for coming."

Miller called out, "Couple more things. The churches at either end of Main are opening their doors and brewing coffee. The diners and the bakery are all open. And we're stringing church speakers out here so you folks can listen to what's going on inside."

As they headed for the rear entrance, JayJay asked the mayor, "Who did you tell?"

"Aw, nobody you'd know. Word just kinda spread."

JayJay was kept from pressing further by the sight of a tawny head of hair crowning a woman whose beauty drew light and attention from all through the back room. He marched straight over and said to the makeup lady working on her face, "Give us a minute, please."

"Sure, JayJay."

Kelly did not object as he led her to as remote a corner as he could find. "I've missed you, Kelly."

She was tight. Subdued. "I shouldn't be here at all."

"I was sorry to hear about your grandmother. How is she?"

"Not good. She's eighty-one and she's independent and she's stubborn. She hated the idea of live-in help. Ran off the nurses we brought in. Refused to move into our home." Kelly scanned the room, searching everywhere but in his direction. "Momma found her lying on the kitchen floor, she'd broken her hip. We can't even say how long she'd been down. But we think all night."

He made fists by his sides to keep from reaching over and taking hold. This was not the place or the sort of lady who'd accept an embrace she hadn't asked for. "I can't tell you how sorry—"

"Grandma's gone all addled. The doctors say it's normal for somebody her age who's had a bad spell." Kelly bit her lip to stop the tremble. "They don't think she's going to get better."

"Oh, Kelly."

"She didn't remember me, JayJay. She basically raised me. My second momma. And here I am, playing games for the camera while she's alone up there. And I don't know how many days I've got left with her."

JayJay tried to hear what she was saying and not just what his heart was telling him. Which was, the lady had moved on and hadn't taken him with her.

"But Daddy said I'd made promises and I needed to keep them. Which is the only reason I came back." Kelly focused on someone behind him. "Guess it's time to get started."

Britt stepped into their midst. "Kelly, you okay?"

"I'm here."

"Well, I'm sorry for your troubles. But we're under pressure and we need to play this like the pros we are. Right?" He took their silence as accord. "Derek wants to situate you out in the crowd now. He needs to light your seat. Wait, I want to run through this since you missed my talk earlier on. This scene isn't just about JayJay swaying the crowd. You are going to hear him, and you are going to *change*. He is going to affect you *very deeply*. Can you handle that?"

Her hesitation was as hard a blow as any JayJay had ever felt. Finally she responded with a very tiny, "Yes."

"We need to see this change in your expression long before you stand up and deliver your line. Okay. Let's go get you settled."

JayJay had a jumble of words and thoughts that welled up as Kelly turned away. Which was why he said nothing at her departure.

He stood there staring at the empty space until a voice beside him said, "What I'd give for a guy like you to miss me like you're missing her."

JayJay faced Claire and confessed, "I've blown it wide open."

"Maybe not."

"I had my chance and lost it on worrying over things I can't control."

"Yeah, I know that song too. Woulda, coulda, shoulda." Claire did not even try for a smile. "But you remember why we're all here?"

He pretty much sighed the words, "I ain't got it in me."

"That's where you're wrong. Remember what we've been talking about? Search your core, find what it is you've got boiling inside, and *use* it. Sometimes it doesn't matter what's churning inside your gut, so long as it's *strong*." She gave that a minute, then, "I've been in this business a long time, JayJay. And I know what I'm talking about when I say, whatever it is that makes for a pro, you've got it in spades."

JayJay really looked at her for the first time. Saw the pain. The lonely hours. And something more. A new light. A calm that had not been there before. "You're a real friend."

Claire tasted a smile. "I guess that will have to do."

Miller was waiting when he turned around. "Thought maybe we should have us a time of prayer."

JayJay did not recognize most of the people in the room. Peter was there. Derek had slipped in and was standing by the door leading to the stage. His two tame grips. Miller. Claire. The other four men and three women were strangers. Not that it mattered. "Sounds good."

"Folks, I'd like you to meet John Junior. JayJay, these are friends. Guess that's about all you need to know right now." Miller said to the room, "Let's go to the Lord.

"Father, we're just so in awe of what You can do when we let You in. Bringing us all here together, setting this man up for our message to get out, why, it's a miracle in action is what it is. And we're grateful. We're scared, we're worried about the future of our towns and our valley. But we're grateful too. Because like the Good Book says, we trust that You have given us the victory. So be with our brother here tonight. Arm him with Your wisdom and Your message. Make him the hero we need to have here. In Christ's holy name do we pray, amen."

JayJay lifted his head to discover that Britt had slipped in and was standing beside Derek. Britt motioned to the makeup lady, who had never set foot in one of their morning sessions and now looked about as out of place as a cat in a cage of wolfhounds. Britt watched her retouch the work she'd done on JayJay's face before they left the hotel, and asked, "Claire speak with you?"

Claire said, "JayJay Parsons is going to do just fine tonight."

Britt nodded and said to her, "Derek's got you a spot marked out."

Claire patted JayJay's arm as she passed and said, "I'll tell you what I'm seeing here, JayJay. You have the whole world just waiting to be on your side."

Britt thoughtfully watched her depart, then said, "Miller suggested this group of leaders should be onstage with you. I like the idea. But it means people seated behind you where you can't see them. If they're up there, you'll need at some point to turn and address them too. We haven't practiced that."

Miller said, "Couple of the mayors from up and down the valley, a county commissioner, some pastors. Just your basic posse."

Britt kept his gaze on JayJay. "It's your call."

JayJay was glad to hear his voice remain steady. "Can't hardly tell prayer partners to go away, can I."

"Derek, get them settled and check the background lighting."

"Sure thing."

Britt held back as the others filed out. The door was open now, which meant they could stare across the stage and through the open curtains and out over the massed audience. Britt said, "I've been in this business a long time. I thought I'd seen it all. A star backstage, with the camera ready and the pressure on, basically they get whatever they want. A director learns to ignore whatever it takes to get them turned on and shining bright. The drugs, the booze, the sex, it's all just part of the business. When I heard about this prayer group of yours, I figured, okay, it's just one more for the books. But now . . . ."

For the first time since seeing Kelly, JayJay felt the clouds part.

Britt kept talking softly to the crowd and the stage and the waiting podium. "In all my years in this trade, I've never . . . The work we're getting in the can is solid. We're ahead of schedule and under budget. All without a finished script. Shot by a DP who's never directed filming. And a star who's never seen the business end of a camera." He shook his head. "I don't know. This is . . ."

JayJay supplied quietly, "A miracle."

Britt just kept staring out over the crowd.

JayJay said, "You'd be welcome to join us some morning."

Britt let the words rest there between them for a moment. Then he turned and looked at JayJay. "You ready?"

JayJay replied, "I am now."

The bombshell came midway through the second take and caught them all unawares.

There had been minor surprises from the very beginning. JayJay walked out and did exactly as Britt had scripted, which was to approach the podium, blow on the mike, and say, "I'm JayJay Parsons and I'm not running for anything."

And a woman's voice called out from somewhere far back, "Honey, you got my vote anyway."

Which was not scripted anywhere JayJay had seen.

Afterward Britt assured them all he had not set that up.

The morning practice had been grueling. But it gave him the space to be two people. The man who worked through the scripted actions with a slow and steady ease. And the man who reached into the cauldron located between his gut and his wounded heart and pulled out the acid. And put it to good use.

He set his hat on the table beside the water pitcher and the glass. He adjusted the mike, and he started, "This is my home. My valley. Y'all are the only kin my sister and I have. We *care* for this place, and for these people. *Our* people. *All* of them. And that's the problem. We've let outsiders come in here and split us up."

The audience was one massive wriggle. There were so many people the air felt compressed. Every kind of face stared back at him, every age. Mexicans, African-Americans, Asians, whites. Angry, eager, skeptical, squinting, smiling, frowning, yawning. Kids bounced on mothers' knees. Ropey-armed farmers prodded their neighbors and spoke behind leathery hands. Derek's lights pointed directly into his face, just as Britt had said they would, bathing his universe with a slightly yellowish tint.

"We've got developers who want our water and our land. And you know what's so awful about this? We're letting 'em do pretty much whatever they want. Why? Because we've forgotten what it's like to be a community. We've got the ranchers, and then there's the citrus growers, and the village shops, and the folks who've settled here over the past few years. All of us roped off and quarreling. Ready to go to war, only we don't know who with. One day it's the 'crats up in Sacramento. The next it's a rancher we reckon might be out to steal our water. The next, and, well, you know who comes next. Don't you?"

He turned around then. Doing what Britt said, which was to look at the semicircle behind him. But it just happened to come as two things occurred. A white-haired lady official started nodding. And not just with her head. With her entire upper body. Rocking back and forth, the motions causing her chair to squeak gently.

Two chairs over, Miller Whitley, the mayor of Salton City, glanced at the lady and then back at JayJay. And gave him a single tight nod.

JayJay held Miller's gaze for a longer time than he should have, gripped by the realization that for these people he wasn't just an actor and this wasn't just a stage.

When he turned back, he'd forgotten his place.

He stood there, frozen by the billion images and sensations, until Claire called from somewhere down to his right, "Say it, JayJay!"

It was all he needed. "Everybody who knows Clara knows I got to obey my older sister." Which got a laugh, and the laugh gave him time to remember where he was in the script. "The developers haven't divided us. They didn't need to. Why? Because we did it for them! We're *comfortable* with our arguing. We *like* pretending we're better than some of our neighbors."

JayJay stopped and took a sip. His hand trembled. But he wasn't scared. He just needed to stop his lips from sticking.

It was then he noticed the first change.

The audience had stopped moving.

The hall was wooden-framed and about seventy yards deep and forty wide. A big U of a balcony ran around the back, supported by wrought-iron pillars painted the same color as the walls. And the place was just packed. A thousand souls, fifteen hundred, the numbers meant nothing. What mattered was the stillness. Like they'd just stopped breathing. All of them. Even the kids.

They stayed that way right through to the end.

And beyond.

When JayJay finished, he stepped away from the microphone. The script said there was to be applause. But the folks out there apparently hadn't read the screenplay. They just stayed right where they were. Tight and quiet.

So JayJay went over to the one empty chair in the semicircle and sat down.

The rustling started then. But not much. Folks talked quietly among themselves. Britt rose from his place between the monitor station and Derek's camera and walked down the central aisle. He climbed the stairs and moved behind the microphone. "Okay, that was great. We're going to need about ten minutes to get ready for the next take. Anybody who's had enough, now's the time."

Nobody moved.

"Right. Fine." Britt started to turn away, then went back to the mike and said, "We're going to release a little smoke for effect. We're using an inert gas. Not much. Don't anybody get alarmed. We're trying to fil- ter the lights a little is all." He inspected the audience a moment longer, then said, "Kelly, all the others, this next time I want to move straight into your responses. No stop between takes. You all ready?"

There was a chorus of assent from the audience. JayJay tried to locate Kelly, but could not with the lights in his face.

"Derek, do what we discussed with the second camera. And get your steadicam ready."

His voice called from the back, "Got it!"

Britt moved to where JayJay was seated. "You okay?"

"Fine."

"Ready to go again?"

"Say the word."

"We can stop for a break." Britt spoke leaning over, his hands planted on his thighs. "But I'd say let's try for one more."

"Fine by me."

Britt said to the mayor, "I'm having our electricians check the out- side speakers. I'm not sure we'll want to try and shift this crowd and then gain this same feeling a second time."

"You're the man with the whistle." Miller cleared his throat. Said to JayJay, "Hoss, you gave me chills."

JayJay asked Britt, "Any word on how you want me to change the next take?"

Britt inspected him a moment, then said, "Can you see the audience?"

"Some. The lights—"

"Forget the lights. Can you *feel* what's happening in here?"

"I guess maybe I can."

"Good. That's what I want. For you to feel what you've done and do it again."

They left him alone. Somebody came over and handed him a cup of coffee. JayJay took a sip and set it down between his boots. The pastor who had delivered Sunday's sermon was seated on JayJay's other side. He opened his Bible and began reading. Just turning the pages and keeping his head down. The rustling paper had a calming effect. The makeup lady came over and did something to his face. JayJay let Derek draw him back to the mike and take a couple of light readings. Derek wore an earpiece attached to his walkie-talkie, so all JayJay heard was what Derek said, which was, "We're totally good to go at this end."

Britt did not even return to the front. He just called from the back of the room, "Okay, JayJay. We're rolling. Just move offstage and walk forward. Whenever you're ready."

But when JayJay was behind the curtain and about to make his entry, the pastor rose from his seat. The reverend approached the podium, bent the mike down a fraction, and said, "Brothers and sisters, I've felt the Spirit move this evening. And I want you to hear what the Spirit has said. Hear, now, the Word of our Lord." He opened his Book and said, "First Samuel, chapter nine, verse six. 'Look now, there is in this city a man of God, and he is an honorable man; all that he says surely comes to pass. So let us go there; perhaps he can show us the way that we should go.'"

JayJay walked out to another dose of silence. He dropped the opening comment. Instead, he adjusted the mike, took a breath, and launched straight in.

The speech read out at three minutes and eleven seconds. Which, according to Britt, came to something like nineteen years in film time. They were going to cut it down. A lot. Maybe transpose some of the words JayJay spoke here to other spots. Such as, show him in the barn working the horses, and feed in a voice-over. That was one idea. As though cowboys couldn't write unless it was on a feedbag with a worn pencil by lantern light with a horse looking on. Britt called it atmosphere. JayJay called it pretty silly. All these things came and went through his mind as he plowed through the talk a second time. He was concentrating, sure. But his mind was racing faster than a herd of spooked cattle. So he was thinking and he was wandering. Looking at how the sunset splashed through the side window. Noticing how Derek had gone to a paler light because of how the sunset was offering natural color. Looking back over his shoulder to see if the lady was still marking time with her upper body. She was.

Then it happened.

Somewhere out beyond the light's barrier, a voice called out, "Now you just hold on there a second."

JayJay faltered, as he could not recall having read any such line in the script. Or having a pause in the middle like that. He wondered if this was one of Britt's little surprises.

Then a spot swiveled over, and JayJay realized he had never seen the guy before.

The man had a shark's smile and a suit to match. Little string tie with a turquoise clasp. Voice that said he was used to being the center of attention. "Name's Whip Mitchum, with Triad Developers. You ask any of the farming families we've turned into millionaires. We're the best friends the San Joaquin Valley's ever had. Now are you going to sit here and listen while this outsider twists things around and—"

Then it was Kelly's turn. "Bub, you remind me of a man desperate to stop the river after the flood's done come and gone."

Which was her line, all right. But due to be said when the ruckus broke out after JayJay was done.

The developer made a serious mistake then. He redirected his smarmy smile in Kelly's direction and gave her lip. "Oh, I see they've planted a few more clowns out here among the *real* people."

"You want real?" Kelly was unique in her ability to make angry look fabulous. She said to the farmer seated next to her, "Mister, do us both a favor and get your feet out of my way. There's a gentleman over there in need of a good shaking."

"Don't bother yourself with this fool, ma'am." The spot shifted once more. This time it revealed a mountain of beard and overalls crowned with a John Deere cap. The stranger reached across the row and hefted the developer by his jacket shoulder. The developer gave a little "ack" as his collar was constricted, and his air with it. The stranger started down one aisle while the developer danced along the next. "My momma raised her boy to take out his own trash."

There was a smattering of applause. When attention turned back to the front, JayJay said the first thing that came to mind, which happened to be, "Looks to me like Elvis has left the building."

He worked his way to the end, finishing with a few words that were all his very own. He hadn't planned on it. But the moment just seemed to pick him up and carry him off. "We're all faced with the awful truth of not being strong enough or smart enough to handle what we're facing. We try to act our way through, pretending we don't have these holes in us big enough to hide Texas. Holes we can only fill one way. By joining together with our neighbors, united by what really matters."

"You tell 'em, JayJay." Kelly again.

JayJay saw the lines there in the back of his mind, the words Peter had written for him to finish on. But something else had taken hold and was pushing him now. What, exactly, he couldn't say, other than the *moment.* "Our community is like ourselves, too weak to last unless we unite in prayer and focus on what matters. Forget party lines and bloodlines and church lines. It ain't gonna stain you none to get along with folks who are different. We need to face up to what's real, a world we don't much understand that wants to rob us of what matters. We need to see what's precious about who we are and where we live, and make it last. Before it's too late and everything is gone. For our children's sake. For the sake of our own heritage. For a world that needs the values that make us who we are."

A voice from the balcony roared, "And all God's children said . . ."

"*Amen!*" There was no telling how many people responded. Or how long they applauded. Before JayJay could head back for his chair, the mayor and the pastor walked up and pounded him on the back and shook his hand. Said things that were lost to the clamor. Then they walked back and seated themselves. Leaving him where he was.

When he turned back around, he spied another man in a suit standing up near the front. JayJay recognized one of the bit players brought in for the scene. Only his lines had effectively been stolen by the real developer. He was midway into turning toward the crowd when a woman shouted, "Mister, don't you dare!"

# Chapter 34

Kelly was there at the edge of the crowd who had clambered up onto the stage. JayJay had no idea if Britt was still filming. He no longer cared. They had worked through two more takes, when the crowd had basically declared they were done. Afterward JayJay shook hands and smiled at words he could not hear.

Kelly still wore the strained expression as she pointed him toward the room behind the stage.

He worked his way through the mass as quickly as he could. He had no idea what he was going to say to her, only that he was going to give it his best. But when he made it into the back room, she gave him a look strong as two hands pushing against his chest. Telling him an approach even in words was most definitely not welcome.

The back room was almost as full as out front. The officials were eager to draw JayJay into their chatter. He was polite but firm, telling them he needed to go do something else now. Finally he managed to draw Kelly to one side.

She told him, "That was real nice, what you said out there."

"I meant it."

"I could tell. So could a lot of others." She turned him so his back was to the room and whoever was approaching. "This isn't the right time. But I want to say I'm sorry for not getting in touch while I was back home."

"No. It was me. I acted like a purebred fool back before you left. That ride, up through the hills that day, well, I don't have any more answers now than when I went out. But I guess maybe I've gotten to where I can live with not knowing."

"I'm glad."

She looked so sad JayJay blurted it out right there, surrounded by a roomful of strangers. "Lady, have I blown what chance I ever had with you?"

Kelly bit her lip, hesitated, then said, "I need to ask a favor."

"If it'll put me back in your good graces, you got yourself a deal."

She pointed toward the door. "I need you to come have a word with somebody."

The crowd filling the street applauded as he accompanied Kelly down the back stairs. He didn't want to be impolite, but he wasn't interested in anything right then but following this lady through a lingering sunset. Then the diminutive AD arrived at his side. "Britt wants—"

"Not now," JayJay said.

"JayJay, the director wants to speak—"

JayJay gave him a ten-second blast from beneath his brows. Enough to stop the next tirade dead in its tracks. "Tomorrow."

He followed Kelly into the Main Street Diner. The two back booths had been reserved by a rope tied across the narrow passage. A woman waited in the rear booth. There was no question who she was. Long before Kelly slid in beside the woman who shared her looks and her stature, JayJay knew.

"John Junior, this is my mother, Edith Channing."

"How do, Mrs. Channing."

"Thank you for asking, Mr. Junior." She managed to turn the booth into her personal throne. She was not haughty so much as naturally dignified. And cold. She froze the air between them. "Please, won't you have a seat."

The waitress appeared at JayJay's elbow and said, "You look like a man in need of a slice of coconut cream pie."

"Coffee will do me good, thank you, ma'am."

"I'll have the same," Kelly said.

Edith Channing said, "Nothing more for me, thank you kindly."

The waitress returned instantly with mugs and a pot. She said as she poured, "I stepped outside and listened to what you had to say. Wish it'd come long before now. But it got said and folks listened. I reckon that's the most important thing." She gave a friendly nod. "I'll make sure nobody disturbs you folks."

"I had the opportunity to hear you as well, Mr. Junior." Kelly's mother wore a short-sleeved sweater set of summer-weight cashmere and a thin string of pearls. Every inch a lady. "You certainly can act up a storm."

JayJay sipped his coffee. "From where I'm sitting, I'm not certain that's a compliment in your book, ma'am."

"I'm curious, Mr. Junior. How much of what you said tonight was your own?"

"A few of the words there at the end, is all. Mostly I just gave another man's work the best I could."

"How interesting. You asked how I was. The answer is, concerned. My husband and I are very concerned about our daughter. Concerned enough that I would leave my mother-in-law's bedside to come down and see things for myself."

"I'm very sorry to hear about the lady's distress, ma'am."

"Thank you for the kind sentiment." She spoke with the silky musicality of the Deep South, but there was no mistaking the frigid edge. "Kelly is our only child, Mr. Junior. And I must explain to you why we are so concerned. You see, my daughter lives for her obsessions. She is now obsessed with this acting business. And it appears she is becoming obsessed with you as well."

JayJay's first response to the news was to leap from the booth and do a jig right through the diner. But there was no room in Mrs. Channing's frigid attitude for joy. Or even a grin of relief.

"My daughter's last male obsession broke her heart and almost destroyed her. I assume she has shared with you the episode that took her to Hollywood?"

"The friend whose role she took in the TV drama," JayJay offered.

"How remarkable. You listen and you remember. Yes, Mr. Junior. The reason Kelly did not notice her friend had gone months without calling was because her life had been shattered by this last male obsession. He was a horrid man. He devoured what he wished of her and left her a hollow gourd."

"Point him out," JayJay said. "I'll shoot him for you."

"That will not be necessary, Mr. Junior."

"I'd be grateful if you'd call me JayJay, ma'am."

"It would be a waste of a perfectly good bullet, Mr. Junior. The man is gone. The damage is done. My task as Kelly's mother is to make sure it does not happen again."

"Don't mind Momma," Kelly said softly. "Southern ladies are brought up to mistake character assassination as polite conversation."

Mrs. Channing chose to ignore her daughter's words. "When my husband heard Kelly intended to tarry in California and continue with this vile craft, he offered her three bits of advice. I made do with just one, Mr. Junior. 'Do not,' I told my only daughter, 'do not under any circumstances fall in love with anyone in this trade.' Do you know why I said what I did?"

"Probably because you're a very smart lady."

"How kind of you to say so. I told my daughter that because such people are paid to lie. They are paid to exhibit emotions that are not their own. They make believe all day and all night. They feign interest. They live a constant myth of their own making. How is it possible to lie for a profession, and then be real at night?"

JayJay could only say, "Whatever real I've got inside me, Mrs. Channing, it's Kelly's. If she wants it."

"The words are nice, Mr. Junior. But I must question the sentiment.

Which brings us to my purpose for coming here. One question, two parts. Are you the least bit genuine? And are your affections for my daughter something she can count upon? I must ask you this because it appears my daughter has chosen to ignore my one piece of advice."

"Ma'am, Mrs. Channing . . ." JayJay looked from mother to daughter. "I would never mean your daughter harm of any kind."

"Work with me, sir. Why is it, then, that my daughter burst into tears the first two times she spoke your name?"

"Because the days before she left I was acting like a fool," JayJay said. "Because I wanted answers to all life's questions, and I let my head get in the way of listening to my heart. Which was telling me . . ."

"Yes?"

"Telling me your daughter is the finest thing that's ever happened to me in all my born days."

Edith Channing disliked his answer. He could tell that. And Kelly did not look his way at all. "Well, you can most certainly act. We've all seen that talent on display tonight. Let me out, daughter."

JayJay rose with her. "I'd just like to say again how sorry I am about the problems y'all are having with your husband's mother, Mrs. Channing."

"Thank you, Mr. Junior." She took a two-handed grip on her purse, and punched him with her eyes and her words both. "I fell in love with my husband because he was more than I could ever aspire to become. My daughter deserves the same. I wish . . ."

"Momma," Kelly said quietly.

Her mother looked down at Kelly, who continued to stare at the linoleum tabletop. She sighed. Once. "I should not have come."

Kelly did not respond.

"Walk me to the car, daughter. Good evening, Mr. Junior. I wish I could say this been a pleasure."

Morning sun filled his room with what should have been a cheery light when he placed the call. "Floyd, it's JayJay. Ahn gave me your number. I hope it's all right—"

The pastor's voice shone with pleasure. "It's great to hear from you, is what it is. How are you, brother?"

The prayer group was over and most everyone had left for the day. Hotel cleaning staff clattered down the hall outside his room. He sat on the floor and leaned his back against one of the beds. "Sore. Feel like I been kicked by a mule, but I doubt Kelly would like to hear me talk about her mother like that."

"Kelly, now, this is the lovely lady someone pointed out to me at the ranch?"

"Kelly Channing."

"Hold on just one second." There was a rustling on the other end of the phone. Then, "All right. The world is on hold over here. Why don't you tell me about it."

So he did. From when Floyd had left. Right through his funk, his ride in the hills, his decision, and Kelly's departure. Finishing with the previous evening's conversation.

"Where is she now?"

"Who, the mother or the daughter?"

"I assume the mother's gone back to tending her sick relative, now that she's sunk her fangs in good."

"That's not exactly what I'd expect to hear from a pastor. Especially not when everything the mother said was right on target." When the pastor remained silent, JayJay finished, "Kelly is out at the fairgrounds. Which is another problem."

"How's that?"

"Oh, some group that brings fun rides and such to country fairs is here putting up their gear. The towns around here are turning my act last night into a reason for a big shindig tomorrow."

"Let's pare that comment of yours down into segments. First of all, from what I hear it wasn't an act."

"You already knew about my talk?"

"I got a call from a pastor friend who was there for the show. But let's hold that thought in abeyance. Why is it a problem that Kelly's gone to the fair?"

"I let slip that the lady's got a voice. She's gonna sing for the camera tomorrow night."

"She's an actress, and she's got a voice. Where's the problem? No, never mind. Son, I've been in the pastoring business for almost twenty years. And one thing I learned early on is this. When it comes to folks having problems with love, you can get yourself so tangled up you'll never see daylight again. So let's forget about Kelly's voice and focus on the real issue here. And it ain't Kelly's mother either. All she did was poke a raw nerve."

"More like sawed it in half."

"The first time you and I spoke, you went on about how you don't have a past to speak of. How everything in your early life was a lie."

"That's not exactly it. I don't—"

"Now just hold on. You been churched enough to know you don't choke a pastor off in midstride. They turn puce and can't breathe proper. What I just said is close enough to the truth for us right now, JayJay. Now I want to tell you about another no-'count ranch hand. His daddy lost some mules one day and sent his son, whose name was Saul, by the way, he sent Saul off hunting. After he and a servant had been looking a while, Saul came upon this prophet by the name of Samuel. And Samuel told him, I hope you're listening good now, because this is important. Samuel told him, 'Then the Spirit of the Lord will come upon you, and you will prophesy with them and be turned into another man.'"

"I believe I heard that story before," JayJay countered. "About this feller who becomes king and gets himself doomed in the process."

"On account of how he doesn't listen to God once he gets there. Like a certain feller who won't let the preacher finish."

"Go on, then."

"All right, I will. Samuel then says, pay attention now, 'And let it be, when these signs come to you, that you do as the occasion demands; for

God is with you.' Long as Saul followed those orders, he stayed in good shape. His downfall came when he got too big for his britches. Pride and wrongheaded arrogance was Saul's weakness. What is yours?"

When JayJay did not respond, the pastor went on, "It ain't pride, son, it's self-doubt. You don't want to believe God can use you. I don't know what you got in your background. And this morning's not the time for us to work through all that. What you need to remember, whether it's affairs of the heart or affairs of the saddle, it's all the same. God has decided to use you. Don't let your weakness be an excuse to turn away."

JayJay complained, but his heart wasn't really in it any longer. "I thought we were talking about Kelly and me."

"We are, if you'd have half a mind to hear what I'm saying. Now the reason I told you about Saul was because of what happened next, and when I finish this time I'm done. The next day Saul met up with some other prophets. Just like Samuel said, the Spirit came into him, and he joined up with them. Folks who saw him asked, 'Who's that guy there? He ain't no prophet, he's just the son of that no-'count rancher.' And another man answered this way. He pointed at the prophets dancing alongside Saul and said, 'But who is *their* father? What makes *them* so special?' You see where I'm going with this? Almost everyone's past holds shadows, son. Everybody carries a stain. Kelly's mother is right about you only if you *let* her. Okay, yes, Hollywood's got more than its share of liars and cheats. But the same could be said of a lot of places and a lot of trades. What we're concerned with is *you*."

# Chapter 35

Martin Allerby sat in the screening room. One lamp glowed on the table next to his podium. Otherwise the room was dark. Martin had broken one of his own rules and brought along his cigarillos. He hated smoke in a screening. The first inspection of a film crew's work deserved conditions untainted by shades filtering the colors. But today he needed the crutch.

The phone by his elbow lit up, and the projectionist said over the speaker, "You wanted to be notified when Mr. Keplar's car arrived at the gates, Mr. Allerby."

"Have him sent straight down. Ask Gloria to bring another thermos of coffee, a cup for Milo, and a fresh one for me."

Martin was tired. Keeping his calm mask in place was proving an almost impossible burden. Every morning he drove his Volkswagen Touareg through the company gates. He attended to the business of running a studio. He had lunch. He negotiated deals. He drove to whatever dinner or cocktail hour he had penciled in for that evening. He felt eyes upon him all the time. Whether the attention was real or just paranoia at work did not matter. He could not afford to be seen as doing anything other than what was totally normal for the CEO of a studio in the business of making quality television. He was not supposed to know anything about a deal brewing. The deal that just might catapult him into the stratosphere of Hollywood stardom.

Milo arrived with Gloria. He settled into the sofa next to Martin and let Gloria pour him a cup. Milo said nothing until the door sighed shut behind her. "I had to cancel a meeting with the exec VP of Paramount."

"This could be important."

"It better be."

"Britt Turner ordered our best digital film editor to drop everything, load all her gear in her SUV, and drive to Salton City."

"You approved this?"

"He made his call on Saturday morning. Got the lady out of bed. Told her she could write her own ticket. But she had to move immediately."

Milo masked his whispered words with a noisy slurp. "Think he suspects?"

Martin continued his conversational monotone. As though to release any worry, any steam at all, would have resulted in an eruption that might well level the office building. "I called him Monday morning, as soon as I learned about it. I explained that the studio had a policy of all editing taking place in-house. Britt made a good case for his move. They are six days ahead of schedule."

"That's impossible. They haven't been up there—"

"Six days," Martin calmly repeated. "They are shooting at almost double the intended rate. They are moving so fast they are outstripping the set designer's ability to get things ready. Using digital means he can check takes on the monitor soon as they are shot. According to Britt, they have not needed more than five takes for any shot all last week. So Britt wanted to take a day with Derek and the film editor and run through what had been done so far."

"Derek? Oh. Right. The new camera guy."

"According to my source on the shoot, Derek Steen is proving to be remarkably adept at bringing the most out of digital filmwork. This has been confirmed in the one report I have received from our editor."

"What else did she say?"

In reply, Martin hit the speaker button connecting him to the projection room. "You have four segments, is that right?"

"Three longer ones and two together that total less than a minute, Mr. Allerby."

"Roll the longest tape."

The lamp beside his chair dimmed. There was none of the flickering start to digital film. For raw footage, the cameraman held the clapper in place longer than normal with film, just to give the viewer something to focus on before the scene actually played.

In this case, however, they were seeing work that had been edited, and thus the clapper was removed. Which meant the light came onto the screen and revealed fifteen seconds of a handwritten scene number. Then the screen came to life.

Both men instantly moved to the edge of their seats as though drawn by the same cord.

The light was far too rich for a midbudget film. The crowd was far too large. The first three seconds declared this to be an epic. Fifty, a hundred million dollars. A *Titanic*-size budget. It had to be. But it couldn't.

There must have been two thousand extras filling the hall. The place itself looked drawn from the twenties, as did many of the faces. Hard, leathery people. The sort of crowd you might expect in a Russian film of the Stalinist era, back when the director could walk through streets and have the commissars pull out every face he liked. The sight hit Martin like a fist to his gut.

And that was just the first image.

The camera swooped down from its perch in one long arc, drawing in absolute professional perfection from the balcony, lingering over a few of the faces, each and every one of them perfectly lit. Then it came to rest upon the man on the stage. A pastor. He spoke a few words. Martin could only assume they came from the Bible. Spoken in simple clarity. The words gave an impossible authority to the man who took his place at the microphone.

Impossible that a completely untested actor could carry himself with this much power.

JayJay Parsons spoke words that Martin could not completely take in. JayJay set his hat upon the table. He talked some more. He drank water. The tremble in his hand caused the water to reflect the light in tight shimmers. But his voice was steady. Firm. He turned and spoke briefly to the people behind him. Martin felt his breath catch. The man looked good from every conceivable angle.

When JayJay turned back, a voice broke in from the audience. JayJay's own surprise was reflected by the camera, which jerked sharply as it shifted and searched. Almost as though the man who spoke had caught them both unawares.

Milo asked, "How did they *do* that?"

Martin lifted his hand for silence. Too caught up in what he was seeing to respond any further. The camera settled upon a member of the audience. No, that was wrong. The camera *gripped* him. The image was so sharp Allerby could smell the man's sweat, feel his nerves. The camera was *relentless*.

Then a woman spoke. Again there was the slight jerk, though Allerby suspected the camera had half anticipated this, because there was no searching for the second speaker. That new actress came into view. Kelly Channing stood in the aisle. She was angry in the way of a truly beautiful woman. Her rage magnified her allure, turning her into some kind of unapproachable magnet, the charisma of a primitive chieftess. A warrior queen. Again Martin was not able to fully capture what she said. Because in truth it did not matter.

The camera returned to JayJay. He finished speaking and just stood there, a terrible mistake in the film's rule book. *Never* release mounting emotion into a vacuum.

But here, this one time, it *worked*.

The camera gripped JayJay as the weariness came and went in a flash of ruthless insight. Here stood a man worn down to the secret essence, the core of truth that few people ever truly saw in themselves, and never in another. Yet here it was. The man wanted nothing more than to live his life on the ranch. Yet he had been drawn into a fight not of his making. A fight that had so drained him he was stripped down to the *bone*. Revealing his true nature.

A hero.

In the instant where the revelation would have become corny overplay, a voice shouted from the balcony, "And all the people said . . ."

The roar came from one voice emitted by a thousand throats.

"*Amen!*"

And it still did not end.

The camera action was Academy Award smooth. Martin knew they had spliced it. The working portion of his brain, the analytical segment that never stopped, told him there was no way they could have done what they did without a cut-and-switch between camera units. Only he could not find one.

The view drew back from two thousand people rising and shouting and clapping and calling back to the man on the stage. Their hero was now surrounded by other men and women who had come forward from their chairs to shake his hand and speak words JayJay probably could not take in. The camera never lost JayJay as its focus moved farther still, until it finally drew back through an open rear window, and turned.

And revealed a crowd even larger than the one inside.

The camera swooped down and connected with a single face. A woman in a waitress uniform shouted and clapped in total abandon. Then the camera drew back. On and on and upward, higher now than the building from which it had just exited. So high it looked down upon the entire crowd filling Main Street from the hall down to a church. The steeple rose into the sunset. The cross cut a brilliant shadow from the setting sun. The same sun that burnished the crowd and the assembly hall and the town with an ethereal glow.

The screen went blank.

Milo slumped back in his seat. He needed both hands to steady the thermos and refill his cup.

Martin shook a cigarillo from the pack. Gripped the lighter with two hands to light it. Took a steadying drag.

The speakerphone light came on. "Should I run the next clip, Mr. Allerby?"

"What do you think, Milo?"

His sales director leaned over and asked the speakerphone, "Is the rest as good as this?"

"I've only seen two more segments, Mr. Keplar. I thought they were hot."

Milo took two tries to get his cup back in the saucer. He said carefully, "We need to discuss how we're going to handle this hit."

"Let's take a walk." Martin rose and said to the projectionist, "I'll be back in ten minutes. Hold the room for me, please."

"You got it."

They said nothing more until they were walking through the stretch of green between the outer wall and the office building. The same Japanese gardeners who handled Martin's home kept this tiny patch looking like a green tuxedo.

Milo saw nothing but what lay ahead. "It's true what you told me in there? They're ahead of schedule?"

"And under budget, if Britt's cost sheets are to be believed, and I think they are."

"You won't ever keep a lid on this. One word from that scrawny projectionist to his pal at the *Hollywood Reporter*, and tomorrow you'll be reading about this over your mangoes and coffee."

Martin flipped his cigarette over the studio wall. "I agree."

"If I show this to Fox, this one clip, I'll have worldwide rights sewn up in about two seconds."

Martin drew a pair of sunglasses from his jacket pocket and settled them on his nose. He did not need them for the light, as the smaze had been building all week and now blanketed the valley in shades of putrid gray. He simply did not want any prying eyes to see how close he was to letting loose the screaming ninnies.

"Scratch that," Milo said. "If Disney sees this and gets a single solitary whiff that the studio is available for purchase, they'll be camping at the old man's front gates with a blank check in hand."

Martin lit another cigarillo. He wanted to feel something. Even if it was the acrid bite of smoke at the back of his throat.

Milo looked at his partner. "That's not so bad, is it? Being able to write your ticket to one of the majors?"

"It is," Martin said with his smoke. "If the original aim had been to own the studio outright."

Milo kicked the grass at his feet. "So what happens now?"

"I want you to go on vacation. Vanish completely. No phone, fax, e-mail, nothing. Make a big deal of it, talk it up, let everybody know I approve. You've been working too hard, need a complete break, and since you're gone your secretary and PA can take off as well. Shut your office down entirely. There won't be anyone for the sniffers to approach. Officially, everything will have to wait. Call when you get wherever you're going and let me know how to make contact."

"What about you?"

"I'll think of something," Martin replied. "I always do."

The woman was stylishly dressed, but about twenty years out of date. Yet her crystal clear gaze and her calm expression said she could not have cared less. She rose from her chair on the other side of the screening camera and straightened her jacket. She wore an original Balenciaga she had pulled from the trunk of a junk dealer's car. She had found it one weekend in La Jolla, just before her husband had gone down with cancer. Probably the last great weekend they had shared together. That was how she liked to dress. In memories as fine as the clothes.

"You're a prince, Chuckie," she said to the projectionist.

"No problem. And you'll do what you said, right?"

"The next opening we get in editing is yours." She walked to the door. "I was never here, okay?"

"Just so you don't forget."

"That's my boy." She started to open the door, then turned back and said, "Strange response from our two top dogs over their latest smash hit, wouldn't you say?"

"Looked to me like they were both kicked in the teeth. But hey, I'm just the projectionist, right?"

She opened the door, checked to make sure the hall was empty, and replied, "Not for long."

# Chapter 36

For a day and a half, Britt worked JayJay with the second team. That was the name he had given Kip and the steadicam. Kip had responded with genuine disbelief at the news, so shocked the feather-weight flapping was stilled entirely. Britt had told them both together. Just, go out there and do it. No further instructions, no embellishments, no nothing. Typical Britt.

They shot half a dozen fifteen-second mini-scenes. They started with JayJay standing on a hay bale or the back end of his own truck, which had been adopted into the cinematic fold. Both the hay and his truck now sported bunting straight from a local printer. Red, white, and blue banners that proclaimed in starry letters, "JayJay Parsons for Mayor."

The same bunting that had suddenly sprouted up all over town.

Running JayJay for mayor being the surprise Peter had worked up and to which Miller had agreed.

The steadicam guy was a solid human brick. With his equipment he measured about five feet square. He wore a biking singlet stretched to bursting by his muscular build. He did not speak. Ever.

Britt had booked a vanload of extras. But they proved unnecessary. Wherever they pulled up, people appeared. The third time it happened, JayJay said to the steadicam guy, "We oughtta try this in the middle of the Mojave. Just hop out and see who pops outta the sand."

The steadicam wore his blond hair cut in a big-city buzz cut. He pushed his bug-eyed shades up on top of his head and rubbed at the sweat.

"Nice talking with you," JayJay said.

The steadicam guy nodded and slipped his shades back into place.

Kip flickered about, setting up shots and then shrilling them to a last-minute halt, wanting a different backdrop, or another face up close to where JayJay stood. The AD was clearly terrified over his first big chance. He bit his nails to the quick as JayJay delivered the same lines over and over, a couple of paragraphs from the same speech he had used in the hall. When he had enough footage, Kip made his hands dance, which was the prearranged signal for the crowd to applaud.

Six stops, six different crowds, and they were into what played for rush hour in Salton City. JayJay asked, "You know what I think?"

Kip did not look up from his rumpled script pages. "Actors can get arrested for thinking on location. It's part of the California penal code."

"I'm thinking you ought to film me walking down Main Street."

Kip dropped the pages into his lap.

"Have the steadicam guy walk beside me. Use that feller with the whatchamadingie—"

"Reflector."

"Right. Have him do his job on the light. Let's just see if the folks keep coming up to say hello."

"No sound," Kip mused. "Just get some footage of you playing actor."

"Politician."

"Same thing." Kip grinned. "This is fun."

"I wouldn't go that far," JayJay said, climbing from the truck. "But it sure beats digging fence holes for a living."

When they showed up at the fair, an extra dressed as a cop directed them down a dusty field into a long line of waiting vehicles. They knew he was an extra soon as Kip rolled down his window and yelled, "We're filming here."

"Sorry, Mr. Denderhoff, sir! I didn't recognize you. Right over there, sir! Park behind the sound truck, please!"

Kip settled back into his seat and said, "Offer them a line of decent dialogue, and an extra will suck up to the exhaust pipe of a cross-country bus."

"Thank you for that Hollywood news flash," JayJay said.

"Hey. You want to survive in the jungle, you got to learn the code."

"Anytime I need a dose of wisdom, I sure know where to come," JayJay agreed.

"What did the crowd say the other night? Amen?" But Kip was smiling. "Unless you wise up, next time you hear that will be at your funeral."

They didn't need to talk it through. They both saw the crowd turning and thought the same thing, which was, why waste the moment? So JayJay let the makeup lady do another touch-up and the lighting guy settle into place with the reflector, and the steadicam get situated by Kip, and he made his entrance. Getting applauded through the fair gates and down the carnival midway. A dusk-streaked sky competed with the carnie lights, splashing the crowd with happy colors.

When Kip spotted Britt watching them, he went back to his splay-footed nervousness. But all Britt said was, "We need to move straight into the first take."

JayJay caught the director's edge. "Is Kelly okay?"

"Kelly's not the problem." Britt's expression was grim. "Kip, they need help settling the crowd down by the stage."

"I'm on it."

"Tell Derek we go in five." Britt turned to JayJay. "Kelly's handling it okay. But it's still her first time singing for a camera. You know what that's like."

"Not the singing part, which is a good thing for everybody. But I can imagine."

"Go help her get ready."

"What's the matter, Britt?"

Britt seemed tempted to tell him. But the director merely shook his head and said, "It has to wait."

They had pulled a trailer up behind the stage. JayJay waved to the roadies working on the musical equipment and knocked on the trailer door. A voice said something he missed because the sound guys started testing the mikes. He entered and said, "Kelly?"

"The lady's in back." The band's leader got up from the sofa and handed his guitar to a buddy. "Mister, I don't even know your name. But I got to tell you, we owe you big-time for this break."

"All I did was tell the folks in the front office what I heard you giving on the stage, which was quality. And you can call me JayJay."

"That's your for-real name?" The guy took a double-fisted lock on JayJay's hand. "We been waiting eight years for this. The head honcho out there says maybe they'll use one of our original songs on the sound track. If that happens, Arista is talking a two-album deal. Anytime, anywhere, you hear what I'm saying?"

JayJay slipped by the band and knocked on the rear door. He heard Kelly say, "Is it time?"

"Not quite." He opened the door a fraction. "Can I come in?"

"Sure thing, Slim. Watch a girl go into full-frontal meltdown."

There wasn't really room for her to pace. But Kelly was giving it a solid try. JayJay shut the door and asked, "Are you mad with me for telling them?"

"I should be. But seeing as how my mother gave you her version of verbal branding, I'm kinda stuck at my own need to apologize." She wrung her hands. "That is, I would be. But right now I can't get my mind past what's about to happen."

"Kelly, I got so many things I want to say I can't hardly get a single thing out." JayJay wanted to reach out, sweep the lady up, give her a hug big enough to rob them both of air. But he couldn't, not without a sign of welcome. So he leaned on the wall behind the door and said, "But I got to tell you, you look about a hundred kinds of fine right now."

She wore a Hollywood version of country cool. Silk top one shade darker than her hair and knotted across her middle. Silk pants made to look like denim, tucked into pale high-heeled boots so soft JayJay reckoned he could roll them up like socks. Her hair flowed across one shoulder, the way he liked best, and tonight there were little sparkly jewels woven into her tresses. Her top and her hair glittered as she turned.

"Kelly."

"What?"

"You want to pray?"

"You say the words, Slim. I'll do my best to pay attention."

"Can I hold your hands?"

She made two more crossings before she finally got within reach. Her hands were cold as ice. JayJay said the words, hardly hearing them himself, just willing his strength into her.

Whatever he'd said, it touched her enough for her to finally look at him. "I've missed you so."

The metal bands that had been wrapped about his heart for over a week loosened somewhat. "You don't know, you can't, how much that means."

She whispered, "I'm so scared."

"I know, and it hurts me to think I'm the cause. But I got to tell you, what you did up there on the stage at Goody's, it was the finest thing I've ever heard."

"This is a totally different animal, Slim. One that's gnawing me right down to the bones."

He had a thought. "One thing Claire's told me is, try and find someone in the crowd to reach through your lines."

Her gaze sharpened. "You been spending time with Claire?"

"Just listen to what I'm saying, okay? I haven't been searching those crowds for just any old face. I looked for *you*."

"Oh, JayJay."

"What I'm thinking is, did your grandmother like your singing?"

Her eyes bloomed with sorrow. "She taught me almost everything I know."

"Well, maybe you ought to try and find her with your voice. Forget the camera and the mess out there behind the lights. Do this for her." When she didn't speak, he said, "That sounds crazy, don't it."

She touched his face. For the very first time. With a hand that was warming rapidly. To match the look she gave him. "There's nothing more dangerous in this whole wide world than a good-looking man who knows the right words to tell a lady."

They took a step apart at the knock on the door. Britt poked his head inside, inspected them both, and said, "It's time."

Britt stepped to the mike while the band limbered up. "Folks, we're so grateful for your helping us out like this. In case some of you missed it, the carnival is on us. Our way of saying thanks to the greatest community it's ever been my pleasure to work with." He waited through their applause and whistles, then went on, "My assistant, Kip Denderhoff, raise your hand, Kip, see him over there? Kip is going to wave his hands when it's time for you to make noise. He'll wave them again and you need to stop right then. But try not to look directly at him, or the cameraman on the platform who'll be aiming at you, see him? Don't look at either of them because we want to get some close-ups of you. Now what we're going to do is have Kelly Channing—"

The applause caught everybody by surprise. No one more than Kelly. JayJay stood beside her just behind the large stack of speakers. The makeup lady was still working on Kelly when they started shouting and whistling. JayJay saw her eyes go wide, and whispered, "Looks like you got some friends out there."

She asked, "Did you set this up?"

"I would have if I'd thought of it, but I been busy wrangling my own bronco." JayJay looked to the makeup lady. "You're my only alibi."

The lady said with a smile, "He's been out on a shoot all day."

Britt finally broke the crowd off and continued, "Kelly is going to do three songs. She'll do them several times. We ask you to please, please be patient with us, and stay in close and try to enjoy what she is giving."

The director hesitated, then added, "Because it feels like we're among friends, I . . ." He had to stop again for the applause to fade. "I want to share one thing with you. Kelly has never sung for the camera before. And nothing can help a new actor more than feeling like the audience is on her side. So when she comes out, let her know what you think of her. That's all. Have a great time. And once again, thank you. Not just tonight. For everything. You are great, great people."

They applauded him off the stage. Britt took up position behind Derek, whose camera was situated on a flatbed truck between two lighting pillars. Britt wound his hand over his head. The band struck a pose, and hit it.

Kelly turned around and wrapped her arms around JayJay. Held him with all the force he had wanted to give her. A strong lady with all the energy in the world at her command. Squeezed the breath from his body.

Then she turned and walked onstage.

The crowd just plain went wild.

The script girl appeared at JayJay's elbow. She wore the standard headset and a frantic expression. JayJay wanted to refuse when she motioned him to follow, but she was having none of it. She gripped his arm and tugged him around to the stairs and down into the crowd. Down to where the spotlight waited.

Which turned out to be a good thing, because when Kelly slipped the mike from the stand and looked at the crowd, she stared straight at him.

Then she turned and looked at the band. One glance. They swung into the Dylan song, the same one that had blown JayJay away at the restaurant. Got to serve somebody. Belting the words with a throaty burr that left him shivering.

The band shut it off with a single solid punch. And waited through a full-throated roar in return. Kelly smiled then. She might have been smiling at him. JayJay liked to think so, anyway. The band used the applause to switch electric guitars for mandolins and fiddle. The drummer went to brushes. A quick countdown, and they swung into the old country favorite, "He Touched Me." Some of the older folks slipped through the barrier and started a country two-step. Kip was in the process of waving them back when Britt punched the air over his head. Let them be. The crowd saw the exchange and took it as all the sign they needed. Folks released the ropes forming the semicircular barrier between the crowd and the stage. The steadicam guy lost his ability to move, but Britt only pointed him up onto the stage.

*He touched me*, Kelly sang, *and He made me whole.*

When the crowd quieted once more, the lighting shifted. A grand piano JayJay had not noticed before was highlighted by a single spot. With the silky night as a backdrop, Kelly walked over and leaned against the piano. The band leader played the opening bars, and she swung into "Love Never Dies" remixed as a torch song. A woman faced with the impossibles of life, promising herself as well as the audience that despite everything, hope would live on. Just her and the piano. As raw and exposed as a woman could be. Letting it all out. Singing to another woman, one locked away in a hospital room some thousand miles away. JayJay felt his face go wet, knew the camera was watching, and couldn't bring himself to care.

They had to wait through a full five minutes before they could start the second take. JayJay clapped and hollered until his throat went raw.

# Chapter 37

They should have gone out racing with the wind.

That was how good JayJay felt. Like there was nothing that could possibly have fit the moment except to pile all of them into his truck, ten, twelve, however many they could cram into the front and back seats. And go tearing around town, burning rubber at the stoplights and shouting at the moon, letting off the joy that turned them sixteen and wild again.

Instead, what they did was troop into the trailer now vacated by the musicians and spread out around the long front room. Peter, Britt, Kip, JayJay, Claire, Kelly, Derek. All the usual suspects. Plus a woman JayJay had not seen before. A woman of age and humor and character, was how he thought of her. Crystal-green eyes and carefully trimmed white hair and a gaze that said she had seen it all and found most of it purely hilarious.

Only she wasn't laughing now.

Britt said, "This is Rhoda Dwyer. Rhoda is chief film editor at Centurion. I've had her camped out here since Saturday so I could work with her on some of the first takes. Just seeing for myself if we had something that worked." He nodded to her. "Tell them."

"About the work so far or what happened back in LA?"

"Both."

"This is highly irregular, I have to say. I can't recall a film editor speaking with actors on location before."

"This entire project," Britt replied, "has been based on broken rules."

"Well. If the scenes I've worked through so far are any indication, I would say Hollywood will be forced to sit up and take notice of your new directions."

They looked at one another, confused by the mixed signals—the woman's words, and the bleak expression she shared with Britt and Derek. Claire finally asked, "They're good?"

"They are better than good. Excellent is one word that comes to mind. Outstanding. Exceptional. Oscar-quality camera work."

Derek covered his eyes. Peter slugged his friend's shoulder. "Way to go, man."

"Some of the scenic structure Britt has envisioned is nothing short of genius. And your acting, Mr. Junior, well, I can only say that it astounds me to learn you have never worked before a camera. You too, Ms. Channing. And tonight's performance moved me terribly."

"Okay," Britt said. "Enough for the buildup. Now give them act two."

Rhoda related what she had witnessed from the projectionist's booth. When she finished, Claire cut through the silence with, "You're sure about that? Martin Allerby was disappointed with our results?"

"I would say he was devastated. He and Milo both."

Britt let that sink in, then, "Tell them what you told me."

"Are you sure that's wise?"

"No. I'm working on gut instinct here. But it's served me well enough so far."

"Very well." She had a schoolmistress's manner, very prim and easy, yet giving off the subtle warning that this was one lady never to mess with. "I have worked with Martin Allerby for seven years. He has the cold, calculating deadliness of a big jungle cat. He gives up nothing until he strikes. But my impression was he sent you out here to fail."

Britt said, "And we've disappointed him."

"You *worry* him. And very few things worry Martin Allerby. Or rather, very few things concern him to such a level that it shows."

Kelly asked, "Why would he want us to fail?"

"That is a question I have been asking myself ever since."

Britt said to the group, "I wanted you to hear this because we are going on full throttle. I want to get as much done as we possibly can. Not just filmed. Edited and packaged. So if we do get shut down—"

"When," Rhoda corrected. "*When* Martin decides to close you up."

"Whatever. I want enough in the can I'll be able to shop this product to another studio. If he forbids it, I'll leak it to the press. I'll alert the Centurion board." Britt had never appeared so angry. "Martin isn't the only one who can play tough. He is *not* going to kill this. What we have is too good."

He studied the room. "But I can't do this alone. What I want to know is, will you back me up? Eighteen-hour days from here on out. Kip will direct what I decide can be delegated so I can be freed up to work with Rhoda. Are you with me?"

Though he dreaded the hours to come, JayJay knew what was called for here. "I always admired a fellow under pressure who can still count his bullets and take careful aim." He offered Britt his hand. "Let's get to work."

The prayer meeting was shifted to five the next morning. Cynthia plied two coffeepots and apologized for not having the equipment for direct transfusions. After Kelly did her Bible reading, JayJay said, "I've got a couple of praise reports and one new request. First off, I got to tell you, give the lady to my right a mike and she'll plumb knock you into next week."

"I'll say amen." This from a yawning Derek.

"Next, I had a nice conversation with Kip yesterday."

That got their attention. Kelly asked, "What did he say?"

"Far as I recollect, something like, 'This is fun.'"

"What was he doing," Claire asked, "sharpening his filleting knives?"

"We were working. He was doing his hand-tango and more getting in the way than directing. But we got some good stuff in the pot."

"Can," Claire corrected. "In the can."

"Pot, can, we took some pictures and I think they worked. And we just chatted. Like two normal human beings."

"Kip is neither normal nor human," Claire said.

"Well, I think we ought to add the little guy to our prayer list, is all."

"You can pray for him all you like," Kelly said. "I'll just hum along in the background on that one."

Peter asked, "You had a prayer request?"

"For Britt."

Those who had been there the previous night just nodded. Britt had ordered them not to talk about what had been discussed. There were spies on location. He knew that because Martin Allerby always had spies. It was one of Martin's trademarks. Nothing went on within Martin's reach that he didn't have his secret sources. Martin fed on information like a worm on dirt.

Britt had chosen them because they were, in his words, the core leaders. If they accepted his move to longer days and faster action without a whimper, so too would the rest of the crew. But nothing could be said outright. The crew would wonder and talk among themselves and probably assume the pressure came from the studio. Which, in truth, it did.

They had scarcely time to pray a round before there was a knock on the open door and Kip said, "Party time is over, people." He clapped his hands like he was herding goats. "Your little fun and games will just have to wait."

Claire caught up to JayJay in the hall and said, "It's not too late to reconsider your plan to pray for Kip."

"The Book doesn't say anything about taking back prayers, sis."

Claire did not see him stop dead in his tracks, halted by the realization of what he had just called her, and how natural it felt.

# Chapter 38

The Beverly Wilshire Hotel coffee shop had once occupied a privileged place in Hollywood lore. Then, to the horror of the regulars, the new Japanese owners tore out the shop's fabled Mexican interior and replaced it with Romanesque columns and marble and gilt and powder-puff pastels. Now the place remained for the most part empty of customers save the usual tourists and the occasional lost soul. Martin might have said the players avoided it out of principle, except that Hollywood had none.

Eight days after he had disappeared, Milo let the dark-suited maître d' seat him and said, "I hear the interior decorator who destroyed this place has a job doing colors for Crayola."

Martin said to the indignant maître d', "I'll have a white omelet with chives, brown toast, and grapefruit juice."

"Same." Milo studied the chalk-blue angels overhead as the maître d' snapped his fingers for the waiter to fill their coffee cups. "I won't be sorry to stop meeting in places like this."

"How was your vacation?"

"It feels like I've spent the last week living in an isolation room equipped with sand and palm trees. Longest I've been out of contact since I started in Hollywood."

"I have an idea."

Milo did not need to ask what about. "It better be first-rate, is all I can say. First call I got when I turned my phone back on was from Paramount."

"And?"

"She was just fishing. Mentioned something about a possible hit, our first time up to bat in the big league, asked if we might be in the market for a long-term distribution deal." He waited as the orange juice was deposited. "She didn't know anything for certain. Yet."

One thing to be said about eating in an empty five-star hotel restaurant was the speed. Their omelets arrived, fluffy and crisp. They ate in silence. Martin liked this about Milo. The man said what needed saying, then shut up. He would wait until Martin was ready to pitch his plan. In this business, timing was everything.

Finally Martin pushed his plate to one side, sipped his cup, and said, "Yesterday afternoon my office extended a personal invitation to the entire Hollywood press corps. We have a junket leaving tomorrow for Salton City."

"How many do you think will show?"

"Everyone. Once they read this morning's front-page article in *Variety*. I owed Alexi a scoop. I phoned her yesterday."

"What'd you tell her?"

"That *Heartland*'s dailies are off the chart. That we may be after the elusive dream, a film that wins critical praise and plays for months in Kansas City." Martin let that sit for a moment, then continued, "I met her in your empty offices. Gave her a chance to view a couple of scenes for herself."

Milo's voice rose a full two octaves. "You're giving up?"

Martin waited while the waiter recharged their cups. "You know better than that."

"Then what—"

"Milo, *think*. You've said it yourself. Six days ago they suspected. Whatever we do, sooner rather than later they'll know." Martin finished his orange juice. "I'm just making sure the word comes first from us."

Milo pushed at his gut with a fist. "This strain, I got to tell you, it's worse than Emmy week." He fished in his pocket, came out with a plastic sheet of pills, took one, chased it with coffee. "What have you heard?"

"The crew has moved into an impossible shooting schedule. Britt spends what time he can spare heads-down with the film editor."

Milo froze in the process of stowing away his pills. "Your spies are sure about that?"

"Spy. Singular. More than one and they spend all their time reporting on each other."

"I thought you were going to call the editor back to the studio."

"I can hardly do that," Martin replied. "Not when I'm receiving dailies that literally take my breath away."

"That good." Milo pressed his fist in harder.

"More than good, Milo. They are phenomenal. We're no longer talking an occasional decent scene. The story is taking shape, and looks to be as good as the camera work and the acting."

"We're finished," Milo declared. "Soon as this gets out, I'll be handling more high fliers than the Dodgers outfield. Your press junket will only fan the flames. Dawes will hear. He'll have his attorney make it known that Centurion is open to offers. The studios will descend on that Ojai ranch like a pack of ravenous wolves."

"They might," Martin agreed. "Except for one thing."

Martin gave him the idea. Midway through relating his plan, Milo's fist dropped from his chest to the table. He began nodding and kept doing so long after Martin finished speaking. "This could work."

"It better."

"I'm thinking I've heard something like this before." Milo's voice had returned to its standard calm. "A while back, what was it . . ."

"*Apocalypse Now*," Martin supplied.

"Sure, that's it." A faint smile played around Milo's mouth and eyes. "They built copies of Saigon and the Mekong Delta from scratch, where was it?"

"One of the Philippine islands, I forget which."

"Sure. First they had to fend off the guerrillas. Then, just as they finished the most expensive set in history, the country got hit by the first hurricane in what was it, fifty years?"

"Something like that." Martin swung the handle of his cup in a modest little dance. Having Milo approve of his idea reduced his own worry load by a ton or so. "Then Marty Sheen had his heart attack."

Milo actually laughed. "I'd forgotten about that."

"Brought Hollywood's most profitable studio to the brink of bankruptcy. All with a film that was generating some of the hottest press in history."

Milo leaned back, a happy man. "You can trust your spy to get this right?"

"I only pay for results."

"What does the little maggot want?"

"What they all want," Martin replied, signaling for the check. "Their chance to grab the big brass ring."

# Chapter 39

Peter closed his laptop and stretched. He rose from the rear table and walked to the windows of the suite's parlor. The night was inky black, save for the glow surrounding the pool. He rubbed his back and watched a pair of bats chase insects drawn to the underwater lights. He checked his watch and gave a weary chuckle. The hands read twenty minutes to five. Even the clock had waited for him. He had just enough time to finish before the crew arrived for prayer.

He turned his computer back on and hit the Print button. When the printer on the floor by his table started whirring, he rose and entered the kitchen alcove. He filled the coffeemakers to brew. He shaved and put on a fresh shirt. He went back to stand over the worktable at the back of the suite's parlor. And took a slow look around.

One basic tenet of Peter's work was that he wrote alone. Other than Cynthia, the only people allowed into his workspace were the characters inside his head. Yet this parlor, which had become home to the first prayer group he had ever heard of on a film location shoot, had also generated some of his very finest work. And most consistent. Every morning, as soon as they finished the prayer time, he returned to the desk and sat down and started anew. No waiting for inspiration. No fighting out the real voices and the real people who had invaded his space. Because in truth it was not an invasion at all. The room was alive with what they had just done, and his own work flowed naturally from this.

As soon as Peter entered the bedroom he knew Cynthia was awake.

She had not moved, but his senses were on full alert. Perhaps it was because of just having pulled an all-nighter. But he didn't think so. He crossed the overlarge bedroom and settled down beside her. She rolled over and asked, "Did you get any sleep?"

"I can sleep later."

She studied him in that calm way that was all her very own. Peter brushed the hair from her forehead, feeling as though he had never seen her as clearly as at this moment.

She did not need to ask. "You had a good night."

"Yes."

"I'm glad." She lifted her arm, her signal for Peter to help her shift over. He took the extra pillow and settled it where it would cradle her belly. "Thank you."

"It's almost time for the group to start."

"I think I'll just lay here for a while."

It was as close to complaining as Cynthia ever came. That was another of the amazing things about his wife. If Peter had a cold, he wanted the whole world to know and suffer with him. Cynthia hated people fussing over her. He asked, "Can I get you something?"

"I'll be fine."

He knew better than to probe. If the doctor was needed, she would tell him. Otherwise she would lie there and shelter her children with her arms and wait it out. He leaned down and kissed her. "You are going to be a super mom."

Cynthia smiled and closed her eyes. "Go say a prayer for your babies."

The first people to arrive were always the same, the silent electricians and one of the lighting guys and a carpenter. The four of them occupied two adjoining rooms, and no matter how early he opened the door and set the latch for the others to let themselves in, this group was already there in the hall. They knew the drill and felt no need for words. They charged their mugs and settled into their accustomed spots along the wall. Within ten minutes the last sleepy stragglers were seated.

Then Britt knocked on the door.

Peter stood there with the empty coffeepot in his hand, feeling for some inexplicable reason that he'd been caught doing something wrong.

Britt asked nervously, "Mind if I join you?"

JayJay must have sensed that surprise had rendered Peter incapable of speech. He leaped from his chair and crossed the room in record time. "You kidding? There ain't no guest list at God's party."

"I had something I needed to discuss . . ." Britt waved away the excuse. "Never mind."

Peter watched JayJay ease the director into a chair far enough back so he wouldn't feel like he was forced into the hot seat. That must have been why God invented cowboys. To handle things that ordinary humans found impossible, like bucking broncos and bosses at prayer time.

Peter glanced Britt's way as he made fresh coffee. Clearly the director had slept no more that night than Peter. He took a mug over unasked, dressed the way he knew Britt took his brew. Britt gave him the edgy look of a guy caught in a situation he totally did not understand. Like a visitor at the zoo suddenly finding himself on the wrong side of the bars.

Things proceeded in the normal fashion, the process so ingrained they could have done it in their sleep. Which, given the hour and the short night, was not too far off target for many of them.

Then JayJay asked, "Britt, you have any special prayer request you want to share?"

Peter watched him sort through the alien data. "You guys would pray for me?"

"We already do." This from Kelly. "Every day."

Britt's eyes tightened. He was a man well accustomed to the Hollywood usage of truth, as in, change it to suit your purpose.

"I know, it takes some serious getting used to," Claire said, smiling. "They even pray for Kip."

"Get out."

Claire's smile broadened. "Prepare to be amazed."

"Okay," JayJay said. "Let's go to the Lord."

When they were done, Britt was the first to rise from his chair. He stood by the wall, gripping the empty mug with both hands, a very thoughtful expression on his weary features. As they started to break up, he said, "I need to speak with the group from the other night."

Peter ushered all but the core group out, and returned to his chair in time to hear Britt say, "Word is out. Today's *Variety* has us on the front page. Last night I got a call from Alexi Campe, their chief television writer. Yesterday Martin had her at the studio, gave her a look at some of our scenes. Alexi normally covers television. But because she's been writing about *Heartland* for six seasons, she's covering our project. She is calling our work on this feature a hit in the making. She asked for my reaction."

Britt's hands shook slightly as he toyed with his mug. "I told her I'd have to check with Martin and call her back. I reached our boss just after midnight. Martin informed me that the studio is setting up a press junket. They're coming out Friday."

"Friday," Derek said. "That's—"

"The day we film the wildfire," Britt confirmed. "Martin thought it would make for a nice intro to the project, see everybody involved in such a major take."

"Hoping we'll fall on our faces, more like." This from Claire.

Britt shrugged. "Maybe. Or it could be I got it all wrong."

"You didn't get it wrong."

The certainty with which JayJay spoke turned all attention his way. Britt asked, "You know something I don't?"

"I know a snake in a suit when I see one. And I heard you and the film editor the same as everybody else. I can't tell you what that feller's got planned. But he's not parading these press folks out here to see anything good." JayJay's face was angry flint. "Shame he's gonna be disappointed again."

Britt's anxious load visibly eased. "We'll give it our best shot."

"We'll do more than that. We are gonna *shine*." JayJay rose from his chair. He straightened up his shoulders. And gave the director the stare. The one Peter had come to think of as JayJay's patented expression. Serious determination. Enormous depths of strength and focus and grit. "We will *not* let you down."

Britt actually smiled. "Man, you're really getting good at this gig. Even I believe you."

"You better," JayJay said. "Because it's the dead-solid truth."

"I'll say amen," Kelly agreed.

Peter let that sit for a moment before saying, "Now's as good a time as any for a little news of my own." He took a big breath and announced, "I finished the screenplay."

Britt asked, "When?"

"About ten minutes before we met."

Britt asked, "And?"

He took a breath, filling himself not with air but rather the remnants of what they had all just shared. "I think it is the best thing I've ever written."

The moment was cut a fraction early by the bedroom door opening. Cynthia appeared and bestowed upon them all an ethereal radiance. "I have an announcement of my own," she said. "Peter, it's time."

# Chapter 40

Even though the limo was outside the hotel, they took JayJay's truck because, as he put it, no kids of theirs were going to celebrate their coming-out day in the back of a Hollywood bus.

The doctors in Fresno had told them the same thing they had heard from the LA team, which was, they were going to cut. So when the preliminary inspection confirmed a cesarean was required, JayJay used Peter's cell phone to ask Britt's permission to hang around. When Peter came back to the waiting room, JayJay reported, "The ladies have organized a prayer team. Two people are gonna be praying round the clock 'til they get the word."

Peter could still feel Cynthia's arms around him, still smell the fresh soapy scent of her hair, feel the imprint of her lips, hear her quietly spoken words of love. He slipped into the chair next to the cowboy, so full of conflicting emotions he wanted to dance and weep all at the same time. Instead, he muttered a hoarse, "Thanks, brother."

They sat together and let the minutes tumble by. Time was marked by quietly harsh hospital noises. When the chair could no longer hold him, Peter paced and stared out various windows, doing his best to shut out the television and the other worried faces. JayJay showed a cowboy's patience and rarely moved.

On his twentieth circuit, Peter asked, "You think it should be taking this long?"

"You're asking the wrong man." He pointed at the nurses' station. "What'd the lady in uniform tell you?"

"'The doctor will be out directly.' She's told it to maybe a million other nervous relatives. I doubt she even saw me." Peter collapsed back into the chair. His mind roamed erratically, seeking something, anything, that would keep him from giving in to fear. He finally came to focus on the man next to him. "Mind if I ask you something?"

"'Course not."

"Back when you first arrived." Not even his worried state could keep him from noticing how JayJay froze. "We were all too busy being glad you'd showed up to ask how you got here."

"Maybe now's not the time."

"What, we got something better to do?"

JayJay looked at him then. His expression said it all. Ask me again, and I'll tell you.

Peter felt torn. He wanted to know, and he wanted to walk away. A portion of his brain or heart or something said that JayJay was right, now was not the proper moment. But the little enquirer, the driving questioner that drilled away at life and fueled so much of what he wrote, would not be silent. "You never need time to study your lines."

"That's right," JayJay said slowly. "I don't."

The early suspicions came back in full force. "They're tied together somehow. Aren't they. The mystery around how you got to be here, and the way you always know the script."

In reply, JayJay simply told his story. About leaving the ranch and taking the bus and sleeping through a huge crash. About waking up in the wardrobe storage room. About getting slotted into the show, and finding himself playing a parody of what he had always thought of as his own life.

For the first time since his wife had stood in the bedroom doorway, Peter was fully focused on something other than what was happening in the next room. "I don't get it."

JayJay spun his hat by the brim and stared at the floor between his boots. "You took the words straight from my own head."

"This is real, I mean, you're not kidding me or anything."

JayJay just kept spinning his hat.

"No. I mean. Of course. You're the straightest shooter I've ever met. How could you not be telling the truth?"

JayJay then related what the Riverside pastor, Floyd Cummins, had told him. About God having planted him there because a different kind of person was needed. Peter nodded in time to the words. "Makes all the sense in the world, in a bizarre kind of way. I mean, you haven't been around Hollywood much. What am I saying, I'm no expert on the place. Writers are semi-tolerated only because their work is required. But if Hollywood ever found a computer that could replace us, we'd have weights tied to our ankles and be dropped off Catalina." He realized he was babbling but couldn't stop. So long as he talked he didn't need to try to get his mind around what he had just heard. Which was, basically, he was seated next to a flesh-and-blood rendition of a character from a TV show. One who had suddenly appeared out of a scene he himself, after weeks of outright desperation, had been unable to complete. "But there's no place in this world for people like you. I mean, the person you're supposed to be playing. No, that's not right, I mean the person you really—"

"Mr. Caffrey?"

Peter was so caught up in what he was struggling to say that it took a moment to refocus on the guy in blue. "I'm Dr. Khandahar. We spoke earlier."

Peter started to rise, but his legs suddenly refused to respond.

The doctor settled into the chair on Peter's other side. "Congratulations. You have two lovely baby girls. My guess is they are identical twins, but it's too early to know for certain."

After babbling away before, he could hardly get his mouth to form the single word. "Cynthia?"

"She is in recovery. We had an unexpected complication and needed to fully sedate her, which is why the procedure took so long." He was a slender olive-skinned gentleman with pianist's hands. His eyes were both deep and expressionless. As was his tone. A calm and softly accented voice that was made to deliver difficult news. "I wish I could wait before discussing this, Mr. Caffrey. But my experience has shown that women have a remarkable ability to sense these things long before they should perhaps be told."

Peter felt JayJay's hand reach over and take his own. It was the first time he had held another man's hand except in prayer. But, then again, that was probably what JayJay was doing now. At least in his heart. Peter's mind was tumbling fast so he could process all these thoughts, while grabbing hold of nothing save the yawning void at the center of his being.

"I'm sorry to have to tell you that your wife will not be able to have any more children, Mr. Caffrey. In a couple of days the three of us can sit down and I will give you both the full details. Right now, what is important is that you need to be there for your wife. You must be strong. You must reassure her, and help her focus upon the fact that you are now parents of two lovely, wonderful little girls."

When Peter could not speak, JayJay said softly, "Thank you, Doctor."

The doctor seemed to find the words coming from someone else, a rawboned cowboy who gripped Peter's hand, totally natural. He rose from his chair. "I'll have the nurse take you back for a moment with your wife."

JayJay watched Peter stumble into the back corridor. He had heard Cynthia talk about them both wanting a big family often enough to know this was not going to be easy. But Peter took the blow to their future hopes with the resilience of one who had to be strong for someone else. Going in to deal with a woman who would wake up soon and look into her husband's face and find what she needed to get through this. The love of a good man who was there for her.

When the doors closed behind the doctor and the husband, JayJay leaned back. He lifted his hat and set it down low over his eyes. Hiding as much of his face as he could from the outside world because he felt as hollow as a well gone dry.

He had seen it in the writer's face. How his tale was both impossible and yet probably true.

JayJay sifted through the tumbling thoughts, allowing one to come to the forefront. And not a thought but an image. Of a woman with hair the color of harvest leaves and a wisdom that came only from standing on solid ground and staring out at horizons as straight and full as heaven's meadow.

How was he supposed to be real for a woman like that? He winced from the ache of knowing Kelly's mother had been right to question him. Truth be told, he was *less* than the actors she detested without knowing them. At least they had a past. At least they could lay claim to a future beyond what somebody else wrote upon the page.

The pocket of his denims started chirping. JayJay realized he had forgotten to give back Peter's phone after calling Britt. He pulled it out and stared at it a moment. Knowing he had to answer. Dreading what he had to say.

Kelly said, "JayJay, I know I told you we'd wait to hear. But I thought, I don't know, maybe you'd heard and had need of somebody else being there for you."

He felt the hot needles sear into the back of his eyeballs. He squeezed them shut. "Oh, Kelly."

"Wait, honey. Just wait a second. Come over here, Claire. Take my hand. Okay, JayJay. I'm ready. Tell us what you know."

Which was the problem. He didn't hardly know a thing.

"Go on, darling." Kelly's voice carried so much love he felt it crimp him up inside, balling him up like a little fist-size bundle of denim and flesh. "How are the babies?"

"Both fine. Two girls. The doctor thinks they might be identical twins."

Her voice broke over the name. "Cynthia?"

"She's gonna be okay. She's got Peter. She's got her babies."

"Wait just a second." Kelly did not mask the phone as she related the news to the others. "Okay, JayJay. Now tell me what's gotten you so broken up."

He sighed around a badly wounded heart. If only he could.

# Chapter 41

P art of him wanted to just get in the truck and drive. Find a high-way exit sign that read "Oblivion." Hammer the pedal down so hard it welded to the floorboard. See how fast he could find the end of that road.

But the truck played like a good horse, holding steady to a modest speed, rumbling down the highway in the direction of home.

Home.

A word with meaning to every human being on earth except him.

JayJay caught a glance of his expression in the rearview mirror. His face was pinched up so tight he could not even see his own eyes. Like even the tiniest pinprick of light threatened to sear his brain.

The only thing that kept him aimed at the ranch was his promise to Britt. His vow to the people that had come to matter so much to him. People who *relied* on him to be there and give his best. Every time the raw wound started to reopen, JayJay pounded the wheel, doing his best to seal it shut. He would not let them down.

Before he pulled into the lot, Kelly had already bounded from the cabin and was racing across the dusty foreground. The sun followed her. A cloud moved aside, so the illumination could rest upon her flying hair. JayJay was frozen in place by her beauty. He could not even reach over and shut off his motor. Not even when he no longer saw her clearly. Just the light that followed her everywhere.

She tore open the door and grabbed him. Not willing even to give him time to climb down, if he could. She reached inside and fitted herself to him. Breathing for him.

Kelly cut off the engine and pulled him out of the truck, all without releasing her hold. She stood there in plain view of the entire company, molded to him. Finally she stepped away and said, "You just come on with me."

She drew him to the corral, where Felicita had Skye and another dappled mare saddled and ready. Though the Mexican wrangler said nothing, her expression showed a remarkable ability to share pain. Kelly stood and made sure he could rise to the saddle. Then she hoisted herself up with a horsewoman's ease. "You want to lead out?"

JayJay took the cottonwood trail. The one he knew so well he could have tracked it blindfolded, backward, in driving hail. They wound by the spring and followed the path along the meandering stream. Along the valley floor, through a sweetly scented meadow and into the orchard beyond. The one he had played in as a child. An orchard he had inherited from his uncle and leased out to a neighbor.

All lies.

When they were surrounded by the carefully tended trees, Kelly said, "Let's hold up here."

JayJay followed her lead. He slipped down from the saddle and tied Skye to a branch within easy reach of some grass. He slipped the bits from both horses' mouths. Kelly gripped his hand and led him back to the last band of cottonwoods. She said, "All right, JayJay. Now tell me what you couldn't manage over the phone."

He had no power of resistance. Though it meant stirring up the whole mess a second time, he did as she ordered. Just started back in the bus and stumbled his way all the way up to the present.

She stood and watched him as he croaked out the last word and just stopped. Unable to move on his own strength.

When Kelly spoke, it was in the same calm voice she used every morning. "Let's say for the time being that all this is true. You've been drawn over from some parallel universe. Dropped into a reality that fits and doesn't fit."

"I don't see how you can be so calm about it. This ain't your normal ordinary past we're talking about here."

"No, it's not."

"But you're not disturbed? Worried? Fretting over standing here with a man who can't exist?"

"But you *do* exist, JayJay. You're about the most real person I've ever met. And the rest of this, well, either I believe you or I don't. And to my knowledge, you have never, not once in all the time we've been together, given me anything but the absolute truth. You don't have any idea . . ."

The first sign of the tumult within her came in the way she wiped her eyes, angrily fisting one and then the other. "Never mind. This isn't about me or my own awful tales. JayJay, listen to me. I've got something to tell you, and I want to make sure you're paying full attention."

"You're the only thing that's holding me together right now, and that's the honest truth."

For some reason, what he said was enough for another quick swipe of each eye. "JayJay Parsons, John Junior, however you got here, whatever past you're carrying. Right here, right now, I love you. With all my heart. With every breath."

"Kelly . . ." His feeble gesture toward her was halted by one upraised hand.

When she was certain he was staying where he was, she went on, "I never thought I would ever use those words again. I thought my ability to love had been cauterized by my own awful past. But here I am. And I'll tell you what I know. What I'm *certain* of. That whatever it is you have to face, I will be there with you. Long as you let me. I'm here for you. Because that is who *I* am."

He felt the confession was going to tear the fabric of his throat. "I'm so scared."

"I know you are."

"What happens . . ." He swallowed, and the effort bunched him over. He spoke to the dry leaves rustling around his feet. "What happens if we start down this road together, and whatever it is that brought me here takes me away again?"

"Then a part of me will wither and blow away." Her voice cracked. She fought her own internal battle and managed to steady herself. "But life offers no lovers any assurance. It's just the way things are. We are together now. We do what the Good Book tells us. Live this one day. Be thankful for the gifts we have. Trust in the Lord for tomorrow and all the days beyond."

She waited for him to object further. When he said nothing more, Kelly went on, "We have to be strong right now. We need to set aside all these concerns, because people are counting on us."

"I know that."

"Of course you do. That's who you are." She moved in then, touched his arms, and lifted them until they were settled around her. When she was nestled in close, she said, "Now the next time you start to worry about how real you are, tell me what you're going to do."

JayJay found the answer there in her gaze. "Reach for you."

"Reach for me. Find what you need right here to reassure you. Whatever else might be happening."

"This is a miracle, Kelly."

"You got that right." She smiled then, and came closer still. "And here's another."

# Chapter 42

Peter's days were not so much frantic as completely and utterly filled. Either he was with Cynthia or he worked with Britt on changes to the script. Pushing through the work at warp speed, because he was literally twelve hours ahead of the camera. He did some of his very best work seated at Cynthia's bedside, scribbling on a yellow legal pad while she slept or held the children.

Their children.

The words were so alien, just to think them meant he had to stop and look over. Drawn from one amazing world to another. Sharing time with this incredible woman who understood him so well his one look in the twins' direction was enough. Because she really was incredible. Able to take the demolishing of her lifelong dream and just set it aside for the moment. Mothering a large family was the first personal goal she had shared when they accepted that they were both in love and contemplating a life together. She wanted a houseful of children. She didn't care how politically incorrect it was, or behind the times, or anything. If she could have twelve children, she wanted them all. But now with everything that was pressing down on both their lives, Cynthia put the shattered dream to one side. Not suppressed it. Just packed it away for a while. Until this current craziness was over, and the kids were home, and she was stronger, and he could be there for her. Then there would be time for tears and prayer and searching for wisdom about tomorrow.

That was Cynthia in a nutshell.

Early Friday morning he took the limo back from Fresno. Gerald, the driver, was nowadays in a perpetual sour state, no doubt bitter over his reduction in status. There was no glory in driving a writer. Nor any gossip he could slip to the tabloids. Only a wonderful woman slowly recovering and taking excellent care of her two new baby girls. What entertainment weekly would care about news like that?

Peter arrived at the ranch just as the sun emerged from the eastern hills. Already the place resembled an anthill whose top had been surgically removed. Lots of nervous bugs swarmed. Kip stood on top of the mobile lighting truck, high enough to be seen by all the workers busy sprucing up the place. His arms whirled so fast they resembled faint clouds of pink. Or perhaps lavender. It was hard to tell with the sun rising behind him.

Britt marched over and demanded before Peter had emerged from the limo, "You finish the rewrite?"

"Both scenes. I'll type them up this afternoon and have them to you tomorrow, as promised."

"What about . . ." Britt stopped when he spotted Kelly and Claire approaching. He asked the ladies, "Where's JayJay?"

"He wanted to spend a while with Skye," Kelly said. "The horse gets spooked when others are nervous. Like now. So JayJay wanted to curry the horse himself. Settle her down before the press get here."

Claire asked Peter, "How's the family?"

Just hearing the word in someone else's mouth was reason to grin. "Great. The doctors are releasing her Monday. We've arranged a nurse to come help out."

Britt was too full of the coming day to share in their pleasure. "I'm still not sure it's a good idea for JayJay to ride in front of the press."

"The horse will be fine, Britt."

"What about JayJay?"

"You can count on him," Kelly said, utterly confident.

"I get the impression something's the matter. But he's not talking. Normally I wouldn't say anything. The work he's done this week, it's . . ."

Kelly glowed. "Good?"

"No. It's outstanding." Britt shook his head. "The man is a star in the making."

Peter and Claire shared a look, for they had both seen Kelly's beaming response. Neither needed to say anything. Both knew this was far more than just the standard location romance.

Britt went on, "That's really all I should be thinking about right now. Just getting it down on film. Using whatever he's going through. But, well . . ."

Kelly patted his arm. "You know what? You have the makings of a very good friend."

"I can't afford the luxury. I'm a director, remember?"

She hugged him. Hard. "I'm glad you're the one leading this shindig. And don't you worry. JayJay is going to be fine."

Whatever Britt was about to say was cut off by Kip's steam-whistle shriek from on top of the lighting truck. "They're *here*!"

Friday was the day JayJay finally learned the definition of the word *star*.

A star was somebody who smiled so strong it convinced folks to smile along with him. A star was the feller who put his entire life in a little box and locked it away. Just shut the lid down so tight his other life, the one that existed away from the work, was just not there. A star lived for the camera, the lights, the moment, the driving urgent demanding all-consuming call to be totally and utterly *on*.

And that's exactly what JayJay was for this crowd. He was pure-t *on*.

When the woman from the entertainment program took hold of his arm and brought to mind the sucker-fish that clung to the bellies of whales, JayJay did nothing but smile until Kelly stepped over and did that woman thing with her eyes. The thing that offered in no uncertain terms to introduce the woman's lower jaw to the next county, all without saying a word.

He stood by the corral and let the cameras go to town. He brought Skye over and clambered up on the fence rail and stroked the horse's muzzle and answered about sixty dozen totally dead-brained questions. For all the world, like he *enjoyed* it. He rode for a while around the corral, then leaped the fence and headed toward the spring. Then turned back, and kept on smiling, even when Skye had the good sense to resist his urging and tried to aim for the hills. He rode Skye into the barn and curried the horse for the cameras, and let them keep on with their silly questions. JayJay even made out like he was reluctant for the interview session to end when Kip and Ahn came over and led them all away.

A star.

The cameras were everywhere. Stills and television both. The only harsh words came when one of the announcers or their team got in the way of another. Then there were the quick hissy fits of two cats claiming the same stretch of road. JayJay never gave any sign he heard a thing. He couldn't afford to. They filmed everything he did. They filmed him attaching Skye's trailer to his pickup. They kept telling him to look this way or that, smile, hold up a second. Until Ahn was sent over by Britt to tell them he couldn't keep stopping, they had to go shoot the main event. Finally they gathered at the entrance, there must have been three dozen in all, and shot him and Kelly and Claire driving beneath the gates. Four different times.

The press and Centurion's PR team filled three buses. They followed the limos and the trucks and the crew's bus away from the ranch, swinging down through town. There they stopped again for a buffet barbecue spread along one side of Main Street. All the locals invited. The press would hole up there and interview anybody who moved while they set up the wildfire shoot. Britt's idea terrified Centurion's PR staff. Forget having a group of LA city folk standing around when they let go with the flames. The Centurion crew were petrified by the thought of what an entire town might have to say about a group of actors on location. But Britt stomped on their objections all the way up to Martin Allerby's office.

They were an hour into their preparations when Ahn arrived at the shoot and announced, "I wish you could see it. Fifty talking heads trying to accept the fact that there isn't any dirt. No scandals. No hatred between the town and the crew. I must've heard a dozen people actually say into the cameras and the mikes that they'd vote for JayJay Parsons if he had a mind to run for mayor."

It had been Claire's idea for Ahn to come up. Saying this was what managers did, back their stars in the pinch. Ahn had dressed for the part, a new suit, silk collarless shirt, Italian loafers. He looked like somebody's kid brother with a fresh haircut. Even so, JayJay was glad to see him. "How's the family?"

"Man, my sister is *so* jealous." If a smile could throw a jaw out of joint, it was this one. "She told me to give you a hug. I said, 'How professional would that look?'"

"Give her one back from me."

"Not a chance in this whole wide world. If hugging Minh was needed to up your take next season, I'd have to take a minute out for serious consideration."

"Yeah, well, I seem to recall a certain brother who blubbered away when he thought his kid sister was hurt." JayJay pointed at the line of buses snaking up the valley road. "Showtime."

Britt's commanding-officer mode was stern enough to make even this crowd behave. That and the fact that half of Salton City's ten police officers were on duty as crowd control. Britt stationed the junket on the crest that had been cleared as a press stand. He ordered the junket photographers to get in place, and said it hard enough to make them obey. He brought JayJay and Kelly over in their fire gear. He explained how they were going to light a controlled burn. He brought over one of the two retired fire chiefs who would supervise. The other was down on the other side of the ridge, Britt explained, in the orchard between the burn and the ranch. This emergency backup team was the last line of defense in case things went south. There to save the ranch and the town both.

All the fire crew were retired firefighters. These Hollywood gigs paid thirty times more per diem than they had ever earned in real life. The firemen brought to the shoot the tight no-nonsense attitude of men who knew what was going down and were going to handle it like pros. Two crews, nineteen men in all. Britt explained to the press how this was customary for a location shoot requiring real flames.

At Britt's request, the police chief issued marching orders to the press. The chief's instructions were very simple. Take one step out of the press area, for any reason, and they would be escorted off the land and every bit of their equipment sacrificed to the fire. Accidentally, of course. But they were going to behave. If they felt they were above taking orders, the bus was ready and waiting to ship them back to Salton City.

The press didn't like it one bit. But they got the message.

"Okay," Britt said. He turned his back on the assembled press and instantly forgot them. A director in full location mode. Able to segment life with a surgeon's dexterity. "Let's make this happen."

Martin Allerby called his partner from the new cell phone, one of two he had purchased for the occasion. Milo answered on the second ring. Martin asked, "You alone?"

"On my office balcony."

"It's going down in a couple of hours. Time to disappear."

"The agent of a star on the rise invited me to a lunch and a private screening. Very hush-hush. I'll be totally unreachable for the rest of the day. You?"

"I'm on my way to Van Nuys. Spending the entire day with our accountants. I'll leave strict orders we're not to be disturbed. Standard ops when we're crunching numbers."

Milo was quiet for a moment. Martin feared he would ask something inconsequential, such as, were they putting anyone in danger.

Instead, the sales director merely asked, "How much is this costing?"

"You sure you want to know?" Good old Milo.

"Tell me."

"Think six firemen set for life. No, seven, because the chief required a double helping. No, eight. Our little on-site mole decided to take a cut." Martin took a choke hold on the steering wheel. "This time tomorrow they'll be shopping for beachfront properties in Bermuda."

Milo said weakly, "Maybe the bar at this lunch will serve me Valium in a glass."

"Don't worry about it," Martin said. "When it's all done but the signing, we'll slip it from the investment account, write it down as part of the deal package."

"What if it doesn't work?"

"It will work," Martin said. "It has to."

# Chapter 43

---

P eter was in the second camera stand with Derek. Peter kept
telling himself it wasn't all that high, twenty feet off the ground.
And that was true, so long as Peter remained focused in the direction
the camera was pointed. But Peter had two little problems doing so.
First, the stand was perched upon a hill that rose like a stony mole
from the ridgeline. As in, the highest point along the high side of a
narrow valley.

The second problem was the real kicker. Which was, the stand's
other side hung slightly over the ridge. The ridge Peter tried not to
think about. The drop was about sixty-eight thousand feet, or so it
seemed to Peter. Straight down a rock face. Peter was certain if he
turned around he could stare out over the valley holding the Parsons
ranch, over Salton City, and right on out to the ocean a hundred or so
miles to the west.

Thinking about how just five skinny poles kept them from tumbling
into the abyss left Peter's tummy swooping with the eagles.

He knew there were five poles because he counted them as he climbed
the ladder into the stand.

The ladder that had started in the pine forest on the slope's gentler
side. The side that masked the drop. The drop Peter hadn't seen until
he was up top.

He asked, "You're sure you can trust the carpenters?"

"Relax." Derek was busy at the portable monitor. He slipped the walkie-talkie from his belt and said, "Britt, it looks real good from this angle."

About a billion cables snaked up through the ladder-hole, fastened to the stadium-size collection of lights over the stand, to the monitor, and to the camera. Peter asked, "What about the weight of all this gear? Are you sure they took that into account?"

The sound guy, hunched over even more equipment, asked, "What's with him?"

"Nothing. Everything's okay, right, Peter?"

"Maybe I should head on back."

"You stay put." Derek vaulted into the camera's hot seat. "They're about to start the burn."

Ahn's head popped into view. "Britt said I could come watch if it was okay with you."

"Join the party," Derek replied, then said into his mike, "Ready to roll."

"Did the carpenters factor in him too?" Peter asked.

Ahn walked straight to the stand's other side. The side with the view all the way to Maui. "Man, this is just too cool!"

Peter said, "I know those carpenters. They have a bad night, they decide the hammer's too noisy, they skip every other nail." Peter motioned to Ahn without turning around. "Get on over here. If we fall, let's slide in this direction."

Ahn asked Derek, "What's the matter with him?"

Derek cast Peter a little grin. "Aw, our fearless writer is just having a slight case of the jitters, is all."

Peter complained, "I want to live long enough to name our babies."

"Mork and Mindy work for me." Derek turned back to the camera and said, "Sound check."

"Go."

Derek hit the trigger on his gear and said into the walkie-talkie, "Rolling."

Britt's voice rose from a stand about a hundred yards away. The echo rolled up from the valley behind Peter like a halloo from the far side. Peter felt his gut swoop again and could not keep back the groan.

Derek said, "Here we go."

Ahn slipped over beside Peter. "I can't believe I'm actually here."

The reason for their position became instantly clear. The burn was started by two guys in fire-retardant gear walking a line from Britt's stand to theirs, down at the base of the nearside valley. The fire, centered between the two camera stands, swiftly towered above the highest pines. The breeze and the slope angled the fire up toward where JayJay and the fire crew stood ready for the shoot.

Ahn asked, "Why is there so much smoke?"

Peter managed, "We doused the trees in chemicals those guys brought with them. I don't know what—"

Derek's voice had undergone a sharp change. "Hold the chatter. We're filming and we need to get this in one take."

Between them and where JayJay and Kelly and the fire crew stood, the steadicam guy stalked the forest like a half-human centaur. A trio of bulldozers lumbered in, thundering along the ridge, clearing away debris. A single chopper buzzed overhead, carting its fire-bucket with eight thousand gallons of water. Derek's other cameraman must have been filming the drop because Derek remained focused on the people below. The chopper dropped its load just beyond the fire line. Peter knew because the flames continued to grow and leap from tree to tree. From the other camera's angle it would appear to be a perfect strike. Only the fire continued to grow.

The smoke rolled up the slope and poured in dark waves over the fire team. But their stand remained in totally clear conditions. Peter's gut calmed with the rising adrenaline rush. He could take in a bit more of his surroundings. The press were clustered upon the next ridge, about four hundred yards farther from the burn. The flames reached up high enough now to lick at the sky. Peter saw where the fire trucks had doused a great V ahead of the burn. The trees angled from the burn to the stand were a much darker shade. The trucks had spent two days drenching the area, so that the burn would be funneled up the hillside yet keep them safe. The cameras were aimed such that they would take in nothing beyond the burn's water-drenched borders.

Ahn said softly, "I never thought I'd want to see another one of these things again. Ever."

The soundman looked over and shook his head. Once. Then he pointed down at the guy with a satellite dish at the base of the stand, directed toward the approaching burn.

Peter nodded. It was strange to be this close. His brain kept telling him he was fine. But the burn looked close enough to touch. And the noise. He had forgotten that the forest fire had a voice. A constant, sibilant, angry, rushing roar.

Then it happened.

One moment everything was working in movie-perfect control. The next, and the world was filled with a single great *WHUMP.*

Peter felt the noise in his chest. Like the world had suddenly taken a great indrawn breath.

Ahn asked, "What was *that?*"

A ball of fire, big enough to look like it enveloped the entire valley, rose with the sluggish grace of a giant rising from slumber. Peter felt the heat crackle against his face.

Ahn asked, "Is this supposed to happen?"

"*Down!*" Derek flipped the catches holding the camera to the tripod, hefted it to his shoulder, and scrambled from his perch. "*Everybody down!*"

When they started lighting the ribbon of fire, the only guy not seriously spooked on the ridgeline was the senior fireman. When Kelly had asked his name, he answered, "Missie, until this is over and in the can, you call me Chief. After that, everything is open to negotiation."

Things ran pretty much to form for the first minutes of the burn. JayJay had no idea exactly how long it took. He was back into fire-fighting mode. Running hard and actually relishing the chance to *do* something.

Then came the noise. To JayJay's mind, it sounded like something between a bomb and the earth clearing its throat. The explosion was more felt than heard. *WHUMP.*

Everyone gaped as flames unfurled overhead. The fireball was so big it rose in slow motion. Spreading out like a great living bellow of rage.

The entire crew just froze up solid. It took all the self-control JayJay had not to run around in tight little headless-chicken circles and to keep his voice from wobbling for the body-mikes as he yelled over, "What was *that?*"

The fire chief jerked to alert status, keyed his walkie-talkie, and said, "Crew Two, you folks better wake on up. Looks like we got us a situation here."

Kelly trotted up. "Was that supposed to happen?"

"It ain't in any script I was shown." The chief keyed his mike again. "Crew Two, come back."

One of his men yelled over, "We're about ten seconds from toasting the dozers!"

"Pull out!" The chief keyed his mike a third time and roared into his walkie-talkie, "Wake up, Drew! We're into some serious business up here and it's coming your way!"

The same crewman yelled over, "Pull back *where?*"

The chief squinted into the billowing smoke. "South along the ridge-line. Everybody *move!*"

# Chapter 44

They aimed for the camera stand between the burn and the summit holding the press. JayJay and two of the younger fire crew helped Peter and Derek and Ahn load equipment onto two bulldozers. The chief, still unable to raise the emergency crew, ordered everyone to find perches on the dozer. JayJay helped the others up, then found there was no more room. The chief directed JayJay to hoof it along the trail to the parking lot and send up a red flag, while he herded the dozers along a longer but broader trail.

JayJay did his finest version of Indian running, as in leaping scrub and trampling trees in his haste to make it through the brush. He had a fleeting impression of a camera sweeping alongside him. But he wasn't sure. Maybe he'd gotten so used to having the ever-present glass eye staring his way, he could render the image out of smoke and drifting embers.

When he finally broke into the clear, he was treated to a spectacle he knew he would draw out and laugh over once this was done.

That is, if *done* was not the word they used to describe his sorry carcass. As in, toasty done.

The image was this: the Hollywood press corps, the most recalcitrant and egotistical and rebellious group on earth, were all doing exactly what the cops ordered. Which was, *Get on the bus. Now.*

The three doors leading to the three buses were a mass of squirming, wiggling, shrieking, wailing humanity. JayJay slowed momentarily, just long enough to embed that vision in his brain. Then he ran harder still.

Which was why, when he finally got to the cops, he had to lean on his thighs for a second and gasp in enough air to tell the cop with the most stripes on his shoulder, "Need your communicator."

The cop was a local, which was good, since it predisposed him not to tell the actor to go play star somewhere else. He simply asked, "This for real?"

JayJay huffed a nod. "We can't raise the backup fire crew. Maybe their walkie-talkies are down."

"Oh, man." The cop wore one of the shoulder-mikes. He thumbed it and said, "Sarah, come in." He listened a second, then, "See if you can raise the backup fire crew."

"Channel eighty-six," JayJay said. He heard footsteps crashing up behind him. "Least, that's what our chief had down as the operating channel."

"Try eighty-six, Sarah." Another wait, then, "Okay, go to eighty-five and seven. Well, try them again. What about our own folks, we got anybody down near them? Okay, patch me through. Earl, you there? We're missing our backup fire crew."

The voice behind JayJay said, "And the three fire trucks they used for dousing the fire line."

JayJay wanted to ask Kelly why she wasn't on the dozer where she belonged. But the cop was talking and JayJay needed to listen. And the portion of his brain that wasn't occupied with the billowing smoke and raging fire told him Kelly would only have given him the extended tongue in response.

The cop said to his mike, "And the trucks? What? Don't give me that, Earl. How hard can it be to miss three red pump trucks? Hold on, Earl. We got us a serious racket here." He frowned in the direction of the lead dozer, which cleared the brush and thundered in the direction of the departing buses. A dozen or so people in fire-retardant gear, and film crew in short sleeves and work boots and radio headsets, clung like limpets to the yellow sides. The cop said, "Speak up, Earl. Okay. Roger that."

The cop waited for the fire chief to join them, then said, "Earl can't find the trucks or the crew neither."

Kelly said, "Martin Allerby. It's got to be."

The fire chief said, "Who?"

"Right now it don't matter," JayJay decided. Only then did he realize that Derek was standing about arm's length away, getting the whole thing down on film. "But we better figure that all our backup are hightailing it for the Tijuana crossing."

Martin surprised himself. After two and a half weeks of sleeping fitfully and only when drugged, he managed to lose himself utterly in the long list of numbers and the accountants' pedantic explanations.

Their first disturbance came an hour after lunch, when the chief accountant's secretary used the excuse of bringing in a fresh thermos of coffee to report, "Mr. Allerby, your office has been phoning in repeatedly."

Martin was careful not to look up from the ledgers. "They can wait."

"Gloria, your secretary, she says it is absolutely critical that you—"

The accountant took Martin's grim expression as his cue. "No calls means no calls. We'll be done here in a couple more hours."

"No. Hang on a second." Martin rose from his chair. Papers and sandwich wrappings blanketed the entire conference table. "Gloria is not the type to panic. Just give me a second."

Martin emerged from the office. He accepted the stack of messages from the accountant's secretary, who had been turned sullen by holding off so many frantic calls. He glanced through them, the word *urgent* becoming ever more stressed and underlined with the passage of time. He looked up and said, "Looks like we may have to call it quits. I'll return Gloria's call from the parking lot."

Martin rode the elevator down to ground level. He had to resist the urge to whistle along with the show tune piped in over the loudspeaker.

Midway across the parking lot, he phoned Gloria. "What do you have?"

"Sir, of all the days not to be able to contact you—"

"We're talking now, Gloria. What's going on?"

His normally unflappable secretary was so frazzled as to require a fresh intake of breath between every few words. Like she'd been running wind sprints all day long. "I started hearing rumors, oh, I have no idea how long ago. There was a call from somebody who heard something. From a PR staffer on location."

"Which location?"

"Which . . . *Heartland.*"

"All right. Calm down. So there's been a problem at the *Heartland* ranch. Was it the press junket? A wreck?"

"Sir, no. There have been reports on the news as well. Wait, it's coming on again. And *pictures.* Oh, Mr. Allerby, this looks *awful.*"

"Tell me!"

"The fire is completely out of control! Oh, here's a flyover, Mr. Allerby, the whole valley is in flames!"

"Has Britt called?"

"No sir. I've been trying his phone all afternoon. And his assistant, Mr. Denderhoff. Oh, I can see the ranch! The fire is—"

"Call the airport and book me a plane."

"Sir, I've tried. We're too late. Every plane in fifty miles has been booked by the newspeople."

"Then I'll drive. I'm leaving for Salton City this very instant. Call me with updates. *Find Britt.*"

# Chapter 45

T he fire chief had aged about six hundred years. Or so it seemed to JayJay.

He kept saying over and over, "That second team were my lifelong buddies. I can't believe they'd do this to me."

Kelly looked at JayJay as she said, "Yeah, well, I guess what they say is true, hang around Hollywood long enough and the rot starts to work under the toughest hide."

The fire chief's face had gone slack as an old hound dog's, his eyes so dulled not even the rising blaze could ignite them. "I *counted* on those guys."

Kelly said to JayJay, "Looks like you're up, Slim."

JayJay punched the chief's arm. Hard. "Wake up there."

"Watch who you're slugging, mister."

"Just making sure I got your full attention. You round your men up and get them down to my ranch. We'll make that the line. I got meadows stretching out to either side with a spring we can use for pumping in water." He turned to the hovering cop. "Better get hold of the forest service."

"Already have. There's a big burn started about thirty miles south of here. They're dug in good. They say it'll be tomorrow at the earliest."

"What kinda units can we get up from the town?"

"The equipment's no problem." The cop responded fast enough to show he'd been thinking the same thing. "The state's been upgrading fire trucks in all the valley towns. But the crews are all volunteer. Mostly retired geezers who use it for a place to hang their checker games. A few college punks wanting a kick."

"Get them to the ranch. They're your responsibility."

The cop nodded. "You taking charge?"

JayJay glanced over, doing his best to ignore Derek and the big glass eye. The chief was moving, but dully. Unfocused. "'Til this guy says otherwise." To the chief he said, "Get your men and equipment down to the ranch pronto. This thing is growing." He turned to Kelly. "Let's go."

Together they trotted to the pickup. JayJay talked as he unhitched the horse van. "Take the truck. Go find Miller at the Ford dealership. Tell him to get everybody he can on out to the ranch. See if they got somebody with clout at the forest service."

She had to shout now to be heard over the rising flames. "What about you?"

He tightened the saddle-girth and slipped the bit into Skye's mouth. "I got to go save me a director."

"Here." Peter came running over with Ahn. Both of them held armfuls of mini oxygen bottles. "Take these."

JayJay pulled two feed sacks from the horse van. He held the necks as they stowed the bottles, then tied the cords together and slung the sacks from the pommel. Then he swung himself into the saddle. "Time to fly."

Martin waited until he was out of the LA concrete spaghetti and aimed up I-5 to phone the only other number set into his new cell phone's speed dial. Even so, he checked around. As if anybody on this desert wasteland of a road would care what somebody in a Volkswagen was doing with his phone.

The phone answered with a rush of what sounded first like static. Then a voice shrilled, *"Help!"*

Martin said nothing. Just listened as the static became a beast's furious roar.

His spy shrieked so high the phone could not handle it. But Martin understood the final two words.

*"We're trapped!"*

He cut the connection and turned off the phone. He could not totally suppress the smile. And who could blame him.

After all, he now had a fat Bermuda account that he could claim for himself.

# Chapter 46

JayJay finally got around to admitting the truth when only Skye was around to hear.

Which was, he was scared out of his wits.

No surprise there. Not with the fire raging up and over the ridgeline, a great blanket of smoke and fury. The fire was moving so fast the rear trees still smoldered, like they were sulking over being left behind. The ridgeline and the left-hand stand, where Derek had been, was basically one solid wall of red. The smoke obliterated any chance JayJay had of seeing the other stand. The one where Britt and Kip and the second cameraman and the script girl and a couple of others had been working.

But it did not look good.

Which was why he raced over still-smoldering earth. Hugging as tight to the fire line as he dared. Cutting the distance, and making better time, because most of the undergrowth was now fiery ash. Skye whinnied with alarm or pain, he couldn't be sure which. But the horse was as steady and trusting as ever, pushing hard and relying on JayJay to keep them both alive.

The earlier drenching was good because it kept the flames from eating too far into the safety line. But it was also bad, because the wet trees were now smoking from the reflected heat. And the smoke was not merely blinding. It puffed in the way of trees that were just begging for the fire to notch up a single degree more. And when that happened, they were going to ignite. Three-quarters of a mile of tree-size firebombs. All exploding at once.

JayJay touched Skye's flanks with his heels. He didn't need the whip. Skye was as taut as JayJay. The horse leaped forward. Not seeing any better than her rider. But trusting JayJay just the same. Twice the smoke pushed aside enough for JayJay to get a sighting of the gray-tainted sun and fix the ridgeline. The third time it happened, JayJay spotted the director's stand, or what was left of it. Fire licked up the near side, devouring the rail and the cables. The stand began to tip over, a reluctant sacrifice to the roaring beast. Then the smoke closed in again. JayJay was fairly certain the stand was empty. Which was all that mattered. He fitted the kerchief tighter over his mouth and nose and nudged Skye forward.

From where JayJay sat, it appeared the only reason they didn't gallop straight over Kip was that the AD gave his best rendition of a steam whistle and drew Skye up on her hind legs.

JayJay figured the little feller was going to go into one of his patented conniption fits. But as JayJay slid from the saddle, Kip threw his arms up over his head and shrilled, "Yippee yee ki yay!"

Britt came staggering out of the smoke. He had his arms wrapped around the terrified-looking script girl, who could not stop coughing. The director's face was streaked with ash and there was a burn mark on his cheek. But he grinned at JayJay and said, "So maybe there's something to this prayer thing after all."

The steadicam guy came staggering behind the others. He got as close to JayJay as he could, and spoke the first words JayJay had ever heard him utter. "Okay, hero, where'd you stash the actor fellow?"

Britt waited until they got the script girl up on Skye's back and they distributed the oxygen bottles to ask the steadicam operator, "You getting this?"

The steadicam guy was back to silent running. He just sucked his bottle and gave the director a double thumbs-up.

Britt was still grinning with weary relief. "Time for act three."

The limo driver was jacked so high by the smoke and the need for speed he actually two-stepped his way around the limo to open the door for Britt, who greeted him with, "I think we're way beyond the courtesy zone, Gerald."

"Hey, you let the dog out, he might never fit back in the kennel." The guy swept into a smoke-streaked bow. "Can I get you anything? Canapés? Champagne? A new charge on your oxygen tent?"

"Just get us to the ranch in record time."

"Caddies have a tendency to sway a little when you do curves at high speeds," Gerald warned the group. "Anybody with funny tummies might want to follow behind in the truck."

They headed downhill in a limo, an equipment truck, and one of Miller Whitley's service department loaners. Skye was safely on her way back to town with a messenger sent to direct volunteers. The limo ride brought to mind a yacht fitted out with afterburners. On curves the limo devoured every inch of road. Twice the crevices to their right disappeared, revealing a fire that appeared to be racing them down the ridge.

Gerald kept up a cheery commentary on the way. "Now that they're far enough from the embers not to have their hair spray go up like fire-bombs, the Hollywood press have gotten all brave again. Your three bus drivers have basically seen their tax bracket hike upward from the bribes. A couple of passing Mexican farmworkers sold their produce trucks for down payments on condos in Acapulco. All the taxis in two counties are just plain gone. Nineteen news choppers are inbound. Along with every rental plane between La Jolla and Seattle."

JayJay had a death grip on the ceiling and door handle. It was the only way to keep from banging around the limo like peas in a soup can. "Long as they stay out of my way."

The spectacle that awaited them when they rounded the final bend and the ranch came into view was good for a serious intake of every-one's breath.

Gerald, however, had seen it all before. "Drinks and charbroiled refreshments will be served on the veranda at six."

The flames formed a crescent that licked its way down the hills. Plural. Once beyond the drenched trees, it had spread in both directions. And soon as they rose from the limo, they all felt the same thing brushing against their faces.

The wind.

Gerald held Britt's door and said, "Is now a good time to discuss my per diem?"

JayJay said, "You best get out of that fancy suit, bub. On account of your services are needed on the line."

Derek came trotting over. With Ahn. And Peter. And Claire. And Kip. And Miller. All of them wore the same wide-eyed smoke-streaked expression. Staring not at Britt. At JayJay.

Derek said, "The fire chief might as well have lost his buddies in the fire."

Miller agreed, "Fellow's gone down like a gut-shot balloon."

JayJay asked, "Where's Kelly?"

Grins pushed through the weariness and the ashes on five faces. Miller said, "Hoss, that is some honey you got yourself there."

Peter said, "She's playing general."

Derek said to Britt, "I got the second camera stuck on her like snot on my baby's upper lip."

Claire said, "Yuck. You think maybe you could find a more appealing way to describe that?"

Derek went on, "My assistant cameraman just got herself promoted. She's up on the roof doing sweeps with the official gear." He poked the tape-strapped camera at his feet. "I'm hopping around with this old clunker."

JayJay asked, "What about the forest service?"

"They're a day out," Miller said. "We're it, hoss. I got my men spread down the creek bed, making us a fire line. Kelly's directing the fire crew down at the valley's far end. The dozers pulled in about five minutes ago. You want to take them over?"

"I'm on it," JayJay agreed.

Derek asked, "Where's the steadicam?"

Britt said, "In the truck coughing up his left lung."

Derek said, "You need to tell him to give me his gear. I've worn one a couple of times. Tell him he'll still get paid. But we need to use it."

Miller still had not lost his grin. "Can't believe you folks are talking about film with this fire bearing down."

"We are not going to let them win," Britt said, hot as the approaching flames.

Miller showed confusion. "Who's that?"

"Never mind." JayJay pointed them forward. "Let's go save the day."

# Chapter 47

JayJay knew it fifteen minutes into his new gig. The army of locals who were still arriving, streaming into the smoky valley and being directed into the fire line by Ahn and Claire and Peter, made no difference. None.

He sent Ahn off to gather the bosses. The ones that mattered. The fire chief joined them. But he was not fully there.

When they met on the porch's front step, Derek said, "Britt, you and Ahn and Peter step out of camera range."

Britt said, "You're giving directions now?" But they all did as they were told.

Then, just as JayJay was getting ready to shape the words, there she came. Stepping out of the smoke like the chieftain she was.

JayJay leaped down the steps and ran over. Kelly sped toward him, as fast as the fire-retardant gear and her load of weariness allowed.

They met in a bulky embrace. And laughed at how hard it was to hug properly when dressed in jackets thick as Sheetrock.

JayJay shrugged out of his coat and dumped off his hat. Slipped inside her jacket and took hold of the woman. Tight hold. And kissed her.

Kelly tasted of soot and fire and sweat and worry. It was the finest flavor JayJay had ever known.

They broke for air and a shared smile. Kelly said, "You look some kind of fine, Slim."

"Funny," he replied. "I was just thinking that very same thing."

"There you go," she said. "Another star stealing his lady's best lines."

JayJay led her back to the others. All without letting go.

Miller said, "I never thought fire clothes could be something erotic. Guess that shows how much I know."

JayJay said to his team, "We need to lose the ranch."

He pointed back up the ridge. The upper ridge and most of the slope where JayJay had ridden were ablaze. The almond orchard was gone. The fire's two incoming arms were sweeping out as well as down, a hundred and fifty yards max from the meadow's border. JayJay went on, "We use the town's trucks and douse the fields. Move the teams back to the other side of the cottonwoods. Focus all our effort on extending the fire line through the orchards to either side of the ranch."

It was Claire who said, "Give up your home?"

"Either that or risk the town."

It was then that JayJay's two worlds finally meshed. Looking into the eyes of this woman who had been his sister and then a stranger and was now a sister again. Different, and the same. JayJay was so very glad to be able to say, "Besides, it's just an old cabin. Full of memories that don't mean nothing to nobody."

# Chapter 48

They had won. Everybody knew it. The fire was still fierce, but was now contained within the valley's natural confines. The fire trucks strung their hoses out from the spring to the portable pumps and shot huge streams of water over the ranch and the surrounding meadows. JayJay split his dozers, two to the denser orchards down below the last meadow, one to help extend the natural break made by the road. Kip played number two both to Miller and to Britt, keeping the road clear, ordering the stream of new arrivals to park well away from the fire and hoof it in, getting all the trucks and gear out of the ranch. Britt remained the director. He was the one man in touch with everyone. He used runners as well as walkie-talkies, since the new workers had no communicators. He watched both the cameras and the fire crew, like he was simultaneously directing two overlapping scenes.

The fire line was not nearly as broad as anyone would have liked. But the spring meant there was a steady flow of water. And the chopper was back repeatedly now, dumping water where Britt ordered via cell phone. JayJay stayed on the dozers, running back and forth between the two lines. Britt and he had racing confabs every time JayJay passed the station. Ahn was his deputy on the pair working the orchard. Claire handled the others.

Derek's clothes were drenched almost black with sweat from keeping up with JayJay.

JayJay waited until the flames started licking across the far meadow to say, "I'd say it's time."

Britt nodded. They were enough in tune now that words from one worked for both. "Do it."

JayJay said to the nearest runner, the square-jawed Ford salesman named Piston, "Tell Miller to clear everybody away from that far side. We're falling back. Let's meet up here." He said to Claire, "I'll go fetch the dozer working the western slope. You tell the machine down the east side to head out."

But as he started out across the meadow, he felt it. The awareness surged like a current through his hands and up into his brain.

The barn was going up now, no amount of water able to keep the dry old wood from burning. JayJay hustled toward where the cottonwoods had been chopped down, the stream framed now by raw stumps. The corral fence was burning. The ranch's drenched roof was smoldering sullenly. The puddled meadows were turning to ash without ever really blazing up.

Ahn must have seen where his gaze was centered, because he asked, "You okay?"

"Not sure." JayJay had not even realized the kid was there beside him. The niggling sensation grew stronger. He did not bother to tell Ahn to go back. There was nothing to be gained from wasting his breath. He started jogging, the heavy coat bouncing hard on his shoulders with each step.

Miller emerged into the clearing, surrounded by a weary, soot-streaked, but satisfied crew.

Then it happened.

The wind did not arrive in the same punching downblast as at the last fire. Instead, there was a quiet sibilant rush, like the trapped fire muttered curses against them and all their efforts.

The valley caught the smoke and clamped it down tight. Blanking out the way ahead. Burning his eyes with soot. The only light was flickering embers, sweeping by in rushing swirls.

Ahn coughed and said, "I believe I've been this way before."

JayJay gripped his jacket and spun him around. "Move! Straight ahead."

They found Miller by colliding with him. The mayor of Salton City had finally lost his smile. "What in heaven's name was that?"

"Downdraft." JayJay snaked out and connected Miller with Ahn. "Link up. One hand in front, one behind. Miller, you head straight on."

"I could blunder into Nevada and not know it."

"Something tells me this ain't gonna last." JayJay started running.

A voice from the gray wilderness called out, "Where you headed?"

JayJay did not bother to reply. All his senses, all his energy, were hunkered down in one tight alarm.

Kelly needed him.

JayJay rode the signal like he was following a scent. He did not have time to figure out what was going on. He could not even afford to hope he was wrong. All the confusing mess of who he was and where he'd sprung from and where he might or might not be headed. All gone. He was surrounded by an impenetrable mist, and the only way he was going to make it happen was if he used everything, the fear and the rage and the weariness and the tension. Everything. And plugged it into the socket where his heart resided. Just another primitive hunter on the scent of game.

Just life and death was all it was.

He used a tracker's lope. Limbs all loose and everything on the move. Dodging branches that appeared at the last split second from the gray choking soup. He passed a few figures stumbling toward him. He checked the faces and in the instant he realized they were not Kelly, he gripped them hard enough to shock them from their fear and confusion. Pointed them straight back and said the only words that registered. Safety is *that way.*

Then he was gone.

His hands were fists in front of his face. His knees came up almost to his chest as he leaped over dead growth. He heard a rising thunder and was amazed to realize it was the sound of his own breathing.

Then he stopped. Fitted the kerchief tighter around his mouth and nose. Clamped it down with one hand. Breathed as shallow and soft as he could. And listened. Not for sound. For the guidance. The link. The compass of his being. Searching through the drifting embers and the searing smoke for the only spark that mattered.

He angled right. Running hard. Straight into the approaching fire.

Then he saw her.

"Oh, lady. No."

She was slumped on the ground. A branch lay beside her. Her helmet was shattered. Which was supposed to be impossible. Her hair was spilled out and covered her face.

He stooped over her. Slid her into her arms. "Come on, Kelly. Let's get you out of here."

She did not move. He could not tell if she was breathing at all.

JayJay reached around her inert form and pulled the kerchief from his mouth. He fitted his own lips over hers. Her face was oily with old sweat and felt so very very cold.

He breathed hard. Again. A third time. And waited.

She did not move.

The fire was so close it sounded like it surrounded him on all sides. The sense of guidance was gone now. He was just another firefighter trapped in a world where he shouldn't be.

"Come on, Kelly, speak to me."

He was talking because he needed to. Not because he expected her to respond. She was too limp. Too still.

He set her back down. Stripped off his jacket and hers. Tossed his hat in the direction he thought the fire was probably coming from. Gave her four more quick breaths. Willing not just his breath into her lungs. But his life as well.

Nothing.

He hefted her again and started walking. Not running. He could not hold her and keep his balance in the undergrowth and run. But he walked as fast as he could. Praying to God and to Kelly both. For one to show them the way out and the other to wake up. The farther he went, the more it seemed as though he was talking the same words to both.

He had no idea how long he carried her. Long enough for his arms to become one solid ache and for his back to grow numb and his legs to begin to stumble. But he was not setting her down. He stopped talking because he could not spare the breath. But the words were still there, slipping out of his brain and his heart in one steady stream. And he had the sense that she was listening. Hearing him talk about love and oneness and the wonder of finding her. How much it meant. How crossing over to wherever he was, the pain of the realization, the confusion, it was all okay. Because of her.

JayJay was not fully aware that he had fallen to one knee until he saw how much closer she had grown to the earth. He pushed himself back upright and saw where the earth had grown bloody. And realized it was his own. And decided it really did not matter so much.

He looked down at the bundle in his arms. And knew that if she was gone, he had no interest in staying behind any longer.

"JayJay!"

He heard the words but could not place them. Like sounds from another dimension. Which was kind of funny. Him being the person he was.

Arms crowded in on all sides. "I got her, JayJay. Let Kelly go. Come on, man. Unlock. *Somebody bring me oxygen!*"

He felt the mouthpiece fitted over his lips. He did not breathe so much as drink. And coughed so hard it felt like his throat tore.

"Easy, big guy. It's okay. We got you."

Ahn. The kid was crying again. The tears streaked his face and tore holes in his words. "The fire line held, JayJay. Come on, let's get you on your feet."

Only then did he realize he was flat on his back. He felt other hands pulling him up. Britt. Claire. Everybody but the one who mattered.

He stared up and realized the sun had emerged.

He dropped his head and tried to pull off the mask. But other, stronger hands kept it in place. He saw a crowd ahead of them make tracks for the road, holding a limp form between them. One of Kelly's hands dangled flaccid and loose between the running men. Like she was waving him farewell.

# Chapter 49

Martin was on the outskirts of Salton City when his secretary called on his normal cell phone. "I have Mr. Turner for you."

"Patch him through. Britt?"

"Yes, Mr. Allerby. What can—"

"What's this I hear about an accident?"

"It wasn't as serious as we feared at first. Apparently one of the fire crews left the fuel they used to ignite the fire line out in the forest."

"The news coverage suggests the town is under threat."

"It might have been. The rising wind was against us. And the backup crew vanished. We still haven't tracked them down."

Martin took the Salton City exit. And kept his foot on the brake. He pulled over to the side of the off-ramp. Set on his blinker. And tasted the air.

His director was too calm.

"You're saying . . ."

"Everything is under control here. The press junket is still fanned out around the town, interviewing anybody who'll hold still. But the choppers have left. At least, I think they have. We're not getting buzzed anymore."

"The radio news still claims the blaze is out of control."

Britt actually chuckled. "You know the press. They hate to give up on a good story, even when it's dead. The fire is still smoldering in places. But volunteers from the town are out hosing things down. We lost the ranch, I guess you heard that."

"No." Martin touched his face. His flesh was numb to his own touch. "I hadn't."

"I'm editing the takes now. Crazy how all this worked out. We scored big-time, is my first impression. Even losing the ranch will fit into the script with a minimum amount of rewrites. Did I tell you Peter finished the screenplay?"

"I don't think . . . No."

"For a first-time feature writer, I'd say he's done an incredible job. Big events, emotive enough to drive us easily through the second act. The high concept is something I've never seen before, a huge payoff I think will catch most people by surprise, but at the same time leave them saying afterward that they could see it coming." Britt was clearly tired, but selling hard. "You know what they say, if it's not on the page it will never be on the screen. Well, it's here. And I'd say we've got ourselves a hit."

Martin leaned his head against the steering wheel. He wanted to reach through the phone and rip the smug calm from his director's throat. "You're sure the fire is out?"

"Pretty much. We had almost three hundred volunteers show up from the town. They were fantastic. Just one case of serious injury and smoke inhalation. Which is a miracle. Kelly Channing is down, but she's alive. The doctors are cautious but hopeful. JayJay saved her life, by the way. He was magnificent."

Martin pushed himself off the steering wheel. But his spine held no strength. His head just kept moving back until it thunked against the seat rest.

Britt went on, "No casualties, more good press, friends all over town talking us up to the Hollywood junket, incredible takes in the can. I'd say we're on a roll here. Nothing but good news at this end."

Martin felt like he'd been fitted with a crank, just grinding out the words. "I'm glad."

"Was there anything else?"

"No. Nothing."

"I'll get back to the edits, then. Maybe I'll drive this lot down myself, take time out to watch them with you. I'd love to see how they play on the big screen."

Martin tossed his phone onto the other seat. He fumbled with his door handle and scrambled out, almost going down on all fours. He staggered away from the Touareg. His fists remained clenched to either side of his gut, fighting to keep himself from being sick.

He stared up at the sky. Amazing how many stars there were out here away from the Hollywood smog. The moon was rising, a huge disk glowing in smug golden shades. Like he'd suddenly emerged from a smoking pit, only to discover a different universe, a different reality. One where his power did not reach.

There was something more etched into the nighttime sky. Written across the face of the moon. Martin had heard it clear as the night air in Britt's voice.

The director knew.

# Chapter 50

JayJay woke up in time to watch the bad moon rise.

The hospital held a somber tone. The room was dark and the other bed was empty. It was just him. Alone in the moonlight with smells and sibilant whispers.

He eased himself upright. The door was rimmed in yellow light, a warning sign wrapped around the frame. Telling him flat out he better be ready before he went out there and got told the news.

But he could not wait. Not even when the pain in his legs was so bad his groan came out like a half-formed scream.

Only then did he realize he was half-naked. Stripped down to his drawers.

Which meant the little black threads snaking over both shins and one knee and the opposite forearm were all visible. Seeing them caused the pain to fully emerge.

Ahn pushed open the door. Saw what he was staring at. And said, "You pass out on us, you miss a lot of the action."

JayJay kept looking at his legs because he couldn't bear to see the kid's face. Not just yet. "Kelly?"

"She's in recovery."

He just dropped. It was a silly thing to do. And of course the kid just panicked, seeing him slump to the floor. But JayJay managed to shush him before Ahn could call for the nurse. "Just find me some pants."

Ahn left and came back with some hospital blues. "Everybody made it out, JayJay."

"Take me to her."

Ahn took a two-armed grip around his middle. "They're not letting anybody in yet."

They pushed through the door. He waved away the cluster of people he did not want to even acknowledge. "Get me as close as you can."

He wore a face tight enough for the others to keep their distance. Just kept going on grim determination and a need not to acknowledge how wobbly his limbs felt. Ahn let JayJay use him as a human crutch, like he didn't mind at all.

Which, truth be told, he probably didn't.

They entered the intensive care unit. The rooms fanned out in a semi-circle around a large central desk. Ahn halted only when a nurse the size of a dozer demanded, "And just where do you think you're going?"

Kelly was near enough for him to smell her. Which was absurd, since the entire place was full of a scent sharp as airborne knives. "I just want to see her."

"Who?"

"Kelly Channing."

"And you are?"

JayJay just looked at her. "Please."

His expression, the way the hoarsely spoken word carried across the empty hall, how he stood there barefoot and clinging to Ahn for support, was enough to melt the woman's stern expression. "I'll let you look in. But you mustn't speak."

"I am much obliged."

"Unit seven." She led the way. The glass door slid open.

There in the gloom JayJay made out a face so pale as to appear unbound by earth or time. Her beautiful mouth was slack. Oxygen tubes snaked into both nostrils. Her eyes were shut. She was cleaned up and the electronic monitor on the bed's other side beeped the message that she was still with them. At least partly.

JayJay waited until the door had closed to ask, "How is she?"

"It's too early to tell. Now I must ask you to leave."

Ahn said, "I heard the doctor mention a coma."

"She is resting well." The nurse had a face that was made to say no with force. "That is all I am able to tell you."

Back at the central desk, JayJay was the first to hear the tapping sound. Someone walked toward them, carried on heels driven with such urgent force they threatened to drive through the linoleum. He knew who it was long before the face came into view.

The newcomer hissed, "You!"

"How do, Mrs. Channing."

She stepped close enough for her breath of rage to blister his soul. "You did this, you despicable little man."

Ahn protested, "JayJay saved her life."

"Only after you got her into this mess. I have no doubt whatsoever of that. Kelly has far too much sense to do anything so *stupid* as to be dragged into a *fire*. Except of course when a *man* is behind it." Edith Channing's fury shook her from her low heels to her shellacked copper hair. "You may stand tall in the lights of publicity, Mr. Junior. But you are a *midget* in my eye. An emotional *dwarf*. A *stunted* human being. You are *forbidden* to have anything more to do with my daughter, do you hear me?"

Edith Channing whirled about. She did not actually shout at the nurse. But only because the force of her rage made up for the lack of volume. "This, this *actor* is *banned* from coming anywhere *near* my daughter. Is that *perfectly* clear?"

The nurse recognized higher authority when she saw it. "Yes, ma'am."

"Take me to her."

# Chapter 51

---

JayJay released himself from Ahn without ever really hearing the excuse he gave. He turned a corner as though headed for the bathroom, then was guided to a rear exit by a small Latina in a cleaning uniform. She might not have understood JayJay's words, but she knew all about the press hanging around the front door, out beyond the police yellow tape. When JayJay pointed to the crowd and the clamor and then shook his head, she nodded and took hold of his surgical blues and led him to the loading platform. All without saying a word.

The more he moved, the easier his body responded. His truck was parked far down the road, just one more fire-streaked vehicle in a long, sooty line. He plucked the safety key from its holder beneath the bumper and drove back to the hotel.

The night manager was watching some LA newscaster breathlessly relate how close a Hollywood wildfire had come to torching Salton City. JayJay snagged two keys from their cubbyholes. One for his room, and the other for Peter's suite. And sneaked away unseen.

JayJay had known what he was going to do the very instant Edith Channing had turned away. Shutting the door between him and the only reason he had to stick around. The only link to this world that mattered.

He entered the empty suite and walked over to Peter's writing desk. The laptop was there, just waiting for him. He sat down in Peter's chair and touched the computer's surface. He felt a bit of stimulation, a softly humming power, strong enough to work through the numbness.

The plan was simple, like all good plans should be. He would find the script. He would type in the words.

He had been written into this world. No problem. He'd sign out the very same way.

He was in the process of opening the laptop when he thought he heard something.

He swiveled in the chair. The room was illuminated by courtyard lights spilling through the windows. He listened, but there was no further sound. Even so, he had the feeling that he was no longer alone.

Then the hairs on the back of his neck started rising.

Gradually the room's shadows began coalescing into figures. Two huge grips leaned against the side wall. A pair of bespectacled electricians sat there beside them. Claire. Derek. Peter. Cynthia. A dozen figures. There and not there. All praying. For him.

And someone else.

JayJay bounded from the chair. With trembling hands he unplugged the laptop and clutched it to his chest. He backed over to the door. One hand scrabbled over the wood, searching for the handle. He let himself out and stumbled down the hall.

Chased by the impossible. Because the murmuring prayer did not cease when the suite's door clicked shut behind him.

Which was why, when he got to his own door and saw the figure leaning against the wall, his neck-hairs tingled all over again.

The guy was so ropey-hard he mocked his own load of years. His forehead and silvery hair were both folded with the permanent imprint of the Stetson he was not wearing. His jeans were saddle-worn, his boots as tough and seamed as his face. He watched JayJay's approach with eyes that had been raised on endless horizons.

"I reckon there ain't no question who you be." The old cowboy uncrossed his arms. "What's the matter, Junior? You look like you done seen a ghost."

JayJay resisted the urge to reach over and poke the man, just to make sure he was real. "Or something."

"There's somebody who wants to see you."

"Can it wait?"

The cowboy pushed himself off the wall. "If it could, you think I'd be out here propping up this wall at midnight?"

"Give me a minute to get outta these hospital drawers."

"The feller who's waiting on you don't care what you got on. You just come with me."

The murmurs were still there. Following them down the corridor toward the front of the hotel. JayJay asked, "You hear anything funny?"

"You mean, other than my boss of thirty-seven years telling me we got to load up and drive to a town on the border of a raging wildfire, then argue with a hotel manager for a room and pay five times the going rate, and then be told to stand outside your room until you show up, no matter how long it takes?" The old cowboy pulled out a key, knocked, and unlocked the door. "Nope, can't say as I do."

JayJay took a tentative step into the semidarkened room. A voice over by the window said, "Come on in, Mr. Junior."

The old cowboy said, "If you're done with me, I'll go get some shut-eye."

The voice by the window said, "I'm much obliged, Royce. Take this chair over by me, Mr. Junior."

He rounded the bed and found himself staring at a man who had shrunk until his skin lay slack as a mottled rucksack. Then the door clicked shut. And the murmurs stopped.

The old man said, "I'm Carter Dawes. You and me got us some business to discuss."

# Chapter 52

Kelly did not wake up so much as swim through increasingly shallow depths. She passed through one level after another. First came a faint sense of her own body, far beyond the level of pain or even concern. Just knowledge that she had a body at all, one tied to a world she had not yet left behind. Then sounds, snippets of voices and electronic beepings that came in quiet waves. Then smell and a raging thirst and faint whispers of discomfort.

Then she opened her eyes.

"Oh, thank the good Lord above."

The voice drew her closer to the surface. Her mother looked down at her. A smile fought through the worry and the shared pain. "Hello, darling. My sweet baby girl."

Kelly knew just one clear thought. A question that could not wait another instant. Even though uttering the one word drew the pain into sharp relief, such that tears seeped from both her eyes as she whispered, "JayJay?"

Her mother's entire body clamped down so tight her hand jerked as she cleared away Kelly's tears. "That man has made you cry for the very last time."

Kelly wanted to speak, to protest, but it was no longer possible to keep hold. Her eyelids fought but would not stay open. She was cast once more into the sea of slumber, carried away upon her wailing heart.

"Eighteen years ago I bought me this podunk studio and threw a dump truck of cash at it. Just paid and paid. I had the money. I own almost a hundred wells, most of 'em solid producers. But I ain't in the business of throwing good money away like that." Carter Dawes' voice held the reedy thinness of a man with no air to spare for inflection. "Did it because of what happened at a prayer breakfast. I was sitting there over my griddle cakes when I felt God reach out and speak to me. Only time it's ever happened. Ain't that the strangest thing you ever heard?"

"No sir." JayJay settled the laptop on his knees and rested both hands on its top. He reckoned he could wait another few minutes and satisfy the old man's need for conversation. "I can't say it is."

"There you go then. I heard tell you were a believer. After all I've witnessed in Hollywood, I figured it for just one more tall tale. But seeing you here, I'm inclined to believe it after all. Which is why I came down here at all, Mr. Junior. The slim chance that this strange thing I'd been hearing was true."

"Call me JayJay, sir."

"Pour me a glass of water there, JayJay."

JayJay had to settle the laptop on the coffee table to do so. He disliked letting go of Peter's computer. But it was right there where he could keep an eye on it.

The old man was so arthritic he needed both hands to lift the glass. He drank and settled it back on the table and declared, "I'm dying."

The truth was too clear in what JayJay saw to be denied. "I'm sorry to hear that, sir."

"I'm ready to go." Carter Dawes spoke with a blunt calm. "Been ready. Lost my wife five years back and my only child eleven months before then. After that sorry mess, life just lost its flavor. Feel like I've woken up most mornings since then, hoping to hear God's call."

JayJay nodded once in response. "I understand you. Yes sir, I truly do."

"I didn't want to make this trip. But I felt God pushing me. Which is a mighty strange thing. On account of how I ain't had nothing from this studio but grief." The tone did not change. But the old man began rubbing his knees. Two circular patterns of old aggravation. "I knew why God wanted me to buy this studio. There ain't never been a time in our nation's history when we needed moral leadership more than now. Not just in politics. In everything. And the truth is, we're an entertainment-driven culture. Which means our young folk look to Hollywood for their guidance. And if these folks have a moral compass, they sure keep it well hid."

The old man took time out for another unsteady sip. He used the edge of the blanket covering his legs to wipe his mouth. Then he continued, "But the fellow I chose to run this studio didn't pan out the way I'd hoped."

"Martin Allerby," JayJay said.

"He was the third try. All of them ran to ways that turned my stomach. At least this one's made me money. I set a board in place that I hoped was gonna keep him in line. Told him he had to start up a program that would have a Bible-reading hero at its heart. A man of the land. A man who knew how to lead by example. Martin Allerby fought the idea tooth and nail. I told him either he did it or he found another job. So he did. And he made money on that too. But even this hasn't turned out the way I wanted."

JayJay recalled Peter's earlier conversation with Britt. "Too many tornadoes and not enough moral meat."

"There you go." Dawes thumped a fragile fist on the sofa's arm. "And that feller they had playing the lead role, he just went from bad to worse. Made a mockery of everything they had on the screen by the way he lived when the lights went off. Then I started hearing rumors. About a new feller they'd brought in. A believer. A man with guts and true grit. A man who walked the talk."

Here it came, JayJay reckoned. The feller's windup was over. The lasso was about to be tossed.

"Now I done seen you for myself, and I believe the rumors are true. So here's the deal. I want you to sign on for the long haul. Not just making more pictures. Representing the studio. Giving it a face. Being the man people think of when they hear the name Centurion. Name your price. A seat on the board, a chance to direct, whatever you hanker for. I just want to leave this earth knowing there's one feller in charge down here who listens to the same higher call as me."

The man spoke like a cowboy. Simple and direct. When he was done, he just stopped. No need to fill the empty space. JayJay had to ask, "You ever live on a ranch?"

"All my born days. Eighty-three years. Born to it, lived it, and I'll be buried behind the house on the same patch as my wife and family, right back to my great-grandaddy." He looked away then. "Including my son. And his boy. All we had. Both lost in a traffic accident six years back. What cost me my wife as well, I have no doubt."

"I can't tell you how sorry—"

"Don't give me sorry, son. Just say you'll help me out in the here and now."

JayJay stared at the laptop. He could feel the energy more sharply now. Drawing him like a magnet tuned to his mortal flesh. "I can't, Mr. Dawes. I don't like telling you no, but I'm set on leaving this place."

Dawes did not show regret. Perhaps he had aged beyond that capacity. All he did was go through the painful process of drinking once more from his glass. When he had wiped his mouth and settled back against the pillows, he said, "Had a call from the lawyer feller in Ojai who handles my affairs. There's been an offer for the studio. All cash. Lock, stock, and barrel. He ain't said nothing, but I smell a rat. One that likes fancy suits and running things his own way."

"Martin Allerby is buying your studio?"

"I ain't got no hard proof. Man's covered his tracks well. But that's my guess." He gave JayJay a look steady as a hunter's aim. "And I'm gonna sell it to him."

"You can't do that."

"Can and will, son. Can and will." The old man leaned forward. "Unless we shake on this."

JayJay wanted to rise. Just get up and walk out the door and down the corridor, back to his room, back to where he could open the computer and type in the words and leave this whole sorry mess behind. But a weight had settled upon his heart, pushing him down, filling him with an unutterable knowledge.

"The fact that you don't want this chore is all the sign I need," Dawes told him. "God's hand is on my being here, and on our talk, and on this offer. I'm asking you with a dying man's certainty. Accept your calling, son. Take on this duty. Become the man our poor hurting nation needs. One voice for good. One Christian who will stand in the false lights of Hollywood and point out a different path. A path toward the *true* light."

# Chapter 53

Peter was back in the Fresno hospital room seated beside his wife when she opened her eyes. "What time is it?"

"Just gone midnight."

She reached over. "How is Kelly?"

He pulled his chair up closer and set the pad down on the bed so he could take her hand. "She's woken up. Spoken with her mom. The doctor says her signs are good."

"The babies?"

"Both sleeping. Like their mom should be."

"In a while." She used her free hand to pick up the pad, which was empty. "Working hard, I see."

"I just got here."

"That's no excuse."

"Now you're sounding like Britt." Peter wanted to add, *The simplest conversation with this woman could be turned into a poem of undying love.* But the look in her eye said she already knew. So he made do with a kiss. "Can I get you something?"

"I'm fine. How is everything?"

Everything being the world of film. "Britt used a conference room downstairs for interviews and planning. When Kelly woke up he left for the hotel. The press are gradually drifting away. They've basically gotten bored with the townspeople saying they don't blame us, they like us, we did our best and fought it with them. And how JayJay saved a half dozen lives."

"Where's JayJay?"

"Hotel, probably. He left a while ago. Ahn said there was a problem with Kelly's mom."

"What kind of problem?"

"Couldn't tell you."

She knew him well enough to read the unspoken. "What is it?"

He hesitated. "Maybe it should wait."

"Tell me."

So he did. About the conversation he'd had with JayJay while she was in the operating theater. What JayJay had said about how he had come to be here. And what the pastor had told JayJay. Peter finished with, "It was amazing, sitting there and hearing him talk about living through exactly what I had written—"

"Why haven't you told me this before now?"

"I don't know, hon. I mean, you're laid up and the babies—"

"Go to him."

The sudden change in her expression caught him totally off guard. "What?"

Cynthia pushed herself higher in the bed. She winced at the pain. But waved away his hand. An impatient gesture. An *urgent* signal. "Peter, you've got to find him."

His writer's mind went into random sort mode. Finally he settled on, "It's after midnight and I don't—"

"*Listen to me.*" Cynthia rarely got this way. Where her tension vibrated in her voice and her gestures and her gaze. But when it happened, there was no denying the dynamic urgency. "Peter, you have got to go to him *now.*"

Peter had exited the elevator and walked past the nurses' station, heading for the parking lot when a voice said, "You sure you want to go out the front?"

He turned to face Ahn. "I thought the press had given up and blown away."

"All but the die-hards." Ahn stepped closer and tightened his gaze, as though seeking to probe beneath the surface. He stated flatly, "Something's the matter."

"I don't know if it is or not." Peter waved vaguely at the floors overhead. "But Cynthia's got it in her head . . ."

"Is it JayJay?"

It would be far too easy to dismiss Ahn as just another unfinished kid. "How did you know?"

"Man, you weren't there. That lady, she just *vaporized* him."

"Who, the mother?"

"I played like a potted palm and Mrs. Channing still blistered me. When she was done, JayJay took off. Said he was going back to the hotel. Man, I'm worried. I tried to tell Britt, but his world has tightened down to editing scenes with Derek and Rhoda. Getting ready in case Martin tries to say we lost it."

Peter liked the way he said it. *We.* Even the agents were claiming a place on the runaway bus. "I think . . ."

He stopped at the sight of Kip scurrying down the hall. "Did you hear what happened to JayJay?"

"Hear?" Ahn snorted. "I was there."

"Bad?"

"I'd rather go fight another fire."

Peter said, "Cynthia thinks JayJay needs us."

Kip hesitated before asking, "Is it true what Britt was saying, about you guys praying for me?"

"Every day," Peter confirmed. "JayJay's idea."

Ahn was already headed for the rear exit. "We can talk on the way. Let's *go.*"

# Chapter 54

Kelly clambered out of the dark, driven from slumber's embrace by a driving, urgent need. One she could not name until she was close to the surface again.

Like the first time, awareness came back to her in stages. Her first conscious connection was her chest rising and falling in steady rhythm. So steady, in fact, she was not surprised to next feel the tube in her nose, pushing oxygen into her lungs. A fact that had escaped her entirely the first time she'd reappeared. Then came the astringent hospital smells, and the beeping, and the sound of a voice saying, "I believe she's coming around."

Kelly's mother gripped her hand. Kelly knew it was her mom, the way she took hold, it was an energy thing as much as the touch itself. Edith Channing said, "Hello, darling. I'm right here. Everything is going to be fine."

The doctor bent over her and gave a professional smile. "Can you hear me, Ms. Channing? Just nod your head if you can. Excellent. Your throat has suffered some burns, and it will be quite difficult for you to speak for a while. And to swallow."

Her mother fitted a tiny sliver of ice between her lips. "Suck on that, dear. It will help the thirst."

Kelly lay very still, gathering herself. Then she swiveled her head. Locking gazes with her mother. Pouring everything she had into the look. All that could not be said. All that needed to be understood. The pure, unadulterated urgency of what had to be done.

Edith Channing's bedside manner disappeared. She might not have caught every component of her daughter's message. But what she saw caused the older woman to drop her eyes momentarily.

Kelly knew the doctor was saying something. And she needed to pay attention. But that would have to wait. Right now there was space for just one thing. She waited until her mother finally lifted her gaze again. Then she spoke. The three words were so painful they seemed drenched in acid. Her voice was unrecognizable. She had to take a shallow breath after each word. But she got them out.

"Call. Him. Now."

# Chapter 55

As soon as Peter entered JayJay's hotel room, he knew. It might as well have been written across the sky in Hollywood-size script. Peter's laptop lay open on the coffee table in front of JayJay's chair. The screen was blank. JayJay's hands lay limp on the chair arms. JayJay did not look over when they entered. He just sat there staring at the empty screen.

Peter walked over and sat down on the sofa next to JayJay. "You can't do this."

JayJay did not look over. Or give any sign he heard Peter at all.

"Look. I know I'm guilty as anybody of doubting you. When you first showed up, I, well, I *mistrusted* you. Ask Derek. He'll tell you. I questioned everything about you." The stress and the tension were so tight Peter felt his consciousness compressed down to this one instant. He had heard this was how it was when somebody tried to talk a suicide off the ledge. Which, in truth, was exactly what he was doing. "And I kept doubting. Right to the evening when you came to my hotel room. What am I saying. *This* hotel room. I was so messed up. Cynthia was sick and I was here and I felt so totally helpless. So scared. I'd been given the chance of a lifetime and the timing was so totally awful. All I wanted was to just go ahead and fail, which I knew I probably would, so I could get back to where I belonged. Beside my wife."

Ahn crossed the room. And Kip. The two of them didn't sit down. Instead they settled against the window. And stared at JayJay like he was a member of the recently bereaved.

Peter went on, "Then you stopped by my room. And what you gave me was *hope*. You were on my side. You cared about my problems. You prayed . . ."

He stopped. He wanted to keep going. But just then his throat was not letting out enough air to shape the words.

Ahn asked softly, "I don't know what he's talking about. But if you leave, you have to answer me this. What am I supposed to tell Minh?"

JayJay winced at the name.

"*Leave?*" Kip almost shrieked the word. "You *can't* leave! Not *now!*"

JayJay looked over and squinted. Like he couldn't place the little man.

"Do you have any *idea* what you've done for me?" Kip's arms started their frantic dance. Like he was back on the set. Only the emotion was real this time, along with the driving urgency in his voice. "I'm the little shrimp on the set. The guy everybody laughs at behind his back. The guy they like to mimic. The guy everybody is paid to *hate*. Okay. If that's how they want it, *fine*. I'll show them. I'll be *worse* than they think. I'll become a *legend*."

He might have scored a swipe at his eyes on that last swing, Peter couldn't be sure, Kip's arms were milling so fast. "And then *you* show up. And you are *nice* to me. Even when I don't deserve it. Even when I'm *vicious*. What do you do but arrive on the set and you *apologize*. And then you take me out with you on a location shoot and you talk to me like I'm *human*. And then, what do I hear?" The AD's chin was trembling so hard he had to clench his teeth to get the words out. "That you've got half the crew *praying* for me. Not once. But every day. Nobody has ever . . ."

By the time the AD had reached the point where he couldn't continue, Peter was back in control. "You're more than an actor on the set, JayJay. You're leading this location crew in a direction they've never taken before. This is one of the laws of Hollywood, how the stars and the director set the tone for the shoot. Not what goes on film. What happens in reality. The prayer group, the harmony, the friendship, the way the town feels about us, this is *real*."

"Let's talk about real." This from Ahn. "Let's talk about the people like my grandmother, who almost wept when JayJay Parsons didn't live up to her ideal. And now, she's got her hero back. Can you really walk away from that? Can you?"

The silence extended out to where time stopped mattering. Dawn became a pale wash upon the window. Birdsong rose from the courtyard garden. Finally JayJay said, "I been sitting here for hours. Staring at this screen. I turned it on twice, then shut it off. Trying to figure out what I was going to write."

Ahn started to ask something. Peter raised his hand. *Not now.*

"Was I gonna make it all go back to how it was before? If I did that, how was I gonna live with what's happened over here? I couldn't. Not unless I wrote in a memory loss. And I could. Just slip in a couple of sentences, right?" JayJay looked at Peter now. "Turn the clock back and make like none of this ever happened. Not the people or the film or Kelly . . ."

It was JayJay's turn to struggle for control. "But I couldn't do that. How could I be sure I wouldn't turn back the clock on everything that happened *here*? What if, what if I wrote me out and wrote everybody back to how it was before? No prayer time, no renewal of *Heartland*, no win in the fight against Allerby. I tried to tell myself that it didn't matter, not with me leaving and all."

"It matters," Ahn said grimly. "I don't have any idea what you're talking about. But I know it matters."

"Too right," Kip agreed. "It matters a *lot*."

"So that's how I got to be where I am right now. Sitting here. Stuck."

Peter waited long enough to be certain JayJay was done. "You want to pray about it?"

JayJay sat there, staring at the screen a while longer. "I've got to stay. Don't I."

"I think that's what you're being called to do."

JayJay nodded slowly. "Stripped down bare as the day I arrived here. Nothing to call my own. So alone my bones ache."

"You're not alone!" Kip cried. "You've got *friends!*"

"Brothers," Ahn said. "We're here for you, JayJay."

"You were there to give me hope when I had none." Peter reached out his hands. "Let us do the same for you."

But just as they reached out to take hold, the phone rang.

When JayJay made no move to answer, Peter said, "Maybe it's important."

"You go right ahead. I'm not ready to face the world yet."

Peter lifted the receiver. "JayJay's room."

"This is Edith Channing."

"Yes, Mrs. Channing." When JayJay gave his imitation of Kip's arm-flapping, Peter went on, "What can I do for you?"

"Is he there?"

"Yes, but he's not—"

"Oh, I don't blame him. I wouldn't want to speak with me either. Would you pass on a message, please? Tell him . . . Tell him, I'm sorry. I think the truth is, I never saw him at all. Both times we met, I was still addressing the man who hurt my daughter two years ago. And that was wrong of me. Very wrong."

"I'm sure he'll be happy to hear that, Mrs. Channing."

"Tell him the doctors say Kelly is going to be fine. Tell him Kelly is awake. And she needs him." Now it was the mother's time to search for strength. "She needs him desperately."

Peter hung up the phone and passed on the message. And waited while the room brightened with more than the dawn.

Finally JayJay looked over and said, "I got a man down the hall who's waiting for my word. Soon as that's done, I guess it's time to go greet a lady. Then we got us a film to finish."

Kip and Ahn did the fist-on-fist thing, which from Peter's perspective seemed to include the rising sun. The AD said, "I've always been a sucker for happy endings."

JayJay reached for their hands. "What say we pray this show onto the road."

378

# Chapter 56

K elly liked to think she sensed the change before she opened her eyes.

"Hello, darling." Her mother squeezed her hand. "Welcome back."

She smiled. Like a child, reflecting on unfinished features in what she saw there before her. Able to do so because she sensed the change in the room. She opened her mouth, dreading what it would cost her to speak. But needing to ask just the same.

This time, however, her mother whispered, "He's just outside. I'll go get him."

Edith Channing rose from her chair. She looked down for a long moment, then said, "It's not just to the gentleman I owe an apology. You were right and I was wrong."

Kelly watched her mother turn and leave the room. She felt a tear dislodge and roll down her cheek. And did not care.

He was there. The light in the outer room silhouetted his form. The massive shoulders, the slender waist. She had not noticed until that very moment that his legs were slightly bowed. Or maybe it was his stance. She could tell he was very tired, even though her vision swam such that she could not really see him at all.

He walked over. "Lady, if you don't stop crying you're gonna have me bawling like a baby."

She smiled again. And felt his hand wipe at her cheeks. First one and then the other. Gentle and hard and soft and strong. The hand came to rest upon her face. She lifted her own hand and held it there.

"I had a billion words I wanted to say." His voice was so hoarse it sounded sandblasted. "And now that I got my chance, I can't think of a single thing. My heart is that full."

She blinked hard. Wishing she could clear her vision enough to see him better. Then she decided it was all right just as it was, because maybe the glow that surrounded him might vanish. And she didn't want that. Not just yet. Not until she had embedded the image deep in her heart.

If only he would lean over and kiss her, the moment would be as perfect as heaven's holy song.

JayJay must have understood. Or maybe the moment held the same message for him as well. Because that was exactly what he did.

# Chapter 57

M artin stood in the center of his office. He paced. Not swiftly. Just hunting. Making sure of what he suspected.

The light that had followed his every move was gone.

Milo sat in the corner, idly leafing through the latest PR sketches for the promotion of Centurion Studio's first feature film. The location shoot for *Heartland* was four weeks away from wrap. Since the wildfire the previous week, the buzz just kept building. The distribution offers were coming in a steady stream.

And yesterday Paramount had made a public offer. Not for the film. For the studio.

Milo glanced his way. He said nothing because there was no need. They both knew.

The Centurion board was meeting in the next room. Martin had been asked to wait for their summons to join them. And Milo. Of course it was the board's prerogative to ask them to wait. Martin was not, after all, a board member. But only twice in his period as CEO had the board ever conducted business when he was not present.

Martin pulled out a cigarette. And put it back. He was not certain he could smoke and keep his fingers steady. He crossed the room once more. And found himself standing in front of his favorite photograph.

His office had no trophy wall. He did not care to boast about people he had stood with, or once greeted, or shaken hands with, or been given awards by. The only images on his walls were a couple of

Davis Bunn

original movie posters, one of Garbo and another of Bacall. And this photo. A black-and-white masterpiece taken of Marilyn Monroe shot by Sam Shaw. The week he had taken this job he had attended an auction and acquired the photographer's proof. Shaw's scrawled notation in the bottom right corner stated that the picture was his choice for *Life* magazine. The photo was taken in 1956 on the set of *The Prince and the Showgirl*. Marilyn stared into the makeup mirror. Another photographer, hidden behind the massive frame of a Speed Grafex, was readying a shot. Marilyn stared into this second camera, revealing that special magic all stars needed and few had. She was known for her singular ability to shine for the camera. Just reach out and *embrace* it. But because the magic was directed at another camera, Sam Shaw's picture revealed not just the magic, but the humanity. He had captured both the star's unique magic and her fragility. Marilyn had never looked so appealing, or so human. So destined to crash and burn upon Hollywood's altar.

Martin's eye tracked left. Upon the wall between the photo and the bookshelves containing his Emmys and other awards was a line of four small frames. Each contained a single sheet of paper. Two were personal letters. One was a page from a private journal. The fourth was a sheet from a reporter's notebook. They contained unique insider takes on Hollywood. Original words in their original form.

He read them again now. Studying them carefully. As though he had never laid eyes on them before.

The first was from Orson Welles: "Everything you hear about Hollywood is true, including the lies."

Then Shirley Temple: "Any star can be devoured by human adoration, sparkle by sparkle."

Then the famous Hollywood reporter Hedda Hopper: "Our town worships success, the goddess whose smile hides a taste for blood."

And finally his prize, the favorite of many from Marilyn Monroe herself: "Hollywood's a place where they'll pay you $50,000 for a kiss and fifty cents for your soul. I know because I turned down the first offer and held out for the fifty cents."

His mental camera traversed over to the awards. Then halted, captured by a dusty volume behind his trio of Emmys. He pushed the shiny brass trophies aside. And pulled out the Book.

Five years it had rested there. He had forgotten the incident entirely. The one time Carter Dawes had visited his office had been the day after Martin had requested the right to plow their rising profits into a feature film. He had thought the studio's owner was coming down to discuss terms. Instead the scrawny old rancher had talked to Martin about his dream for the studio. And his ideals. And the faith behind it all. Then he had given Martin the leather-bound Bible. And asked his CEO to study it. And to call when he was ready, or if he had any questions.

Not about the film project. About religion.

As if religion had any place in Hollywood.

Martin carved a design in the dust. This was the enemy, he knew. What had kept him from his goals. What had stood between him and everything he had fought so hard to obtain. Not the board in there. This Book and what it represented. He'd burn it if he could. Burn them all.

"Mr. Allerby? Mr. Keplar?"

He set the Book back on the shelf and turned to face his secretary. Gloria might be inscrutable to others. But one glance was enough to tell him all he needed to know.

"The board is ready for you now."

# Chapter 58

M ilo's sharp intake of breath was the only sound as they entered the boardroom. Martin moved forward on legs he could no longer feel. He floated on a Novocain blanket. Like a soldier whose body refuses to accept the fact that he has been mortally wounded.

"Please sit down, gentlemen."

Milo slumped into a seat. Martin remained standing by the back wall. The *Heartland* movie poster would serve well enough when the bullets started flying. He would meet his end without blindfold, and on his feet.

The board members were drawn tightly back around the oval table's other side. Their seats were scrunched closely together, placing as much distance as possible between them and the pair who had just entered.

Behind them, against the far wall, were seated Britt Turner, JayJay, Kip Denderhoff, and Gloria. Even before they started speaking, Martin had all the data he would ever need.

The pastor was their chosen spokesman. He addressed them with a tone suitable for a funeral service. Which, given the fact that Martin lived to make films, this was.

The pastor picked up a sheet of paper and read, "Acting with the full approval of Carter Dawes, the Paramount offer to acquire Centurion Studios has been turned down. Instead, the studio will be set in a trust, to be administered by an extended board. Britt Turner is to become the new acting CEO, pending full approval in twelve months' time. Kip

Denderhoff is to take over as Mr. Turner's replacement upon the set of *Heartland*, but only after the feature project is completed."

Milo protested, "That's insane."

The pastor chose to ignore him. "Gentlemen, I will come straight to the point. We have spoken at length with Amber Hill, the script girl who admits to acting as your spy on the location, Mr. Allerby. And also as your go-between to the fire crew who ignited the blaze that almost took out the town. The authorities in Salton City have been notified. You gentlemen may wish to speak with your attorneys."

Milo groaned and covered his eyes.

JayJay Parsons leaned forward in his chair. "What this feller is trying to tell you folks is this. We've just declared open season on skunks."

# Chapter 59

T he estate was not overly large by Hollywood standards, a couple of acres surrounded by a waist-high brick wall topped with ten feet of iron spikes. Planted in the grass outside the wall were shields warning intruders of an armed response. JayJay's windows were rolled down and the truck was full of eucalyptus scent. The shaggy trees dominated the cul-de-sac off Mulholland that contained Neil Townsend's home.

Kelly said, "Remind me again why we're here."

"I'm trying to do what I feel God has asked of me. You, I'm still trying to figure out."

"There was no way I was going to let you do this alone." Kelly's voice still held a raw quality, one that sounded to JayJay's mind like honey-coated sandpaper. "Leastwise, that's what I was thinking when we left the ranch. Now, I'm not so sure."

"I could take you back to your apartment."

She reached over and took his hand. The day was warm and she wore a T-shirt from Goody's. Her forearm was still bandaged from where the hospital drip had been inserted. "I told you once before, Slim. I don't run."

JayJay used his free hand to cut the motor. "One of my new life-long goals is to try and find a way to show you just how much those words mean."

The bandage was off her head and the bruise to her forehead had started fading. Kelly had her hair pulled back in a ponytail that accentuated the shape of her neck and ears. She looked both nineteen and a very wise ninety. She gave him a smile that did not need to touch her mouth. "What say we ask for the only help that matters."

He did so, then followed the amen with, "I don't want you coming up to the house with me."

"That makes two of us. But I'm not happy with the idea of you going up there alone."

JayJay opened his door and climbed out. "I won't."

The drive was sealed by twenty-foot-high metal gates. There was no house number, no name, no mail slot. Just a buzzer atop a security camera set in the right-hand brick pillar. A handwritten sign wedged above the loudspeaker read "Playpen," but the "Play" had been crossed out and replaced with "Pig."

He pushed the button, then waited long enough to have a decent reason for turning away. But his gut told him the house was not just occupied, but watching him.

A voice over the loudspeaker finally said, "What do you want."

"A friendly word is all."

There was another long wait, then the gates swung silently open. JayJay glanced back at where Kelly sat in the truck watching him. Then he started up the drive.

The lane was paved in multicolored brick. The house was stone. The windows were tall. The lawn sparkled with electronic water. The palms whispered a Hollywood greeting, all empty rattle. JayJay climbed the stairs and found the front door ajar. He glanced back again, but the truck was blocked now from view. So he looked upward, taking in a final glimpse of sky.

He stepped inside. "Neil?"

The house was silent. JayJay crossed the marble-tiled foyer with its thirty-foot domed ceiling and fancy chandelier. He descended the four limestone steps into the living area. He started to call again, when he spotted the actor through the rear glass doors. JayJay crossed a carpet broad as a small lake and stepped through the sliding doors. "Mind if I join you?"

The actor sat with his back to JayJay and the house. He stared through wraparound shades at the sparkling pool. His shirt was unbuttoned, revealing a bloated belly the color of boiled shrimp. "Grab a drink, why don't you."

JayJay pulled another padded iron pool-chair around to where he faced the actor. "I'm good, thanks."

The actor shifted his head a fraction. "Come to gloat?"

"No, Neil. I didn't."

"I'll be back. You'll see." The voice was as robotic as the arm that raised the glass to his lips. He almost gargled the words. "The show is gonna bomb without me. They'll crawl back, begging. You watch."

JayJay felt like he'd left all his air out front. There was scarcely enough left to breathe. Certainly not enough to speak proper. Hardly enough to remember how to pray. "I got a cowboy's way with words. Short and choppy."

The actor sneered at the pool and plied his drink again. "What, you think I'm gonna offer up my trade secrets?"

"What I mean is, I . . ." JayJay stopped then. He lowered his head so he examined the glaring white pavement at his feet. "Nah, this ain't right. I'm trying to take hold of the reins myself."

He clenched his teeth together. And prayed. Or tried to.

JayJay lifted his gaze. Neil Townsend had returned his attention to the pool, almost as though he'd forgotten JayJay was there at all. The actor's features had ballooned out to where his face looked flattened by a frying pan. A big fleshy circle that pinched up around his sunglasses, poked his mouth into a constant pout, and spilled down over a chin that had all but disappeared. The only real sign of life was the hand that lifted and lowered the glass.

JayJay started over. "I ain't got no business being here at all."

The ice tinkled as Neil tipped his glass. "You got that right."

"What I thought early on, how the miracle was all about me showing up, I was wrong as wrong could be. The great miracle is *not* the act of breathing life into dust. God does that with every baby that cries. He does it each dawn. We open our eyes to a gift we don't deserve and haven't earned. Another day, another hour, another *breath.*"

He watched Neil drink again, then set the glass on the table and almost miss the rim. Neil shifted his head another fraction, as though even that motion required too much effort. He used a pudgy finger to push the glass back a hair. "This got a point?"

JayJay kept talking because he knew, whether or not the actor was listening, his words were being heard. "The greatest miracle is taking the emptiness of life and filling it with eternal meaning. It's an *invitation*. The King of all lets us *choose*. We're given the miracle of life and told, do with this what you will."

The actor tilted his sunglasses up and rubbed at one eye. He dropped his hand. The glasses remained skewed.

"That's what I came here to tell you," JayJay said. "That if you ask, God will not only restore you to life. He will give you a reason to be joyful."

The actor might have been asleep. His chest rose and fell. The fingers of one hand twitched. His angled glasses remained focused upon the empty pool.

JayJay rose to his feet. He looked down and saw not an actor, or not just an actor. There before him sat himself. JayJay asked, "You mind if I stop by again?"

The actor remained somnolent for a time, then muttered, "Whatever."

JayJay settled his hand upon the other man's shoulder. "Good-bye, brother."

When he reappeared, Kelly did not bother to ask how it went. Already she knew him well enough to see in his face that he needed time to sort through the whirlwind of emotions. So all she did was take his hand and say, "Come look at what I've found us."

She led him back to where the cul-de-sac met the main road. There a path cut through a narrow park leading to the reservoir. On the lake's other side rose a tennis club and the sound of kids playing in a pool. JayJay started to remark on how it was interesting he could not hear anything inside the actor's home. Then decided he didn't want to bring any of those shadows out here with him.

They claimed an empty lakeside bench. They sat there beneath the twin oaks and watched the setting sun turn the lake to a cauldron of molten gold. JayJay had a lot he wanted to say. But his heart was still wounded by what had gone on inside. And what he wanted to tell this lady was so important it had to wait until he was whole.

So he said the only words that could not wait. "This is one cowboy that ain't riding off into no sunset."

Kelly took that as the sign she had been waiting for. She closed the distance between them. She gripped his hand in both of hers and drew it around her shoulders. And spoke in a voice that managed to sing and whisper, all at the same time.

"My hero."

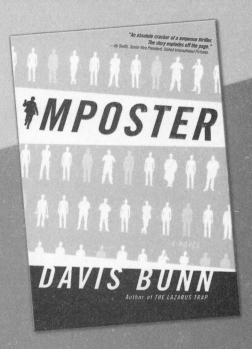